Date Due

THE CRIME OF
OVIDE PLOUFFE

THE CRIME OF
OVIDE PLOUFFE

ROGER LEMELIN

Translated by Alan Brown

172673671

McClelland and Stewart

The Canadian Publishers
McClelland and Stewart Limited
25 Hollinger Road
Toronto M4B 3G2

Canadian Cataloguing in Publication Data

Lemelin, Roger, 1919-
[Le crime d'Ovide Plouffe. English]
The crime of Ovide Plouffe

Translation of: Le crime d'Ovide Plouffe.
ISBN 0-7710-5260-X

I. Title.   II. Title: Le crime d'Ovide Plouffe.
English.

PS8523.E53C713 1984   C843'.52   C84-098942-3
PQ3919.2L45C713 1984

Every reasonable attempt has been made to attribute copyright material used in this publication. Information regarding inadvertent errors or omissions of copyright information would be welcomed, and efforts will be made to correct same in future editions.

This translation was completed with the support of the Canada Council and published with the assistance of the Ontario Arts Council.

Printed and bound in Canada

The fictitious characters in this novel are, like their adventures, purely the author's creations. He has tried to give a just portrayal of the institutions and public figures mentioned as the plot develops; the attitudes and political commitments of these public men, now a part of history, are here used for novelistic purposes, so that the real and the imaginary are intertwined throughout the book, in which the events that stirred Quebec in 1948 and 1949 serve as a backdrop to the action.

To all those who, over the years,
honoured me with their confidence
and friendship

Part One

"Cheerio, Madame Plouffe!" cried pretty Rita, waving her be-ringed hand as she rushed off down the stairs.

Joséphine Plouffe, nose pressed to the door-screen, stuffed in her apron pocket the package of Sweet Caporal cigarettes her daughter-in-law had left for her, listened to the fading staccato of high heels on the steps, and shouted:

"Bring little Arlette around by seven, I want to curl her hair. And don't come home too late!"

Sniffing the cloud of Chanel N° 5 that floated behind the stylish coquette, Joséphine watched the departing form of this superb creature, married (alas!) to her second son Ovide eight years ago. Her motherly instinct had not led her astray when she warned him against the match. Poor Ovide! Things weren't going any better for him, he was still a clerk in a record store at a wretched salary, even working evenings at times, but he stubbornly went on living in the upper town, and the Lord only knew what his wife did there all day! Too often Joséphine was called upon to look after their little daughter, Arlette. To-night, for instance! While her husband was stuck behind the counter of the record store, Rita was invited by a cousin to accompany her to the restaurant Chez Gérard to hear Charles Trenet. Joséphine frowned. The couple wouldn't last long at that rate.

They had gone through their worst crisis last spring when, unknown to her husband, the lovely Rita had been chosen Miss Sweet Caporal. What a to-do! Her photo was put up by the manufacturer all over town, showing her in the little corporal's uniform with its tight tunic and short skirt, bare thighs and white knee boots. And that provocative smile that spoke volumes! What a rage Ovide had been in! Despite his wife's tears and supplications he had cancelled her advertising contract. But the company kept sending the persecuted majorette cartons of Sweet Caporals, and Rita never forgot to keep a few packs for her mother-in-law as a reward for looking after Arlette.

Joséphine dismissed an ugly thought: could it be that Ovide had an unfaithful wife? The other day as she was on her way home from church she had imagined she saw her daughter-in-law beside a smartly dressed man, her hair flying, in a white convertible with the top down. It was all the fashion, these open cars. Ovide would never in the world be able to afford such a thing! And Rita made no bones at the family dinner on Sundays about deploring in front of the whole clan the fact that her husband would always be a poor provider, saying she'd rather have had him less cultured but more practical, and as well-off as his older brother, Napoléon. But Ovide never complained. This, however, was not enough to reassure Joséphine. He had the same drowned look that had come over him once before, when he gave up everything to join the order of the White Fathers of Africa.

What on earth was bothering Joséphine today, disturbing her usual serenity? After all, it was just early October 1948, the birds were still singing, it was as warm as summer, and all the leaves in Canada had turned red, yellow or gold, or all three at once. Could it be that her faint distress was a kind of rheumatism of the soul, announcing the coming winter? She was wide awake just the same: she grabbed the fly-swatter and whacked a large bluebottle; then, pleased with herself, went and sat down in the rocking chair, which groaned and creaked as she set it in jerky motion. She ripped open the Sweet Caporal package and lit a cigarette, inhaled it too rapidly, coughed, now thinking less about Rita than her defunct Théophile. She stared hard at the gold-plated ring he had given her on their wedding day. She hadn't taken it off in the twenty-five years that followed. Her fingers had grown so fat that the ring, nearly buried in yellowed flesh, peeked out as a gilded sliver, intact despite a thousand washdays. Joséphine remembered the tumour in her side that, in the latter days of their union, had given her an excuse to repulse the advances of her over-frisky spouse. Oddly enough, the moment he died, her lump had begun to grow smaller, and disappeared completely. No doubt the good Lord had sent her that ailment to protect her from sexual excess? Rita glided back for a moment into Joséphine's consciousness. Followed by an obsession – the face of that Ramona with whom Théophile was supposed to have sought relief in the days of the tumour. A scandalmonger, a Lady of the Holy Family, had kindly informed her about it one Sunday after Joséphine had triumphed as soloist at high mass, singing "Bless thee, good and powerful mother." How often Joséphine had shed tears after that! But her grief was old and worn now; a kind of cellulitis had overgrown it until it was almost as hidden as her

12

gold-plated ring. The phone was ringing loudly. Her hand waved away the smoke that stung her eyes, and reached for the receiver.

It was her oldest, Napoléon, asking about Guillaume, her youngest. Had he written? What day was he coming back, exactly? She had no idea, but he'd turn up as usual with no fanfare. Charles Trenet? Chez Gérard? Thanks for the invitation, but she had to look after little Arlette. Joséphine hung up and wandered around the kitchen where an electric stove and a big freezer were ensconced – gifts from Napoléon. She smiled to herself as she lit a second cigarette.

What a lot of changes there'd been since Guillaume, the baby of the family, had got back from the war! She could still hear the voice of her eldest son ringing in her ears. At least *he* was making a go of it! In no time at all, riding the boom after 1945, he had grown too big for his job as a hired plumber and roofer's helper, and became a contractor overnight. Now he had a big yellow brick house and had built a spacious shop with the most modern tools in the back yard, he owned three trucks, was getting contracts from the Duplessis government, and on Sundays drove around in a convertible with his wife Jeanne and their five children. Napoléon! Joséphine had gone along a few times, but soon had enough of having her dresses ruined by the brats taking turns on her knee in the back seat, while Jeanne, who had put on a little weight, reigned in front beside her husband like a successful social climber. The whole bunch of them slurped innumerable ice cream cones until they had no room for more.

Joséphine shook her head. Napoléon spoiled his kids. He was doing too well in his business. It couldn't go on this way. He'd offered her a fine, sunlit room in his house, but no, she preferred to live with her old-maid daughter, Cécile, forty-nine, in the same place where she'd brought up her brood, faithful to her memories and familiar sights. Even Napoléon, overflowing with good intentions though he might be, would never succeed in getting around his sly old mother. She knew very well that if she accepted she'd be a perpetual nurse and baby-sitter while the contractor and his fat wife went out all the time, spending their money in those post-war inventions of the devil, the night clubs, where you could get gin and scotch and maybe even a Singapore Sling. What a revolution! And in those clubs you could hear and see in person people like Lucienne Boyer,

13

Charles Trenet, Maurice Chevalier, Roche and Aznavour. They even allowed boogie-woogie, that crazy new dance that had them jigging and jumping around like monkeys. Joséphine went no farther than Maurice Chevalier: he sang "Louise" so nicely, and wore a boater, like Théophile's on their wedding day.

She flicked her ash and made a face at the electric sewing machine Cécile had bought herself the year before. Joséphine preferred her old treadle machine that still stood in its old place by the window. Poor, dear Cécile! For a long time she had been unable to get over her loss of Onésime Ménard, the married bus driver who had been killed on duty in a traffic accident. From the widow of this man she had so loved, she had obtained permission to put Onésime's oldest son Nicolas through school. Cécile thus cherished the illusion of having had a child by her pusillanimous lover, and had recently seen the boy accepted to college, where he was learning his Latin and Greek with a view to becoming a lawyer. Thus the old maid had belatedly found a cause to live for.

Passing the table Joséphine admired the basket of wax fruit in their many colours, dominated by orange, presented by Major Ephrem Bélanger. Cécile had her little diversions after all, like this discreet flirtation with the commander of the parish Zouaves, a widower in his late sixties who wore his uniform with style. Joséphine, a glint in her eye, approved of the relationship, Ephrem seeming to be a kind of improved Onésime, whose greatest charm consisted of his tendency to lavish more conversation on the mother than on Cécile. The daughter was annoyed with this at times, but Joséphine always reassured her, explaining this harmless anomaly by the things sexagenarians had in common.

Joséphine sat down, only to get up again at once. Why was she so restless today? She opened the freezer, but closed it at once as if shocked at the sight of the smoked salmon and cuts of game that filled it to the top. When would Guillaume get it into his head that she had enough?

Madame Plouffe turned the knob on the radio, but cut it off on hearing ". . . and he strikes out! . . ." All afternoon there'd be nothing but play-by-play of the semi-finals in American baseball. Which fact brought her back to the complex problem of her youngest. She went over to where his picture hung on the wall and stared long at the soldier with his medals, in the photo that hung between those of the late Théophile and Father Folbèche.

Finally Joséphine dropped wearily into her rocking chair again. She was at the end of her inventory of the family, at the point where it gave her the greatest worry. Poor little fellow! Guillaume, who had always been such a happy, good-natured boy, was now an unhappy child. Joséphine couldn't fathom his odd behaviour. Had he killed too many men with his grenades? Covered with decorations, he had come back from Europe taciturn and melancholy, refusing to talk about the war where he had been a real hero for a good five years. What interesting stories he could have told! And the American baseball teams had come back on the attack, offering him a try-out again for pitcher, but all he did was clam up, saying only, in a rage, "I'd be scared I'd kill somebody." It was true that the speed of his pitches could have cracked a batter's skull. No, baseball was out.

For months after he came back they'd watched Guillaume sink into a profound depression. He was uninterested in women and frightened of marriage, concerned, no doubt, about bringing into the world children destined to die at the front. What was worse, he refused to live with his mother and rented the apartment on the ground floor for himself. It had been given up by Napoléon when he bought his house. Trained to military discipline, he kept the place as clean and neat as a new nickel. With the tidy sum of his wartime savings he could afford to take his time and indulge in long, staring daydreams and the perverse pleasures of melancholy. He went out only when Napoléon dragged him along on the pretext he had some job calling for superhuman strength, appealing to his pride and wakening him out of his lethargy.

After a year of this the soldier's depression seemed to be getting worse. Sometimes, tossing in his uneasy sleep, he would sing a snatch of "Lili Marlene," or wake up in a sweat and pound the wall with his fist, terrifying his mother and sister upstairs. Sometimes his straight left would go right through the partition, but Napoléon knew a plasterer who patched the holes promptly. Guillaume was failing fast. Every time his sister-in-law Rita arrived, he would disappear – to Ovide's astonishment. Dark circles appeared beneath his eyes, his hands got the shakes, he was losing his appetite, and sometimes at meals he would heave a sigh, almost a groan, from the depths of his being, in the midst of the prevailing jollity.

A family council was called. Ovide went on about the world-weariness that Alfred de Musset had once described. Napoléon didn't know what he was talking about. The cure for Guillaume, he maintained, was sports, but he didn't want to play any more. Joséphine, for her part, knew: her son was suffering because he had killed human beings.

The solution came from Uncle Gédéon, a farmer from the Beauce and brother of the late Théophile, known in the family for his unflagging vigour and his love of women, whom he referred to, his mouth watering, as "those lovely creatures." Uncle Gédéon had a son, Aimé, nicknamed "Ti'-Mé", who showed the same taste for solitude and melancholy as his decorated cousin. This love of silence, this desire to get away from it all, the need for broad horizons, lakes, rivers and life in the wilds, is often to be found in French Canadians, inherited no doubt from their ancestors, the French colonists who left their homeland for the Great Adventure. Well, Uncle Gédéon suggested that Guillaume join forces with his son, Ti'-Mé, who spent each summer and fall as a hunting and fishing guide on Anticosti Island, working for visiting American millionaires and friends of the Government. No doubt Guillaume, with his sense of precision and his experience as an infantryman, could become a first-class hunter. As far as fishing was concerned, he had caught so many smelts in the St. Lawrence, so many trout in the creeks and even so many chickens in the neighbouring coops (with the help of a hook and a wriggling worm) that he would beyond a doubt become an expert angler and fly fisherman for Atlantic salmon! What's more, he could learn English from the Americans. Perhaps the language of Shakespeare would help cure his distress?

Guillaume agreed, and off he went to the open-air life under the protection of head guide Aimé Plouffe, the odd cousin. This was his second season leaving Québec for the giant island from June to October, returning loaded down with smoked salmon, venison, small game and Menier chocolates: Henri Menier, the famous French industrialist, had taken over Anticosti for a number of years and left a general store behind. Joséphine was soon overwhelmed by the abundant supplies sent or brought by her son. She passed some on to the priest, her whole family, the churchwardens, and the choir in vain: the freezer stayed full.

Joséphine smiled. Her Guillaume would be home in a few days. Oh, if only he'd come back cured! Before the war it was poverty they had on their backs, she reflected. Now, despite their troubles, they had too much of everything.

She got up again and returned to the soldier's photo. He'd be spending the winter with her, filling the long evenings by tying salmon flies with their delicate nuances. At night, from her bedroom just above his, she would hear him snoring and would be able to drop off to sleep, happy and reassured.

But a disagreeable memory popped into her head. A month earlier, Guillaume had been offered a ride to Quebec in the plane of an American millionaire for whom he had organized a miracle of fishes and had two unexpected days at home. Joséphine, sitting alone as she was now, had rocked herself to sleep as she said her rosary, humming the hymn "In heaven, in heaven, in heaven." Napoléon and Guillaume had come in on tiptoe and, seeing her dozing, had lifted her, chair and all, on to the kitchen table, where she, still half asleep, went on rocking and humming. The two villains, still boys at their age, had knelt on the floor and joined their hands in prayer, groaning, "Saint Joséphine, pray for our souls!" Waking with a start, she saw them and at the same time became aware of her ridiculous position. Instead of laughing at herself she grew furious, rose to her full height and, her head almost touching the ceiling, stretched an accusing arm at the two brothers, and pronounced these solemn words:

"When two children make fun of their mother that way, terrible things can happen!"

As soon as the sentence had fallen all three of them had felt a chill. Guillaume thought, I could be killed by a stray bullet in the woods of Anticosti, or drown in the rapids of the Jupiter. Napoléon saw his business bankrupt and refused even to think of the tuberculosis from which his wife had suffered once and which could descend on one of their children. Joséphine herself thought of Ovide and Rita, and their marriage on the rocks.

The two brothers, with less dash this time, took their mother down from her perch, said they were sorry and tried to change the subject. But the seed of anxiety had been sown. They went off crestfallen toward Napoléon's shop, leaving Joséphine unhappy that she had succumbed once more to her mania for dramatizing everything and prophesying the worst, thus traumatizing her children.

When, for goodness sakes, would she get over this tendency to play the broody hen, when would she let them fly with their own wings, and take the courage to be alone and look to her old age?

She tried to turn her wedding ring. It refused to move, and her finger hurt. What if her prophecy came true? What if frightful things happened to her sons? She should never have uttered that grandiloquent threat. All too often fate obeyed the apprehensions in a mother's heart.

2

Being a fishing guide on the Jupiter River with his amazing cousin Ti'-Mé Plouffe was a sweet exile for Guillaume.

The Jupiter flows in the dreams of the great sport-fishermen of the world, not the least of whom was the son of Charles Ritz (in his suite at the Paris Ritz in winter he would practise casting into a Jupiter of his imagination). But the Island that holds that river to its breast is a place of mystery and legend. Humpbacked, an immense immobile cachalot, it guards the mouth of the Gulf of St. Lawrence, two-headed, one facing the Atlantic and the other looking to America. Two hundred and twenty-five kilometres long and seventy-five wide, covered with dense spruce forest, scored by salmon rivers of which the Jupiter is the queen, it has a population of over a hundred thousand red deer, descended from a few head imported by the Frenchman Henri Menier and his gamekeeper Martin Zédé early in the century. First granted by Louis XIV to the explorer Louis Jolliet as a reward for his exploits on the Mississippi, this island (which has several shipwrecks on its conscience) became famous for its legends of pirates and buccaneers.

Early in this century the chocolate manufacturer Menier, tired of being a businessman and ably assisted by Martin Zédé, outfitted a ship and sailed in search of a virgin island. This wealthy Crusoe, after ploughing through many seas, at last discovered Anticosti. He bought it, built a wooden castle at Port-Menier, furnished it in the European style, and began to reign over his possession as an absolute monarch. He taught discipline to the natives and made them into a class of suave domestics. He built a railway and sold lumber from the forest. How privileged, those guests from Paris to whom he offered two-month visits to his paradise!

The Port-Menier store was overflowing with Menier chocolates. A flourishing handicraft industry in deerskin slippers and handbags sprang to life. But in 1917 Menier, grown obese, suddenly died, and his brother, who had been grumbling for years about the fortune the family was throwing away in this far-off paradise, sold the island to a big Canadian lumber company. During the depression of the thirties the president of the company burnt down the castle as an economy measure. From then on Anticosti remained exclusively a sanctuary for rich anglers and hunters from the States, or captains of Canadian high finance, or politicians and their cronies. In 1937 a group of Germans, self-styled scientists, with instructions from von Ribbentrop, surveyed the island with a view to purchase. But the Prime Minister of Quebec, the sly Maurice Duplessis, scenting the danger (what a splendid location for submarine bases!), alerted the government of Canada. The Germans took off.

On that Friday evening at eight-thirty, Anticosti the magnificent, the immense emerald, was exposing its most sumptuous flaw, the Jupiter River, to the gaze of the moon. As far back as Indians could recall there had never been an early October like this, with not one flake of snow. On the contrary: if it hadn't been for the multi-coloured foliage you'd have thought it was July. The Jupiter curled crystalline past the stratified rocks of the shore, toward the sea twenty kilometres farther down. The dark patches of the salmon pools ended in rapids silvered by the moon. The steady purr of the water was a part of the silence, was its complement. From time to time, here and there, came a cracking of branches where a deer was running, or the perfunctory howl of a sated wolf.

The hunting lodge, a shocking intruder in this Eden, lights ablaze, was loud with the shouts and songs of the happy hunters, still sitting over dinner. Along the walls of varnished spruce logs hung head-down a dozen deer, the too numerous descendants of those imported by Henri Menier in his ark, fifty years ago, when he mistook himself for Noah.

The guides had almost all taken to their quarters for an early night. The hard day began at four next morning. But two of them were still awake. As if drugged by the river, Guillaume Plouffe and his cousin Ti'-Mé were sitting on logs facing pool number twelve, the most famous, the most magical, the most prodigal of its salmon, the favourite of Henri Menier and the great men of this world, lying at the foot of a limestone rock twenty metres high. The two men seemed to join in a religious silence, the better to meditate with awe on the struggle of the salmon up toward the pools of his origin . . . his back, as it split the current, lighting the waves with flashes of bluish steel.

As the two sat staring at the flank of the great rock they seemed to be reliving the miraculous catches of the summer, when *Salmo salar* weighing six to eight kilos, well hooked, leapt in fury out of the water, twisting to get free. Now the fishing season was over. For Guillaume and Ti'-Mé hunting was nothing less than butchery, as the deer were too plentiful and made an easy prey. But the salmon! With him you had to fight, use all your wits and, if you caught him, earn your catch. After twenty minutes of struggle, feints, and mad, desperate rushes, the fish could still, though he was almost ready to fall into the landing net, free himself with a wild flick of his tail. Then the fishermen would curse their luck (it was always the biggest one that got away), but Guillaume and Ti'-Mé, grinning broadly, would salute the victor with raised hat.

Ti'-Mé lit his pipe. As tall as his cousin, but skinnier, he had a tanned, innocent face with restful green eyes. His old soft felt hat, stained with oil and grease, its blackened band crimped with multicoloured salmon flies, seemed too big for his head. Ti'-Mé must have been forty. He spoke slowly in his deep voice, almost in monosyllables, and when he wanted to show affection for a woman he would call her "my little squirrely." His whole world was reduced to fish and game. Ti'-Mé exhaled a puff of blue smoke and glanced across at Guillaume, whose face was framed by his blond beard. He was getting close to thirty and had become a real man, a kind of Tarzan in hunter's garb, a god of nature disguised as a hired hand. In summertime the tourists' wives wanted no guide but him. And yet . . .

From the lodge came the response song "Alouette," enough to set your teeth on edge with the off-key voices flat with weariness and booze. Ti'-Mé made a face.

"Why don't those noisy buggers go to bed?"

Guillaume shrugged.

"They pay to howl, we get paid to put up with it."

Ti'-Mé lit his pipe again.

"Sure, you're used to it. The war, like, and the soldiers always in a gang."

"I never liked that," said Guillaume. "Never liked gangs. I don't know what gets into those Yanks. As soon as you get a bunch of guys together they start drinking and shouting and singing as if they just got out of jail. The Germans are like that, too. I like the Americans better when they bring their wives or daughters along fishing."

Ti'-Mé nudged him, half suppressing a throaty laugh.

"We know about that, eh? Remember that blonde from Philadelphia? You didn't miss out, down there on the big flat rock just below the rapids past pool number nine."

"What are you talking about?" Guillaume demanded, with a faint show of indignation.

"I got good eyes, even at five hundred feet."

"Forget about that."

There was a pause. They were the kind of men who never boasted about their conquests, out of decency, or respect, or to protect the honour of those they had compromised. But it was true that both of them had sharp eyes. They could see things that others missed entirely. Beside the darkest pool they would shade their eyes and say, "Cast there, there's ten salmon. No . . . Make it a foot upstream."

The ruckus in the lodge was slowly growing quieter, as the fire in the great hearth burned low. Ti'-Mé had often marvelled at Guillaume's luck in not being shy with women, thinking of all the chances he himself had bungled with pretty guests as he stuttered and froze in their presence. He knocked his pipe against a stone.

"You glad to be going back home?"

"So-so."

Of course Guillaume would be glad to see his mother again. But the others? He was still fond of them, and yet . . . Take Napoléon: he'd changed so much. He was always restless, excitable, talking about nothing but getting rich, about using his political influence or grabbing all the plumbing contracts in the province of Quebec. Cécile, for her part, persisted in buzzing around Guillaume like an indefatigable fly. And Ovide? Every time Guillaume thought of his brother he felt guilty. Alas! He had been the first to go with Rita behind Ovide's back, and now she was certainly carrying on with other men. What a

21

whore she looked in her ads, with that Miss Sweet Caporal uniform! Guillaume felt Ovide's unhappiness so keenly, he preferred not to see him. What was it the war had killed inside him? As an adolescent he had been so carefree, so quietly happy! He supposed that after living through that extraordinary tragedy for five years, little everyday joys were no longer the same.

"Hey! Look at those two fine squirrels!"

Ti'-Mé had automatically reached for his rifle.

"Don't shoot!" said Guillaume, pushing down the barrel.

On the top of the cliff two deer stood silhouetted, their antlers hooked to the dark.

"Well, aren't you some ass-backward kind of a guide, eh? And you the best shot on the Island!" complained Ti'-Mé.

"They're like us. They just came for a look at the Jupiter. They're here because they know we won't kill them."

"I wouldn't have fired, you know that."

"I don't like killing for no reason," Guillaume grumbled.

"But you've no pity for the salmon."

The veteran wondered why. The salmon was a stranger in from the sea, indifferent to the world of men. It seemed a fish didn't suffer from the hook buried in his mouth. But a deer, now! He'd look at you with eyes like a frightened child. Guillaume remembered a sick one, his lower jaw taken off by the bullet from a Winchester. He was wandering alone from one thicket to the next, his eyes dull. Guillaume had held him by the neck and caressed him. Then he had fed him small handfuls of oatmeal. After that the animal had come back often in the early morning, loitering around their cabin. He shook his head to get rid of the thought of the mutilated beast, trying to think of arrogant, vigorous stags, leaping like fauns, which he would catch with a lasso, cowboy fashion, when the tourists couldn't see. He would hold his prey by the neck in his powerful arms, undo the slip knot and, laughing, send the astonished animal back to the forest with a slap on the rump.

Guillaume's life was neatly divided in two: there was the comic-book period, in which Tarzan loomed large, and which had made him cruel and irresponsible; and there was the five-year war period from which he had returned kind and gentle. Ti'-Mé had often tried to get him to talk about those years in Europe, but Guillaume was always upset and evasive and would go off to bed. Maybe he'd loosen up tonight – such a beautiful night!

"Guillaume, I don't understand you. You're so chicken hearted, how could you kill all those men at the front? Guys your own age!"

Guillaume turned pale and got to his feet.

"Don't ever talk to me about that."

He sat down again. His heart was bursting. He had to shout or scream. His vehemence seemed foreign to the beauty of the river and the calm of the night. Was it a cry of liberation or despair?

Suddenly the words spilled out.

"We were just like a herd of sheep. We had no choice. It was you or the other guy. When you're young it's like a sport. The more you kill the more batters you strike out, like baseball. You don't see them, they're too far away. It's as if you're not guilty from far away. But it's not a game any more when you see your chums die all around you. Then you go crazy, you're scared and the whole world seems like a hell. You realize what you're doing. And you kill and kill, and later when you see the ones you killed lying there, young like you are and they've got wavy hair like you, even the Germans, you want to cry and you wonder what you're doing on this earth. And that's why I like it here on Anticosti."

Guillaume was trying to suppress the quick sobs that were shaking his broad shoulders. Ti'-Mé sniffled and wiped a cheek with his sleeve. He suddenly felt great respect for this extraordinary grief.

"I'm a dumb bugger," he said. "I shouldn't have brought it up. It's terrible. But I know what you mean."

Guillaume was started now.

"The worst thing I remember, Ti'-Mé, was in Germany. A beautiful blonde, about twenty years old, she took me to bed with her. But I was on the lookout. I slipped my .38 under the pillow. An' a good thing, too. All of a sudden two armed Gerries bust out of the clothes cupboard. I was a little faster. I got them both."

There was a pause. They heard a loud slap and a splash. The great salmon had jumped two metres out of the water.

"What about the girl?" murmured Ti'-Mé.

For the first time Guillaume confessed it, reluctantly, ashamed.

"I shot her, too."

"Yeah," said Ti'-Mé sombrely. "That's something."

Why was Guillaume thinking about Ovide just then? He had

just imagined his brother shooting Rita if he caught her in bed with another man. Ti'-Mé laid a hand on his arm.

"Look, you had no choice, that's for sure. And you might as well get it out of your head if you want to be your old self. It's like being born again."

"The older you are, the harder it is to be born again."

"Never say that," persisted Ti'-Mé, filling his pipe. "Take me, now. I've got my troubles, too."

His partner seemed not to hear. He was haunted by the face of the dead Rita, caught sleeping with another man. He remembered now that the German girl had appealed to him because she was the image of his sister-in-law. Ti'-Mé went on in a monotonous voice.

"D'you think I had it easy? My old man never liked me. You know what he's like. Never satisfied. My brother Alexandre is a Dominican. That won't do, he should have made it to bishop. Dad's mayor of the village, it's no good, he wants to be a member of parliament. I'm the dummy of the family, the shame of the land. Just because I have no ambition and I like to live a quiet life in the wilderness, the old boy's ashamed of me. When he shouts at me I jump like I was a kid. At my age! I'm in no hurry to get home. I think I'll go work my ass off all winter in the lumber camp, Price Brothers, two hundred miles from our place."

Guillaume got up, shivering. The air had grown chill. He looked at his Bulova, taken from a German soldier's wrist. Friday, nine o'clock. Ovide would still be behind his counter in the record store. Napoléon was just arriving with his politician friends at the Chez Gérard night club to hear some French chanteuse and drink John Collins highballs. And his mother and Cécile and Major Bélanger would be playing cards at home, sipping lemonade.

Before going back to the lodge the two guides cast a final look at the Jupiter flowing down toward the sea.

3

And indeed! Napoléon, his wife Jeanne and an influential couple close to Maurice Duplessis' Union Nationale government were living it up in Chez Gérard's cabaret-restaurant, right across from the railway station in lower town. The owner, Gérard Thibault, had been the first one to realize it: in this exciting post-war period, in a world where communications were beginning to extend their infinite tentacles, people in Quebec who a few years before didn't own a radio or even a telephone were now greedy to enjoy their new-found prosperity, including music-hall shows they had previously only seen on film. From the closed ghetto of the kitchen or the parish, from the narrow pleasures of the amateur performance, they were branching out into entertainment on the international scale. From the dull existence of the past they had escaped at last, opening their arms to the new amusements offered.

Gérard Thibault had started up business in the shady section of the city, guessing that the good burghers of the upper town would hasten to nibble the forbidden fruit. He was right.

That Friday there was a line-up at the door of the cabaret, which was already packed with fun-loving spectators drinking and guzzling their drumsticks or pepper steaks heaped with French fries. Let joy be unconfined! They were there to hear Charles Trenet sing "*Boum*! When my little heart goes *boum*!" and "The sun has a rendezvous with the moon," and "When I was small," and "Ménilmontant." Charles Trenet's genius symbolized gaiety and youth, relegating pre-war songs to the mothballs and anticipating Presley and the Beatles.

Napoléon and his guests had a choice table near the stage, under the spotlights. At the time he did the plumbing for the restaurant, he had reduced his invoice sufficiently to get in to the Friday shows free and include his politician cronies. In return they saw that he was given a little contract here and there. In his naive way Napoléon practised his public relations with all the subtlety of a demolition team, but it worked!

That evening he was being extra demonstrative, greeting everyone around and offering drinks to customers at the neighbouring tables. His wife Jeanne seemed uneasy. They had fallen in love when they were poor and times were hard. Would prosperity change Napoléon to the point where she would lose him or he would lose himself? For Jeanne these nights at Chez Gérard were something out of a fairy tale, but at times she felt a vague fear that the tale would have an unhappy ending. She came from a poor family and had worked as a housemaid: was she not intended to live poor and die poor? Would she not be punished some day for defying destiny? She tugged at her husband's sleeve and whispered:

"Don't talk so loud! Everybody's looking!"

He pinched her chin and nibbled her ear.

"That's how it is when you're well known and you have a good pair of lungs. Ever since I took up the trumpet my voice is like a bull's. The more I play the better my wind is. Eh, old Jeanne?"

She blushed at this unequivocal evocation (backed up by an enormous wink) of his conjugal exploits, which often took place several times a night. He shouted, calling the waitress:

"Marie! Another round! Long live life!"

Marie came toward their table, followed by the lustful gazes of the men and envious glances from the women. She was a superb young woman in her twenties, French, from Paris, and newly arrived in Quebec. No one knew much about her, except that she had been recommended to Gérard Thibault by an influential person, a follower of Marshal Pétain during the occupation.

Tall and dark haired, with big green eyes and full, attractive lips, one could imagine, under her sky-blue uniform, hips that were broad despite her wasp waist, and, plain to see, legs whose shapely curves aroused the gentlemen customers and vexed their wives and companions. Everybody wondered how long a beauty like her, with an education into the bargain, was going to stay in a place like Chez Gérard. It was inevitable: Gérard Thibault was going to lose her soon. Marie kept her distance from everyone and did her job with tact and diligence. Reserved in manner, she seemed unaware of her charms, paid no attention to vulgar remarks and, with the elegance of a butterfly, avoided the exploratory hands of customers who had drunk one too many. As she was writing down the order Napoléon laid one hand on hers. Jeanne, scolding, pulled it away.

"Let her be, you're embarrassing her, silly!"

Marie smiled her gratitude and went on her way, accompanied by admiring looks from all.

"If I was allowed a second wife, she'd be the one – just as long as you didn't mind, eh Jeannie?"

"Just let me catch you!" she said, pinching his biceps. "What about our kids, eh? I knew you'd start getting that idea one of these days, with all these drinks and evenings at the restaurant."

He laughed and caressed her leg beneath the table. Blushing, she pushed his hand away. Napoléon took an open joy in his life as a prosperous plumber. Sentimental complications and furtive dreams of romantic adventure never amounted to much with him.

"Oh, never mind that, now. Let's have fun!"

And he clinked glasses with the politician and his wife:

"Honourable Assistant Deputy Minister of Public Works, under the greatest politician the world has ever known, Maurice Le Noblet Duplessis, I declare to you, and to you, too, Madame Deputy Minister, that this lovely creature Jeanne, my little wife, was thin as a rake and dying when I met her. Between the two of us we cured her! And five children after that! She weighs forty pounds more than the day we were married."

"Don't make me burst!" protested Jeanne, and the others had a good laugh.

"Which means, when I take on a contract, I fulfil it to perfection," said Napoléon, adding in a stage whisper: "By the way, that contract for the jail, you won't forget it, eh?"

The Deputy Minister's wife turned away and her husband said "Shhhhhh!" and looked around uneasily. But nobody was listening. They were announcing that Charles Trenet would be on stage in five minutes. Napoléon tightened his grip, his whispers grew incisive and his eyes burned like coals:

"My ten per cent for the election fund is ready, I pay cash in advance! And I work well, day and night, cheaper than anybody! My prices are the best!"

The orchestra came on, the violins were tuning up. Suddenly nervous, Jeanne jogged Napoléon's elbow. "See the table at the back!" Rita, their sister-in-law, was clinking glasses with another woman and two well-dressed, fortyish men. One of them was Stan Labrie. Napoléon turned pale and he clenched his teeth.

"What's she doing here with Stan Labrie, will you tell me? And Ovide still working at the store!"

"I suppose she needs her bit of fun," said Jeanne, indulgently. "She likes going out, too, you know."

Napoléon growled:

"Ever since she was Miss Sweet Caporal there's no holding her back. She looks at all the men like a slut."

"She didn't change," Jeanne corrected him softly. "She always was Miss Sweet Caporal, deep down."

As if she had heard Napoléon's words and felt his hard gaze on her, Rita turned and saw her brother-in-law. In the full splendour of her thirty-odd years, she was indeed the same girl who had dazzled Ovide ten years earlier, but her seductive talents had since reached a stunning degree of efficiency. The moment a masculine glance touched her own, her lips grew moist, she crossed and uncrossed her superb legs and her whole body underwent a subtle undulation of disturbing abandon. Did she owe this accomplishment to the thrilling experience of last spring, when Stan Labrie had her chosen as an advertising symbol for the Sweet Caporal company? Over Ovide's protests she had agreed to dress up as a majorette and ride on an allegorical float in the Saint-Jean-Baptiste parade. The crowd whistled its admiration for her shapely hips, her little round bottom that almost forced her mini-skirt out on a tangent, her breasts, firm and aggressive under her tunic, her delightful face, her long and graceful neck, her lips made for the ecstatic smiles of love and her languorous eyes ready to roll at the slightest caress.

Her success was immediate. The company offered her a thousand dollars if she would allow her photo in costume to appear on billboards throughout the city. This was where Ovide, when he saw them, fell into a rage and issued an injunction to the president of the firm with threats of a suit for alienation of affection and a denunciation in *Le Devoir*, a paper known for its respect for moral principles. The contract was cancelled and Rita had been sulky with Ovide ever since. But the damage was done. Everyone knew her now, in the street, in restaurants and at church; and all the gents were mentally undressing her so that they could, after a decent pause, imagine her in her Miss Sweet Caporal garb.

Damn the Plouffes, anyway! Avoiding her brother-in-law's inquisitorial eye, Rita managed to control her embarrassed vexation. The germ of a plausible explanation for Jeanne and Napoléon floated up and took form. If she stood up a few minutes from now as if nothing were wrong, she'd easily attract as much attention as that flashy Marie, if not more. She smiled to herself: she'd been invited to Chez Gérard by her cousin and the latter's boyfriend, an insurance agent. Stan, who was there already, had insisted on joining them. What could she do? She'd tell Ovide the same story and everything would be hunky-dory.

28

Relieved, she undulated her way toward Napoléon's table.

A few hundred metres away, on the Boulevard Charest, glimmered a neon sign, Au Royaume du Disque. The owner of the record store was cashing in on the public's craze for French singers, aroused by radio programs and the great Parisian stars who passed through at Chez Gérard. This was why he kept his store open late on Fridays, catching the patrons from the first show who would come in warmed up by the melodies they had just heard, awkwardly trying to hum their favourites. Of course most other stores were closed, but a dollar was a dollar and it was his business if he wanted to work late Fridays.

And didn't he pay his manager, Ovide Plouffe, the lordly sum of forty a week? The boy wasn't an ideal salesman, but he attracted a clientele that was faithful to classical music and opera and appreciated Ovide's good advice and his encyclopaedic knowledge of the great singers. As for popular songs, Ovide learned with time to conceal his contempt for this second-rate music. But to his surprise he had recently taken an interest in Charles Trenet's creations, which were brimming with joyous rhythms, freshness, poetry and optimism.

Ovide, alone in the store, was lost in thoughts that capered in all directions. They were talking about raising the price of *Le Soleil*, the daily, from three cents to five! What were things coming to? And there were the political problems: Louis Saint-Laurent, a great lawyer from the city, and minister of Justice . . . was he going to become Prime Minister and succeed Mackenzie King, who had been taken gravely ill during a visit to London? That would be a great honour for Quebec City! During the last few months Ovide had felt in himself the awakening of a social conscience of which he had been unaware. The community was developing quickly, and all sorts of troublesome evidence pointed to mysterious upheavals. There were all these proud intellectuals, graduates of the Social Science faculty of which the dean and founder was Father Georges-Henri Lévesque, a disciple of the French Dominicans Maydieu, Delos and Dominique Dubarle: what kind of society did they really want? And these progressive journalists with their European ideas and their idol, the editorialist André Laurendeau; the Christian trade-union movement and its inspiring leader,

the young orator Jean Marchand – why were they all so fero-
ciously opposed to Maurice Duplessis' absolute power? In the
name of democracy and pluralism? Ovide would like to know
them all, to share their passions and join their battle. But he
was only an obscure record salesman!

Mechanically he wiped the dust from a trombone whose brass
shone in the electric light. He dreamed of chalices and mon-
strances of gold studded with precious stones, thought of the
Polish treasure and once again of Duplessis. At the start of the
war, in 1939, the Polish authorities had sent their treasures to
safety in the most Catholic Province of Quebec, where they
were kept hidden in the vaults of the Provincial Museum. Now
Duplessis was refusing to return them (perhaps at the request
of the clergy in Warsaw) on the grounds that the present Polish
government was of the communist persuasion. Ovide scratched
his head. What would he do in Duplessis' place? Those Communists were becoming more and more threatening! Mao Tse
Tung in China was on the point of kicking out Chiang
Kai-shek. In France they were stirring up strikes in every industry. What was de Gaulle waiting for? Why didn't he upset
the Queuille government, which didn't know how to stand up
to the Commies?

These grave world problems depressed Ovide. Suddenly he
felt weary. When would the first show at Chez Gérard get out,
anyway? Encores, no doubt. Rita, standing up, clapping like
mad: she'd be the one to shout for more. Ovide hadn't changed
much, except for a few white streaks in his dark hair. His jaw
line had grown harder, more determined. His teeth were always tightly clenched, even when he slept, a defence against
profound and chronic worry. His eyes ranged over his inventory. The records were neatly classified according to type. A
few musical instruments took up half the store, mainly electric
guitars, very popular with the young. Adolescents, alas, responded with a disquieting passion to disorderly rhythms, a
passion Ovide had never experienced and could not understand. The whole world seemed to be falling victim to St. Vitus's
dance, Lord help us!

One astonishing thing was the increasing number of trumpets he was selling, doubtless because of the popularity of Louis
Armstrong and other American jazz trumpet players. These
protégés extracted such sounds from their instruments that the
result was more a kind of acrobatics than an art. Ovide won-

dered how really musical all this was when it depended so much on lungs, puffed-out cheeks and protruding eyeballs! But what a surprise, his brother Napoléon had dropped in and bought a trumpet! To give Ovide a boost, perhaps? But Napoléon never did things by halves. He was serious about learning, and when he went out on the veranda after supper, while Jeanne was doing the dishes, and began to torture his instrument, the neighbours tore their hair. They came over to beg him to go learn his art in the parish hall or the nearby fields. Ephrem Bélanger, major of the Zouaves, the friend of Cécile and Joséphine, saw in Napoléon a future recruit for his bugle band, but the plumber was evasive, playing hard to get.

Ovide gave a little contemptuous laugh. It often happened when he was alone that he indulged in thinking of himself as Siamese personalities: an admirable Ovide and a despicable Ovide. Tonight he felt no admiration for the latter. Rita was right to get impatient with his wretched salary and his inability to improve their situation. The example of Napoléon's success, the whims he indulged, his convertible car aroused predictable expectations in Rita. With increasing frequency he felt guilty about her and caught himself envying his brother. And how rightly she must think of him as an inveterate killjoy! And how cruel he was to her! In the name of his own detestable vanity he had deprived Rita of her true *raison d'être*, that of showing off and being admired. He had caused her a grievous disappointment by cutting off her brilliant career as Miss Sweet Caporal. Things had not been the same between them since. They were separated by an ill-healed wound, which opened a little from time to time. What should he do? At least she must be having fun tonight with the cousin and her boyfriend. Great! She'd be in better humour tomorrow. He would try to share her enthusiasm for Charles Trenet, he'd even promise to switch to a new and more spectacular future. You could lose your wife if you didn't become the champion she hoped for. Ovide tried to puff out his chest but his shoulders sagged at once and the momentary flash of aggression in his eyes gave place to the expression of a drowned man.

A more spectacular future: but where, and in what? He wasn't much of a businessman and the only trade he knew was that of leather cutter. That, never! He'd die before he'd go back to the factory. He felt his bowels weaken, laughed again at Ovide the despicable and went over to the turntable where he put on

31

Pagliacci by Caruso. Alone, he sang and sobbed with his idol. Two euphoric couples burst into the store. Caught *in flagrante delicto*, Ovide choked off the tenor and assumed his pose as a serious sales clerk.

"What can I do for you, ladies and gentlemen?"

"We want all of Charles Trenet's records!"

He stayed there until half-past eleven. Obviously Rita had forgotten him, absorbed as she must be in her pleasure at Chez Gérard. And he certainly wasn't going to disturb her at the cabaret. Something told him that he might suffer for it, but he preferred the noble attitude of the husband who allows his wife a certain amount of freedom: if you love and respect her, you trust her, don't you? He closed up and set off for his apartment in the upper town, at the top of the stairway in the rue de l'Alverne, just beside the Franciscan monastery. It was there, against the wall, that he had hurled himself at Rita one evening long ago, a Rita who didn't put up much of a fight, by the way, after several Singapore Slings absorbed in the Château Frontenac bar. Afterwards, mad with remorse, he had tried to join up and go die for democracy.

Where did he get this mania for sticking to the symbols that had marked his life? Hitched to this procession of memories, he dragged them after him, head bowed, with no view of the horizon. Only last week he had phoned Brother Léopold, his cell neighbour in the monastery of the White Fathers of Africa, to see how he was getting on. Perhaps Ovide was only good for remembering all kinds of things, especially arias and monasteries.

He lived in a small four-room apartment modestly furnished. Forty dollars a month: he observed the wisdom of "one month's rent, one week's pay." Of course his salary didn't allow for a car. But Rita had a tendency to buy clothes on credit. He was always begging her to give up the habit, but she was so mad for the frills and furbelows that suited her so admirably that all he did now was apprehensively open the mail, most of which was bills. Yet Rita had become more reasonable about these things in recent times. It was almost midnight. He hung up the phone. Granny didn't want him to come for little Arlette, now five years old and Joséphine's darling. Rita could fetch her in the morning. Ovide pinched his nose, wondering. His mother had said something enigmatic about Rita: "You're giving her too much rein. If she learns to trot she'll gallop. See to it, Ovide. Think about what I'm telling you. Your mother has a nose for these things."

He went over to the window and pulled back the curtain. Twelve-fifteen. Really, Rita was going too far! Maybe she'd had an accident. Nervously he paced the kitchen, furnished in pink arborite with chrome legs and arms. This was the fashion, but Ovide hated these horrors, they made him feel as if he were living in a metal box. In the small living room stood the piano covered with books and nearby a small radio/record player, paid for in thirty-six monthly instalments. This was where Ovide forgot about his life and plunged into Verdi, Puccini and Leon-cavallo. Heavy armchairs in beige plush took the rest of the space in a room where the lamps barely had a place to stand.

Rita came in at one.

"Poor you! Aren't you in bed yet?" She felt genuinely sorry for him, but her voice was tough and her eyes were excited.

"You know I can't sleep till you're here," he complained.

She laid her purse on the arborite of the table.

"Phew! What an evening! Charles Trenet! Tall, blond and handsome, curly hair and sky-blue eyes!" she enthused and started humming *"Ménilmontant, mais oui, Madame . . . "*

Ovide tried a feeble smile.

"I prefer 'When I was little, I loved you madly . . .'"

She chucked him under the chin. "You mean, when you were big, dear liar!"

"Have you been drinking?"

Rita whipped around.

"You know, there were two shows! Oh, it was so nice! And you just have to have a drink. You have to. Oh, Ovide, we had such fun. My cousin had her friend Fred along, he runs an insurance office. I tell you what, the money just drips through his fingers."

"That's easy when you've got it."

Then she covered her rear:

"Oh! I almost forgot! Am I dumb! Just imagine who came over to our table? Guess! Go on!"

"Napoléon?"

Rita put on her pussy-cat face.

"No! He was there, sure, with Jeanne and his friends in the Party. Oh, you'll never guess. Stan Labrie in person."

The whole past episode broke over him. Ovide's rival, once

Rita's fiancé, the impotent Stan Labrie, the man responsible for the Miss Sweet Caporal contract. Stan Labrie, orgy-broker, maybe even a white-slave trader, was once more prowling around Ovide's wife.

"I forbid you to talk to that low-lifer. I've told you that before."

"What could I do? I was cornered!"

Ovide found himself ridiculous. Apparently calm, he asked: "Did you drink any Singapore Slings?"

Her laugh was a cascade of pearls:

"Singapore Slings are for you, only with you. They're out of fashion now, people are drinking John Collinses. Poor Stan, he looks so sad and lonely, you know? That's normal, it must be discouraging for a man who can't do anything to a woman, eh? Listen, have we any gin left? You and I could have a li'l nightcap."

"You've had enough for tonight. Haven't you? Let's keep our money to buy vitamins for our daughter. That's more to the point. When I saw you weren't coming I phoned mother to keep her there for the night."

She made a schoolgirl face and slapped her forehead:

"I forgot all about her! God, it's boring sometimes to be stuck with kids when there's so much going on in the world."

She yawned.

"Well, let's go to bed and have lovely dreams!"

She disappeared into the bedroom. Ovide thought of Napoléon, and friend Fred from the insurance office, and money slipping between their happy fingers. He stared at Rita's purse forgotten on the kitchen table, then felt for his own wallet in his back pocket, took it out and opened it. Just thirty dollars. Poor little Rita, he thought. She loved to laugh and have fun. She was the wholesome one! How boring she must find him! And she was behaving better lately. What about a nice surprise for her? He'd slip a twenty-dollar bill in her purse and she'd be all tenderness for him when she found it. On a scrap of paper he wrote: "Use this any way you like, my darling. Your Ovide." And he folded the money inside it. He opened the purse to put the paper inside and his eyes nearly popped out of his head. Amid the usual collection of articles to be found in a flirt's handbag he spied three new fifty-dollar bills. Orange coloured. Stupefied, he counted them. A piece of cardboard from a book of matches – Chez Gérard – fell on the table. There

34

was a phone number written on it. Ovide didn't dare jump to any conclusions: his whole being froze in a pose of horrified defence . . . But his mother's warning was pounding in his brain. Stan Labrie had turned up again . . . As if in a panic he shouted:

"Rita!"

She came out in her bathrobe, saw the open purse and the three bank notes in Ovide's trembling hand, and his face, white and waxen. She too grew pale and almost lost her breath.

"So! Now you go fishing in my personal things, like a spy. Is that it?"

"I wasn't fishing. I wanted to give you a surprise, I was putting twenty dollars in. But where did you get this money, Rita?"

"I . . . I've been saving it up out of the household money for months, and Arlette's family allowance is in it, too! I changed it all into fifties. It takes less room and I feel better than with a roll of ones and twos. And what did *you* think? With that look on your face . . ."

She went on the attack and he began to stammer:

"Listen, I'm sorry, I'm going crazy, I must be. It's just that I'm so tired these days . . . "

The worst was over. Rita grabbed the bit of cardboard with the phone number.

"And that's a number I'm supposed to call about a job."

He was choking. His wife, Ovide Plouffe's wife, working? This was a direct attack on his pride.

"Never! If I can't keep you and make you happy I'd rather die!"

She shrugged. She was sobering up, and now she spoke gently to him, attentively, like a nurse:

"Ovide! You've got to be sensible. I can't bear to see you drudging yourself to death. Let's be realistic. We live like a poor couple. I could have Arlette looked after or put her out to board for a while. It'd be one more salary coming in. And I'd love it! We'd be a going concern again instead of falling to pieces from one day to the next like now. Look, I could get a job as waitress at Chez Gérard tomorrow. And the tips, eh? You'd see that French thing, that Marie, where she'd get off. And the way she looks down her nose at us, with her precious accent! She'd see what I was made of. And the money would roll in, I'll guarantee."

Ovide felt weak in the knees. His Rita, waitress in a night club! A worse humiliation than seeing her as Miss Sweet Caporal in the parade!

"Don't ever do that to me, Rita! I could never look myself in the face again."

In a toneless voice he was begging like a child, ready to go on his knees to her. But he pulled himself together and said roughly:

"Go to bed. We'll talk about all that tomorrow."

"You're always against everything!" she complained.

Trying not to sob aloud, she ran to the bedroom and slammed the door behind her, then curled up in bed and covered her head.

Ovide sat down at the end of the table, elbows on the pink arborite, chin in hands. His life was just one long tribulation! He had a pain near his heart. His head was swimming. For some minutes he felt close to losing consciousness. Then he managed to get to his feet, tottering a little as he murmured his act of contrition. He drank a glass of warm water and went to lie down beside Rita, murmuring:

"If I die, have me cremated and get married again. You'll be happy at last."

Next day Ovide rose early, carefully so as not to wake Rita, drank some tomato juice and went to the store. He felt less unhappy there than at home where the sight of his wife against that mediocre background was a constant reminder of his dismal life. Here, among the records (many of which, completely foreign to his customers, allowed him to escape into a dream world) he found the respite his inner peace required, a peace that was constantly threatened by events.

The owner came in, looked at him and asked if he felt ill. He congratulated him, however, on being first in the shop. Ovide explained that he had become an early riser in the monastery. As for his wan face, he pretended that he had slept badly because of some stewed pork hocks Rita had made, she knew very well he couldn't digest that fine-grained meat and most of the time it was full of bacteria anyway . . . .

"If this keeps up we're going to run out of Trenet!" said the owner, checking the stock. "You're a good saleman, you know what you're talking about, but you're absent minded, you forget to re-order the hits. What's more, you spend too much time listening to records with your finicky free-music fans, and they end up buying nothing. And you've ordered too much sheet music. Young people aren't learning to read music these days. They play and sing by ear. Well, that's a word to the wise, young fellow."

Ovide's pale cheeks turned red. He had a fierce desire to hurl all the records within reach at the owner's head in an act of total rebellion such as had led him some years earlier to knock out his torturer, Brother Léopold of the White Fathers' monastery, after which he had given up the frock and married Rita. But this time he would run away alone and for good. He would write a farewell letter to Rita, to his mother, to his daughter, confessing his utter failure. He would ask their pardon and beg them not to look for him, to think of him in the future as an anonymous atom in the totality known as the human race. He would turn vagabond and end up as a bum under the bridges of the Seine. Or he'd come back, out of the blue, after years of absence, a millionaire in his Rolls-Royce, smoking a big cigar. Before his eyes danced the three fifty-dollar bills in Rita's purse. Her explanation rang false! Ovide's perceptions were keen after the fact. When he remembered certain harmonies in Debussy they would astonish him, suddenly revealing their marvellous originality.

"Answer me when I talk to you!" said his employer impatiently.

Ovide did not tell him that the recollection of certain orange-coloured bank notes had just deflated a fierce desire to stage a memorable scene of farewell. He seemed to be startled out of deep thought.

"I was just thinking about the future of your business," he said, as if fascinated by a sudden vision. "If I forget to re-order stock on time, and I admit it, that's because I'm the kind of man who's good at long-term planning."

The owner stared. Long-term planning! What kind of aberration was this, coming from his odd-ball manager?

"All these 78 records we're selling like hot cakes, you know, well, they're on their last legs."

"What? We'll not sell any more? Oh, boy, you have some pessimistic days, don't you? If we're going broke, why not close down now?"

"I didn't say that," replied Ovide solemnly. "I merely mean that research is being done that will revolutionize the record and playback industry. First there'll be 45 rpm records, then 33s. Do you see what that means?"

The owner's eyes opened wide.

"On the 33 rpm's," Ovide continued, "there'll be eight or ten songs on each side and you'll have twenty minutes of music before you turn over the record."

"I'm not so sure I like that. We'll sell a twentieth as many records, am I right?"

Ovide shrugged. What calm wisdom he brought to the contemplation of other people's future!

"In that case you charge twenty times as much! They'll take a lot less room. And there'll be a market for sophisticated playbacks that today's merchant cannot imagine."

The owner, shaken, was thinking hard. The boy was really astonishing. Great things awaited him, no doubt of that. And he was going to lose this precious employee one of these days. What if Ovide decided to open his own store? He'd better cater to his feelings, butter him up a bit, maybe even . . . give him a raise . . . .

The door opened and a ravishing beauty walked in. Ovide was paralyzed at the sight of this superb creature, the most beautiful woman he had ever seen in his life. He thought of Bizet's *Carmen*. Those eyes, that hair, that body, those legs! Had he been present at Chez Gérard last night he would have recognized Marie the Frenchwoman, about whom Rita had spoken with such envy, hoping to steal her act.

Seeing Ovide helpless, the owner rushed over to their customer. She said she was looking for a classical record. A Frenchwoman! Ovide's heart gave a leap. What a lovely accent! What a disturbing voice! Her contralto tones placed her: sensual as Eartha Kitt, less tragic than Piaf. She asked, seeming almost certain of receiving no for an answer, whether they had any songs by Francis Poulenc.

"Francis Poulenc?" said the owner, hesitantly, and turned prudently toward Ovide.

Eyes rivetted on the girl's pretty face, Ovide nodded, his throat dry, preparing to control his Quebec accent. Marie's face lit up with childish joy, and Ovide smiled.

"Of course, Francis Poulenc," he gulped. "At the Royaume du Disque we have everything. Ah, Francis Poulenc, the great

38

French composer born in 1899, influenced by Debussy, Chabrier and Ravel. Eminent member of The Six, his talent mainly directed toward the art song and the theatre."

The owner puffed out his chest proudly and approvingly.

"Exactly, indeed," the girl confirmed, astonished to discover here a kind of language she had not heard in Quebec. "Would you by any chance have 'Les Chemins de l'amour' sung by Yvonne Printemps?"

"Ask and you shall receive!" said Ovide gaily.

He began to hum "Oh paths of memory, pathways of our love . . ."

The girl nodded, absent-minded, her gaze lost in her own past. The owner was admiring Ovide's performance, feeling like an outsider in his own store. Ovide was launched:

"Of course we are familiar with Yvonne Printemps for her 'Pot Pourri' by Alain Gerbault, and because of her marriage to Sacha Guitry. But here in any case, alas, only a very few are aware that 'Les Chemins de l'amour' was composed for her by Poulenc after a poem by Jean Anouilh.

"Oh, Yvonne Printemps!" Ovide went on, "an inimitable voice! Such sensitivity, enough to make one shiver – like your own voice, Mademoiselle!" he added gallantly, " but in a deeper register. Ah, excuse me! I must hasten to find this masterpiece for you."

The girl smiled at her discovery of a French Canadian such as she had never encountered in all her months in Quebec City. There was something comical about him, but at the same time something engaging and kind that enfolded you like the smell of incense. Marie never lingered over this kind of analysis, but Ovide, though he had disappeared into the storeroom at the back, seemed still to be with her.

"That boy there is the greatest music expert in the country. We've got everything at the Royaume du Disque, and we've got the best."

Ovide returned with his treasure.

"I found it! It's only been played once, and that was by me."

Ovide wore the marvellous, gentle smile, full of goodness and delight, that illuminated his face when he was happy. He started the record player and half-closed his eyes out of respect as befitted a music lover who knows how to hear and appreciate high art. The girl's attitude encouraged him in his pose. She herself was deep in meditation, her expression nostalgic, as if

Yvonne Printemps' voice brought back fond memories.

Ovide didn't dare ask her any questions, though he saw that her eyes were moist. He simply murmured:

"What a performance! What subtlety! And what an admirable song! Do you not agree?"

Carefully, he slipped the record into its brown envelope.

"You're French, are you not?"

She nodded, but her gaze was still distant. She opened her purse . . . .

"It is almost as if you had known Yvonne Printemps . . . in person!" he ventured.

"Yes. In Paris, at my mother's place, years ago. Very well, I'll buy this record."

She was too reticent and Ovide too tactful to pursue the question. Suddenly he felt a touch of panic. What if he never saw her again?

"May I invite you to come back? We have a great many fine recordings. I would be happy to play them for you."

Could he believe his eyes? She was smiling at him with tender gratitude. She was about to pay for the record, but he pushed her hand away.

"No, let me make you a present of it. I'll put it on my account, sir," he said to the owner.

Suddenly he grew pale. He was overcome by the same dizziness he had felt last evening after his scene with Rita, but more intense: he felt he would surely die. Was it the sight of the open purse, reminding him of his wife's, or was it just that this lovely girl had smiled at him with such tenderness? Or was it both at once? He fainted as if struck by lightning and lay stretched out full length upon the floor. "Good heavens!" said the girl. "I'll be hanged!" exclaimed the owner. "It must be that stew again."

Marie, distressed, kneeled beside him and gently slapped his face. "Monsieur," she cried. "Monsieur!"

And there was the owner with a damp towel.

"Good grief, and he was that pale this morning! He's too fond of music, when he gets talking about it you'd think he was about to die. What a thing to happen!"

It was a curious sight: a young Parisian beauty and the owner of the Royaume du Disque kneeling beside Ovide Plouffe, who was lying flat in the midst of all the trumpets, guitars and record shelves and electric organs. What if customers came in! Gently,

40

Marie moistened Ovide's cheeks. "Monsieur! Monsieur!" At last his eyes opened, rolling wildly. "There, that's better," she said, relieved, for she had thought for a moment he was dead.

The owner mopped his brow. At least he wasn't going to lose this extraordinary sales clerk, this long-term planner, this dreamer of tricks for commercial success. Ovide had already suggested to him that he sponsor a radio program to be called "Records are trumps at the Royaume du Disque!"

In the presence of this magnificent young woman who, like Ovide, knew who Poulenc was, he suddenly felt his heart expand to fit the dimensions of a French magnate.

"You're getting a ten-dollar raise! Wake up!"

Ovide's eyes, still unfocussed, still glassy, remained open. Marie went on moistening his neck and cheeks. "Come, come, what's the matter, then?" Before sinking back into oblivion he succeeded in murmuring, "Thank you, thank you so much!"

"This is an ambulance case, hurry!" said the proprietor.

4

Ovide had been hospitalized on the "medical" floor at Saint-Sacrement Hospital. Any ailment that didn't end up in surgery was relegated there, acquiring an aura of mystery when the doctor declared it "a medical case."

In the public ward with its row of forty-odd beds, patients with every possible illness were cared for. The Grey Nuns, owners of the immense building, and a squad of devoted student nurses under the eye of hardened graduates and doctors, and all subject to the iron hand of the Mother Superior, watched over their charges jealously, indiscriminately, as if they had been victims entrusted to the Grey Nuns by the Good Lord himself. In 1948 the sick still inspired a respect that had its roots in Christian humanism. The organism was thought of as a complex whole that was also susceptible to psychological disorders. "Specialization" was rampant in the United States, but Quebec doctors, trained in the European clinical tradition school, stubbornly rejected the concept, which tended to treat the human body like a balky car that only needed a few parts repaired. In the Saint-Sacrement Hospital, prayer and faith in God were as important as the most powerful remedies.

In Ovide's ward many different complaints were to be found, from hypertrophy of the heart to eczema, leukemia disguised as anemia, pleurisy, coxalgia. Side by side were cases of diabetes, gonorrhoea, hemorrhoids, cancer and uremia. Here was a young man quietly dying of a sarcoma of the knee, now spreading to his lungs. He was strumming his guitar in his corner bed in a melancholy way, just next to the office of the head nun, while drunkards, prematurely old, shared tales of trouble, packing their pipes with strong Canadian tobacco as they sat around the radio waiting for the square-dance program.

Ovide in the hospital! By ambulance, with its howling siren, its long, tragic, strident wail! The Plouffes were profoundly anxious. Until that moment ambulances had been for other people, in Joséphine's mind. She rushed to the hospital but was turned away. No visitors! Ovide was resting, under observation in the emergency area. Rita also was refused admittance. Joséphine hauled her off to church to light a few candles and made her kneel beside her for ten minutes asking Saint Joseph to cure the patient. Monsignor Folbèche promised to say a mass for him the following morning.

His prayers were answered. Twenty-four hours later Ovide was lying in bed number fourteen, looking well and still puzzled by that sudden weakness. They had found nothing wrong with him except the slight heart murmur the army doctor had already noticed when Ovide, in despair, had tried to enlist in 1940. But Ovide wasn't too surprised. In his soul, his mind and his body strange things were going on that no one would understand. Two o'clock: almost visiting time. A nun came to take his pulse, scrutinized him closely and said:

"Is something about your life bothering you? Your heart seems to be too sensitive. Your pulse jumps ten beats if a person asks you if you have family or work or money troubles."

He looked away.

"Talk to me about music and you'll see it go up by twenty."

This nun paid particular attention to him after she discovered he had spent some time in the monastery of the White Fathers of Africa.

"Maybe you weren't made for marriage," she sighed. "At least you're a good boy. Not like . . ." (and her voice descended to a near-whisper) ". . . not like that French atheist in number thirteen beside you. Between you and me, he's next thing to a scoundrel. He never goes to confession or communion, not to mention the rest of it."

Her face turned hard with a sovereign dignity as she went on to number fifteen. Intrigued, Ovide turned toward thirteen. Since the morning he had frequently observed this despicable individual out of the corner of his eye.

The man had a clean-cut face, a thick head of greying hair and, above all, extraordinary, steely, piercing eyes that chilled and penetrated like the needle of a syringe. Ovide, startled, wondered how a Frenchman from "sweet France" could have such a stony look about him.

Crutches stood at the head of the injured man's bed. Ovide had never seen him up and around. He spoke to no one. A jeweller's glass screwed into one eye, he spent his days examining and repairing watches of all kinds, skilfully manipulating the most delicate tools. Precisely, with never a trembling of his hand, he would penetrate the works of watches brought in by an individual with the look of a gallows bird. He would glance furtively around to see if any of the nuns were looking, then slip a bottle of De Kuyper gin under the Frenchman's pillow.

A scoundrel, the cripple? Ovide suspended judgement. He knew how intolerant some Quebec Catholics could be, especially monks and nuns. If you weren't a believer you were a black sheep, automatically. But it seemed to Ovide that it took some courage to admit to those who had the faith that you didn't have it. A Frenchman! How had he landed in this hospital? Ovide thought of Marie and recalled with emotion his last vision of her, leaning over him and gently moistening his face. This daydream of Marie began to occupy the foreground of his private cinema, chronic dreamer that he was, while the image of Rita faded away against a storm background in which she was dancing a coquettish ballet, barefoot, in a rain of banknotes. What was happening to him? Was his mind going to become the prisoner of a face he might never see again, of a woman he dared not even dream of as his true soul mate, until now undiscoverable? It was unfair of life to give him that brief gleam of hope, a moment of promise bound to vanish, forever!

He heard a gentle commotion in the ward. It was time! Friends and relatives invaded the room, but it was Rita who attracted the attention. Aware of the admiring interest she aroused, in her white dress and red shoes, the combination that reminded Ovide of their engagement eight years ago, she was smiling at him from afar. As she walked toward him she tried to tone down the suggestive wiggle of her hips, but it was second nature to her and she only half succeeded. A number of patients cranked their beds up higher, others whistled discreetly.

"Ovide!" she said, holding his head in her hands and giving him a kiss on the forehead. "What a fright you gave me! There's nothing wrong with you, is there? Just tired? That's what sister told me. I want you to hurry and get out of here. You'll see how I'll take care of you! Oh, you'll be spoiled, honey!"

Ovide, touched, saw a Rita that he had not seen for a long time. As he toyed with a lock of her hair he noted that his neighbour, number thirteen, had put away his strange monocle and, with his steel-grey eyes, was watching Rita's legs and hips as she stood by the bed, examining those charming mechanisms whose movement, no doubt, was better perceived with the naked eye.

"But darling, can't you tell me what happened to you?"

A feeling of happy tranquillity washed over Ovide. This was the old Rita from the first days of their marriage. What a delicate, loving gesture, wearing her white dress and red shoes! He could have hugged her tight in gratitude. But was he going to have to faint from time to time in order to keep her like this? Seeing her so sincerely worried and distressed relaxed him, gave him such a feeling of safety that a little melody rose to his lips: ". . . the paths that go down to the sea."

"That's a good sign, now! You're singing!"

He started, ashamed of his absent-mindedness.

"And how's our daughter?" he asked, serious again.

"She's at the neighbour's. She was looking for you this morning to give you a kiss. I didn't want to upset her, I told her you'd gone to New York."

Ovide mentally noted that lying had come to be second nature to Rita, as constant as it was skilful. She was holding both his hands as if to warm them, and now was sitting at an angle on his bed, so that the bird of prey in number thirteen could get a better look at the perfect arch of her knees, as her tight skirt had slipped above them.

"I just hope the doctor's going to order a rest for you. Oh, if you weren't so stubborn! I'd go work fifteen hours a day if need be, and I'd finally be able to prove to you that I'm some use and that your wife can take over if anything goes wrong."

"Please, Rita! Don't start that again!"

The nun appeared at the door of the ward. Ovide, nervous at his neighbour's fascination with Rita's exposed knees, murmured a suggestion that she take a chair. She did so with bad grace. Her husband wasn't biting at her proposal to work. What a jealous fool! She pouted.

"It's stupid, really! All the money I made would go into the Caisse Populaire, I have an account there already. I put in my hundred and fifty dollars. We could look in our little savings book every week and see it go up and up and up! Wouldn't that be exciting? Oh, you could make me so happy, if only you wanted to!"

She turned on her hungry, spoiled-little-girl look and almost succeeded in melting him. But he must be firm. Ovide Plouffe was not about to be kept by his wife. In self-defence his refusal was harder than intended:

"Rita, I tell you again, it's out of the question. That would be the best way to make me really sick. Stay home, just be patient, I'll come out of this test a stronger man. Lying here in the hospital I've been taking stock of myself, and not only that. I've been working out some positive plans that I can't tell you about just now. And from the money point of view I have no real problem, I'm still getting paid and I'm getting a ten-dollar-a-week raise. My boss was a real brick!"

Rita was sulking. That very morning, stunned by Ovide's hospitalization, she had had her interview with Mr. Thibault of Chez Gérard, who, delighted at the prospect of hiring the ex-Miss Sweet Caporal, had told her she could start that Friday. Her bitterness was on the tip of her tongue, but she said nothing. She couldn't go weeping at him, he might faint again. Maybe he'd die! She shivered with horror at the very idea. All her life she'd have to bear that responsibility along with the burden of her three crimes at fifty dollars each with Bob the architect, and the lawyer and the engineer Stan had introduced her to. It had been fun with each of them at the restaurant, and the sequels had taken place in luxurious bachelor quarters where, after drinks and caviar on toast, she had been unfaithful to her husband.

At first these escapades had seemed almost harmless. She hadn't even stayed out all night! Moreover, she hadn't for a second forgotten her deep feelings for Ovide. On the contrary, she had regained her self-confidence from the certainty that she could make conquests of the handsomest men at any level of society. But if Ovide should die, these peccadillos of a single evening would turn to crimes! Ovide must live. And she had to play for time.

"I know I'm stubborn," he said, almost repentant, stroking her auburn hair with its highlights of fire. "But when I get out of here I'm going to get my life in order and we'll go off to Paris together."

Rita's eyes shone again a moment, then took on an anxious look.

"Paris! But that costs a fortune! And you say we have no money?"

Ovide was flying high:

"Bunkum! We'll go into debt and pay afterwards. When you've travelled nobody can take that away from you. Remember the part from *Manon*, '. . . we'll go to Paris, just we two . . .'?" (They hummed it together softly.) "I'll be your Chevalier des Grieux, we'll go to all the famous restaurants, and the cabarets and theatres and symphonies and the operettas and the opera. We'll even go to hear Yvonne Printemps!"

She listened spellbound, caught once more by this magician of a husband, following him into the dream that he opened up before her like a book of fairy tales.

"Look, here comes your mother!" said Rita, sitting up properly and trying to look dignified.

A group of five people with Joséphine Plouffe in the lead were making their way toward Ovide's bed. In Joséphine's wake came Napoléon, Jeanne, Cécile and Major Ephrem Bélanger. Ovide had to smile at the anguished determination with which his mother approached, taking him by the shoulders but not giving him a kiss.

"Oh, you big booby! You gave your mother a scare!"

"I can tell you right now, mother, there's nothing wrong with me. I think I'm even getting out tomorrow."

Awkwardly, clumsily, Rita excused herself:

"I have to go. I have to pick up Arlette at the neighbour's. I've been here a good half hour!"

"That Arlette is the most baby-sat kid in Quebec City," Joséphine broke in curtly.

Rita blushed.

"Well, at least there's no need to worry. I haven't seen Ovide in such good shape for a long time. We're even supposed to take a trip to Paris maybe. Eh, honey? Here's a big kiss. I'll be back tomorrow. Bye Cécile, bye Jeanne, Napoléon, bye Major, bye Mom!"

She spun around, arranging her body into a noble, dignified posture, avoiding Napoléon's heavy, accusing gaze, but unable to escape the burning, grey eyes of the patient in number thirteen: they had been scorching her consciousness throughout her visit.

The usual kind of conversation now began between Ovide and his nearest and dearest. Rita's presence had inhibited Joséphine from showing her tears at the sight of her son, who, for his part, stiffened at the sight of the major, whom he did not think much of. Now Joséphine was ready for battle, like a ship's captain in a storm. Cécile was thinking that marriage creates all sorts of problems for the heart and the pocketbook, and that it was just as well for her that her (by now) lukewarm need for the company of men was satisfied by Major Bélanger's visits. He brought to her and her mother his wise and tranquil masculine friendship (it had been his idea, on seeing their nervous state, to accompany them to the hospital). Jeanne and Napoléon were there because he felt he must soon intervene in Ovide's life, as he had done in the past. Despite his goodwill, his generosity and his wish to help his brother, Napoléon, caught up in so many calculations and contracts, found it increasingly hard to sympathize with the lot of others, though his own success stung him with guilt every time he thought of Ovide's unhappy situation.

"Hospitals know nothing," declared Joséphine, after receiving a description of the events that had landed him there. "I'm your mother and I know what's wrong with you. I brought you into this world. You never used to cry. But sometimes you'd swoon and seem unconscious. Mostly in the autumn, when the leaves fell, and that went on till you were two. And you'd get yellow. It's your liver, my boy. You've got the bile. Too much bile. The whites of your eyes are yellow and this is the fall."

"If you go to Paris, with the money that'll cost, you're going to have the bile but good," said Cécile.

"It's very simple, son, what you need is a good purge. I brought you a bottle of castor oil to clean you out and a bottle of cod-liver oil to build you up. Don't tell the sisters. They'd all be down on me," said Joséphine, smiling. "I'll stick them here in your drawer. And here's two boxes of fudge I made you."

As she turned she noticed patient number thirteen. The faces of tough guys did not impress Mrs. Plouffe.

"You got no visitors?" she asked.

The cripple grumbled, disconcerted:

"I've been sick too long. Visitors got tired, then they forgot about me!" he said with a thin, ironic smile.

Joséphine was sad:

"Poor you! Look how lucky you are, Ovide. A family, that means something. Don't you ever forget it!"

She retrieved a box of fudge from the drawer and held it out to the neighbour.

"Nobody ever comes? Lord, can that be? Well, let's just say I'm your visitor today. Take this, you're welcome to it. Let me know how it is. You don't mind, Ovide?"

Stupefied, number thirteen turned the box of candy over and over in his agile hands, looking at every side. He looked long at Joséphine. "Thank you, Madame." Cécile smiled at him:

"Bet you never ate any that good, did he, Ephrem?"

"Indeed, sir, Madame Plouffe's fudge is candy worthy of a general."

And, noticing the crutches, the Major asked:

"War wound?"

Number thirteen replied with a ferocious stare that left the major speechless. Napoléon was emerging from extensive thought.

"Ovide, I've been thinking things over. You could be my partner. You could make the contacts with the ministers, for the big contracts. I can't do that. You put up a good front, you're a smooth talker, eh?"

Ovide looked at him, touched and grateful.

"You'll never change, Napoléon. You'd give a fellow the shirt off your back. No, dear brother, your business is in good shape because you run it your way. What if I hurt you more than I helped? I haven't what it takes to go after plumbing contracts. I'm more of a moralist!"

"Ovide's right," Cécile agreed. "He has so many scruples! And he'd never ask a cent of me to get started in business."

"Nor did I," said Napoléon curtly.

"No, but the fact is, that's why we get along," Cécile concluded. "Oh, you know, Ovide, that clever boy, Nicolas, he got eighty-five in his first exams at the College? He's just like you, smart, intelligent, you wouldn't believe."

"The difference is, Nicolas gets to go to classical college," he said sadly.

Silence fell. Jeanne, in her gentle voice, suggested that Ovide shouldn't worry about his weakness. She herself had suffered from tuberculosis and she'd been desperate, but look at her today! The healthiest and happiest woman in the world!

"That's for sure," said Cécile. "While there's life there's hope."

"You should come and stay with me while you're getting better," said Joséphine. "It's not Rita's going to look after you. I'll make you a bet, I'll have you back on your feet in short order."

"Talk about feet, I'm really gettin' ahead with that trumpet," said Napoléon. "I'm playing 'Stardust' now."

"And if you want to make me a Christmas present, you'll join my band in the Zouaves," said the major. "I mean it, you know."

"Yes, why don't you?" begged Cécile softly.

Napoléon, his mind already back on business, was thinking about a troublesome contract. Absent-mindedly, he replied, "Well, we'll see . . . ."

"What about it, Ovide? You come and spend a month with me," Joséphine insisted. "Guillaume gets back from Anticosti next week. We'd be cosy as mice."

Ovide was trying to listen, but their words fell like echoes from Mars. He shook his head, and with a touch of weariness said:

"I'm grateful for your kind concern. But I need to get my wits together again, a certain balance. I have to settle my problems myself, according to my own nature. Mom, I have to cut the umbilical cord one of these days."

"Cord or no cord, you'll still be my boy."

Ovide sighed. Cut the cord? He had never in his life felt such a desire to bury his head in Joséphine's lap and cry like a baby while listening to "The Pathways of Love."

In the next bed the Frenchman was sucking a piece of fudge and listening to every word of the Plouffes. His mind, sharp as the image in his jeweller's glass, was now examining the infinite complexity of wheels within wheels in an ambitious project, one that the pendulum of time would link with Ovide's destiny.

5

After supper Ovide thought he should introduce himself to his neighbour, number thirteen.

"I'm glad you liked my mother's fudge. My name is Ovide Plouffe. I'm a record salesman."

His neighbour hesitated:

"Yes, so I gathered. I'm Pacifique Berthet. Watch maker."

Ovide smiled:

"Pacifique. That's a reassuring name."

"The joke's been made before," his neighbour cut in, roughly. "There aren't many called Pacifique Berthet. Nor Ovide Plouffe, for that matter."

Ovide was too intimidated to pursue the conversation. This surly fellow clearly didn't want to. Ovide resigned himself to watching this odd individual out of the corner of his eye, patiently wiring his alarm clock to the radio that stood on his bedside table. All evening Pacifique Berthet said not a word, lying with his hands behind his head, chain-smoking, his gaze vague with the loneliness of the chronically ill. It was lights out at nine o'clock and some patients were already asleep. Here and there a burst of snoring could be heard, or a cough, or a gentle groan. You'd think the sufferers felt freer to complain once it was dark. Ovide, completely cured, saw himself as an intruder in the place. Yet it did him good to lie resting this way in a strange bed, protected from the rest of the world with its assorted troubles, all of which would be at his heels the minute he left the hospital.

Ovide observed how Pacifique Berthet, after casting a searching glance at the dark entrance to make sure none of the sisters was lurking there (he had already been expelled for possession of alcohol during a previous stay), carefully took the mickey of gin from under his pillow and drank greedily from the bottle. "Want a slug?" Ovide refused politely. He didn't like De Kuyper gin, especially after fudge. This seemed to be no obstacle for number thirteen, who had already gone through half of

Joséphine's delicacies. He emptied half the bottle at a single go and hid it again under his pillow. This was the best means he had found for knocking himself out each evening. Almost all the money he earned from repairing watches was blown in this way, along with the profit he made from the sale of stolen jewels. Ovide, flabbergasted at his performance, watched with wonder as, just minutes later, the man fell into a profound sleep.

Ovide's own sleep was uneasy, and he woke in a sweat after a dream in which Rita had caught him kissing the young goddess he had met at the store: Marie, in a sarong, like Dorothy Lamour. Then, around three in the morning, he had a nightmare. He was being rolled away to the morgue from the ward where he lay. From his own bed he could see his long, thin remains being propelled toward the dissecting room. He was dead! He sat up in bed, staring hopelessly. Wow! But then he slept again. At six o'clock the jingle of a small bell woke him for the third time. The chaplain, assisted by a nun, was giving communion to all who would take it. Very few patients refused: it looked bad to say no. Really, this hospital was not the place for a good twelve-hour sleep. Shortly after, Pacifique Berthet, still under the influence of alcohol, dropped his bedpan on the concrete floor. Ovide picked it up for him. Around seven, just in the middle of a healing nap, he was startled awake along with Pacifique Berthet by the sound of fiddle music. The cripple, seeing his astonishment, pointed to his alarm clock and its connection to his bedside radio.

"I'd rather open my eyes to the sound of a violin than the racket of their damned communion bell," Berthet sneered.

Impressed, Ovide found the man most ingenious. After lunch two medics came to change the dressing on Berthet's hip. He was suffering from coxalgic tuberculosis. There had been an open wound there for years, which would almost close for months at a time but always opened again to suppurate worse than ever after weeks of all kinds of excesses committed by Berthet. The man was a volcano. When he had no alternative, he would go back into hospital. The hip joint was consumed and he could only walk, with crutches, at times when the eruption grew calm. But when the fury of the disease broke out again he was confined to bed or his couch.

Newly shaved and with his wound freshly dressed, Ovide's neighbour was suddenly in excellent humour.

"Have a good sleep, Mr. Plouffe?"

"Not as well as you did, Mr., er . . . Pacifique, er . . ."

"Berthet."

"If I'm not mistaken, you are French."

This didn't seem to flatter him excessively.

"Yes, I'm a 'damn Frenchman' as you people say. From Grenoble. I came here a good fifteen years back. I was starving to death there as an apprentice goldsmith and jeweller. Here in Quebec I was doing fine, in spite of the depression, and bang! this cursed sickness got me, and will never go away. It came from a fall on an icy street. But I keep alive! I can repair watches, even lying down. I specialize in Walthams. So I have a little business going. I buy from the wholesalers. But how do you find new customers when you're stuck in a wheelchair or hobbling on crutches?"

Ovide was touched, and his face imitated Pacifique's mask of disgust and resentment, as if the cripple's bitterness had rubbed off on him. The man's troubles made Ovide feel triumphant, generous and sympathetic, despite his own defeats.

"I was thinking about our two given names just before I went to sleep. Mine, 'Ovide,' suggests the great Roman poet, and yours is that of the biggest company in the country, the Canadian Pacific, ha ha ha!"

The cripple failed to get the joke but succeeded in hiding his vexation, as he had already begun to meditate on a project in which Ovide was to play a leading rôle.

"Come, come! Have a laugh, friend and French cousin! Laugh, won't you? Pacifique Berthet! That sounds splendid! It's one of the finest names I ever heard. Not Dupont, not Durand, but Pacifique Berthet, like Napoléon Bonaparte! You should be proud of it, believe me. They've often made fun of my name, Ovide Plouffe, but I wave it like a flag. It's come down to me from ancestors and relatives who were brave and proud and defended it nobly." (In vain Ovide tried to recall some of their lofty deeds.) "Even my wife holds it against me. But I'm like granite. Long live the name Ovide Plouffe! Unfortunately my brother Napoléon, on the advice of some of his politican friends, dropped the Plouffe from the name of his plumbing business called Napoléon and Sons. Of course, this amputated form is short and snappy, and people might laugh at a plumbing firm called Plouffe because it has a certain bathroom sound. People are so vulgar."

Suddenly Ovide was struck by a half recollection and began to murmur, "Berthet! Berthet . . . ."

Pacifique continued his observation of Ovide, evaluating him. He was waiting for the right moment to make Ovide a proposal he had been saving up since the previous evening. During the visit from Rita and the family he had not missed a word, and knew all the record-man's problems, among which his wife, that superb creature about whom he had dreamed libidinous dreams all night, was surely not the least. Ovide must become a part of Pacifique Berthet's life. Would Rita come again today?

Ovide, his eyes vague, lost in the previous century, sent his phenomenal memory rooting among the disorderly heap that remained from his reading. Suddenly he burst out:

"Eureka! I've got it! Grenoble, Grenoble! Antoine Berthet! Of course!"

"What? What about Antoine Berthet?" asked Pacifique frowning.

"But of course! I remember now!" Ovide exulted. "Antoine Berthet, the young man Stendhal read about in the Gazette of the Courts: it gave him the plot for *The Red and the Black*, and it all takes place in Grenoble. Antoine Berthet had shot a society woman he had seduced, shot her with a pistol. Could you be a descendant of that Antoine Berthet who had his head cut off in eighteen hundred and something?"

Pacifique, who had never heard of Stendhal, let alone Antoine Berthet, grumbled:

"That's right, give me a guillotined ancestor. I wouldn't be surprised if I was a scion of the damned, what with this bloody life I lead."

Ovide grimaced in regret, ready to trip over himself with apologies. Once more he had let himself be carried away by the desire to show off his learning, without realizing – he the sensitive one – that he might be hurting the cripple. He leapt out of bed and held out a hand to his neighbour.

"Forgive me, and let us swear *pax*! I acted like a swine. You must understand, that kind of association of ideas is such a stimulant to my mind, which is starved for cultural commerce! Imagine, a Berthet, in the next bed to Ovide Plouffe! What a meeting! I beg you again, forgive me, I didn't mean to hurt you."

The cripple accepted his hand. Ovide made a face as his hand was crushed in an iron vise. Pacifique released him.

"When you walk with crutches your hands get too strong. I always forget. With my thumb and four fingers I could break a man's neck with one hand."

Ovide coughed cautiously and backed up to sit on the edge of his bed. There was a long silence. Pacifique, cold and efficient once more, returned to his plot.

"Ovide Plouffe, you are a remarkable young man."

Ovide, flattered, smiled in protest.

"Yes, yes, remarkable, much superior to anyone I've met in Quebec in the last fifteen years. It was none of my business, but I couldn't help hearing what was said around your bed yesterday afternoon."

The record salesman clammed up like a bivalve, sensing some hidden peril. Pacifique's tone grew gentler.

"How could I shut my ears? A man of your calibre, and in financial difficulties! Simply unacceptable! You seem to me much smarter than your brother, and he's running a business!" he sighed.

"I know, I know," stammered Ovide. "But what can I do? I have no degree and no head for business."

Pacifique shook his head, smiling.

"Believe me, there's a lot to you, but you doubt yourself and fail to see the great things you could accomplish. You have no perspective on yourself."

"Do you really think so?" breathed Ovide, hooked, straining forward.

"Yes, Mister Ovide Plouffe, upon my word. One great advantage cripples have is their ability to size people up. Because we're seeing from outside, like wallflowers at a dance!"

Ovide drank in his words. It took a crippled Frenchman from Grenoble, a namesake of Stendhal's model, to appreciate him! Pacifique Berthet paused to let the compliment sink in. Then he aimed at the bullseye:

"I know how you can make a lot of money."

Another pause, giving weight to his phrase.

"On the stock market?" Ovide finally asked.

"Not at all. I'm looking for a partner. You could be the one. I haven't decided yet. There are two other men waiting for me to make my mind up. Watches are a gold mine."

"But I know nothing about watches!"

Pacifique smiled.

54

"That's my job. We'd need a shop with at least two rooms: the store in front and the workshop and office in the back. Repairs will pay your rent and the phone. But that's not where the money is. The money's in watches and jewellery you buy from the wholesalers."

"People don't buy a watch every day," Ovide remarked.

"That's not the point. Just think, if we organized a sales network all over Quebec with salesmen on commission, we'd really be in business! And did you know it's the people in the villages and the countryside, and the North Shore Indians who buy the best watches and the shiniest jewellery?"

"Could be," Ovide mused aloud. "Jacques Cartier got around the Indians with glass beads."

"In jewellery you make a big profit on every article. Around fifty per cent. If you sell a thousand watches at forty dollars apiece in six months, you'll have a profit of twenty thousand dollars. That's ten thousand each, in a fifty-fifty partnership. With that kind of money you can buy a convertible and live it up, you're your own boss, you can travel by train or yacht or airplane. I'm telling you all this, Mister Plouffe, but if the idea doesn't interest you we'll not mention it again. No hard feelings."

"No, no, by all means, let's talk!" Ovide protested.

Ovide's imagination was galloping off in all directions. At last Rita would be proud of him. He could take her on trips and spoil her in so many little ways. It wouldn't take him long to learn the jewellery business. Like Jules Romains' Doctor Knock he would stick little red flags into a great wall map to indicate his points of sale. And later they could expand all over Canada. Ovide tried to curb his enthusiasm but with little luck.

"It's a splendid idea!" he exclaimed.

"I know," said Pacifique. "You might find it hard at first, but you never get something for nothing. I'd be doing repairs in the back and my partner would hit the road setting up sales points all over the province. In your case, if I choose you, your wife could look after the store. It might be slow for a few months, but you have to clear the land and sow the grain to get your harvest. And once it started to roll, it would really roll!"

Something was bothering Ovide. He got up his courage and asked:

"How much money would it take to get started?"

"Oh, ten thousand dollars or so would do it. For an idea like that the bank would give us a loan."

"Yes, yes, I see," Ovide murmured, thinking that Napoléon would tell him how all that worked. Napoléon was always throwing around his five and ten thousands as if he was talking about tomorrow's weather.

"My partner is going to have to become a public figure. He'll have to give lectures on the different makes of watch, get invited for radio interviews, make friends with country priests and newspapermen and lumbering and mining companies, you name it."

"My brother Guillaume could sell a lot for me on Anticosti, with all the fishermen and hunters and lumbermen he knows up there. It's funny, all of a sudden I can see buyers growing like bean sprouts."

"See! And the more I think about it, the more I believe it's right down your alley."

Pacifique Berthet had him on the hook. Feeling success at hand, he grew open and jolly: hope had begun to shine in his wretched life. Ovide was thinking about the Royaume du Disque. He'd miss his customers, and it wasn't going to be easy switching to watches. But this lack of money that was souring his life was the first thing to be remedied if he wanted to recover his dignity in his own eyes and those of others. He felt a surge of energy, he was Cortes before the conquest.

"When do we start?"

"Think about it, think it over. Don't decide on the spur of the moment. And besides, I have to be fair to my other two applicants."

"When I make up my mind, that's it!" cried Ovide impatiently.

"I like your attitude," said Pacifique pompously. "In a partnership like this you have to get off on the right foot and draw up a contract with a notary, and look for a location across from a church if possible. You always get pedestrian traffic there and they'll all stop at our window."

"You do think of everything!" said Ovide admiringly.

"Are you a Knight of Columbus?"

Disconcerted, and looking slightly foolish, Ovide admitted he was not.

"It's indispensable to become a member and try to reach the

fourth degree as fast as you can, it's the most important one. They're a real brotherhood, they stick together and help each other out. There are thousands of Knights of Columbus in Quebec. And you have to go to the service clubs like the Rotary and the Kiwanis and the Richelieu, make contacts everywhere. With your charm and personality and that vocabulary of yours you'll be a celebrity, and in a year you'll be in clover!"

Ovide found the project stupendous and full of possibilities, yet his heart was heavy. His boss, for example – how straight he'd been with Ovide, and how disappointed he'd be to lose him! Perhaps he could take the odd evening off and work for nothing for his former employer, serving his faithful music-lover friends. But what bothered him most was this new career of contact-maker – a career for which he felt no affinity because of his stubborn individualism. He tried to find fault with Berthet's project.

"Do you drink a lot of De Kuyper gin?"

The cripple had seen this one coming.

"If I choose you for this undertaking, I'll go on the wagon a hundred per cent. And in a couple of weeks my sore will be healed enough for me to get out of here."

Enough of these weakling's scruples: Pacifique's idea was a great one, with fabulous possibilities. At thirty-six it was time for Ovide Plouffe to get in the game. Would he ever have such a chance again? It wouldn't be twenties and fifties he'd bring to the bank, he'd be counting in hundreds, maybe thousands! He held out his hand in solemn confirmation to Pacifique, who took good care not to crush his slender fingers.

"Shake on it, Pacifique old boy, we'll call the firm Ovide and Pacifique!"

"I'm honoured by your confidence. So! Should I tell my other two candidates I've chosen you?"

"You certainly should!"

Ovide felt like a great ship launched in search of the Holy Grail of financial and social success. Those who had taken him for a loser would watch his triumph open-mouthed. His wife, and Cécile and Napoléon too, would learn to take him seriously. He seemed to grow, and his chin grew firm:

"I'm getting out of here at noon. There's nothing wrong with me. I'll give my notice to my boss and start looking for a store. I'll join the Knights of Columbus and see the bank manager."

"See the banker first!" said Pacifique, wagging a finger.

"Of course, but that'll be easy. Let's get your sore healed up. I'll wait for you. You should give me your mailing lists and catalogues and fill me in on the watch business."

"I'll draft a contract for our partnership," concluded Pacifique, who had not expected Ovide to be so precipitate.

Pacifique too was bubbling with impatience. Oh, if that damned sore would only heal! He felt a sting of pain in his side and controlled his grimace. He was convinced that this partnership would be a success. At least he would be able to afford a prettier whore from time to time, and maybe even a wheel-chair with an electric motor! And when Ovide was on the road he could spend whole days looking at Rita's legs and behind, or her breasts, in profile, or . . . or . . . (his dreams were taking form).

"Don't do anything final without my approval," said Berthet. "I have the experience. And don't forget, we'll work together like Siamese twins."

"That I'll swear, old partner."

Ovide rubbed his hands together, cocked an ear and repeated, "Ovide and Pacifique." It sounded so fine!

"Just as soon as I leave the hospital I'm going to give my wife the good news!"

But then he wondered if he shouldn't perhaps talk it over with his mother and Cécile and Napoléon. But Joséphine and Cécile had always been used to regular salaries, and they'd likely try to talk him out of taking such a risk. Napoléon would understand. But would he want to interfere, maybe talk to Pacifique? He'd ask so many questions to protect Ovide's interests that Berthet would get cold feet and find himself another partner! Oh, if only his childhood friend were there to advise him, as in the old days. But no, Denis Boucher had been in New York since the war's end, working for *Time* magazine.

"I'll give Rita a surprise, first of all. She's my wife, eh?"

He had never spoken a truer word.

"Say hello to her for me," smiled Pacifique.

And Ovide, humming a hit from the thirties that had been sung by la Palma de l'Empire ("Just say hello for me"), headed for the office of the head nurse.

6

Rita, looking annoyed, brought a gin and orange to Stan Labrie, former baseball pitcher, envious rival of Guillaume Plouffe's and, into the bargain, Rita's former fiancé. He was making himself at home, sprawled on the beige plush couch in the living room. His jacket lay on the floor and his tie was loosened. His feet rested on a low chrome-legged table. He gazed at Rita in tender admiration.

"You shouldn'a come here, Stan, I don't like that."

He accepted the glass and kissed her hand. Still handsome, almost beardless, he seemed younger than his forty years. His caddish face was distorted in a sneer.

"You got no gratitude for your poor Stanislas, and after I introduced you to some good-lookin' guys who know how to look after a girl? Your Stan who got you chosen Miss Sweet Caporal?"

"For Miss Sweet Cap, OK, but for the other I hate you, I feel real bad about that. I'd had a bit to drink, but I'm not an old slut. I'll never do that again. When I saw Ovide yesterday in his hospital bed I felt like a criminal."

"Aw," he said, sipping his gin, "you need a little fun now and then. When ya get to know guys with class like that you can appreciate your husband better afterwards. You'll find your superman Ovide cuter than ever."

"You're a real devil, Stan! I wish you'd leave, it bothers me. It's as if Ovide could see you here all the way from the hospital."

Tense, sitting facing Stan, her knees tight together, she was cracking her knuckles. She examined the soft, regular features of this man who, though impotent, had occupied such a prominent place in her life. Ever since her marriage, Stan Labrie's destiny had taken an odd tangent. Scarred and humiliated by that unforgettable evening when she had broken up with him because he was unable to prove to her that he was sexually normal (Denis Boucher, Ovide's friend, had warned Rita's parents), he had dragged the shame of his fiasco like a ball and chain. Since then his only thought had been of revenge, of proving Ovide as impotent as himself, but impotent in another way: incapable of making Rita happy. Stan had practised dozens of professions, but had finally landed in the one that responded to his deeper tendencies: he was a pimp.

He began to practise "public relations" in a somewhat disreputable way. Stan had mobilized an impressive lineup of girls and married women who were ready for brief adventures with no follow-up except payment. He called them his "escorts." That era saw the birth of the "escapade" fashion among many of the ladies of Quebec. Ten years earlier they might have submitted to a caress in the back seat of a car. Nowadays they went much further.

Stan had a remarkable nose for ferreting out his recruits in the popular bars, among the office girls from the Legislative Assembly or the pretty operators from the Bell. He had a key job in government: special duties with the Minister of Commerce. If there was a convention in Quebec, Stan was the boy who rented out his troop of "escorts" to the American or English-Canadian delegates. Their services, ranging from the strip-tease to the quickie, were marked more by drunkenness than desire. Stan loved his work, which, because of his host of satisfied customers, brought him vicarious pleasures he could never directly know.

He would never have dragged Rita into these adventures, as he had preserved a real attachment for her, which tugged at his heart each time he thought of Ovide, that Don Quixote, who didn't deserve such a wife. Unable to cuckold Ovide himself, he had introduced Rita to three highly placed professionals, respected citizens, whose gratitude might be useful to him some day.

"You know, the architect, Bob, that good-looker? I think he's crazy about you. He wants to see you again."

"Oh, I know I can still get them going," she said, batting her eyelashes. "It's true, Bob's a classy guy. He's nice, and tactful, and he has such nice manners. If I'd known him before I got married . . . ."

But she shook her head and refused to pursue the thought to its conclusion.

"No! It happened three times, and that was three times too many. It's all over. My husband don't deserve that."

He drank the last drop of his gin and orange.

"Will you tell me what you see in that guy, that skinny broomstick, that nincompoop, that . . . that . . . ."

Rita was thinking.

"You couldn't understand. He's not like anybody else. With those words of his he can invent a different world where everything is nice. But I hate to see him sad and worried so often."

The door opened and Ovide appeared, his arms raised theatrically.

"Hallelujah! I'm cured! Today a new life begins for us. At last, we're going to be rich!"

He held out his arms to her. What? She was awkward, motionless, didn't run to give him a hug? She nodded toward Stan Labrie.

"Here's to you, chum," said Stan.

Mocking, Stan raised his glass. Ovide turned white. His arms fell to his sides and he stammered:

"Wh . . . what are you doing here in my house, with my wife, and me sick in the hospital?"

Stan's voice was plaintive, his expression innocent.

"When I heard you were sick I was real upset. I just came by to ask how you're doin'. What a reception! That'll learn me to worry about my friends. Gratitude, eh?"

Ovide ground his teeth. Rita was terrified.

"That's the first time, you know, honey, Stan ever came here. I swear it!"

"And it's the last time, too!" Ovide roared. "Now, get out! Scram, will you?"

Rita, in a cold sweat, thought she was going to faint. If there was a fight between these two men, and if Stan, to get even with Ovide, let it out that thanks to him Ovide had been cuckolded three times at fifty dollars a time . . . . Stan guessed Rita's anguish and reassured her with a glance. He would never betray her. Too discouraged to put up a struggle, he looked at her with affection; he understood her better than her husband. His voice was quiet, with a touch of regret.

"Cool off, Ovide, cool off now. I think that's not very nice of you. It's selfish, see? Do you know how you're acting? You're feelin' better, you shout Hallelujah we're rich, and then you give me hell and treat me like the lowest of the low. That doesn't seem very fair. You got Rita by default, you know that and you should thank me for it, at least you should understand how I feel, you're the guy that understands so much. If there is one guy you shouldn't worry about, it's me. Even if I spent the night in bed with her you could sleep sound. And the worst part of it is, it's Rita you're hurting."

Disgusted, Ovide picked up Stan's jacket and tossed it to

him. Stan, getting up, caught it. He shrugged, stared at Ovide and made for the door.

"It's a heartless world. Bye, Rita."

"Good luck, Stan," she murmured.

He had already closed the door behind him.

"And the devil take you!" shouted Ovide.

He grumbled away, trying to recover his composure.

After a long, embarrassed silence, Rita risked an explanation.

"I just haven't any luck," she groaned. "It wasn't my fault, I swear it. I told you he came over to our table at Chez Gérard the other night, and all of a sudden the doorbell rings here a few minutes ago. I thought it was the postman but there he was. I couldn't throw him out! We knew each other so well at one time. And you know he's not dangerous."

"I don't like it at all," he fumed, growing slightly calmer, however. "A casual visit like that is a bad sign. First, he starts hanging around again in Chez Gérard the other night. And now I find him in my own house!"

She flung her arms around his neck.

"The main thing is you're well again! I'm so pleased!"

He stroked her hair gently.

"Too bad that swine spoiled my homecoming."

"Don't talk about him any more. Did you say we're going to get rich? What's that about?"

She had put him back on the rails. He began to boast:

"We're leaving this place. I'm going into business. A real gold mine."

"Hurray!" she applauded.

Rita hated embarrassing situations. She had a natural talent for the small successive joys that stimulated her narrow brain, the lucky series of nice surprises that give you the impression of an almost continual bliss.

Ovide was boasting again.

"The doctor said I was in perfect health. He thinks the fainting spells may be psychological spasms, a very rare condition, found only in patients with acute sensitivity and powerful imagination. That's normal, understandable. Just wait for my new career, I'll be making at least twenty-five thousand a year."

"Twenty-five thousand? Incredible!"

"Probably more. Get ready for a life that's bustling with travel and discoveries and all the joys I never gave you. And we'll celebrate it all at Chez Gérard on Friday."

Was she dreaming? She snuggled up close to him and kissed his cheeks, his forehead, his nose.

"Now, tell me everything about it!"

He explained the proposal Berthet had made and the size of the projected watch and jewellery business. He was already ripe for profit-taking and would have liked to start the very next morning.

Rita at first found the idea of moving to the lower town disagreeable, and winced at the idea that this cripple, Pacifique Berthet, who had burned holes in her with his stare during her visit to the hospital, was going to be Ovide's partner. The company name Ovide and Pacifique bothered her, too.

But Rita quickly forgot the disagreeable parts and fell in easily with the evocative magic of Ovide's dreams when he turned loose his fancy. How glad she was of standing her ground with Stan! But Ovide in the jewellery business! She saw herself encrusted with diamonds, almost for free! She'd be the first to try out all the novelties.

Yes, she'd work in the store. They could count on her to make record sales.

"With our first thousand dollars clear, we'll buy a convertible."

"Let's run home!" Ovide could restrain himself no longer. He was in his seventh heaven. "I can't wait to see what Cécile says, and mother, and Napoléon. They'll be thunderstruck!"

"You go on, I have to stay here. It's almost noon."

Of course she had to stay. What a fine little wife he had!

"Lock your door," he warned, smiling, as he went out, "I'm always scared you'll get kidnapped!"

7

Ovide set off for his mother's house with long, stiff strides, as if his renewed rage against Stan Labrie had affected his knee joints. What an uncouth lout the fellow was! Ovide's anger was mixed with a vague anxiety. Ever since the Miss Sweet Caporal affair he had hoped that Stan had vanished forever from their landscape. And here the villain was again, with his cynical smile! Ovide was sure that Stan's visit to his house, while he himself was supposedly still in hospital, augured some ill for the future. Rita was so naive and vulnerable!

With a ten-minute start on Ovide, Major Ephrem Bélanger, whistling a martial air, was on his way to the same destination. Ovide, who considered this shop-window officer as the most insignificant of creatures, was obscurely shocked by his attentions to Joséphine, as if it were treason against his late father, Théophile.

But Ephrem Bélanger cut a fine figure in his uniform of the neighbourhood's Papal Zouaves, with all those gold-braid chevrons on his left sleeve. On this particular day his chest glittered with all his decorations, including the *Bene Merenti* medal of the Federation of Parish Guards of the Quebec City Area, of which he was president; that of the Association of Former Churchwardens; and that of the Saint-Jean-Baptiste Society. He always blushed with false modesty when his claims to glory were cited in his presence, but this also launched him on a dull and protracted recital of the motivations, deeds and petty victories that had occasioned this shower of honours. Because of the length of these monologues (his listeners were often tempted to cry, "Get on with it!"), people took care not to trigger the litany.

A former, now retired, streetcar conductor, he had known and esteemed the defunct Onésime Ménard, his ex-*confrère* and late beloved of Cécile. Ephrem, a childless widower, found this autumn of his life both happy and fulfilling. Commanding his Papal Zouaves, performing the duties of his varied chairmanships, taking part in parades and making speeches at various banquets – all this left him little spare time: just enough to make his daily visit to Joséphine Plouffe and her daughter Cécile.

That was to be his first call of the day, as he strode along in his dress uniform, sword dangling at his side, and under his left arm an enormous white bag that looked like a pillow. On leaving Joséphine's he would walk to the bus stop two blocks farther along, oblivious to the mocking smiles of passersby and gossips hanging out their windows. He considered it perfectly normal that an officer decorated with such pomp and circumstance, marching like a general, his scabbard dragging and clattering on the boardwalk, should have to walk to the bus, or even run to catch it!

On this chilly, sunlit October day he was going to bid a good day to his two lady friends and give a happy surprise to Joséphine.

He enjoyed recalling with her the memory of Théophile, whose photo held a place of honour in the Saint-Jean-Baptiste Society's parish headquarters, immortalizing the patriotic act of the deceased in refusing to hang out a flag during the visit by the King and Queen of England in 1939. This lofty deed of daring had led to the loss of the brave Théophile's job, and then to his paralysis and death.

Cécile had just arrived home from the factory and was sitting down to her bowl of soup, puddling suspiciously in it to make sure it harboured no particle of onion.

"I hardly put any in," said Joséphine, who loved them.

"But you know very well I don't want any in my soup!"

"Winter's coming. Onions make you strong, my girl," preached Joséphine. "If only Ovide ate more of them! This year of all years. Onion skins are thick, it'll be a hard winter."

She was going to see Ovide this afternoon at three. Had he taken his castor oil and cod-liver extract?

Ephrem knocked discreetly and came in.

"Come and have a nice bowl of soup with us," said Joséphine, fussing.

"My land, isn't he handsome today!" said Cécile admiringly.

"No, dear ladies, I cannot linger. I am lunching with my eight Parish Guards commanders. I am attending as President of the Federation. We have an important decision to make: in what order are the Quebec Guards to march in the processions of Saint-Jean-Baptiste, the Sacred Heart and the Fête-Dieu next spring."

Processions, parades and religious ceremonies had always been Joséphine's favourite shows, and she also, of course, had a weakness for gaudy uniforms.

"I hope you'll let the Zouaves lead the parade," she said. "After all, they defended our Holy Father the Pope against Garibaldi. And anyway, the other Parish Guards are too dull."

"What've you got in that bag?" asked Cécile between spoonfuls.

Ephrem had left his bulging pillow-case in the rocking chair. Pleased with himself and all smiles at the fine surprise he had for Joséphine, Ephrem extracted a couple of military tunics from the sack.

"I have a contract for you," he said, "if you're interested. A contract that pays."

A contract? Nobody had ever offered one before to Joséphine.

"That's right, sewing gold-braid chevrons on the left sleeves. You've got a sewing machine, haven't you, Joséphine? And you're a good seamstress, eh?"

"Mama's worked enough for one in her lifetime," said Cécile. "She's not going to start her treadle going for the parish Guards! What's more, don't forget I have a sewing machine, too! Electric, no treadle like mother's."

"Let him talk, why don't you?" said Joséphine, all ears.

"The Federation has over three thousand members," said Ephrem proudly. "We've got a big problem with the chevrons. The wives or sweethearts often sew them on upside down, or else they don't want to sew them on at all. But the more boys we get in the more promotions we have. We can't keep them down to private more than two months. The world's in a hurry. They all want to start up the ladder right away. So, we make them corporal, that's one stripe, and after six months it's sergeant, that's two stripes, and then we push them up to second lieutenant, that's three stripes. But wait a minute: at first lieutenant we start getting tougher. You can't take just anybody for that. A man like Ovide, say. What do you think? He might even make a good first lieutenant, eh?"

Cécile was doing mental arithmetic. Three thousand members, corporals, sergeants, first lieutenants, a continuous turnover of three thousand times three chevrons, that made nine thousand units. She said:

"Well, with my electric machine I could do them for you at twenty cents apiece. That's cheap, isn't it, Ephrem?"

Ephrem was talking only to Joséphine:

"Twenty cents!" he exclaimed, growing to the dimensions of the commander's statue, "for stripes that are well sewn and straight and solid, I'll give final orders that you're to have the exclusive contract for the whole Federation at fifty cents a stripe. We supply the material."

As the magic number exploded in the air it seemed to have left a hole in the atmosphere of the kitchen. The gallant gunner who had fired the salvo was waiting for its effect, arms akimbo and smiling proudly.

"Nine thousand times fifty cents! Four thousand five hundred dollars a year!" exclaimed Cécile, pushing away her soup plate, while Joséphine trotted over to her sewing machine and took the cover off.

"Are you interested, Joséphine? It would give you a little something to do all day, and you could afford a few luxuries."

"Four thousand five hundred dollars!" Joséphine was gasping. "Why, that's twice what Théophile was earning before he died! I'll take your contract!" she said firmly. "Thank you, Ephrem. I'm very pleased."

She was thinking of Ovide, to whom she could give part of her profits. And he'd be happy again and get well. She loved him more at the very idea of giving him money. Cécile didn't want to look greedy. In a honeyed voice she said to her mother:

"Mummy, just think! At your age! You're not going to go and ruin your eyes sewing as if we were hard up? I'll take the contract myself. We'll put part aside for Nicolas, and then when he gets his degree and wants to open his law office the money will be there."

Joséphine was not to be moved. For the first time in fifty years she'd be earning money!

"There's nothing wrong with my eyes. I see things you don't. The days are long in wintertime and I like sewing, especially those nice golden chevrons on their left sleeves. And you, Cécile, you work hard enough at the factory. When you get home at night your eyes are so tired they have bags under them."

Cécile restrained her impatience as best she could, but a word of protest got by:

"I know, you want to give all that money to Ovide. And that Rita, as soon as she gets a whiff of it, she'll go and squander it on plastic shoes and short skirts and John Collinses in the night clubs."

"I know what I'll do," said Joséphine, her mind made up. "We'll divide the contract, fifty-fifty."

Major Bélanger had never expected to trigger such a bitter struggle. He wanted to leave. Cécile, satisfied with the 50 per cent concession, rushed over to him.

"Really, Major, you can't go to your official dinner with your sash all crooked like that! That's how it is when there's no woman around to help you get dressed."

Ephrem hung his head, blushing. It was true. His broad sash, five metres long, had been rolled on in a most haphazard way, unworthy of a dashing Zouave. An officer as strict as he was could not afford such sloppiness, for he dressed down his troops unmercifully for their inattention to the art of wearing the sash.

"Take off your sword-belt and unroll," said Cécile.

The two women grasped the end of the sky-blue sash and the Major, having leaned his chrome scabbard against the wall, began to spin like a top, ending up beside the sink.

This scene would have given a laugh to Théophile or Guillaume or Ovide, who had no use for such falderols. But there was something touching about these two women and their insistence on perfection, unwinding their Zouave and winding him up again. From five metres away, he began his return movement, stiff as a capital I, rotating on his own axis with such gravity that the operation took on a sacred character.

Ephrem had come within a distance of two metres of the ladies when Cécile cried, "Stop! It's going crooked!" She went over to Ephrem, who had frozen in his tracks, and undid a half-turn, then, holding him by the waist, spun him along to Joséphine who, for her part, was gripping the end of the sash with total concentration. Ephrem sailed into port with his bellyband pukka as never before. "Hooray!" shouted the two ladies, very proud of themselves. Just at this moment, as Joséphine was reminded by their exploit of her own dexterity in changing her babies' diapers in two shakes of a dead lamb's tail, Ovide, supercharged, wearing a Chevalier boater, burst into the kitchen.

"Salutations, women of the Plouffes!"

"What! You're out of hospital!" exclaimed Joséphine, astounded and delighted.

"Why, sure, mother. All cured and ready to take a bite of the future!"

"And wearing a Maurice Chevalier straw hat!" said Cécile admiringly.

"Just like your father on our honeymoon! And you took your castor oil and your cod-liver extract, right? What did I tell you? Those hospitals are useless."

Joséphine, with a reaction that sprang from her very entrails every time one of her sons came to visit, ran to the stove, which she still called "my range."

"You're going to eat with us. I'll warm you up some soup!"

Ovide, put out by the presence of the major, drew the sword, and, flourishing it, cried:

"Fie upon this earthly nourishment!"

"Take care, it's just been sharpened," said the major, shocked by this frivolity.

"Sharpened? Whatever for!" sneered Ovide.

Had he been drinking? He sliced at the kitchen air with the stage ardour of an opera tenor, feinting, lunging, spitting invisible enemies on his blade, his eyes sparkling with fun. His audience, petrified, dared not make a move for fear of entering the field of operations of this rapier gone mad.

He was savouring their consternation, especially the displeasure of the major, whose presence violated the memory of a father. Ovide, impelled by his great joys and deeper pains to grandiloquent gestures worthy of the heroes of swashbuckling novels, took advantage of his own clowning to make fun of the major and give him a piece of his mind and, at the same time, to give his mother and sister clearly to understand that their friendship for this Zouave was no credit to the family. And that, if there was an immortal soul, Théophile himself most certainly didn't deserve to be cuckolded post-mortem. Still waving his weapon, Ovide began to sing:

"Toreador, don't spit on the floor!"

And he bore down on the major as if to run him through. Ephrem, livid with fear (the boy had always seemed to him slightly unbalanced), backed away to the wall where Théophile's photo hung. Holding the sword-point to the breast of the terrified major, Ovide added, still paraphrasing Carmen:

"And never forget, an angry eye sees your every move!"

"Ovide!" shouted Joséphine and Cécile together. "Will you stop that?"

Was he really going mad? He imagined himself slicing Stan Labrie to bits. But he abandoned his victim and pointed the blade toward the ceiling, declaiming:

"The new Lagardère, I pledge myself to a brilliant destiny in which I shall lop the head off defeat and pierce the heart of despair. The error of my life has been to think there was no place for Ovide Plouffe in this dark vale, eternal victim of fate that I was. Thus I made myself drunk, I wept, and entered the monastery!"

"And then you married Rita Toulouse," Cécile couldn't resist adding.

Ovide turned pale and accepted the blow like a man.

"I'm turning over a new leaf," he cried. "In a changing world I'll prove, in black and white, that it's the Ovide Plouffes, the misunderstood ones, the misfits, the private soldiers" – here he cast a piercing glance at Ephrem – "who, in their hideouts as incorruptible partisans, are preparing to take over the world!"

69

"Talking about privates," said Cécile, "mother and I just got a contract to sew on chevrons for all the corporals and sergeants and second lieutenants in the three thousand members of the Parish Guards."

Ovide listened flabbergasted to the account of the offer, in which the major seemed to want his mother to have the lion's share of the contract. Four thousand five hundred dollars! Anything could happen in this funny world! He burst out laughing, to the chagrin of the Zouave who had firmly decided now to hate this man for life, this enemy of all that was dear to his soldierly heart. Ovide, sensitive to Ephrem's feelings, lowered his weapon, stuck its point in the linoleum and said, staring the major right in the eye:

"I just wanted to check the courage of a soldier who's never been to war, who is decorated like a parade float, not to say a wayside shrine! My congratulations, you did quite well, and I'll never know if I was wrong, your pants are floppy enough to keep your secret."

"What do you mean, floppy?" stammered Ephrem, still in shock.

"That'll do, son!" Joséphine interrupted severely. (She didn't dare go too far with her reprimand, feeling her position weakened since the reference to "an angry eye.")

"Your floppy pants," Ovide repeated, enjoying himself. "Do you know, Major, why you are wearing this wide and endless sash and those baggy trousers? The reason is, in the desert necessity gives birth to invention. What, you still don't get it?"

The major shook his head jerkily, staring at the sword-point stuck in the linoleum.

"All right, I'll tell you. The Zouaves were originally a regiment of heroes in Africa. Field Marshall Lyautey relates in his memoirs that the relentless sunlight of the Sahara had disastrous effects on the digestive process of the soldiers. Hence the baggy pants and the sash!" he went on, laughing. "An intestinal problem! Ha ha!"

"Oh, that boy, he's up on everything," said Joséphine, trying to smooth things over. She found Ovide's explanation logical, if somewhat disrespectful.

Cécile, who always had a hearty laugh ready for scatological references, managed to restrain herself. As a precaution she took the sword and shoved it back in the sheath. Without a word, pale with humiliation, the major hung it at his side again.

He didn't want to hurt Joséphine and Cécile by flying into a rage, because he cherished their friendship and his visits to their kitchen. He was, after all, alone in the world, and so highly placed that he couldn't even drop in on his subalterns. Furious and miserable, he left, and Ovide winked at Théophile's photo as he went out, striking a final blow that stopped Ephrem cold on the door step.

"And let me tell you, sir, that not one Canadian Zouave died in Italy, except one, from a venereal disease!"

Ovide sighed, and concluded in a tone of boredom:

"Now, Major, you see I'm not one of those who marches in step with the mob."

"Thanks for the contract!" shouted Joséphine and Cécile, seeing the discomfiture of their friend.

Major Ephrem went down the stairs, tears welling in his eyes. He was a gentle sort of man who, in his rôle as a Sunday officer, found the opportunity to exercise an authority for which he was not equipped by nature. Ovide, in five minutes, had destroyed his hard-earned self-confidence in front of the only two friends he had. He thought of his sash, his baggy pants, his rank, his medals in the midst of the desert and its dysentery. "Old fool, old fool," chanted his scabbard as it rattled down the steps behind him.

"It's all very well to say you were sick, but I think you're mighty cruel," said Joséphine sadly.

"You were worse than mean, you were a real pig!" Cécile insisted. "Ephrem did nothing to deserve that. And before you came in he even said you'd be a good candidate for lieutenant. He'd even appoint you right away if you liked. And it might do you good."

"Me! A lieutenant in the Zouaves! That's a good one!" cried Ovide, insulted.

But then he began to think it over. It was true, he had gone too far. What on earth had got into him? He was always the one who worried about people's feelings. The unexplained presence of Stan in the apartment with Rita had provoked a rage that had broken out and been aggravated at the sight of Ephrem's over-familiarity with the two women in Théophile's absence, so to speak, for in Ovide's heart his father was still alive. But the real reason for his folly remained repressed: he was beginning to panic at the thought of his jewellery project with Pacifique Berthet, and he had sought a diversion from his

71

fright in this curious behaviour. What a coward he had been to take out his spite on this defenceless, good-hearted major! Overcome with remorse, he said:

"You're right. I'll go and tell him I'm sorry."

The two women, relieved, agreed that that was their good Ovide, in spite of his mean, unexpected behaviour. And Ovide ran after the major, who, on seeing him, laid a hand on the hilt of his sword: was the enemy about to charge again?

"Major, my apologies. I behaved like a mannerless lout. I know that you are a man to be esteemed, and I'm grateful for your kindness to my mother and Cécile."

Poor Ephrem could have cried.

"Think nothing of it, think nothing of it, and thank you, sir."

Ovide trotted back to the house. He was beginning to remember why he had come to see his mother, and that this was the most important thing in the world. But before beginning his story he said:

"There, I apologized. He's all happy, everything's forgotten. Not another word."

Ovide, when he started explaining a plan of his, was easily carried away by his exuberant imagination. As he talked, his mother made a valiant effort to see him as president of a jewellery chain selling thousands of watches across the province. While Rita flounced around behind a counter and had her fill of seeing strange men. And what was this about the cripple in the back of the shop? That sounded somehow strange and unnatural.

"But . . . aren't you well off where you are? You have a secure job and a decent salary doing something you like, in the music business, right?"

"You can like what you're doing and find you like it no more when you're starving to death. Amen!" Ovide protested, clinging to his project as to a life-buoy. "Anyway, I like the idea of being Mr. Berthet's partner. I'm proud, even, to treat a handicapped man as my equal. And I'm happy to take second place to a man of great ability and not to feel the kind of pity that would hurt his feelings. By the way, he loved your fudge."

Joséphine didn't dare say too much against Ovide's new project, guessing that it might help his conjugal situation.

"And that's not all," he continued. "I'll be moving back to this parish and renting a store opposite the church. There's a lot of foot-traffic there. And people with less money buy more jewellery than the ones who are well off."

"Why didn't you say so?"

Joséphine's face lit up. Coming back to the parish was re-joining the family! She would get after the Ladies of Saint Anne and the members of the choir to "encourage" her son. One watch apiece. And she'd be able to keep a better eye on Rita without seeming to do so, every time she went to the grocery or the church. Cécile was thinking hard.

"If our little brother's making so much money, you don't need to sew on stripes to help him out."

"Help me out?" shouted Ovide. "Not on your life!" He was already having trouble with Rita, who was obsessed with being a waitress at Chez Gérard and pretended it was to help him out! "The women in my life aren't going to make me a kept man! Thank you very much!"

Joséphine was delighted. She was one of the "women in his life"! She glowed with pleasure.

"We'll split the contract, Cécile, just the way I said. I always like to have a little something to fall back on."

Cécile knew when she was beaten. Her calculating mind was already working on a new equation.

"Doesn't it take money to start a thing like that?"

"Just ten thou' or so, at most," said Ovide nonchalantly.

"Ten thousand dollars!" cried Cécile. "Well, I'll tell you, I can't touch my capital, it's already loaned out at high interest." (Her savings by now were up to twenty-six thousand dollars.) "I can't even guarantee a loan for anybody. I can take no risks. I'm thinking about Nicolas and my own old age."

Detached as if touching Cécile's money were an unheard-of idea, Ovide declared:

"Sister, dear, that never crossed my mind! I'm going to see Napoléon's bank manager. The very size of my project will convince him. My signature is good, but what's really going to guarantee it for him is the idea itself."

"And how much is your Frenchman going to invest?" asked Cécile.

"Oh, we'll see, we'll see. But for now his contribution is his experience and his present clients. That means a lot."

"Well, you have a word with Napoléon, then," said Joséphine, concerned and vaguely anxious.

8

Napoléon's children, except for the two oldest who had left for school, were playing in one of their father's three trucks, while the employees sat outside the plumber's shop, their backs to the wall, Coke bottles in one hand and sandwiches in the other, lunch box between their legs, eating as they admired and wondered at the next-door family's washing, including that of the fourteen sturdy daughters, all unmarried, aged from seventeen to thirty-five. It was washday in this sultanless harem and the fourteen pairs of panties and brassieres bellied in the wind.

Jeanne was doing the dishes, and Napoléon, his feet up on the veranda railing, was blowing his trumpet, regaling the atmosphere of this early afternoon with strident howls and painful burps. The phone had rung several times with neighbours complaining, and it was Jeanne who bore the brunt. But her Napoléon, who had to go through such troubles with his business, found that his instrument brought him a relaxation that was well earned as he played after every meal. Jeanne came out on the veranda.

"Poléon, it's bad for your digestion playing the trumpet like that and you all bent in two."

And she added timidly:

"It bothers the neighbours, too, they're phoning to complain."

Napoléon showed all his teeth in a happy laugh and pinched her on the bottom.

"Just wait till I can play, they'll be phoning to beg me to go on. They can afford to suffer a little now."

His hand had slipped down to Jeanne's knee. She escaped, laughing, gave him a shove and scolded him gently:

"All right, lunchtime lover, don't start that."

Smiling, with a leer in his eye, he wiped the trumpet's mouthpiece with a finger.

"It's the dainties on the clothes-line next door. They give me ideas."

He sat up abruptly.

"Isn't that Ovide? You're out already!"

Ovide did a little dance.

"As you see. Completely cured. There was nothing wrong with me! How are you, Jeanne?"

She was very fond of her brother-in-law and his fine manners. She complimented him on his healthy appearance and his straw boater, but disappeared to the kitchen when she saw that Ovide wanted to talk to Napoléon "man to man." She was an excellent woman, generous and sensitive, and loved her husband's family, to whom she owed everything: her life, her happiness, her comfort and her lovely children.

Napoléon was waiting for Ovide to talk. Patiently he played with the trumpet valves, which made Ovide think of his Royaume du Disque.

"Do you play by note?" he asked.

"No. By ear. But I'm coming right along."

Then Ovide brushed aside the problems of trumpets and valves, and, before an astonished Napoléon, laid forth his project, causing the unheard-of financial possibilities of jewellery to glitter before his brother's eyes.

Napoléon's objections were not the same as those of their mother and sister. His decent and naive heart believed in the infinite chances given by North American society to those ready to calculate their risks and take the plunge. He hoped sincerely that Ovide would succeed, because he felt guilty about making so much money while Ovide, who was head and shoulders above him, merely vegetated.

Napoléon's thoughts, thus stimulated, went back to old times:

"You're not afraid of throwing it all over before you get anywhere? Don't you remember, when I tried to persuade you to bike uphill to prove that you could make it to the top? You'd always give up half-way there."

Ovide floundered a little. He swore, waving his long arms, that life had forged in him a will of steel, and that he had purged all that was erratic from his character.

Now it was time for him to take his destiny into his own hands. Oh, of course there was no question of his borrowing money from Napoléon. He only wanted to be introduced to Napoléon's bank manager. He was terrified at the idea of approaching a stranger for a loan, something he had never done. Napoléon's presence would reassure the banker and give him confidence in the obscure brother of this prosperous contractor. Moreover, Napoléon could keep an eye on Ovide and give him good advice.

"OK, we'll go and see him when he gets back from lunch, about half-past one."

What a good old brother! Ovide wanted to give him a hug. Instead he jumped out of his skin. Brakes squealed and a white convertible with red leather seats skidded to a stop in front of them, the lady driver tooting gaily. Rita, in person!

"Don't sit there like a pair of statues. Come see what I bought!"

Ovide's heart dropped to his boots. With Napoléon he went out toward the street. Rita was exultant, leaning nonchalantly on the open door of the car as she had seen the pretty models do at the Auto Show.

"You don't mean it? You really bought this car?" said Ovide.

"A '46 Dodge! A good year," Napoléon pronounced, looking it over with a connoisseur's eye.

"Sure I bought it, Ovide. Don't make such a face! At half past twelve I walked into the garage and fifteen minutes later I owned a car. And here I am! It's a terrific bargain! Eight hundred and fifty dollars, with only a hundred fifty cash and the rest at sixty dollars a month. When you start out as a big businessman you don't take the bus any more, eh, Napoléon? And there was my hundred and fifty dollars doing nothing at the Caisse Populaire and us walking all over town!"

Horrified, Ovide was thinking about the insurance premiums and the gasoline, the flat tires, and the repair bills that were going to flood through his letter slot. Rita, pouting prettily, caressed his chin:

"Don't you see, it's white with red leather seats, just like my dress and the shoes you liked so much, back when you were so crazy about me you couldn't see straight? Come on, get in! Try it out!"

He climbed in behind the wheel and turned it right and left. He must look smart with his boater! He began to grin without reserve, though his ever-present anxiety quickly showed. He really must get that watch business going.

"Let's drive to the bank!" he said to Napoléon.

"Hit them up for all the money you can!" said Rita cavalierly. "It's meant to be spent!"

Jeanne came out and admired the car, tried out the front passenger's seat and looked delighted as a child.

"And it has hardly any miles on it. It was never driven in winter. Hey, Jeanne, we'll go for drives in the afternoon, eh? Us two girls, when the weather's fine?"

"Jeanne won't have time," said Napoléon, who was not convinced of his sister-in-law's virtue. "But congratulations, Rita, you made a good buy."

Rita neglected to mention that it was Stan Labrie who a month before had told her about this bargain offered by a dealer who used the "hostesses" in Stan's network during a recent Chrysler dealers' convention at the Château Frontenac . . . . She also forgot to say that this white convertible had belonged to Bob, the architect with whom she had been unfaithful to Ovide one night.

"Come on, I'll drive you to the bank!" decided Rita.

Napoléon was ill at ease.

Ovide's heart soared like a swallow as he sat with this banker to whom Napoléon had introduced him as the brain of the family. Ovide talked and talked, evoking the great bankers of history, the Medicis, the Rothschilds (those were the only ones he knew about). But this man, the manager, leaning back in his black leather chair, kept bringing him back to more immediate preoccupations. No, Ovide had never run a business; no, he had no capital; yes, he had a marriage contract with separation of property; no, he didn't know anything about the jewellery business, still less how a watch worked; but there was Napoléon brushing aside these objections with the back of his hand, proclaiming his confidence in his brother's future. He offered to guarantee a loan of ten thousand dollars, just like that, with his eyes shut, so anxious was he for Ovide to make his dream come true. The manager stood up and asked Ovide to leave him alone with Napoléon.

Nervously, Ovide strode up and down, hands behind his back, in front of all the tellers flipping through their enormous wads of bills with astonishing virtuosity. He supposed there was not such a wad awaiting him. He was sure Napoléon would fail. And there was Rita, waiting at the door in a car that wasn't paid for. He was in a sweat of anxiety.

"Monsieur Napoléon," the manager was saying, "I forbid you to back your brother in this fancy venture. He's no businessman. He may know a lot, but what has he made of himself, at his age? A fine talker he is, but he's no man of action."

Napoléon insisted:

"I have confidence in him. I'll pay the money out of my own pocket if I have to. Us Plouffes are winners. Come on, chief, say yes, eh?"

"I'm saying no," he said curtly. "I have to protect you from yourself. What's more, I have to remind you that your own line of credit is stretched as tight as a drum. It's time you started to collect your debts. You're too soft on people."

Napoléon explained that the government took ages to settle its bills, and he wasn't going to send the bailiff after honest customers who were short of cash and wanted a little more time; and he'd been very smart, stocking up on copper piping because copper was going up, etc., etc.

"I know all about that," the manager cut in, "but if I catch you investing in this thing of your brother's I'll cut your line of credit. You know what that means!"

The plumbing contractor, president of Napoléon and Sons, went out swearing to himself that he'd find some other way to help out Ovide.

"Come on," he said. "The bank don't like having two brothers at the same branch."

"I knew it," said Ovide softly.

He felt like a weakling, steered this way and that by his family and friends – by everybody. A chronic ne'er-do-well. A simple soldier who'd never get his stripes. How had he dared make fun of Ephrem Bélanger? He was deflated, pitiful.

Guessing at his despair, Napoléon clenched his fists and said:

"I'm not giving in, Ovide. You don't know me. I have a plan." (He had no plan.) "First of all we're going to celebrate the founding of your company. I'm taking you and Rita to Chez Gérard, there's a violin trio from Broadway there, they play classical, popular, everything. They just make their violins cry and everybody cries along."

Ovide was comforted. Maybe his anxieties were the normal prelude to a great leap into the successful future . . . . Hope made you pay dearly sometimes. Napoléon smiled:

"You know Guillaume's coming back from Anticosti one of these days. When us three brothers get together we'll have the world at our feet. We'll talk it all over then."

Suddenly he had a real idea:

"Hey! There's Uncle Gédéon, Ti'-Mé's dad, he's got money comin' out of his ears. And he's your godfather, remember?"

Ovide's optimism was on the rise again.

"We'll go to Chez Gérard, all right, but it's on me!" he cried, giving Napoléon a powerful slap on the back that made him cringe. Skinny old Ovide, a real Plouffe, eh?

9

While Ovide was writhing in the tangled skeins of fate, two free men, brown as a copper, were chatting happily as they lay near the prow of a coaster loaded with pulpwood. The captain had picked them up at Matane with their abundant baggage: four deer just starting to freeze in the ship's refrigerator; salmon, smoked trout, small game, haversacks, a rolled-up tent – in short, a whole collection of what a hunting and fishing guide brings back from his season's work when he returns to town or is preparing to head for the lumber camps in the forests of Quebec.

The ship was sailing past Rimouski. You could smell winter coming, though the weather was superb on this day in early October. The waves were choppy, now dark, now silver. Enormous porpoises, in their pursuit of the capelin, a small fish that is their favourite food, performed a marvellous ballet, diving with astonishing grace for creatures their size.

At this point the St. Lawrence River is some fifty kilometres wide, and from the middle you have to squint to glimpse the misty shores. Formations of wild ducks and Canada geese flew past high above, fleeing southward in well-formed flights, calling loudly as they went. Around the ship glided dozens of hungry gulls waiting for Ti'-Mé to finish his banana and throw the skin overboard.

"We've got a real beautiful country," Guillaume murmured, thinking of the muddy Danube he had seen in wartime.

"Sure do," growled Ti'-Mé, "but I can't wait to get up to la Malbaie and Baie Saint-Paul and Petite Rivière Saint-François. That's where heaven starts."

There was a long silence.

"When we get to Quebec, that's heaven," Guillaume corrected him. "I'll never forget coming back after five years away.

I jumped onto the dock and kissed the ground and bawled like a calf."

"That's because your lovin' family was waiting for you. And anyway, you're a city boy, that's not the same thing."

Ti'-Mé grimaced and grabbed his head in his hands.

"What a headache! I think it's goin' to bust. My throat's burning! And my crucifix is burning my arm."

"That'll teach you to tie one on like a Kraut. So suffer, put up with it, you earned it."

"Don't give me a hard time," said Ti'-Mé, "it's not fair."

He examined his left arm on which a Lebanese in Matane had, for twenty-five dollars, tattooed a crucifix. Despite Guillaume's objurgations this tattoo artist had dragged his cousin on a monster jag that lasted two whole days, from which Ti'-Mé emerged with misty memories of a bed and a pretty, athletic Gaspésian girl with a sumptuous bottom. Guillaume, furious, had had to wait in their hotel while Ti'-Mé made up for his long months of chastity on Anticosti. When Ti'-Mé took off, he did so in style. Almost all his season's earnings had gone down the drain. The tattoo artist, the girl, the bar of the hotel where he had broken all the glasses – all this had relieved him of some six hundred dollars! Poor Ti'-Mé!

Guillaume, still marked by the strict upbringing he had received from his mother, disapproved of this kind of folly, and put up with the throbbing desire, regular as a toothache, that he felt for women. In Europe, where he had been the handsomest fellow in the regiment, had he not easily conquered the most exciting French girls – who saw in him, of course, a kind, blond giant come from Canada to liberate them? And then he had had that experience with the German girl, Rita's double, whom he had killed with a .38 bullet. How could he have done it?

Since then, because of this trauma, he had let many chances pass him by. On the few occasions when he had possessed a woman, the memory of the dead German girl had tortured him and saddened his violent pleasures. Except this July, when he had been guide to a blonde American woman at pool number nine of the Jupiter. After they had made a meal of a young salmon, grilled fresh from the pool, and washed it down with a Pouilly-Fuissé of which the wealthy tourists had brought an ample supply, the couple had stretched out for a siesta on a great, flat rock. Instead of a siesta Guillaume had made love

80

three times to the young girl who later wrote him three letters of three pages each as if in celebration of those marvellous moments. He was thinking about her when he said to Ti'-Mé:

"You know, cousin, I don't understand you, blowing your whole summer's earnings in two days."

"When you've got no kids," sighed Ti'-Mé, "and your parents don't like you, and your life's goin' past like a river, and nothing ever happens to you, and you're shy, and you got no friends but the squirrels, what the hell's the difference? And oh boy! that was a fine, fat squirrely I had in Matane!" he chortled. "I sure made her cage go 'round!"

"Dirty old Ti'-Mé!" said the other, giving him a friendly dig in the ribs.

"Hey, don't bust me in! I got a bad head already. Tell me, Guillaume, what are you going to do this winter?"

"Make salmon flies, as usual. And help Napoléon with his contracts. Can you imagine, he's getting after me to start playing hockey. He says I'd be just as good as Maurice Richard of the Montreal Canadiens, world champions."

Ti'-Mé grew very sad all of a sudden. He was comparing his own skull, covered by a battered felt hat bristling with home-made angler's flies, with Guillaume's magnificent head. The forehead was bound by a red handkerchief tied in the back, Indian fashion, decorated with the motley feathers of birds imported by Henri Meunier to populate the paradise of Anticosti by the thousands. It was a headdress that would give his mother a laugh. Guillaume was suddenly in a hurry to see his family.

"You couldn't keep me at your place for a week in Quebec, could you?" he begged, humble because he was afraid of being refused.

Guillaume couldn't fathom his request. Why wasn't he in a hurry to see his own relatives, his village, his friends?

Aimé shook his head stubbornly.

"When I leave your place I'm heading straight for the woods. I'll chop trees till spring. And then we go back to Anticosti. You're coming, eh? Next year? You wouldn't leave me in the lurch? We have to build that log cabin near the lobster crick before the tourists get there."

Guillaume's eyes lit up at the mention of their project. The two of them had decided to build a secret cabin in the forest, not far from the sea and facing a creek where, in knee-deep water and by shifting stones with a stick, you could take as many lobsters as you liked, weighing two kilos each. The cabin, known only to themselves, would be well stocked with dried fish, smoked meat, jam and green tomato pickles made by Joséphine, and powdered milk. If the rest of the world let them down or disaster overtook them or an atomic war broke out (there'd be no Hiroshima on Anticosti), they'd take refuge in their Eden, far from everyone and protected from every harm.

Ti'-Mé tossed a whole banana to the seagulls.

"That's for sure I don't want to go home. Can't you just see my old man when he hears I blew my summer's earnings with a young 'creature' in two days?"

Guillaume shrugged.

"You're exaggerating. Your dad was a wild one in his day. He'll have a good laugh at your story. Why are you scared of him, anyway? I find your old man, my uncle Gédéon, funny as hell. And soft-hearted! Why don't you have a good talk with him, once and for all?"

"I tell you, he scares me. I can't do a thing about it. He gives me the chills."

Guillaume found this situation regrettable. Uncle Gédéon had a sawmill, a big farm and plenty of up-to-date machinery. He was proud of his herd of cows, the best milkers in the Beauce. What was more, he was the township's chief organizer for the Union Nationale, the party in power; and Duplessis, premier of the province of Quebec, called him "Sir Gédéon" (to which he replied "Sir Maurice" as fresh as you please). Ti'-Mé's father was a master chorister, kept seventy-five deals going at the same time and was feared by many who saw in him the most powerful man in the Beauce. Guillaume sighed. A man like that could make his son happy if he took him in on one or another of his activities. He said as much to Ti'-Mé. And the latter finally admitted the cause of his distress.

"Father wrote me a letter last week. Imagine, he's started up a coffin factory and he wants me to run it. Can't you see me? Hey! Anything but that!"

Guillaume couldn't believe it. His uncle would begin anything.

"Just think, Guillaume, there I am with dozens of coffins all lined up on the floor, on inventory! I'd always feel as if there was an epidemic on. I'd think about nothing but death and I'd start drinkin' like a fish. I know me."

Guillaume, on second thought, burst out laughing.

"You could work yourself up to being an embalmer and then an undertaker. You'd be your own boss. I can see you now, all in black, your hat on your arm, leading the funeral procession saying, 'Relatives first!'"

But the more he laughed, the sadder Ti'-Mé became.

"Come on, don't make fun of me. My dad says you can make a fortune in that business. Instead of ordering coffins in Quebec, we make them there, with the sawmill and all, and the better things go in the Beauce the more people there'll be, and, of course, the more will die. Dad says in the long run we could handle all the dead in the region, right down to the American border."

Guillaume thought this profession wouldn't suit him either. He'd seen enough stiffs on the battle field. He understood Ti'-Mé's reaction: his cousin loved life so much, and health of every kind. Yet Guillaume admired his uncle Gédéon, especially when compared with his own father, the late Théophile.

"What a guy, that father of yours! Seventy years old and going strong, ready to start a new business!"

"And he's not so crazy, either!" Ti'-Mé said proudly. "The bottom of the coffins is made of thin plywood. He has the exclusive agency for the whole of the Beauce. Did you know that plywood comes from somewhere out west, near the Pacific?"

Guillaume was thinking about Ovide, and Napoléon, himself, Cécile, his dead father – champion cyclist – and said:

"There's all kinds to be found in families."

There was a long silence, broken only by the rapping of the coaster's diesel. From the still-damp piles of pulp logs rose the rich, heavy smell of resin. Far ahead they could see the Ile Verte.

"We'll be in Quebec tomorrow night," said Guillaume. "It's OK, cousin, you come and spend a week with us in my apartment. But no booze, eh? You know my mother."

Happily, Ti'-Mé began to smile.

"I'll be a wooden saint," he vowed.

Clay pipe in his mouth, Gédéon Plouffe was contemplating the vast extent of his lands in the Beauce with an emperor's pride. He gloried in his land as if it were a pretty woman, and on that day was thinking about the hard labour of a whole lifetime spread out symbolically before him, as far as the eye could see. Older brother of the late Théophile, he had never understood how that brother could desert and go to the big city, where Théophile had chosen to become a printer's apprentice. It was true that Gédéon had been the one to inherit their father's land, and that his possessive temperament made it hard for a weaker soul to live with him. Even his sons had left him to take up all kinds of careers, but his daughters, married in the village, seemed quite able to put up with his tempers. They were not unlike him. Gédéon's wife, Démerise, had died three years earlier of acute indigestion after a too self-indulgent meal at which twelve hearty eaters had consumed two suckling pigs. Poor Démerise! After menopause she had suffered a veritable martyrdom in her conjugal relations. The whole business had never meant much to her, but Gédéon as his years advanced had remained unflagging in his appetites and his capacities to an extent that would have been the envy of Victor Hugo.

Still gazing at his lands, he relit his pipe, then shook his head. The trouble was, after a lifetime of success, that he could not settle down to an absolute enjoyment of his wide, fertile fields and his herds. He was waylaid on all sides by different projects, by his pursuit of the "creatures" and by his plots and schemes as a political string-puller in the village. His reign extended to so many people and activities that he found no time to enjoy any one of them to the full. Intrigue and peasant cunning spoiled his deepest joys. He suffered from the scattered diversity of his small triumphs, but fell on his feet like a cat each time and chased his melancholy with good, coarse pleasantries in doubtful taste. He filled his pipe from a pouch made of a pig's bladder, unfailingly using a mixture called "Saint Jude's Fart," that he made specially from local tobacco. It was famous for its powerful and repulsive odour. He marched off to his barn singing, "I've two great oxen in my stable . . . ."

But his pace slowed again. He was thinking of Ti'-Mé and wondering if he'd see him soon. Ti'-Mé, who had always run away from him. Gédéon had never known how to behave with that boy. He'd tried every approach. But if he adopted a soft, conciliatory tone, playing the father who wants to get closer to his son, he fell out of character after five minutes. If he complained of his son's lack of ambition, Aimé would make some droll gesture or come out with some outlandish remark, triggering his father's impatience and fury, and pop!– his Ti'-Mé, on the loose again, went off to the lumber shanties.

This new coffin factory, already flourishing, had been launched by Gédéon for Ti'-Mé's benefit. The father had thought, naively perhaps, that the daily sight of coffins would make his great good-for-nothing son think twice about his life, would settle him down and make him contemplate his future and his last days. More realistically, he had imagined proudly that on his own death he would be buried in a coffin made by his own son. Instead of visiting his lowing herd in the stable, he made his way toward his macabre factory.

There was a comforting racket of hammers and squealing of saws, along with the smells of strong glue and the perfumes of varnish and green wood. After the war there was such a demand for construction lumber that dried wood was not to be had.

The village carpenters had quickly become familiar with their new specialty. Today alone some twenty coffins had been built and stood ready on the factory floor for varnishing.

"Everything all right, Josaphat? Our cadaver boxes coming along?" said Gédéon to the foreman, a lean and irascible man.

"They're coming along the way they're fetched," he said enigmatically.

Josaphat rapped a knuckle on the bottom of one of the coffins and got a fragile reverberation.

"That bottom's too thin, boss. One of these days it'll fall out."

Gédéon blew this remark away with a puff of Saint Jude's Fart that set the foreman coughing.

"Always the dark side, Josaphat. Most people die thin, especially these days with all the cancer. No use making the bottom thicker, it's going to rot in the ground anyhow. Think of the living, think of the poor businessman who wants to make his profit and keep his costs down. That's how we can beat the competition: save on transport and save on wood. Plywood's not thick, you know, and I have the exclusive agency for it and don't you forget that. Think of the prime cost and don't be a Jeremiah, you make me tired."

Josaphat grasped the threat, but this time he was ready for Gédéon:

"Boss, there's Elzéar Cliche . . . ."

"What? Was he looking for me?"

Josaphat didn't answer. Gédéon grew pale at the solemn expression of his foreman:

"You don't say . . . Not Elzéar?"

"Right. The churchwarden, Elzéar Cliche, your good friend, just died in his bed. An apoplectic fit. I just got the message on the phone."

Gédéon gulped. Elzéar, his childhood friend, his fellow chorister, his acolyte during their wild excursions to Quebec City, where they often went to deposit funds with the Union Nationale's treasurer! Elzéar, a giant, an authentic blackleg (a nickname for inhabitants of the Beauce)!

"I know that hits you hard, boss, but that's how it is. The good Lord comes and gets us one by one and mostly when we least expect it."

He was falling into his professional style, which he gravely adopted each time a tearful customer came by.

"Elzéar! It's incredible! I'll tell you, that gives me a jolt!" said Gédéon, saddened. "Elzéar, my old chum, and just a youngster! Barely sixty-seven! It's not fair. My great friend!"

"Hey, boss! Did you ever think Elzéar is the biggest and fattest man in the township? Six foot four and three hundred and fifty pounds. He's got to have a coffin made to measure. And solid!"

Again he rapped a knuckle on the coffin floor.

"You're right, Josaphat. Elzéar's a friend, we've got to make a special. Put three thicknesses on the bottom. And use screws instead of nails. And four coats of varnish. But I tell you, Josaphat, the exception is not the rule. Remember that. Dead men are thin. As a rule."

Deeply moved, he turned on his heel and went to pay his respects to the dead. He pondered that no one was exempt from accidents like this, and the same thing would happen to him one day without a word of warning. Strangely enough, this reflection aroused in him a carnal desire of which he was proud.

10

That same evening Ovide and Rita, tense and ceremonious as if they had been going to a high-class concert, drove their guests, Napoléon and Jeanne, to Chez Gérard in Rita's new car. She had insisted on putting the top down despite the chilly air. On arriving, Napoléon proved to have sufficient drag to get their party past the line-up.

As this was the only cabaret in Quebec City to offer music-hall shows of international calibre, it was always packed on weekends. Post-war euphoria and the birth of a new era found their expression there, in passion and delight. Some people even went two or three times a week. This was liberation!

In the bustle and racket that preceded the show, customers were encouraged to finish their dinner and order their drinks before the artists came on stage. From their choice table Napoléon loudly introduced his brother to the regulars, despite Ovide's whispered protests but with Rita's blessing. She, for her own part, greeted everyone around with her most alluring smile. Jeanne was happy to have Ovide and his wife at the table instead of the usual back-room boys Napoléon invited.

Excited, Rita siphoned away at her John Collins with a straw that was already smeared with lipstick. She was satisfied with life. At last Ovide had agreed, for this evening at least, to give her the life she loved and deserved. Her hungry, roving eye had already flirted its way around the room. No sign of Stan, thank goodness! But . . . but . . . ! Who was that? Back there, wasn't that Bob, the architect, with his wife (he'd shown her a photo, afterwards) and a couple of friends? From afar, while Ovide wasn't looking, she greeted him discreetly, but he pretended not to know her.

Ovide, on the defensive, kept his hands folded and his gaze lowered, as he did whenever he ventured outside his own universe into a new and hostile situation from which he hoped to emerge intact, as if it had never happened. But suddenly he felt that he was being dull, and took a sip of gin. He drank sparingly, knowing that too much alcohol could plunge him back into acute depression. He felt that, in any case, everything was lining up against him. He was under no illusion: he was indulging in this excursion in the hope of stilling his anxiety by drowning it in an atmosphere of factitious festivity. Ten thousand dollars! An enormous sum, practically out of reach. Pacifique Berthet, before whose eyes Ovide had painted an El Dorado, must be dying of impatience in his hospital bed! And Rita had begun madly spending money they didn't have and most likely never would! What nonsense, buying that car!

Jeanne, radiant, touched Rita's wrist.

"It's so nice going out with you, dear. We don't see enough of each other. We should do this more often," she said, to Napoléon's approving nod. He had suggested that she use her influence to rein in Rita's conduct to something less disquieting for Ovide.

"Why, I'd just love to!" said Rita. "Why not once a week, eh, honey?"

"We'll see, we'll see," said Ovide pompously. "Pleasures that become a habit turn boring, you know!"

Rita pouted.

"You see, Jeanne? I'm not like you. I didn't marry a good sport. Come on, let's go powder our noses."

As the two women left together Napoléon, guessing his brother's worries, shook Ovide's arm, with a gesture of his head toward their wives.

"Look at those two. Did we get beautiful women or didn't we?"

"I don't like washrooms that open right onto a dining-room," Ovide decreed curtly. "Before they go inside the women automatically pinch their dresses and the men grab their flies. How are you supposed to eat after you see that?"

Napoléon laughed.

"I'll be darned, you notice everything, don't you? Hey, loosen up! Relax! Have a little fun, like everybody else! Have a night out, and you'll sleep like a baby. That's when your problems get solved, while you're asleep. Everything's goin' to be all right, just leave it to me. I'm making money every day, we'll find enough for you, believe me. Look at all these people: they're laughing, they're alive, and they've all got their troubles. You're spoiling it for Rita, you make everybody freeze up."

Ovide was vexed with himself. Napoléon was right. But then

he caught himself inspecting people's wrists: every single one had a wrist-watch. Quebec had an adult population of at least three million. He'd be satisfied with five per cent of that number, a hundred and fifty thousand watches. The figure triggered his good humour.

"You're right, I'm a party-pooper. I leave the money problem to you, Napoléon."

"There, boy, now you're talkin'!"

Ovide gaily tossed back a large gulp. The women were coming back, and Rita was totally absorbed by the effect she was producing.

"We got the best looking broads in the whole joint," said Napoléon, giving a one-armed hug to Jeanne's waist.

Stage hands were busy preparing for the show.

"You're going to like it, Ovide, I'm sure of that. Three violinists from New York. Hey, don't make a face, they don't only play jazz. They do classical as well. Just you wait."

The late shift of waitresses was taking over. Rita was the first to notice Marie, the French girl. Ovide, who had let his thoughts wander back to Pacifique Berthet, didn't notice her at first; but at the very sight of her a jealous gleam had burned in Rita's gaze, while the same vision produced a contented smile in Jeanne.

"Hello, beautiful!" said Napoléon, tenderly cordial. "Two John Collins for the ladies and two gins and tonic for my brother Ovide and me."

Ovide and Marie had seen and recognized each other in the same split second. Ovide froze, incredulous. Marie forgot her order pad and pencil, saw nothing but Ovide lying on the floor of the music store where, a moment before he sank to the ground, he had made her a present of the record "Les Chemins de l'amour." She had thought he was near death and had moistened his face and patted his cheeks.

"That's my brother Ovide, the great musician!" said Napoléon, not at all surprised that Ovide was able to stun with his first glance a pretty foreign girl, and a French one at that.

"Ah! He is your brother?" murmured the girl.

Astonished and suddenly suspicious, Rita stiffened. Ovide and Marie seemed to know each other! Was he hiding things from her? And just look at how that Marie creature was looking at Ovide, her husband!

"I see you are cured?" said Marie, smiling timidly.

"Oh there was nothing wrong. I want to thank you again, you were so kind."

Marie, embarrassed by Rita's hostile looks, took their order and went on to another table. Rita's aggressive glance followed her a moment, then came the attack on Ovide:

"You two know each other?"

"She's a customer, a very fine person," he stammered.

Napoléon was delighted, and said to Jeanne:

"Well, whaddaya think of that! Ovide knows our wee Marie!"

"How did she know you were sick?" insisted Rita.

He explained briefly, as if it had no importance, that he'd been selling a record to Marie at the time of his fainting spell. As he came temporarily to his senses he had noticed her moistening his face. Now the jealousy scene had something to feed on. Rita's voice grew biting:

"Well, if that bit of fluff saved your life, the least you could do is introduce her to your ever-loving wife! I'd have got down on my knees and thanked her!"

"Rita, don't get carried away!" Ovide defended himself feebly.

"When I think how you cross-examine me, I'm stupid if I don't twist your arm a bit!" she cut in.

Ovide's uneasiness was growing. Rita had some right on her side. He did hide certain things from her, such as this first meeting with Marie, which he had buried in his most secret self. In a way Rita's instinct put her on the right track, and she had some reason to be angry. Knowing her, Ovide thought how she would leap on him like a tigress if she knew that since his fainting spell the marvellous, aureoled face of Marie had often been superimposed over that of his wife. He tried to cool the situation down:

"My poor Rita, you always go imagining things! The girl is a customer and I saw her exactly once. I didn't even know she worked here. I admit her accent and culture and her taste in music impressed me. It was the first time anybody came into the Royaume du Disque to ask for 'Les Chemins de l'amour' by Francis Poulenc, sung by Yvonne Printemps, whom she knows in person. As you can imagine, I was struck by that! And it just so happened that I fainted when she was there. And then I find her here, a waitress! You could have knocked me over with a feather."

90

Rita smiled spitefully, sure that her intuition was not deceiving her. Ovide was making his excuses so feebly and his voice sounded false.

"It doesn't shock you to see such a well-educated, distinguished French girl waiting on table in Chez Gérard?" she asked. "What degrading work!"

Ovide was doing a slow burn, to the consternation of Napoléon and Jeanne, who would have liked to be elsewhere.

"If I say it shocks me," he snapped, "you'll accuse me of having a crush on her. As she means nothing to me, I can state without any ulterior motive that I am astonished to find her here as a waitress. She must have her good reasons, probably economic in nature."

"So we don't have any economic reasons, I suppose!" said Rita, clenching her teeth. "Just that your wife, a miserable little Miss Sweet Caporal who wants to help you out, though she hasn't much education and isn't French-from-France, your wife, when she wants to become a waitress, that's degrading, is it?"

Ovide felt cornered.

"But you're my wife! That's different!"

Napoléon thought he saw a way out.

"Rita, we know Marie, eh? She's a well-brought-up kid, an orphan I think, and she keeps her distance from the customers."

"It's true what Napoléon says," Jeanne chimed in. "We love Marie," she added, wondering how Ovide could be so secretive with his wife, while she and Napoléon told each other everything.

"Sure, sure, you break my heart with your Marie. And wouldn't I keep my distance? Eh?" Rita was almost in tears.

"Shhhh! The emcee's coming!" said Napoléon, relieved. "The show's starting."

The customers, as if they were about to see a religious rite, turned and settled down in their chairs. At Napoléon's table the silence and immobility were tense with embarrassment. Rita abruptly emptied her own glass, then Ovide's, and retreated behind the mask of a pouting, unhappy face.

For a public they had won over before they even started to play, the violinists performed a pot-pourri of jazz, popular or semi-classical songs and selections from operas and operettas. The whole crowd hummed along as they did the "Toreador's song" from *Carmen*.

Ovide smiled, thinking of the scene he had made in front of Major Bélanger; but Rita thought he was being condescending about the off-key singing of some drunken spectators. Then the master of ceremonies, who had waited for the applause to fade, announced that as an encore the trio, by special request, would play a very pretty melody much appreciated in Europe. "A first performance in Canada, and dedicated specially to Mrs. and Mr. Ovide Plouffe, 'Les Chemins de l'amour,' by Francis Poulenc!"

Ovide and Rita stood up to acknowledge the applause, bowed, surprised and flattered, and sat down, blushing to the roots of their hair. Napoléon and Jeanne couldn't believe it. Ovide, who had no self-confidence! No sooner had he set foot in the place than he became a star! With a song dedication! He was a real Plouffe! Rita, delighted by this turn of events, preened herself as if she were the mayor's wife. Ovide listened religiously to the music, dedicated by Marie herself, he was certain: she must have made her request to the first violin. He listened, eyes closed, observed by the whole crowd, which was hardly accustomed to this subtle music, and closely watched by Rita, whose cerebral mechanism (like her car) was low on mileage, but at this moment high on revs.

When the piece came to an end and the crowd was applauding politely, Ovide, with a nod, thanked the musicians and Marie, whom he glimpsed in the distance. She reciprocated in a friendly way, and Rita intercepted the exchange.

"You know her better than you let on, that Frenchwoman. She practically made a public declaration of love to you!" She smiled sarcastically. "My name was just an excuse."

Still swimming in the tones of Poulenc, Ovide barely heard his wife. He was stupefied by Marie's kind thought. In her charming way she had just thanked him for making her a present of the record. And perhaps she was at the same time wishing him a happy convalescence.

"That 'Chemins de l'amour,' that must be the record you sold her. Or did you give it to her? I know you, Ovide Plouffe," said Rita. "I heard you whistle it a few times around the place. I'll bet anything you gave it to her."

Ovide's embarrassed silence confirmed her suspicions. He explained feebly that Marie had done no more than demonstrate the kindness of a sensitive person. And what was all the fuss about? The piece had been dedicated to Rita, too, hadn't it? Exasperated, he concluded:

"I never thought you could be that jealous. If you keep this up you'll start giving me ideas about that girl! Anyway, that's enough. The incident is closed."

Rita knew too much about tricks of this kind. That Marie was a clever devil. The violinists' set was over and Marie was back at their table, blushing at all the thank you's. Rita, seeming to show the effects of all the alcohol, grabbed the order pad and offered Marie her place beside Ovide.

"Here, take a rest and have a chat with my husband, since you know each other so well!"

And before the brothers had time to intervene Rita was wiggling and swaying her way among the tables toward Bob, the architect, who stiffened in anticipation of the worst.

Ovide had never been obliged to act with such presence of mind. Seeing Marie's distress, he became a man of action. Racing after his wife, with a false smile he caught her arm and hissed:

"Are you crazy? Come on, we're dancing!"

Dragging her behind him, he recaptured the order pad and, with an apologetic glance at Marie, laid it on the table between Napoléon and Jeanne.

In fact, there were couples going out on the dance floor between shows, dancing to the juke box, where sentimental slow tunes alternated with the savage rhythms of a new kind of contortion called boogie-woogie, which Rita adored. Stirred by alcohol and the discovery of an unsuspected side to her husband's sentimental life, she let him lead her to the floor, then clung to him voluptuously to a song from *Le Quai des Orfèvres* sung by Suzy Delair: "Dance with Me!" She was almost weeping on his shoulder.

"I just know it, you're unfaithful. You don't love me any more."

Ovide trembled. This was his revenge for his own sufferings over thoughts of Rita's infidelity, imagining that she might have made love, at least in her imagination, with other men. He threw out his chest, because she was holding him so tight and cuddling against him.

"It's true that the human heart has unsounded depths," he said, "but don't worry. I still love you and I'm still faithful to you."

A boogie-woogie record took the place of Suzy Delair. The dancers were going mad. Couples came together, then separated, changing partners between jumps. This fashion had just reached Quebec. It started on the dance floor, sometimes by dancing with a total stranger, and the exchange extended right to the boudoir. Couples ready to practise this new sport were just forming an exclusive club, to the great scandal of the Church and all right-thinking citizens.

Rita always acted with a disarming spontaneity. Ovide, for his part, was stomping stupidly, marking time but unable to catch the rhythm of the new barbarism. As they passed close to Bob, the architect, Rita suddenly abandoned her husband's uncertain grasp, separated Bob from his wife and shoved her toward Ovide:

"Try her, I'll take the husband."

No sooner said than done, but the two men and the other spouse were stunned, and went on uneasily stomping. Napoléon, with his partner, Jeanne, left the floor shocked, telling his wife this was intolerable. Jeanne agreed and told him of her fears for Ovide's marriage.

Napoléon grew even more concerned. If Ovide was so close to the brink in his conjugal relations, how could he hope to run a province-wide business that would call for all the energies of a man's heart and mind?

The ride home was a stormy one. Ovide accused Rita of hoisting her leg so high in the boogie-woogie that you could see her panties. She wept loudly, accusing him of being in love with that Marie, who was no prettier or sexier than Rita. She locked herself in her room, and Ovide was powerless, despite his appeals for less noise from her sobbing and shouting. Shattered, he thought she would surely ask for a separation, and wondered what would become of him in that case. Then, at two in the morning, the night and their weariness put an end to the argument. After long minutes of silence he suddenly heard Rita's plaintive call:

"Are you coming to bed, darling?"

He went in on tiptoe. She was stark naked, standing up in bed and holding out her arms. He couldn't help thinking of the famous aria "Woman is fickle."

That night he tasted unexpected pleasures. Rita demonstrated such refinement in their embraces, such science in their love, that she seemed to have reinvented it all under the spur of jealousy. She was extraordinary, a genius, and Ovide, bowing under the storm of this voluptuousness, wondered if she were woman or demon. He thought it would be worthwhile to make her jealous from time to time. Between two stints of passion they had a cigarette. Ovide, absentminded as ever, began to hum "Les chemins qui vont à la mer."

"Ovide, you bastard!"

And she hurled herself at him with renewed vigour, and the rest of the night was such that he was like a wounded thing in the morning. His brain was wiped. His plans for a jewellery company faded. Why didn't he forget about it and disappear for a year with Rita, sleeping in tents, living and loving like noble savages, thinking only of pushing their experience to its limits.

He decided to go to the hospital and explain to Pacifique Berthet the enormous difficulties the watch business involved for him.

Rita insisted on driving him there.

11

What satisfaction to stride as a visitor, glowing with health, into a hospital ward where only yesterday one was lying in the fear of death! Rita had preferred to wait in the car, because Pacifique Berthet's eyes terrified her. This strange man aroused in her a fear that she could not define. Ovide, still under the effects of his astounding night of love, walked blithely toward Pacifique's bed. To think that he had dreaded this meeting after his encounter with the banker yesterday!

In fact, nothing obliged him to come here. He could have written a note dropping the whole project, blaming his enthusiasm on a touch of fever and forgotten Pacifique Berthet. But Ovide was a man of integrity and insisted on being let off his promise by the Frenchman from Grenoble in person. Julien Sorel would have done no less.

Ovide felt capable of anything today. He could see himself living a bohemian life. Had his boss not offered him two weeks' paid holiday, and was he not about to take off with no fixed destination for the countryside, with Rita, her hair blowing in the wind, in their luxurious, second-hand, white convertible? And last night, ah, last night! Had not Marie the waitress paid him the tribute of casting a tender, troubled eye in his direction, and dedicating to him the song by Francis Poulenc? How could a man live without the love of women? He smiled to himself in gentle self-reproach. In his night-long frolic he had at times imagined that he was making love to two beauties, even-handedly switching images from one to the other. A Don Juan was emerging in him. Was he, without knowing it, a gifted charmer?

Boater hat in hand, he arrived at Berthet's bed. The patient gave a start. A small writing-pad on his good knee, he was deep in mathematical calculations. His face, normally so churlish, lit up at the sight of his visitor.

"Ovide! At last!"

Ovide began to have an odd feeling in his stomach. Pacifique Berthet was clean-shaven and smelling of after-shave, and his carefully combed locks were freshly washed. He pushed a chair toward Ovide with an outstretched hand.

"My dear partner, do sit down. Our project is going ahead by leaps and bounds."

He was talking fast, as if to hold Ovide, guessing that this trifler had changed his mind. What genius and energy must a cripple put to work to immobilize a man with legs!

"Coming right along, are you?" asked Ovide, hoping to be wrong. Charity forbade him to dash the hopes that beamed from the cripple's face, that face Ovide had seen darkened by hatred.

"Have I been working!" Pacifique exclaimed. "I've done all the figuring and been in touch with all my contacts. Three salesmen for wholesalers in Swiss watches have been in to see me and they're ready to deal. I told them all about you. At the very least, in the first year we can each count on a profit of thirty thousand! Oh, what a life! And how did you get on? What about the bank? And the premises?"

Thirty thousand dollars! Ovide found himself teetering back into the project he had decided to abandon. Pacifique Berthet seemed so convinced! And a man like that would do the work of two, his handicap prevented him from wasting his days on the time-consuming captivations of love. He said cautiously:

"I put out some feelers. My relatives aren't rich. I can't risk their savings. And the banker I saw, a hard nut, he's Napoléon's banker, my older brother, you know, well, the banker didn't think much of our kind of notion. But I'll admit my

96

brother believes in it and he's ready to go to work to show us how to raise the ten thousand."

Pacifique's features hardened.

"Don't pull out! The idea's too good! Above all, don't give up. And what about the location? Where's it going to be?"

Ovide felt cornered.

"Er, I haven't got that far yet. I'm getting places, but I'm not the wind, eh? No, I've had no time to look for a place."

Pacifique Berthet swallowed his saliva. Was Ovide slipping away from him? He sighed, an anguished sigh. Which ended in a fresh attack:

"When two men like us get together, it's the chance of a lifetime. And when they have an idea like ours, they mustn't let it cool off, they have to force on at top speed. In pursuit of Fortune, Mr. Plouffe! Here, look at this map of Quebec!"

Leaning on his elbow, he spread out the map and with feverish gestures indicated the phases of his offensive. The cities of the North – those that would be the first to profit from the extraordinary expansion transforming the province: Hauterive, Baie-Comeau, Sept-Iles, Mingan, Labrador City, Rimouski, Matane, Rivière-du-Loup. In the east, these would be the strongholds of their clockwork empire. Great dams were planned for the Manicouagan, they were about to exploit the fabulous deposits of iron ore in the province's northland and Ungava. Glittering prosperity was about to descend on this land of Cain. It was about to live through a new industrial era with unheard-of-consequences. Were Ovide Plouffe and Pacifique Berthet about to let this opportunity slip between their fingers? What folly!

Ovide, his eyes popping out of his head, could well imagine these fantastic developments: he saw already the hosts of pioneers, shovels on their shoulders, gold watches on their wrists, pouring into immense and empty territories, building their camps, followed by towns and cities, from which trains would leave in all directions loaded with iron ore. He felt proud to live in such an El Dorado. He, Ovide Plouffe, was he going to go on vegetating unknown in Quebec City, at its best an attraction for bureaucrats and tourists? Fascinated, he followed the agitated finger of his partner jumping from one red cross to the next on the map, inked in to indicate the first bastions of their business.

"Why, it's crazy, all the possibilities out there," cried Ovide.

"Crazy?" Pacifique was indignant. "Let's say it makes your

97

ambition get up and go. The money's just waiting for us. Life always starts tomorrow. Think of the pioneers who decided to build the Canadian Pacific across the Rockies! They were just like us, attacked and laughed at by the cynics."

Pacifique was clinging fiercely to his sole remaining hope.

"I, a Frenchman from Grenoble, I believed in Canada, I believed in the settlers and adventurers of this country. The misfortune you know of has kept me from being one of them. But now I've found another sort of adventurer: you, Ovide Plouffe!"

Ovide's intention to disappoint Pacifique was dwindling fast. It was true, he belonged to that race of Canadians who had built such a great country, though with too few people! Was he going to sneak off like a wretch and ignore the riches Canada had to offer, content to die a simple shopkeeper?

"What you say does my heart good," he said. "You're right to remind me of certain duties."

"Look!"

Pacifique raised the covers and showed him his wound. The dressing was much smaller, and unstained.

"It's healing!" he said jubilantly. "As I promised you, I stopped drinking myself to sleep. Because of my determination to leave this hospital as quickly as I can, and my enthusiasm for our project, my wound has been reduced almost to zero, it's barely suppurating except for a few serosities, and I'll be a free man by next week. The doctor can't get over it. I even took communion this morning, to be nice to the sisters. But I know that if I'm better it's because I met you, and you've made a new man of me, you gave me a reason to live."

This time Ovide was thoroughly hooked. He saw himself invested with a responsibility that resembled a sacred calling. Thanks to him, Ovide Plouffe, Berthet was fighting a successful battle against tuberculosis. If he could do that much, he could certainly succeed in business, however complex it might turn out to be. He'd show those businessmen he knew, including his brother Napoléon. Them and their high style!

"Good thing I came to see you, Pacifique. Solitude is a bad counsellor. I was thinking too much."

"Oh, I'd rather not hear about that. It would be a real crime not to go ahead with our project, Mr. Plouffe. I need you, you need me. And here's the proof that I'm serious. I have a cottage on Lake Saint-Augustin and it's worth about three thousand dollars. It's all I own in the world. I love it, it's the apple of my eye. But: I'm ready to put it up as security to a lender!"

Pacifique's proof of good faith did the trick. It left only seven thousand to be found. He, Ovide, couldn't mortgage his furnishings: he had given them to Rita in their marriage contract. And he hadn't even a cottage by the lakeside! But he could walk, and the other man was a cripple, and the cripple was putting up security. Who was he, Ovide Plouffe, to be so fussy?

"Put it there!" he said, grasping Berthet's hand. "I'm off this minute to find a store and the capital we need."

"And come and see me every day," insisted Pacifique, with the caution of a fisherman who can tell by the way a salmon fights that his prey is hooked only by the lip. "In the meantime I'll put the finishing touches to the draft contract. I have a notary already."

Ovide ran out to Rita, who was chatting animatedly with a young intern catching a bit of fresh air between operations. Ovide excused himself for interrupting, but asked his wife to drive on.

"Where to?"

"We're going to mum's place. I have to talk to the family. Our plans have changed again. That Berthet is a genius. He's even contributing three thousand dollars' security. His plan is perfect, faultless and almost ready to go. There's a fortune to be made. We mustn't miss the boat, my darling."

She pouted.

"So our lover's trip to nowhere is all off!"

"Unless you really insist," said Ovide, uncertainly.

But she didn't insist. She had already begun to think about the long evenings they'd spend stuck with each other in boring village motels, far from the action. Weren't Roche and Aznavour coming to Chez Gérard next week?

"You're the boss," she said, "and you're right. Our future is more important. I'd even say it's urgent! And anyway, it's no good for a married couple to hang around boring hotels every night. You and me are the kind that wants action!"

She offered to leave him at Madame Plouffe's, but Ovide begged her to be present, so as to tighten up her rather slack relations with the family. He needed the clan behind him before diving into the unknown. At that very moment the notion of his mother's generous bosom caused a surge of feeling: one of absolute security.

99

12

Ovide and Rita were to discover, on opening the door, a kitchen scene bubbling with joy and animation. Guillaume and Ti'-Mé were back. Four frozen deer weighed down the table, but Joséphine, in her joy at seeing her son again, forgot to protest. Like a portly slave blissful with love and admiration, she followed him around the kitchen, attentive to his slightest wish, and enraptured.

"Lord, isn't he handsome with his red kerchief. A real god of the woods!"

"Am I going to have to get dressed up like an Indian for you to love me that way?" teased Cécile.

But she too admired her brother. In all her life she had never seen a handsomer man. Oh, that Newgate frill of a blond beard! Guillaume noticed her admiration and gave her a tender hug, just for two seconds. She had tears in her eyes. He had never done that before!

On the linoleum floor lay boxes of smoked salmon, frozen sea trout and small game. The luggage of the two guides was piled in a corner. The snow-shoes Ti'-Mé had made for the coming winter, as well as the barrel of his rifle, peeked out of the heap. As word got around of Guillaume's return, everyone had come post-haste: Napoléon and Jeanne, Cécile, Major Bélanger, and the priest – Monsignor Folbèche – a lover of smoked salmon. Ti'-Mé had opened a bottle of Hollands gin and was passing it around, crying loudly between refusals:

"I need a little something to rinse my scuppers."

"Don't go off on a jag again, now," warned Guillaume, fearing his friend's excesses under the influence. "You do, and you won't stay two minutes in my place."

"I'm just happy!" protested Ti'-Mé, waving the bottle and proudly showing his tattooed arm to Monsignor Folbèche. "Like my crucifix, padre? It never leaves me, not by so much as a hair, through thick and thin."

"I'd advise you to join AA," said Monsignor with a mocking smile. Ti'-Mé was of little interest to him, not being a parishioner of his.

Joséphine, hands on hips, looked around at the game and shook her head:

"Now what do you make of that? Four deer and thirty-odd smoked salmon. How can I get through all that? Enough is enough."

"No problem, Mrs. Plouffe," said the priest, holding up an index finger. "Just say the word and we'll take it all off your hands, right, Napoléon?"

"You bet, Monsignor. Tell you what, I'll take the deer's rump!" he said, slapping Jeanne on the bottom.

"Are you nuts?" she shouted, making her getaway. "Napoléon! In front of Monsignor!"

Guillaume grabbed his mother and waltzed around, to the hilarity of all. Reassured, she barely moved her plump legs.

"Here's to our little mum who's always scolding! *Alouette, gentille alouette,*" he began, and sang as Joséphine smiled, delighted.

"Some day you're going to fall with her," said Cécile, who was showing Ephrem a Zouave tunic on which she had sewn their contract's first golden chevron.

Ephrem was giving her work a careful going-over. Splendid! The work of an expert! Monsignor admired the salmon and patted the hooves of the deer. Napoléon did likewise. Cécile remarked that she could sell the game for a good price, but Guillaume was indignant and said his gifts were not for sale. Major Bélanger, seeing the snow-shoes, praised their workmanship and took the opportunity of suggesting to the two brothers that they should join the Zouaves snow-shoeing club. There was sure to be a white winter this year.

"Forget the snowshoes, Major," Napoléon interrupted. "They make you walk with your legs spread. This winter Guillaume and me are goin' to play some hockey."

Into this happy crowd came Ovide and Rita.

Joséphine and Cécile gave them a faintly chilly reception, as Major Bélanger retreated to the other end of the room and made himself inconspicuous. He would never recover from the ridicule Ovide had heaped upon him when he arrived from hospital. Rita, ill at ease, wondered why the two women snubbed her, but Jeanne saved her by recalling how much fun they had had at Chez Gérard the night before dancing boogie-woogie. Rita, she thought, was a real champion at it.

101

"Can you do that dance?" cried Cécile. "You can? Oh, you're so modern!"

Ti'-Mé offered Rita a swig from his bottle and declared she was the prettiest little squirrely he'd ever seen. Even prettier than last spring, when she had come to the sugaring-off in his father's maple woods in the Beauce. He had been very attentive to her, loading and re-loading her wooden ladle with taffy, until by the day's end Rita's fine suit was smeared from top to bottom.

"Comin' out to the sugar camp next spring, cousin?" he asked.

She passed a tender finger over his black moustache, gave him a flirtatious peck on the cheek and said:

"I hope so! You're such a big teddy bear!"

Ovide took Napoléon aside for a moment to tell him the project with Berthet was progressing quickly, and that he wanted a heart-to-heart chat. Then, after long contemplation of the salmon, he began his little lecture:

"Salmon," he said, "is the king of cold-water fish, and contains the highest protein count. During the French Revolution the Jacobins demanded that the *salmo salar* of the Loire and the Seine should no longer be reserved for the nobles and higher clergy, because the poor of the country also needed protein. The lock keepers, on the other hand, complained that they had nothing else to eat. The common people are nowhere content." Guillaume, who had already heard this dissertation, grabbed Ti'-Mé by the sleeve to put a halt to his impetuous caresses of Rita's neck and shoulder.

"Come on, dumbbell, I'll show you my apartment downstairs."

Repentant, Ti'-Mé left the company like a great, disappointed bear cub. The two men carried their gear below stairs. The boy from the Beauce, his gin bottle stuck in the pocket of his checked jacket, admired the tidy interior, measured the large kitchen with a critical eye and seemed to be working out a schedule for his stay. When Guillaume showed him his room he made a face. He was sure he'd suffocate there after the wide open spaces. Suddenly he needed to be alone.

"Look, I can take care of myself. Go visit with your ma."

But Ti'-Mé had his own reasons for staying downstairs. A burning desire aroused by Rita racked his body. Ovide, shocked by Ti'-Mé's advances to his wife, had begun to stare sternly at him, and told Rita to watch her step. Guillaume had only one worry: would Ti'-Mé take advantage of his absence to knock back the rest of the Hollands gin? Oh, let him do what he wanted. Guillaume was not his guardian angel. He ran up the stairs two at a time and joined the family. Father Falbèche was about to ask the Plouffes to do him a small favour.

"I've been hearing just now about your evenings in the night club, and I said to myself, there's a striking example of the faithful deserting the Church. Now, the Plouffe family are my best and most loyal parishioners, but there are others who are starting to neglect their religious practices."

"That's true," sighed Joséphine. "When I go to church on weekdays it's like praying in a deserted barn."

"I beg your pardon, Joséphine!" the priest cut in, offended. "A barn! Really! Such a lovely church! And our Lord is always there, in his most powerful presence, and you have him almost to yourself!"

"We get on fine, him and I," said Joséphine, smiling. "That about the barn, my tongue slipped."

"Well, let me come to my point," said the Monsignor. "To-night I'm starting a series of twenty-six holy hours Wednesday evenings from eleven to midnight. I would like to ask you to join me in them. Your good example will attract others."

"I can't promise you I'll be at all twenty-six," said Napoléon, "because of my contracts. But we'll do the best we can, eh, Jeanne?" Mentally he set aside a few Wednesdays for hockey and Chez Gérard.

"What about my contract?" the priest complained. "Hardly anybody comes to vespers, and low mass on weekdays only brings in a few old folk. Remember what I said a few years ago: the parish is dying a slow death. Dark days lie ahead. When we lose God we lose our only defence against tempta-tion."

They all promised to help, except Rita and Ovide, who lived in another parish. Monsignor Folbèche had grown old, and the fighting tone his listeners had so admired during the war had given way to an almost plaintive sadness:

"I've tried everything," he said, "bingos, guest preachers, masses with deacons and sub-deacons and bishops, nothing happens. I put in air conditioning, it's the only church that has it in Quebec City, and new Stations of the Cross painted by an artist from hereabouts . . . ."

103

Joséphine and Cécile frowned. Like the rest of the parish faithful, they detested those Picasso-style Stations of the Cross, where Jesus had but one eye and feet that were longer than his legs. But they didn't dare criticize them in front of the Monsignor, who seemed so proud of them.

Mysterious, trying to create suspense, Monsignor went on:

"Well, this evening I have a little surprise for you. Do I hear a guess?"

No reaction. A few years earlier they'd have been begging like children to know his secret. Now they were polite but indifferent. The old priest felt like a boxer dreaming that he has to punch a cloud. He sighed. Maybe it was time for him to become a doddering chaplain to a convent full of nuns. He lifted a giant salmon by the tail.

"I've invited the suffragan bishop for Sunday. What a treat for him! I'm going to organize a feast that'll drive away all my troubles – old, forsaken pastor that I am."

And off he went, his back bowed, with a thank you and a blessing for his Plouffes.

Guillaume and Napoléon went downstairs and stood horrified as they entered the kitchen. Ti'-Mé had pitched his tent there, set up a lighted lantern and, seated Indian fashion with his greasy felt hat hanging down as a visor and the bottle of Hollands gin at his feet, was holding one hand to his brow to scan the horizon:

"You know, at sundown I just gotta get some sleep."

"Put out that lantern and have some supper. We have to sober you up," ordered Guillaume.

At a quarter to eleven the family, yawning and dragging their feet (this holy hour seemed like a counterfeit midnight mass), left the house for the church where Monsignor Folbèche held his "surprise" in store for them. They had all supped together on an enormous fresh salmon. Everybody was making jokes and Cécile and Ephrem had even gone so far as to drink two apéritifs from Ti'-Mé's supply of Hollands gin. Rita had behaved with great charm, winning her way back into family favour by being the repentant little girl. She even said to Joséphine:

"I should see you every day, Madame Plouffe. I'd get to be perfect!"

Joséphine's face must have shown some scepticism, because Jeanne chimed in:

"You can believe her, Madame Plouffe, I know my little sister-in-law, she's got a heart of gold. And she's a good girl, you'd be surprised!"

Cécile, grown generous with her second gin and the thought of the twenty chevrons she'd sewn on that afternoon, nodded in agreement:

"All she needs is another baby."

Rita cast down her eyes modestly, and Ovide, whispering about his watch business to Napoléon, glanced obliquely at her in a way that seemed to say, "That's right, that's all you need!"

Major Bélanger, who had never had a baby, reflected aloud that in these modern days people were giving birth with decreasing frequency. This was an attempt to soften up Ovide. Guillaume was observing Rita and wondering what he'd seen in her in the old days. Now her presence embarrassed him, as if it were superfluous and she should have disappeared along with her double, the German girl he had been forced to shoot in Europe at the war's end. It was too abrupt a change, coming here after months of solitude on the Jupiter. He couldn't get used to the flood of talk and the uproarious family life, what with his years of absence and months in the forest. By ten o'clock his eyelids were drooping. When he saw his cousin starting to act up again he decided to lead the way to bed.

Ti'-Mé, patting Rita's cheek (after trying Cécile's: she had pushed him away, calling him a pervert), had concluded:

"Cousin Cécile, there, when you've once had a taste of a man you'll be eatin' out of my hand like a little squirrely!"

Cécile blushed. It was true, she'd never tried a man.

"You're getting a little high, Ti'-Mé," said Rita, ducking away from him. "Guillaume's right. You better go to bed."

Guillaume declared he was too sleepy to go to church and disappeared down the stairs holding his cousin by the arm. But Rita had the last word:

"Ovide, we're going to church, too! It'll do us good to pray."

All eyebrows shot up except Joséphine's, who looked down in contentment.

"I wonder what the Monsignor's surprise is going to be!" she said.

Around a quarter to midnight Ti'-Mé crawled out of his tent in the kitchen and lit his lantern. He had been asleep with all his clothes on. With a frightened look and haggard eyes, he called Guillaume, once, twice, three times . . .

Guillaume, rubbing his eyes, appeared, yawning, in his bed-room doorway.

"What is it?"

"Didn't you hear? There's a bear prowling around this house. Listen!"

"A bear? Are you crazy?"

"Listen, will ya?"

Ti'-Mé himself was listening, a hand cupped to his ear. There was nothing to be heard but the October wind howling outside and the occasional squeal of brakes.

"Hey, you're still pissed. You've got another bottle of Hol-lands going," said Guillaume, disgusted.

Ti'-Mé, in a thick, submissive voice, admitted his guilt.

"You know, I was so glad to see the family. Listen, there it is again!"

"It's the wind, nothing but the wind and somebody honking his horn," said Guillaume impatiently.

Ti'-Mé thought he was still in Anticosti, in the forest. In his drunken state he was hearing the animal sounds that make the night there more alive than day.

"Don't you hear the Jupiter roaring?"

"That's not the river, you fathead, it's a bus pulling away."

There was a sound of car horns. Ti'-Mé scrambled to his feet.

"Moose! Didn't you hear the call of that bull?" he cried, grabbing his rifle.

Guillaume snatched it away from him and checked to be sure it wasn't loaded.

"Come on, go to bed, you damn drunk!"

Ti'-Mé gave in, making a show of submission.

"Just the same I can hear the wind in the trees. Leaves are falling. Winter's coming."

"There's no trees in this parish," Guillaume replied, exas-perated.

"Never mind, I saw some," Ti'-Mé insisted mysteriously, wagging a drunken finger.

Guillaume pushed him violently back into the tent where he at once pretended to snore. When Ti'-Mé was drunk he became incredibly crafty. This was a continuation of the jag started in Matane.

When he was drunk all his frustrations surfaced, especially his unsatisfactory relations with his father. That made him suf-fer. Tonight he was brooding over the coffin factory Gédéon

106

had started for him. Horrified, he saw himself fleeing the paternal monster, running to a lumberman's shanty in the woods, far from his village, far from the city, furiously attacking the forest with his brand-new chain saw, greedily knocking over the spruce trees, beating all records, cutting the trunks in four-foot lengths, ready for devouring by the pulp factory.

He snored for ten minutes, then awoke again, hating himself and his inability to live a normal life and be happy like everyone else. He was taken by a furious desire to cut down trees. Oh, if that fine big girl from Matane had been there, she'd have kept him in his tent, but he was alone, answering the call of destiny. On all fours he crept from his shelter along the pale pink linoleum, got carefully to his feet, and, noiselessly, carrying his shoes and glancing stealthily toward Guillaume's room, took his chain saw and made it to the sidewalk without waking his cousin.

He took a deep breath of the clean night air and laughed to himself, the laugh of a drunken escapee. Guillaume, that liar! Who said there were no trees here?

What were all those cedar poles if they weren't trees? He saw them with his own eyes, lining the sidewalks, street after street, in all directions! Their wiry branches (a multitude of telephone and hydro wires) rattled, beaten by the wind. Of course, their leaves had fallen.

Ti'-Mé, in love with his chain saw (not long ago he'd still been using a cross-cut), tried to remember the weight of a cord of cedar – was it a ton? – and spruce, that was a bit more. With a sudden, savage desire to feel his freshly sharpened saw bite into the standing forest, he rushed at the nearest phone and hydro pole, which soon gave way, dragging down its skein of wires and causing them to break. All the lights in the neighbourhood went out. Ti'-Mé went at the next pole.

Monsignor Folbèche, pleased as punch, was showing off the surprise he had for the Plouffes. At the end of the holy hour he had asked them to stay on as his special guests to see his "electrical purgatory," which was set up next to the stand for the votive lights. This illuminated purgatory was shaped like an aquarium two metres long and two metres high, was designed to reproduce the eternal flames, in which souls like enormous, frightened spermatozoa fluttered and tried in vain to flee.

"General Electric made it to order for me," he said, proudly. "What do you think of that, now?"

"It's enough to give you the shivers," said Rita, thinking that's where she'd go if she died that night without confession.

"It's a very good electric purgatory if it makes you think that way, my girl," said Joséphine.

Ovide was thinking about his monastery days. He was upset by the sight of this unusual, macabre machine. It brought too clearly to his mind the realization that his soul was already burning. Monsignor Folbèche was enchanted with the reactions.

"Look at these suffering souls, twisting and contorted, you'd think they were alive, you can almost hear them weep as they expiate their sins and wait for the day of deliverance. I hope our flock will be impressed."

"A little sad music wouldn't be bad with that," said Napoléon, who loved to patent all sorts of gadgets.

Jeanne gave him a pinch:

"Behave yourself, you!"

"If it can be done," said Cécile, "no purgatory, thanks. I'm going to fix it so I go straight to heaven."

Suddenly all the lights went out, and purgatory as well, which remained visible only as an immense catafalque.

"Drat! There's a power failure!" said Monsignor Folbèche, starting to light a few votive candles.

"That's good, the poor souls can take a rest," said Ovide mockingly.

"Your Voltairean instincts are still active?" said the Monsignor curtly.

Meanwhile, the provincial police, alerted by the local gendarmes, armed with flashlights, discovered the epicentre of the catastrophe. Accompanied by representatives of the phone company, they found Ti'-Mé perched triumphantly on a cord of cedar pulp logs cut in four-foot lengths. He was singing, *"Un Canadien errant, banni de ses foyers,"* song of the exiled French Canadian, "banished from his homeland." When he saw them he shouted, "Here come the measurers! Look here, guys, I cut a cord in ten minutes. That's a record!"

They arrested him, put him in handcuffs and projected him into the van. He was slowly coming to, but from a long way off.

"Hey! You guys aren't measurers! I know, you're the game wardens!"

13

Ti'-Mé's odd misdemeanor caused serious problems for his father, who already had enough on his hands preparing the funeral of Elzéar, his great and oversized chum.

Gédéon, burping and hiccoughing, was a shade unsteady on his feet when he arrived home late that night. There'd been a little celebration at Elzéar's place, as this was the last night of the wake before the funeral. Friends and relatives had gathered in the kitchen. People cast a casual glance at the enormous deceased, lying there in a casket made to measure by Gédéon, who was proud of this first coffin he had made for a friend. There had been one rosary said, then, with the priest leading the way, the assembly had got into the caribou, glasses filled to the brim, and trotted out their broadest stories. The dead man had been on show for three days now, and people talked about politics, crops and plans for the winter—everything but the corpse. The women were busied about the cast-iron stove, frying eggs and "ears of Christ" (thin slices of curling bacon). You'd have thought you were out in the sugar cabin in spring, when they harvest maple sap to make what people in the Beauce say is the best syrup in the world. Gédéon had absorbed at least a litre of caribou and munched away at several ears of Christ, eaten five or six eggs and chased all this with toasted bread dunked in maple syrup.

Around midnight he announced that he had to go to bed if he was going to do justice to the two hymns that had made him in such demand for burial masses: "Stop here, O passer-by" and "Yet another friend on the bier." To tell the truth, he had the beginnings of a headache.

After slipping on his night-shirt and covering his skull with a night-cap, he climbed into the wide, conjugal bed, and he quickly fell into an uneasy sleep. As on other occasions when he had eaten and drunk too much, his stray left hand went searching in vain for the thigh of his late wife Démerise who had kept him company for so long. Just before his eyes closed he had made the fatal mistake of thinking of his friend Elzéar, his immense weight and the three layers of plywood that formed the floor of the coffin. Was that going to be enough? A few faces came and went in his dream and then he was in the village church, in front of the catafalque, his big hymn book open in his hand and his three acolyte choristers around him, hoarsely bellowing in a voice shaken by uncertain tremolos, "Stop here, O passerby, gaze on this tomb." Then the choirboy's little bell rang three times.

Groaning, Gédéon tossed and turned in his bed. The bell of his dream was in fact his phone, but as he thought he had reached the *Sanctus* he didn't wake. Whoever was ringing must have concluded he was still out. The phone on the wall fell silent.

But the dream went on. After the mass Gédéon saw himself and his acolytes walking backwards as Elzéar's coffin advanced down the aisle. Why wasn't it on the shoulders of the bearers? Were they holding it by the heavy bronze handles? Obviously Gédéon had put strong grips on his handiwork, and handsome ones, intended to be removed and kept as souvenirs by the family. But what about the screws? The dream was turning to a nightmare. They hadn't thought about the size of the screws for Elzéar's coffin, and think of the weight of the man! Surrounded by tearful relatives, anxious about the solidity of the fittings and screws, Gédéon sang on at the top of his voice: "Yet another friend on the bier . . . ."

A sudden cracking sound was heard (in fact it was the barn door flapping in the wind) and the corpse slid to the ground. The plywood bottom had given way. Elzéar lay calmly on the church floor, his hands crossed, with no pants on, while the bearers, the priest, the choristers and the assembled relatives and friends remained frozen with horror. This spelled ruin for Gédéon's casket works.

Then he awoke in a sweat, his eyes popping out of his head. He wiped his forehead. "Oh, God be thanked!" Whew! Only a dream . . . . He poured himself a glass of water from the porcelain pitcher on his night table and swore that never again would he eat or drink as much at a wake. It was impossible to fall asleep again. Gédéon, who recovered as a rule so quickly from the worst attacks of pessimism, was surprised to find himself for no good reason the victim of a vague and depressing anxiety, as if the nightmare had been a premonition of some great trial to which he would be subjected. Indeed, the phone was still ringing. His heart was beating like a kettle drum. "That's it," he said to himself, trembling, "one of my children has died!" He dragged himself to the phone and in a voice that was not his own said:

"Hallo!"

Then came what was almost a joyful shout:

"Ti'-Mé! Oh, thank goodness, I thought you were dead! What? You're in jail? Is that all? Look, as long as you're alive, that's all that matters. What have you been up to this time, you little bugger?"

He was talking like a father, with a father's pity. As Ti'-Mé's story unfolded Gédéon's face turned sombre, and he shook his head in grief.

"So you tied one on again after you left the Island, eh? Is that right?"

Ti'-Mé was telling his story drop by drop, cautious as a hunter whose prey has been warned.

"What! You cut down some telephone poles? Have you gone mad? We could be sued for a hundred thousand dollars! Not to mention jail. This is serious, son!"

Gédéon was sweating again.

"Is your lawyer there? Put him on."

The lawyer who had been assigned to Ti'-Mé at the police station came on the line.

Gédéon was almost himself again. When he talked to a lawyer he became a big boss majestically sailing through his natural element. He had been through so many lawsuits, they were his favourite sport! He loved them as some men love gambling.

"Make sure Ti'-Mé says nothing and signs nothing till I've seen him. I'll take the first bus and go and see 'to whom it may concern.' Who's that? Never mind, just do what I tell you. Understand? Put my son back on."

Ti'-Mé was on the line again.

"Don't worry, son, I'm coming. In the meantime sober up, drink lots of water and don't sign anything or answer any questions, have confidence in your dad while you've got him. You know big Elzéar died of apoplexy, funeral's at nine to-morrow. I won't be at it. So appreciate your father while he's

111

alive. Try and get some sleep, I'll go see the big boss for you tomorrow morning. This is one sonofabitch of a jam! Wait for me and get some sleep.''

He hung up, his forehead furrowed with twice as many wrinkles as usual. He'd go and see Maurice Duplessis himself, premier of the province of Quebec, indebted to Gédéon for the recent election of Poulin to a seat in the provincial assembly, winner against the Liberals who had too long held his lovely Beauce county in submission. Duplessis, who called him Sir Gédéon; Duplessis, of whom he had never asked a personal favour – surely he would save Ti'-Mé? Luckily these were the days when the premier was obeyed by all, even the provincial police!

Stubborn as a ram, Gédéon went about his business at dawn, taking the bus to Quebec City. To the disappointment of all, he had been obliged to cancel his appearance at his old friend's funeral. It must be some unusual emergency that would take Gédéon Plouffe away from his duties as soloist and loyal surviving friend of Elzéar's.

The elite of the village, early risers all, were stunned at Gédéon's surprise departure. Was Duplessis about to recognize his services and appoint Gédéon to the Legislative Council? Or was he after a contract to pave roads or build a modern bridge over the Chaudière River?

A moustachioed sphinx, his gaudy tie flapping in the wind, his hip pocket stuffed with paper money, his gold watch chain spanning his thin chest, checking to make sure that his pipe and his pig's bladder pouch full of "Saint Jude's Fart," his favourite home-made tobacco, were safely stowed away, Gédéon said to the curious who had come to the bus terminal to verify the rumours:

"Sleep in peace, my children. The future of our lovely village is in good hands. And I promise you to greet Maurice on behalf of all of you!"

While Gédéon rode toward Quebec in the bus, working out his plan of attack for swaying Maurice Duplessis, Ti'-Mé, sober now, sitting in his cell, his head bursting and his throat like sand, began to realize the enormity of his escapade as he gazed at the crucifix tattooed on his left arm. Squatting on the edge of his bunk, he turned away from the silhouette of the policeman outside the iron bars of his door.

"Whaddaya want to eat, dumbbell?"

He looked at the bars on his window. The more he dreamed of freeing himself from this society the more he felt imprisoned. How he longed to build that log cabin in Anticosti! He'd run away and hide there for ever. He heard birds singing. Getting to his feet, he went over and grabbed the bars. Just in front of him stood an immense walnut tree, losing the last of its golden-yellow leaves. Its nuts lay strewn on the ground, and two squirrels were busily gathering them, preparing for winter.

Ti'-Mé would have loved to be a squirrel.

14

Maurice Duplessis, premier of the province of Quebec, had left his suite in the Château Frontenac at eight o'clock and was walking up St. Louis Street toward the Parliament. A bachelor in his late fifties, he liked to take this walk every morning, cane in hand, cigar in his mouth, his soft felt hat worn Humphrey Bogart style; slightly paunchy, his gold chain glittering on his vest, he greeted passers-by with a thin, mocking smile over-hung by his long, aquiline nose. At times he would stop to give a nickel to a kid, or be accosted by some mother of a distressed family who wanted to tell him her troubles and beg for help. Occasionally a Cadillac would pass and the driver would shout, "Have a good day, Maurice!" Such a driver was undoubtedly a Union Nationale supporter, because the Liberals, their party in the opposition, had the short end of the stick and most often settled for taking the bus.

Maurice had been not only the premier for a good number of years: he was also leader of the Union Nationale party, which he himself had founded, and which held a crushing majority of seats in the legislature. Duplessis was the emperor, the all-powerful master of French-speaking Quebec. He exercised per-sonal power over the Church, education, trade unions and business. He also held the portfolio of Attorney General, so that even justice did not escape his grasp. A highly intelligent lawyer, with a sense of humour that enjoyed the crudest pun and the most subtle sally, he had lived his life in and for politics. Pitiless to his enemies, he heaped favours on his friends. If by chance he helped an adversary, it was only to humiliate him more completely at a later date. Whether they hated him or loved him, all French Canadians felt that they knew Maurice personally.

The great political stand of this tough conservative consisted of a ferocious defence of provincial autonomy and the cultural integrity of a French Quebec on this Anglo-Saxon continent, a French Quebec that would succeed in surviving and progressing in an orderly way, maintaining its traditions within Canadian federalism. Having this tribe of five million souls behind him, full of their folkloric charm, provided him with a powerful weapon in his highly effective wheeling and dealing with the central government in Ottawa. Every ideological innovation likely to threaten his primitive, introverted cottage-industry society put him into a frightful rage and caused him to unleash all the forces of his political and constabulary kingdom.

On that particular morning, all kinds of symptoms announced to the clear and vigilant brain of Maurice Duplessis that there were dark clouds on the horizon. Various indications convinced him that ideological termites were starting to gnaw at his still-absolute power. He had to combat the Jehovah's Witnesses, who were overrunning the province and menacing the one and indivisible Church. And these Catholic unions, who had nothing Catholic about them but the name! Formerly controlled by the bishops, this group of unions now had at its head the proud democratic leader Jean Marchand, champion of justice for the worker and friend of a whole generation of young intellectuals: Pierre Elliott Trudeau, Maurice Lamontagne, André Laurendeau, Gérard Pelletier. Duplessis accused these little bantams of wanting to replace him with the purpose of introducing pluralism and socialistic ideas. They were trying, he believed, to launch society into an adventure it could not afford: Quebec, once freed and deprived of its beloved "Chief" (himself), would commit every possible folly, go in debt with a very Latin light-heartedness and fall prey to external forces. And in the end, the French-Canadian people would slip gradually but surely toward extinction.

Maurice Duplessis had a thought, and turned red with anger. The thought was about his arch-adversary, that wretched Dominican, Father Georges-Henri Lévesque, founder and dean of the Faculty of Social Sciences at Laval University, popular with the young people and the women, and supported by influential members of the clergy in France. How could he be muzzled?

The priest, with his progressive, almost communist ideas, appeared to Maurice Duplessis as public enemy number one. He had to be gotten rid of, by whatever means.

And it just so happened that his first visitor this morning was the Superior of the Petit Séminaire, who had the university under his thumb. The man would get a post-breakfast earful that would make him think. Maurice Duplessis had them well in hand, the gentlemen of the Seminary. No obedience, no money. Had they gone mad, these secular clergy? Giving such a highly politicized position to a Dominican like that? That devil in his white soutane! Wasn't he in the process of training a cohort of young men who were fanatics for liberty, with the purpose of destroying the great works of the Union Nationale and making him, Duplessis, look like a medieval tyrant?

Then he smiled as he thought of the American steel companies that wanted to exploit the immense deposits of iron in Northern Quebec. To lead them on he had promised docile manpower. The Americans would pay only a ridiculous royalty of a dollar a ton. His adversaries protested, but Maurice thought the important thing was to get the work under way. What an economic boom this mining project would trigger up there in what they called the "Land of Cain"! He thought like Pacifique Berthet on this subject. Other Americans, owners of large asbestos deposits in the Eastern Townships, had recently complained to him that the union boss, Jean Marchand, was getting ready for a strike at their mines, despite the promise Duplessis had given them, that he would make that revolutionary see reason. He had to be brought to heel, the young cub; but he seemed to have a tough hide.

Majestic, the parliament buildings appeared in the distance. This was his true home. Oh, if only God would let him live long! His diabetes seemed to have stabilized, and he felt reasonably well. He thought of Mackenzie King, Prime Minister of Canada, about to be replaced by Louis Saint-Laurent, a great lawyer from Quebec City. Yet another blow for the federals against the nationalists! To what extent, he wondered, would the election of another loved and respected French Canadian to the country's top position undermine the prestige and authority of Maurice Duplessis? Quebec's autonomy would be more vulnerable than ever. And to think people said Father Lévesque was a friend of Louis Saint-Laurent!

He made a face. In his politician's mind, organized like a computer, a host of problems and personalities paraded past. The machine ground to a stop at the name of Gédéon Plouffe who had phoned him at the Château Frontenac this morning at seven to ask for an urgent appointment. What on earth could "Sir Gédéon" want? He smiled to himself. Duplessis had more esteem for his farmer organizers, people like Gédéon Plouffe, than he had for his cabinet ministers. Himself a native of Trois-Rivières, a semi-rural area, Maurice knew how much he owed his power to these stalwart village barons. He loved their peasant cunning, their loyalty and their devotion to the party. And supporters like these didn't come too dear! A wooden bridge, a stretch of gravel road, a scholarship, a clerical job in parliament, a tavern licence—these trifles were a gold mine to the country faithful. In Montreal and Quebec City people were out for big contracts or important sinecures. Yet you had to keep the electoral kitty fat! And these pretentious city slickers didn't realize that the Gédéon Plouffes of the province put more money in the party strongbox than all the urban big-timers put together. Maurice, still thinking about Gédéon, absent-mindedly greeted two delighted street sweepers. Didn't the Union Nationale owe Gédéon the election of Poulin as member for the Beauce? He had snatched the seat away from the Liberals and their candidate, Edouard Lacroix, the rich industrialist of the region. Well, it would be pleasant to see Gédéon anyway: he was one of the few Duplessis organizers who could give the Chief a good belly laugh. According to Maurice, Gédéon Plouffe was the kind of man who builds greatness in a country.

The premier strode through his secretary's office (Auréa was her name, and she was in her fifties), entered his own, hung up his cane, tossed away the butt of his cigar and lit another. He shrugged as he realized he had not had a greeting for the anxious churchman sitting in his antechamber. That impulsive fool in his black skirt didn't deserve it.

By this time Gédéon Plouffe was just leaving the provincial police headquarters. He had reassured Ti'-Mé and ordered the police to treat his son with respect, because he, Gédéon, the father, was about to meet with the "Chief" from whom he would no doubt obtain immediate release of the prisoner.

A little later Guillaume and Napoléon came by to find out what was happening and got permission to visit their cousin. They had brought him a bag of peanuts, which he loved, and some enormous smoked salmon sandwiches made by Joséphine. She had also sent along a quart of milk and six bottles of spruce beer, with the message that if he stuck to those two drinks he would never again fell a telephone pole or get sent to the pokey. A zealous cop was a little too casual with Guillaume, but when he fell under the man's hard blue gaze and saw his veteran's medal for five years of war, he went back to his game of whist. Then Guillaume said to Ti'-Mé:

"You damn fool! For a guy who likes his freedom the way the squirrels do . . . Well, look at you now! Behind bars! Isn't that smart!"

"Don't rub it in," said Ti'-Mé piteously. "I was hoping for a little moral support. And I came out ahead one way. Dad had tears in his eyes when I talked to him just now, and he promised me I wouldn't have to work in the coffin factory."

Napoléon was looking around. He'd have liked to try out his brand new acetylene torch on these bars. He shook one to check its solidity, and concluded:

"It'd be easy, you know. And anyway, don't worry, cousin. We have friends all over the place in politics."

"That's what dad said. Seems I'll be out of here by the afternoon. He wants us all to have supper at your ma's place to see the whole family. And he'd like Rita to make an orange pie like last year."

Rita? Guillaume and Napoléon frowned at each other. An orange pie? It must be the only pie she knew how to make, the way she kept Ovide so skinny! She was starving the guy, look at the way he kept fainting! It was true that Uncle Gédéon alway liked to give her a pat on her pretty little bum. And she'd laugh and never scold him, unlike Cécile, who always let out a squawk like a chicken plucked before it was scalded. They agreed to meet at Joséphine's.

Old Gédéon went into the parliament buildings with the determination of a Viking invader. He marched down the middle of the corridor as he would along a furrow on his land, with a self-assured step, toward the premier's office, carrying a heavy box in his hand. The secretary saw him coming and smiled.

The woman, blindly loyal to her boss, had been serving him since the start of his career in Trois-Rivières. She had dedicated her whole life to Maurice Duplessis.

"I have a little present for you, Mademoiselle," said Gédéon. "Six quarts of syrup from my own sugar bush. The best spring run."

She placed the packet on a table used for presents of this kind brought by visitors aware of her influence with Duplessis.

"Have a chair, Mr. Plouffe. Did you have a good trip?"

He replied that he hadn't even noticed, he had so many other things to think about.

"Fine warm autumn we're having," he said.

"Indian summer. It's always like that," she sighed.

He looked at her closely, wondering how a woman could spend her life in an office answering the phone and writing letters, keeping impatient visitors in order. It had never occurred to him to wonder how his late Démerise, with never a word of complaint, had raised her big family, got up at five every morning to help him with the milking and spent her life a prisoner of housework and meals, three hundred and sixty-five days a year.

"Why don't you get married, Mademoiselle Auréa? It freshens the blood."

She blushed and scolded him. She was happy as she was. The minister of Lands and Forests, a thick file under his arm, came in to ask if he could see the boss.

"Not before two," said Auréa.

The minister seemed disappointed. Gédéon, examining him, had a sudden notion and wanted to speak to him, but the minister was already on his way, being unacquainted with the powerful organizers of country ridings. The office fell silent. Gédéon began to grow anxious. What if Maurice himself was powerless because of the gravity of the offence?

The secretary picked up the phone.

"Mr. Plouffe is here," she said, and hung up.

Gédéon grinned to himself. Maurice was waiting for him! A few minutes later the distinguished churchman emerged from the inner sanctum, crestfallen as a schoolboy who's had a lecture from the principal. Maurice, his face still hard, appeared behind him in the doorway and hurled a final admonition:

"I'm telling you, shut that man up or your grant is going to shrink. This province has had enough of being taken for a fool!"

Gédéon didn't know that he was talking about Father Lévesque and the Social Science Faculty. The prelate nodded acquiescence, but his nod merely signified his helplessness in the face of the tidal wave of new ideas. As if this visitor were suddenly dead and buried, Maurice held out his hand and invited Gédéon inside.

"Greetings, Sir Gédéon!"

"Greetings, Sir Maurice!"

They sat down, eyeing each other. Gédéon took a home-made cigar from his pocket.

"Try a new kind. Taste that, will you? A cigar specially made for you."

The premier crushed his Havana in the ash tray, took Gédéon's cigar, examined it and held it to his nose.

"Smells funny. You didn't put any dynamite in it, I hope?"

Gédéon's indignation was convincing:

"You're not a Liberal, after all! That cigar, Maurice, comes straight from the heart. Made with 'Saint Jude's Fart' and rolled in the best leaves of my tobacco."

With a twinkle in his eye, he added:

"And rolled between the thighs of the Mother Superior!"

Duplessis tried to keep a straight face. Sternly, he snapped at Gédéon:

"Don't laugh at the sisters, Gédéon! They're good people! It's our nuns and teaching brothers and the lower clergy that educate our children and look after the sick. If we lose them our future is in danger. I don't make jokes about that, Gédéon. You know, don't you, at the start of the war the Poles entrusted their treasure to me. We keep it in the museum. Today the Polish government's asking for it back. The answer is no, I'm going to keep it here till I get orders from the Vatican. That government now is communist, that much I know. Let the papers print what they like."

"Well, well, we have to have a laugh sometimes," said Gédéon, filling his tongue-scorcher. "Go on, light up, don't be afraid, I'm smoking the same tobacco but I use the pipe."

The two columns of smoke rose at the same time and their wreaths seemed to entwine in the air. The premier managed to conceal his distaste for this bitter, acrid taste. He willingly admitted that Quebec lagged somewhat behind Cuba in the quality of its tobacco. Gédéon guessed what was in his mind.

"You have to get used to it, Maurice. Smoke that for a month and you can't get on without it."

The two sons of the soil sat there sizing each other up like two horse dealers at the fair. Gédéon said:

"I never laugh at the religious. Don't forget my oldest is a Grey Nun and my Alexandre is a Dominican."

Duplessis started.

"I suppose he couldn't have chosen Jesuit, or secular?"

Gédéon sensed danger and advanced taking evasive action.

"The Dominicans have a fine white robe like the Pope. Very distinguished and optimistic. Black is not what you'd call encouraging."

Duplessis didn't want to reveal his thoughts more fully on this subject. He hinted at the hope that Father Alexandre stood far from the revolutionary faction of his order. His eyes glittered, and he pointed at a chunk of iron ore on his desk.

"We're rich, Gédéon. See that? It's iron, from New Quebec, the Land of Cain. We're going to build cities in the wilderness of the North, we're going to build a great port at Sept-Iles, and factories, a railway, all kinds of new industries, mark my words!"

Gédéon hadn't much time for minerals, especially since the parish priest, a Liberal into the bargain, had talked him into buying shares in an outfit called "Saint Teresa's Gold Mine." The priest, of course, had been the victim of unscrupulous promoters; but as he had proclaimed from the pulpit that this mine in the far North lay under the protection of Saint Teresa of the Infant Jesus, a number of parishioners had bought a bundle of shares and lost their savings. Even Gédéon lost ten thousand dollars.

"I'm more for wood, myself," said the farmer.

"And coffins!" said Duplessis. "How's the factory going?"

"By God, you know everything!" cried Gédéon, impressed.

"Have to, have to. I've got an eye on everything!"

Gédéon relit his pipe, a cruel glint in his eye.

"And the better the factory runs the more Liberals are dyin' off. We put the boots to them, didn't we, Maurice? At last we've got the beautiful riding of Beauce. They'll never get it back."

Duplessis, informed about Ti'-Mé's offence by the Chief of Police while Gédéon was waiting in the outer office, admired the old farmer's skill as he tacked toward the object of his visit. The "Chief," however, was patient. He wanted to extract some information from Gédéon now that he was here. What did

120

people think of Duplessis in the Beauce? Had it become an impregnable fortress for the Union Nationale? Would the rising star of Louis Saint-Laurent in Ottawa eclipse his own? In his darker moments Duplessis wondered if his party, after a few years of power, wasn't showing some signs of wear, weakened by the post-war boom. In recent times he had sensed the fermentation of factions within his cabinet and could easily identify those who hoped to succeed him. For a much later date he himself had chosen the soldier, Paul Sauvé, and after him the charming and ambitious Daniel Johnson. Maurice even asked about Gédéon's village. The farmer had to light his pipe yet again.

"The priest gets my goat a bit. He's speculating in mining shares and getting everybody to lose their money. He's a simpleton and a Liberal. Spends his time blowing about Sir Wilfrid Laurier and Alexandre Taschereau, our two worst enemies in the past. Ugh, those Liberals! Good thing you were here. If you weren't, Quebec would have been a war casualty and the English would have rubbed their hands in glee. Am I right?"

Duplessis smiled. In fact he rather liked the English, especially the ones from England, and to show his esteem for someone he would decorate him with the title of "Sir." He protested good-naturedly:

"Oh, some of the English can see straight, you know."

Gédéon prudently adapted his strategy:

"Coming back to the priest, he's on my executive committee in the Caisse Populaire – you know I'm the chairman – and he's always in the way. Whenever I want to give a loan to one of our friends he makes up all kinds of objections. But if it's for a Liberal . . . oh, boy! Then he'd give the house away. Look, Maurice, couldn't you get him moved?"

Duplessis didn't re-light his cigar. He laid it to rest in the ash tray. Good old Gédéon! Maurice fixed him with a gimlet eye, muttered an evasive, "Maybe, we'll see!" and then:

"Is that all you wanted to ask me?"

Fearing that Maurice Duplessis might terminate their meeting too abruptly, Gédéon hastened to make a point:

"You mentioned my coffin factory, Maurice. I want to sell it to my assistant organizer, Fart-in-a-mitt, the little guy with the short legs. It's not that it isn't a money-maker . . . and I was keeping it for my son, Ti'-Mé, you know, the one that's a hunting and fishing guide. But my witless wonder don't want it. Well, the Caisse Populaire would lend the money to Fart-in-a-mitt, who already owns the village hearse. That'll make him feel important, he hates being such a little guy. We'll set a price that doesn't hurt me and leaves something for the party fund, the usual ten per cent, in fine green bills of the Dominion of Canada."

Duplessis appreciated Gédéon's genius.

"But look here, that business is making money! If you sell it, what do you want in return?"

Gédéon squinted.

"I wouldn't mind a lumber concession along the Chibougamou road to the copper mines. You've given some away but I know there's a few left. That's where I'd like to settle my Ti'-Mé."

And that was where Duplessis was waiting for him. With gentle irony, he said:

"If Ti'-Mé ever gets out of jail."

That knocked the wind out of Gédéon. His careful preparation was showing cracks. He put down his pipe and gave himself a few seconds to recover. The premier had him eating out of his hand now, and secretly rejoiced, because he would have liked nothing better than to spend the whole day fencing with this old fox. He was by a long shot more interesting than all the sleek city lawyers who came to lick his boots. Mysteriously he said:

"You see, your 'Chief' knows everything."

Gédéon's breathing was getting back to normal. After his visit to the jail, where he had dropped a hint that he was about to see the "boss," word had skipped up the telephone chain through the hierarchy and reached the premier's ear.

"By golly, you really are in charge," said Gédéon. "With your organization and a head like yours the Liberals are never going to put you out of power. The Union Nationale is here till the world's end."

The farmer who had shed tears on seeing his Ti'-Mé behind bars because he, the father, felt the blame was his, said in an altered voice:

"Get him out of there, Maurice, and I'm your slave for good. You're not a father yourself, but you're a great man and I know you understand."

Duplessis felt a tug at his heartstrings. It was true: he, the bachelor, had no heirs but a pack of over-ambitious politicians. He shook his head slowly.

"It's serious, what your boy did. Cutting phone and hydro poles! Do you realize? He could have killed pedestrians, electrocuted people, cut off the power in a hospital with an operation going on, or I don't know what! You've got to think not only about a civil offence, he could face criminal charges!"

Gédéon grew pale and his voice broke:

"I know that! That's why I came here. You know the boy's strong as an ox when he gets out of the bush after four months as guide? In Matane he got into the De Kuyper pretty heavy, got a big crucifix tattooed on his left arm. He's such a died-in-the-wool Catholic, my Ti'-Mé. He got plastered and went wild. He was still pissed when he got to town here and started seeing trees with no branches and no leaves – that's the poles, eh? – and that got him depressed, just like the coffin factory. And anyway he wanted to try out his new chain saw . . . . You can see, it'd be right up his alley to have a forestry concession. Oh, if you could let me have one!"

Duplessis listened, enchanted, to this unfamiliar Gédéon, puffing and pathetic, who proceeded to make a serious blunder:

"You know what it's like, Maurice, the crazy things a man can do when he's had a drop. You can understand that, eh?"

Duplessis' face darkened and his gaze turned hard. And Gédéon thought he had lost. A few years ago the famous politician had indulged in a few celebrated jags in the privacy of his hotel room, but the doctors, having discovered his diabetes, succeeded in converting him to mineral water.

"Oh, I shouldn't have said that, boss. Excuse me! But when you're trying to defend your child you say whatever comes into your head."

Duplessis was thinking: he had to be in the House in ten minutes.

"Do you realize, Gédéon, that on the civil side alone we can have an action against us by the Bell and by Quebec Power? They use the same poles! The damages can be high, Gédéon!"

"I'll pay the damages!" the farmer exclaimed. "And on the criminal side, you're the Attorney General, aren't you?"

Duplessis remained silent and Gédéon knew he had gone too far.

"Even about the damages, you could fix that. I know it, it's you sets the rates for those companies. Two phone calls, eh? They'll understand. And don't forget," he said, gaining confidence, "Ti'-Mé is Union Nationale! One of your best men!"

Duplessis had no use for softies, he admired tough, determined men. He thought for a long time, then rose and stood in front of the old man from the Beauce.

"Sir Gédéon, apart from the fact I'm your 'boss' as you say, I'm going to ask you one question: are you my friend?"

With a cry from the heart, and almost in tears, the old man said:

"I'm your friend, Maurice, and ready to die for you! As sure as you see me here!"

Duplessis cleared his throat. He disliked showing emotion, but when he was moved his voice grew nasal.

"Go back to the jail. Your Ti'-Mé is waiting for you on a bench in the Chief's office. Forget about all the rest and continue doing a good job for your party and your premier. That's all I ask."

Gédéon tried to kiss his hand. At the next elections he'd run all over the province, if need be, to serve his master.

Duplessis took evasive action, laid a hand on his shoulder and accompanied him to the door.

"That's the way we are in the Union Nationale. We look after our friends."

Gédéon heaved a long sigh.

"You won't forget, eh? The lumber concession? And the priest?"

15

The Plouffes, in times of fortune or misfortune, behaved like bees: they rushed to the hive and assembled around the queen, Joséphine. They were all there for the triumphant return of Gédéon and his son. Rita showed the greatest zeal on this occasion. Others noticed that she had never been so charming with the whole family, especially to Joséphine, who was almost prepared to reconsider her prejudices against her daughter-in-law, and anyway it was Ovide's happiness that counted. And girls nowadays were exposed to so many temptations, you had to be more tolerant – especially of the very pretty ones, thought Joséphine, who were more vulnerable than the others.

Rita, charming and vivacious, ran from the oven to Gédéon

to Joséphine, her tiny apron flying. Pretending to disapprove, she would give a little tap to Gédéon's wandering hand. Jeanne, Napoléon's wife, was also dutifully attentive to him, but he only had eyes for Rita. Poor Jeanne, so transparent and generous, was she a little hurt? Major Bélanger, not unaware of this sideshow, had a vague impulse to pat Joséphine's hind quarters in imitation, but at that very moment he caught Cécile's angry eye, angry not at him but at Rita, as much as saying, "What on earth is that one up to?" Ovide, Napoléon and Guillaume had all gone off with Ti'-Mé to admire the new poles the company had set up overnight, immediately following the incident. Rita opened the oven door.

"Uncle Gédéon, you asked for an orange pie. You're going to get one, with sugar on top. It's already getting brown."

"And the haunch of venison is going to be the best you ever tasted," said Joséphine.

Jeanne didn't want to be left out:

"I'd be surprised if you didn't like my bean soup," she said.

Cécile, who had nothing to offer, said to Gédéon:

"If this goes on I'm going to have to take cooking lessons. My job and sewing chevrons and cooking into the bargain – I won't even have time to sleep. And I thought as I got older I could take it easy!" she sighed.

Rita smiled, and Jeanne said, "Just let us do the cooking, Cécile. We're young, we like doing it."

"Well! I'm not that old!" Cécile protested.

Joséphine was dreaming, thinking about the past. The old family warmth, which she thought had cooled for ever, seemed to be coming back. Today it was because of Guillaume's return and Gédéon's presence. She watched him pacing the kitchen as he brandished his pipe.

"Maurice, he said to me, and he put his hand on my shoulder, and he said, 'Anything you want, Sir Gédéon! Three telephone poles chopped down – what's that amount to?' And there's bigger favours to come if I want them."

Major Bélanger didn't dare ask whether his influence extended to getting a grant for the Parish Guards. Gédéon marched over to the photo of his brother Théophile and addressed it:

"Poor old Théophile! If you hadn't been crazy about newspapers and bicycles and nothing else, and if you'd listened to me and had confidence in yourself, you'd have gone in business with me and made a pile of money."

"And he might be still alive," remarked Cécile.

Joséphine, embarrassed, set the record straight:

"My husband followed his calling and his own tastes. We were happy together. If he'd listened to you he might never have married me, and you wouldn't be here blowing your own horn, Mr. Smarty!"

This was the Joséphine that Gédéon liked: always ready to defend her nest, for better or for worse. He remembered the wrath that had descended on his late Démerise when she dared to make a remark about Joséphine's washing drying in the wind:

"Joséphine, your washing's yellow! Mine's always white as snow."

"My washing may be yellow but it's clean! Some get it looking whiter and it still smells like dirt. It must be the soap."

Rita came over and gave him a pinch and a peck on the cheek.

"What a wonderful uncle you are! What a dear! Can I talk to you for a minute, just the two of us, next door?"

"Why, of course, pussy cat!"

And she marched him off to the parlour, an arm around his waist, and closed the door behind them.

"It's no use talking, she's got what it takes," said Cécile. "She wants him to pay off her car, I'll bet you a dollar."

"Ovide won't like that," said Joséphine, shaking her head.

Jeanne saw deeper than both of them. She smiled:

"Now I'm sure Ovide's going to get to open his watch business."

And in fact, when Ovide came back with the other men his wife threw her arms around his neck.

"I'll bet you won't even thank me, you old grump! Just listen what Uncle Gédéon is going to tell you."

Gédéon was taking over operations:

"Get a move on, godson. We're goin' to the Saint-Sacrement Hospital to see your partner."

Napoléon was jubilant, but Ovide was far from it. In fact, he felt embarrassed at being rescued by a peasant supporter of the dictator Duplessis (Ovide was a Liberal Pluralist), and at the same time felt an undefinable panic as the thing became possible. He could no longer pull back.

Pacifique Berthet was able to get out of bed now and hobble around the ward on his crutches. Now, sitting crookedly on his chair, it occurred to him that he had had no news of Ovide for three days. What a vacillating weakling he was, unstable – and an opera lover! Pretentious, and penniless. Pacifique had been stupid to attach any hopes to such a spineless wonder. One more day and Berthet, who had kept his promise not to drink, would fall off the wagon. And this time he'd down a whole litre of gin at one go. His wound would open again and the tubercular infection would flare up worse than ever. What was the use of being half cured if you were totally miserable? Ovide and Gédéon, at the foot of the bed, watched him in profile.

"Pacifique, this is my Uncle Gédéon."

Pacifique jumped, and his heart leaped. After the introductions the two foxes began to size each other up. Pacifique realized at once that he had his hands full. Gédéon reserved judgement for later. His first reaction, however, was one of aversion to this crippled creature from France. The old farmer judged people as if they were horses at the fair: he opened their mouths, examined their teeth and the colour of their gums. Then he decided if the horse had the strangles. He felt an urgent need to submit Pacifique to such a test. This Berthet! If he could have walked maybe he'd have been a little too fast!

Pacifique deftly removed the farmer's gold watch from his vest pocket.

"May I? Oh! A Waltham 1900! The best make of all. The train-conductor's favourite," he went on, listening to it tick. "And in perfect running order. Like music!"

He put it back in its place, sure that he had scored a point, but Gédéon remained expressionless. He said:

"I always did know the time of the day. And the man that wants to cheat me better be an early riser."

Ovide looked from one to the other. He hoped Gédéon would find a weak point in Pacifique Berthet's armour. But Pacifique started off about the Beauce in France, which he knew well, and the Beauce in Quebec, which he had never seen because of his infirmity. Gédéon assured him that the Canadian region was twice as beautiful and three times as big as the French province of the same name, though he had never been in France. Then Gédéon had had enough of beating about the bush. And he wanted to impress Ovide:

"I hear you want to start a watch business with my nephew. Tell me about your plans."

127

Pacifique went into the routine he had done for Ovide. Rita would look after the store and he, Pacifique, would tend to repairs and book-keeping in the back of the shop. Ovide would make contacts in influential circles, do public relations and set up a chain of salespeople in the province, especially around Sept-Iles, which was bound to boom because of the mining of enormous deposits of iron in that Land of Cain. Feverishly Pacifique opened out the map, where red crosses indicated the nerve centres and outposts of their future business. Gédéon, distracted for a moment, thought he was hearing Duplessis' voice. No doubt this jeweller was a visionary like Maurice! Could it be that his nephew had come across the chance of his lifetime here? A chance that would make his fortune? Ovide, listening to the cripple's convincing line, was regaining confidence in the undertaking. He even dared to make a remark:

"We could earn thousands and thousands of dollars a year!"

Gédéon knew all about that. He cut the palaver short:

"You need ten thousand to get it going? You mortgage your cottage for three thousand, right? I can lend you the money out of the Caisse Populaire in my village. I'll guarantee the rest."

"Then you're going along with it?" Pacifique panted.

"Going along? Why, sure! But it's a sixty per cent share for Ovide and forty for you."

Ovide found this very hard, and his heart bled at the sight of the cripple in revolt.

"But this is unfair, Monsieur Plouffe! I contribute my knowledge, my skill, my cottage, and your nephew nothing! You're taking advantage of my defenceless state, I . . . . ."

Gédéon got to his feet. He had no intention of arguing.

"Think it over. Business is business. Give me your answer tonight because I have to get back to the village tomorrow morning."

Consternation, fear and despair burned in Berthet's grey eyes. Gédéon held out his hand.

"Take care, my friend. And take council with the Holy Ghost. Come on, Ovide!"

Ovide glanced contritely at Pacifique as if to excuse his uncle's brutality. But Gédéon didn't even look back, he merely slowed down slightly thinking of his pretty little niece Rita who had made him an orange pie. She'd be disappointed, she'd stamp her tiny foot at him and the family and accuse him of giving

Ovide false hopes. He stopped and looked back. Pacifique, on his feet, his hands clutching the grips of his crutches, was leaning, stretching toward him. Gédéon, in a hurry to get out of the hospital and light his pipe, returned to him and said curtly:

"Fifty-five forty-five: is that a deal?"

"It's a deal!" exclaimed Berthet.

The three shook hands.

16

There are scenes that call for the film-maker's camera rather than the painter's brush or the writer's pen. Manet's *Le Déjeuner sur l'herbe* would have paled beside the sumptuous picnic Gédéon had improvised to celebrate Indian summer and the happiness of the family, on the banks of the Jacques Cartier River forty kilometres from Quebec.

Nature and the Plouffes together offered their thanks to a bounteous heaven. Gédéon, his arms crossed, leaning against a wild cherry tree, proudly surveyed all this beauty. The leafy forests of Quebec on this early October day shone red and gold in their setting of dark green spruce. The Jacques Cartier River, big as a major waterway, leaps down from the hill country, flashing silver, swollen by the dozens of lakes that feed it in the Laurentian Park. A joyous traveller, it arrives in the plain where its banks are studded with steeples and tamed by white-washed houses, to pursue its quieter way toward the great St. Lawrence.

It was just where its stream left the mountains behind that the Plouffes gathered by this superb river. Gédéon, sucking on his ever-present pipe, felt as sure of his power over the Plouffe family as Duplessis did of Quebec. In a quiet eddy Major Bélanger was rowing clumsily while Cécile, his passenger, clucked with terror at the notion of the skiff being drawn into the rapids. Ti'-Mé was fishing a dark pool (out of season) to round out the catch already destined for the barbecue. Napoléon was tootling away to his heart's content on his trumpet, blowing toward the river in a personal salute. Guillaume, in a canoe, was paddling as elegantly as an Indian, much admired by Rita, who sat facing him and was finding him increasingly attractive. With a few curt words he told her to behave herself. He believed he could still have some influence over her.

The clan's two trucks and two convertibles were lined up in the shade under golden maples. Squirrels in their branches let their droppings fall on the red leather seat of Rita's white automobile, and from an oak tree acorns fell with a tinny sound on the hoods of the trucks. Cries of joy and squabbling children's voices came from a large birch where truck tires had been hung for swings to occupy the brats.

Ovide, a happy man, was playing woodsman. With a hatchet he was cutting chips to feed the campfire burning in a circle of stones built by Ti'-Mé. Sweating copiously, he carried his chips in little armfuls to this improvised stove on which Napoléon had laid a sheet of metal that already was red hot. The big, black iron pot was hissing with boiling lard, waiting for the potatoes which Jeanne, sitting on a log nearby, was skilfully cutting into French fries and piling in the hollow of her skirt. The guest of honour, Pacifique Berthet, had been settled in a comfortable camp chair. He smiled as Joséphine said to him:

"It's a great life, isn't it? Just wait till you try my French fries and my trout with bacon. And don't hold back, just help yourself as much as you like!"

Despite the cold looks he darted from time to time at Gédéon, the cripple appeared cautiously content. He found it hard to fit into this happiness meant for others. That was how it was when you couldn't walk. You were a creature apart, a kind of pariah.

Ti'-Mé came back with his string of trout, and Pacifique said to himself that a stick of dynamite would kill more fish and faster.

"Ready to fry the spuds!" Joséphine shouted to Jeanne. "Napoléon, call everybody!"

Napoléon turned his trumpet toward the children and played the call to arms. The boats hastily turned toward the bank, the children scrambled out of their inner tubes. Jeanne tossed her potato chips by the handful into the hot lard spitting in its cauldron, and Gédéon swaggered up to the campfire, singing in his hoarse but powerful voice the *Peasant's Creed*:

"I believe in thee, Master of all nature . . . ."

Part Two

17

The month of May, 1949, arrived. That year, a great one for French wines, was also exceptional in the chronicles of Quebec and in the life of Ovide Plouffe. How many changes, what swift developments in the space of a few months! Maurice Duplessis had seen it coming: his absolute authority threatened on all sides, he was the witness, despite a ferocious struggle, to the separation of Church and State in the province. In the Asbestos mines a spontaneous strike by five thousand miners had been festering since February. Led by the Secretary-General of the Catholic unions, Jean Marchand (who was in favour of deconfessionalizing his organization), the strike had become as much a symbol of emancipation among the young intellectuals, as against the American mining company exploiting the deposits and against those civil and religious powers that were hostile to all change.

Maurice Duplessis felt the ground crumbling underfoot. Louis Saint-Laurent, now Prime Minister of Canada, overshadowed the Duplessis legend, and, like Truman in the United States, preached social justice for all citizens. Duplessis was made to look very cheap by comparison, with his calls for caution, conservatism and economy! Even the clergy, until now his most powerful ally, was split into two clans, as in 1940 on the conscription issue; but this time the nationalists were demanding justice and democracy. Duplessis had seen it coming: the two undisputed leaders of this revolution in Quebec were the Dominican, Georges-Henri Lévesque, dean of the faculty of Social Sciences at Laval, with a following among his students; and the young Jean Marchand who, with his thirst for justice and his energetic leadership, was pressing forward in this changing society. It was, Duplessis thought, as if a great host of Quebeckers were marching against him, like the fanatical soldiers of Mao in China, who, after the Long March, were about to put the Kuomintang to flight.

But morals were degenerating. Divorces were still a rare phenomenon, but many couples were breaking up. Wives went to meet their lovers in the afternoon, and husbands stayed out until dawn. The Duplessis police stepped up their raids against the news-stands, confiscating daring magazines from the USA and tracking down the few pornographic reels of film that were circulating under the counter. The film censorship board, prodded by Duplessis, took the scissors to the latest French films. Oh! Monsignor Folbèche had been so right in predicting in 1940 that French Canadians would come back from their experience abroad an uprooted people, completely changed. The war had not killed as many young people as it had transformed into enemies of the established system.

Even the most conformist – such as Joséphine and Cécile Plouffe – did not escape this tide of change. At eight o'clock that Monday evening Cécile, all spruced up, dressed to kill, took a long drag on her cigarette before putting it out in the ash tray. She didn't dare smoke in the street: not yet.

"I may be a little late tonight, mamma," she said as a precaution. "You don't mind, do you?"

Joséphine was rocking, a cigarette in her mouth.

"Take your time, have fun, nobody's old at forty-nine, time past never comes again. I'm going to listen to *Ceux qu'on aime* on the radio. There's so much love in the soaps these days. It builds up at the end of the season. I like that, you know!" she said inhaling deeply.

"I notice you're smoking more than I am, mamma. You should cut back!"

"Ha! I'm smoking myself, like a salmon. I'll taste better for the worms," Joséphine jested.

"There she goes, talking about death! You're going to live till you're a hundred," said Cécile as she checked her slapdash make-up for the third time and paused to correct her lipstick. "It was less boring for you when Major Bélanger came every evening," she added.

"Poor old fellow," sighed Joséphine. "Ever since the scandal about the chevrons he's embarrassed, you know. Too bad, it was such a nice way to make a little money."

The scandal of the chevrons had been one of the great events in the life of the Plouffes. It had broken the previous January. Major Bélanger had had to resign his presidency of the Federation of Parish Guards, accused of patronage and favouritism. Oh, shame! He had exploited his Sunday soldiers to extract from them almost two thousand dollars that went to Joséphine and Cécile. Of course he had been denounced by an envious rival who, incidentally, became his successor, and whose wife charged twenty cents a chevron instead of fifty. Since that time

Ephrem had suffered from depressions and, humiliated, had never again dared to visit the Plouffe ladies' house.

"You're right, Cécile, I'm going to speak to him Sunday at the high mass for the Asbestos strikers. Ephrem will certainly be there leading his Zouaves and keeping order. It's to be a whole mass with a public collection and loud-speakers. How your dear father would have loved to be there! Strikers! But what are you dawdling about? Take off! Out you go, Cécile!"

"All right, I'm leaving. It better be a nice film. You don't usually see much of a movie in a private house."

"Time's are changing," sighed Joséphine. "Imagine people buying a projector and showing a movie at home. It's a wonder Napoléon hasn't bought one!"

At last Cécile was on her way. It was as warm as July outside. The soft spring breeze filtered through the screen door, caressed Joséphine's plump face and drove away the blue clouds of cigarette smoke. Luckily Monsignor Folbèche hadn't caught his favourite parishioner smoking yet!

Joséphine, rocking slowly, thought back over the six months she had just lived through. Apart from the chevron scandal the winter had been uneventful. Napoléon and Guillaume, like two young boys, had played a lot of hockey, and as usual Guillaume had made the newspapers because of the goals he chalked up in every game. He was bruited as a recruit for the Montreal Canadiens and comparisons were even made with the famous Rocket Richard. But Guillaume laughed at his own successes and said he was too old. In fact, he had left for Anticosti with Ti'-Mé before the usual date. Enthusiastic, in a rush, the cousins wanted to use the extra month of May to build their spruce-log cabin in a secret corner of the Island.

And Ovide! How he had prospered in that short time! His business was flourishing, and he was heard every week on the radio, where he had bought a five-minute spot Tuesday evenings. He did his own commercials for the jewellery business, and then indulged in commentaries on subjects dear to his mind and heart. Ovide was now a personality! In October 1948, he had joined the Knights of Columbus and had quickly grown so influential that in no time he had acquired the "third degree." In short, everyone said, "Ovide Plouffe is a boy who's made it!" How good Providence had been in allowing him to meet Pacifique Berthet! And Rita! She was behaving like a good, grown-up girl behind her counter in the store and turned out to be a superlative saleswoman.

Joséphine thought of Napoléon and smiled. He had become so expert on the trumpet that his neighbours, far from complaining, gathered around the house to listen after supper. Joséphine almost laughed aloud to herself as she remembered the midnight supper after mass on Christmas Eve, when she and Cécile had revealed to all their secret vice: they were smokers! And had proved it, scandalizing the assembled relatives!

Gédéon? They'd barely seen him. The great thing was that Ovide had already paid him back. Rumour had it that their uncle from the Beauce made frequent trips to Montreal, where he was suspected of courting a sexagenarian widow.

It was almost like the good old days. Monsignor Folbèche was coming to life again, inspired and rejuvenated by the great demonstration organized for the following Sunday. Ovide was all excited about it. Joséphine gazed at her late husband's photo:

"Yes sir, Théophile, you'd have had a fine set-to with the priest, wouldn't you?"

Then she switched on the radio, thinking that in two or three years everybody would have a television. If only she could live till then! She sat up straight, proud of her health and vigour. She was good for a long time yet!

Cécile was still dazed when she arrived home at midnight. She had been caught in a trap, a hateful trap. With twenty or so other girls from the factory she had gone, as if to a picnic, to the house of this widower foreman who owned a 16 mm projector that was to show them rare and exclusive films, so he said, direct from the United States.

For these working women, aged twenty to sixty, who drudged on their production line or work bench from Monday to Saturday noon, the evening promised to be a real première. How privileged they were! They quickly wolfed a few sandwiches washed down with Coca-Cola, then helped to arrange the chairs and set up the screen. The lights went out. In a church-like silence the projector began to hum, the screen lit up and characters appeared. Knees tight together, hands joined, Cécile leaned forward in anticipation. Would it be a beautiful love story? A hairy male entered the bedroom of a vulgar-looking, buxom woman who proceeded to undress. Cécile frowned. Naughty giggles were heard here and there from the younger guests.

Feeling herself observed, Cécile sat stiff backed. What on earth was happening! The man was taking his clothes off, too? She uttered a cry shaped like a capital O when she saw the enormous sex of the male.

"What on earth is that?" exclaimed Cécile.

A few of her companions were laughing their heads off. Cécile made a move to get up and leave as a grand gesture, but despite her growing indignation her eyes remained glued to the obscenities being performed on the screen. Had she lived almost fifty years only to see such things now? She had never even seen her brothers naked! Her temples throbbed. She remembered as if it were yesterday the time when, with her whole class at school, she had been taken by one of the nuns to see the Provincial Exhibition. At the stall where a lordly and superb black stallion held court, property of the Black Horse brewery, she had been stupefied at the sumptuous erection the horse dared to indulge in before their eyes. "Help!" the little nun had cried, and pushed and shoved her girls in panic out of the stable. Sometimes in dreams Cécile had seen that image again. It had also floated in her mind, strangely enough, during the burial of Onésime, the bus driver she had loved. She did not leave crying scandal. One can get used to anything. Grumbling from time to time and condemning with all her heart the showing of such swinish behaviour, she stayed but could not understand how human beings could lose their dignity to that extent. She left, stunned, after this ambiguous torture to which she had submitted for the last two hours.

She tiptoed into the house, feeling as if she needed a bath. Slowly, absent-mindedly, she washed her naked body with lukewarm water. Then, with new curiosity, she began to examine it. She concluded that it wasn't so bad, compared to those scandalous women whose obscene frolics had first horrified, then troubled her mind. A cold emptiness entered her belly. Soon she would be fifty and her body had never been used, had never known love! There was a discreet tapping at the door.

"That's a late bath, Cécile!" said her mother, concerned.

"Yes, it was so hot in that house. Next time I'm going to a real movie, it's cooler there."

Joséphine went back to bed and Cécile began to envy her sister-in-law Rita. Tomorrow she'd go and see her and tell her all about this evening.

137

18

The following morning at the radio station, Ovide Plouffe, president of the jewellery company Ovide Plouffe Inc., was recording his weekly five-minute talk, as he had to leave Quebec City for Sept-Iles that evening to meet his regional representative there. In the script he boasted about the advantages of dealing with his company, to be sure, but he used most of his air time to express the most varied opinions and show off his musical and literary knowledge, growing sentimental over the beauties of French culture and even going so far as to pass judgements on the political situation, which sometimes aroused great nervousness in Claude Saint-Amant, the well-known announcer. Saint-Amant re-sold to various advertisers, in five-minute blocks, the two hours he had bought from the station owners. Because of the originality of Ovide's spots, filled out with his curious comments, the name of this literate jeweller with the eccentric ideas was becoming quite well known. Ovide Plouffe had grown to be a familiar and respected name.

Adjusting his earphones, script in hand, Ovide was waiting for a signal from the technician, who was smiling behind the heavy glass partition. Ovide was eager to read his piece, which he was sure would be much discussed. They would start recording in three minutes. Ovide was thinking what a good decision it had been not to call his business Ovide & Pacifique or Plouffe & Berthet. It was Uncle Gédéon, on the strength of his ten per cent share in the business, who had insisted that only the Plouffe name should appear. Ovide had almost succeeded in convincing his disgruntled partner that it was better this way. A company name must never sound funny. Ovide & Pacifique would have reminded people of Robinson Crusoe or Paul and Virginie. He had even wrung a smile from the cripple by mentioning a bookstore called Booker & Reid, and a funeral parlour called Berri & Paradis.

The technician raised a hand. Ovide spoke gravely about his jewellery business, his low prices and his province-wide distribution network, its phenomenal expansion after less than a year's operation, and the plans he had in mind for extending it across the whole country. Before getting around to his commentary, he concluded his commercial as follows:

"Of course it's this jeweller's dream of beauty to see a watch gleaming on every wrist, a watch coming from Ovide Plouffe Incorporated, jewellers. Perfect and guaranteed repair and maintenance is done for YOU by a French expert of international repute, M. Pacifique Berthet of Grenoble. If you want the right time, it's high time you bought a watch from Ovide Plouffe Incorporated, jewellers.

"And now, dear listeners, let's get around to a few thoughts on politics and social matters. In this Canada of ours we see our fellow Quebecker, the great Louis Saint-Laurent, Prime minister of the country, championing some very generous social measures, and we see Harry Truman, President of the United States, doing the same thing. And what do we see in Quebec? We see the incredible stubbornness of Mr. Duplessis' government, which persists in not understanding the poverty and despair of thousands of Asbestos miners who've been on strike for the last three months. Yet it seems to us it would be possible to oblige the American owners to accept an honourable settlement! It is becoming more obvious every day that this cruel strike is the symptom of a more profound conflict. That is the open war between Duplessis and the Catholic Unions. The Asbestos miners have become the scapegoats of a hateful and archaic autocracy. It is they who are paying for the difficult advance of brave new ideas like pluralism and social justice. Well! Let's not leave them alone to bear the burden and pay the price of this worthy struggle! It's been said that all the high clergy are behind Mr. Duplessis. It's not true!

"Just think of the great public collection on behalf of the strikers, to be made at church doors throughout Quebec Province next Sunday. At Monsignor Folbèche's church – and he has organized a special demonstration for the occasion – we will have Father Lévesque and Jean Marchand in person, as well as famous intellectuals and journalists from here and from Montreal. Bravo, Monsignor Folbèche, and three cheers for the Asbestos miners, our brothers, who are giving us a marvellous example of courage and tenacity! And so, dear listeners, until next week, this is Ovide Plouffe speaking from Quebec City."

Out of tact he had not mentioned that Napoléon was going to lend his three trucks for the loud-speakers, rented and paid for by Ovide Plouffe Inc., jewellers, that were to scour the town inviting the population to come out in droves to Monsignor Folbèche's church on Sunday at ten thirty. Replying with a smile to the technician's approving nods (he too was waiting to be unionized some day), Ovide left the studio and bumped into the famous announcer, Claude Saint-Amant, who said, point blank:

"Mr. Plouffe, there's more ways than one to be daring. You're going too far! Don't get me wrong: I agree with you. But we can't say everything we'd like to, especially with a government as powerful as this one. For an attack like that on Duplessis the station owners could be forced to take away my two hours, or . . . or . . . I tell you, I'm not sure if I can let that go on the air."

"Then you'll lose me as an advertiser. I hope we still have freedom of speech, or do we?" Ovide replied sharply.

Ovide didn't realize it, but Claude Saint-Amant was intimidated by him. Lose an advertiser like Ovide Plouffe? He was good for the station's ratings, too! The announcer sighed:

"I just hope it doesn't get me into trouble."

"Never forget, courage always pays in the long run, Mr. Saint-Amant. Good day!"

He went out, carefully folding the script of his talk.

Monsignor Folbèche, in his office, smiled contentedly as he read the script, of which Ovide had left him a copy. What a fine boy! Generous, intelligent, well informed despite his sketchy schooling; and now he had become sensitive to the true problems of the day, almost as much so as Monsignor Folbèche himself! The old priest had begun to enjoy life again. He had gone through some sad years that had bent his back and turned his hair snow white, years in which his flock had deserted him and the parish had crumbled despite his efforts. Then, all at once, the struggles that were agitating Quebec brought him back to life. His former passion as champion of the all-important parish unit was transformed into a fierce thirst for social justice. Processions and ceremonies were losing their interest? Too bad! But next Sunday's high mass with its political significance was going to be a great day in the re-direction of his obsessions. Of course, he had received an order from his superiors to avoid sensationalism or any attack on governmental authorities. But they would see what they would see! He rubbed his hands. Jean Marchand was going to speak from the priest's very pulpit.

The best-known intellectuals in Quebec province would be present! He regretted the absence of his protégé, the reporter Denis Boucher, who would have admired the new progressive spirit of his grumpy old priest.

The good old days of collective fever were coming back. Monsignor Folbèche was expecting eight to ten thousand worshippers. Of course, they couldn't all get in the church, but there was plenty of room outside! The public address system was already installed and he'd been testing it for the last three days, cocking his ear like an expert. His dried old fingers tapped on the desk top. It was going to be a fabulous collection. He was hoping for at least five thousand dollars for the poor striking miners. The amount would be splashed on the front pages and Mister Duplessis – and some bishops he was acquainted with – were going to be furious. He wore his old-delinquent smile. In his sermon at this grandiose ceremony Duplessis would get an earful, and certain prelates, too. Monsignor Folbèche would certainly be punished. So what? A man of God who fails to end up on a cross is unworthy of Christ. He rang for his second vicar, the young Father Marquis, who was responsible for press relations, but he was still out. The priest shrugged. The little whipper-snapper was probably hanging around Ovide's jewellery store gawking at that flirt, Rita Toulouse Plouffe. He must do something about that. People in the parish were starting to talk. Monsignor glanced at his gold-plated Bulova, bought wholesale at Ovide Plouffe's on receiving a supplication-command from Joséphine. It was almost noon.

That was exactly where Father Marquis was: chatting over the counter with Rita, to whom he had just brought an armful of the first lilacs from the garden behind the presbytery. From the street you could see her face plunged into the cluster of fragrant flowers.

The jewellery store of Ovide Plouffe Inc. was located just across from the church in a new two-storey building of bright-red brick. The shop door opened right on the sidewalk, and the building was flanked by the parish Caisse Populaire. Ovide had made a clever choice: the traffic to and from the Caisse Populaire and the church gave many pedestrians the opportunity to stop and look at the display, artfully arranged by Rita, with shining watches of many shapes and sizes, necklaces, rings and earrings glinting behind the iron bars and the heavy glass of the window. Ovide had re-joined the parish by renting the five-room apartment above the store. He was now one of the most important men in his milieu, proving once again that a fellow who makes a go of it in the business world becomes impressive because of the fact, and enjoys a sure prestige in the world of the working man. They were proud of this little guy from their neighbourhood who had done it all in a few months and now was getting rich and talked once a week on the radio!

When Ovide started in business he had continued on his free evenings to clerk in the Royaume du Disque, but soon his own swelling sales took all his time. Following Berthet's plan, he already had salesmen on the job in Baie Comeau, Sept-Iles and Rimouski, where business seemed to be flourishing and kept Ovide on the road quite frequently.

His customers from the record store became buyers of watches and jewellery. Then, the whole Plouffe clan was so anxious for him to succeed that all their friends and acquaintances felt almost obliged to "encourage" Ovide. The same was true of the repairs. Pacifique Berthet, installed on a chaise longue (his hip hurt when his leg dangled) worked twelve to fourteen hours a day and began to complain of fatigue, turning up in the foulest of humours, which was most upsetting to Ovide.

After six months of operation, as the cripple had predicted, the initial loan of ten thousand dollars had been repaid and the bank account showed a balance of six thousand. And as Berthet complained, there would have been more if Rita, after two months as a volunteer, had not demanded a weekly wage of fifty dollars, and if Ovide hadn't run up extravagant restaurant bills entertaining customers. But Rita, afraid of Berthet and his constant nagging, tried to curry his favour by driving him home in her white convertible with the red leather seats, at least on certain evenings when he had been overloaded with work and had stayed late at the shop and when Ovide was away on business.

Rita had been a good girl all winter. She hadn't said a word about Chez Gérard or Marie the pretty French girl. When they went out it was to dance at the Château Frontenac, where Ovide's new prosperity made him a natural customer. Her husband had changed so much! Ever since his success he smiled often and spoke with great self-confidence. But the more he achieved this peace of heart and mind, the more his wife felt fenced in and hog tied. With the coming of spring she caught herself, at her counter, dreaming of vague adventures in which she charmed and excited attractive men, newcomers to the parish. Now it was May, and she had the itch to do something. For the moment she buried her face in this bunch of lilacs, and in doing so aroused a turmoil in the young priest who hung before her, purple with emotion.

"Oh, if you weren't a priest you'd be a real lady killer," she said mischievously.

Staring down her daring neckline, the vicar was getting up the courage to tell her that she so occupied his thoughts that he was thinking of asking for a posting to another parish, when Cécile came in like a windstorm, her hair wild, her eyes sparkling with joy.

"Rita, I have something terrific to tell you! Oh, excuse me, Father!"

The young priest scuttled out as if caught *in flagrante delicto*.

From the doorway he said:

"Don't forget, it's a Roamer 22 karats I want for my father!"

He made off at a rapid pace toward the church. Cécile leered at Rita:

" 'Pears he comes around quite often. They say you've got the little vicar on the string!"

Rita, amazed, quickly adapted to Cécile's new style.

"It's fun to get a young priest all excited. Well, come on, what's this you've got to tell me? You have a thrill or somethin'?"

In a whisper, glancing left and right to make sure no one was listening, Cécile told all:

"Just imagine! Last night I really got taken for a ride. I went to see a movie in a private home. Well, my dear! I almost fainted! The very first pictures . . . well they were simply filthy!"

"Dirty movies! Hey, you've gotta tell me about that!" exulted Ovide's wife. "Come on upstairs to my place. We'll have lunch together and you can tell me all about it. But I just can't believe it! Our Cécile seeing pornographic films!"

"Quiet, you little nut! Somebody could hear us!"

And in fact someone did hear them, and see them, too. It was Pacifique Berthet, who could spy on all visitors from his little corner. Unknown to his partner, he had drilled a hole in the partition between the store and his workshop big enough to allow him to hear all conversations and to peek at will. The moment the doorbell rang he would lift up his calendar, open the tiny trapdoor that masked his peep-hole, and listen and spy.

In this way Pacifique Berthet had invented and imposed upon himself an almost constant torture. Maddened by a growing desire for Rita, he made errors in his work, and often had to start over again. Whether she was simpering at the young priest or stroking her breasts in front of the mirror, believing she was alone, or hoisting her skirt to adjust a garter, revealing her magnificent thighs garnished with lace, he would boil with jealousy, helplessness and unslaked passion. The two women traipsed up to Ovide's apartment. Berthet groaned. That damned Cécile Plouffe could have told her story here! He would so much have loved to see Rita's reaction to a spicy tale!

Life was stingy with its pleasure so far as poor Pacifique was concerned. Oh, occasionally he'd have a taxi-driver bring him a prostitute, either at his cottage on Lake Saint-Augustin or to the sordid quarters where he lived. But the more his passion for Rita grew, the greater was his disgust at himself and these vulgar women. He hated his incurable disease and his lameness, which made him so dependent on others and so marginal in life. He didn't deserve such a fate. With his well-shaped head, his fawn-grey eyes, his distinguished features and his powerful shoulders, he would have been most presentable. He kept having dreams in which Rita was his partner. There was another dream, most curious and completely platonic, in which he was climbing Mont Blanc, leaping like a chamois, pulling Rita by the hand. On awaking he was shattered by the sight of his crutches standing in a corner, seeming to jeer at him and say, "You're ours for ever!" He cursed life for abusing him this way, but far from thinking of suicide, he gradually felt welling up in himself a kind of murderous madness, a universal hatred hungry for victims. He was sure that Rita had already deceived her husband, but in the six months he had been spying on her he had observed only harmless flirtations, nothing that could be used to blackmail her. Yet he had been driven to the point of considering that as the ultimate means of possessing her. Still, he wondered: was he not being too timid, did he not under-estimate himself? She wasn't such a bad girl, after all. Perhaps he should be nice to her and exploit her pity for the infirm? She had a good heart. . . . But no. Impossible. She always seemed on edge when she saw him, and she only came into the back of the shop to bring him watches to be repaired, saying no more than she had to and fleeing his ardent gaze. He would never possess Rita except by force.

Noon. He opened a bottle of Coca-Cola and bit absent-mindedly into a sandwich. He would have given anything to hear what Cécile was telling her up there.

Cécile and Rita, seated face to face at the corner of the table, seemed electrified by a common current that excited them and lifted them out of their everyday existence. Cécile exclaimed:

"And that filthy film lasted over two hours, my dear! I don't know why I didn't leave after five minutes!"

"Good grief!" exclaimed Rita, her eyes shining, "you should have taken me along! I've never seen anything like that!"

"Did I know it'd be like that? Sure it's just a joke they played on the senior women at the factory, the old fussy ones, eh? But we showed them, we stuck it out."

Rita didn't notice that the soup was starting to stick. Her mind was far away from her cooking!

"They really showed everything, right down to details?"

"In close-up, my dear! You know about that, you're married. Pure filth! When I think about it! The police could have come! Can't you just see me? Cécile, sitting in jail!"

What on earth was Rita dreaming about, chin in hand? Cécile sighed:

"Anyway, as soon as I got home I took a bath. I felt so dirty! And you know, I had a look at my body. It's not so bad, for my age! I'm not comparing myself to them, after all they were actresses, but laugh as much as you like, I thought I was better looking than they were!"

"Why sure!" cried Rita. "You're a well-built woman, you're elegant!"

It was the first time anyone had said such a thing to Cécile. She blushed, and felt like giving Rita a kiss.

"Oh, nothing like you are, of course. Even when I was your age. Those were hard times. You had to work ten hours a day, six days a week, for peanuts. You couldn't afford to get dressed up. Oh but you were lovely, Rita, in your Miss Sweet Caporal costume!"

Rita was on her feet, clapping her hands like a little girl:

"I still have it, Cécile. You're going to try it on!"

"Are you crazy?"

"I'm just telling you. You're no bigger than me. It'll fit you like a glove. Come on in here. Oh, god, Cécile, this is fun!"

Cécile stood up, still hesitating, her heart beating fast.

"Why shouldn't we have a little laugh. Come on, we know it's crazy!" said Rita, dragging Cécile toward the bedroom.

Ovide, still thinking about the script he had just read for the radio, was striding toward his jewellery shop. Napoléon's truck pulled up beside him.

"Hey, get in, little brother! We're going to my place. I've got good news."

Considering Ovide's new status, it was simply not done to climb into a plumber's truck with its greasy seat. He spread out a handkerchief and sat on it.

"Good news?" he repeated, as his brother drove off.

"Right! At last I got the contract for the Plaines prison. The roof, the paving stones and the whole heating and plumbing system."

"We're heading for the zenith of financial success," Ovide smiled. "Congratulations!"

Napoléon gloated:

"You too, eh? Everybody's talkin' about you. It's your radio program. You're a hit! I'm real proud to be your brother. You deserve it all."

There was a pause. Ovide felt that his elder brother was holding something back. Was he going to come again with his suggestion of mentioning Napoléon and Son on the radio? At a stop sign before the parish school the plumber cleared his throat and said:

"Long time since we saw you at Chez Gérard!"

Ovide hesitated, thinking of the quiet times he had experienced with his wife since they had taken up the Château Frontenac cabaret instead, on Saturday evenings.

"Chez Gérard was giving Rita ideas about being a waitress. I hated that. It got her upset every time. She's just getting over it."

"Sure, well, you do what you see fit," said Napoléon approvingly. Then, point blank, he put Ovide on the spot:

"Remember Marie, the pretty little French chick?"

For a fraction of a second Ovide could remember nothing

else. Poulenc's song, "Les Chemins de l'amour," surfaced in his mind. He asked:

"Has she gone back to France?"

"Nope. She's still at Chez Gérard. She often asks about you. She listens to your program. Finds you real intelligent. She told me so again, just yesterday."

"Oh? That's nice. A very pretty girl. Say hello to her from me. Maybe I'll drop by one of these nights and say hello to her."

Marie's image filled his thoughts again. He had almost succeeded in forgetting her, he was so busy with his business and his radio show and his new passion – politics. But he didn't want Napoléon to guess his feelings. At last his older brother told him what was on his mind:

"This prison contract, er . . . you know, I think it would be better if you didn't use my trucks for the loud-speakers, announcing Monsignor Folbèche's collection next week."

Ovide grew pale with indignation.

"You're just like the rest of them! You're afraid Duplessis will retaliate! Oh, he's got you all by the short hairs, the tyrant!"

The plumber defended himself:

"I can't talk on the radio to explain what I do," he said. "And I have a big family, don't forget, and debts to the bank. You've got to see that. Rent cars and I'll pay the bill, cash."

Ovide sighed, mollified.

"I see what you mean, but it's a shame anyway."

Father Marquis flew down the presbytery steps, holding tight the one-minute radio spots Monsignor Folbèche was sending to Ovide, who was to pay for them. The jeweller would bring them to the station and negotiate the best time for broadcasting these brief but vibrant appeals to the population, twice a day, every day until Sunday. Monsignor Folbèche was preparing his ceremony as if it were going to be the coronation of a new pope. But the young priest was thinking only of the sweet pleasure in store for him: he had a legitimate excuse to see Rita in her apartment! What did he care that her husband might be there?

In Rita's flat, Cécile, deeply moved, was disguised as Miss Sweet Caporal and marched up and down in front of her sister-in-law, whose delighted squeals were only slightly overdone, as she suggested to Cécile certain bumps and grinds the older woman never would have thought of on her own. Cécile threw out her chest, arms akimbo, in front of the full-length mirror where she could admire herself from head to foot. Was this really Cécile, so haughty in her pillbox hat and her tight tunic with the gilt buttons, her tiny skirt and her long curvaceous legs which showed to their best advantage in those high-heeled half-boots? Choking with surprise and pride, she discovered a Cécile younger and prettier than she had been twenty-five years before. And in the same moment, she felt that she had let herself be robbed of her best years.

"What did I tell you?" hooted Rita. "You'd turn the heads of all the guys if you walked down the street dressed like that! Just like me!"

Rita put a record on.

"Just for laughs. Let's have a boogie-woogie."

The savage rhythm of this music of the moment filled the kitchen and loosened Rita's limbs. Despite Cécile's giggling insistence that she didn't know how to dance, Rita pushed and pulled her in a fiendish romp. Rita shouted in surprise as she hopped and clapped. Was it Cécile's disguise that freed her to adapt to this primitive dance in which she was even inventing steps?

Father Marquis, whose efforts to raise someone by buzzing the bell had been drowned out by the Bacchanal in the kitchen, came in anyway. He stood stock still, his mouth gaping. It was Cécile who saw him first. She froze, red with shame, her hands trying feverishly to pull down her skirt.

"Oh! Father!" she stammered.

Rita turned down the volume.

"Er . . . excuse me, the Monsignor asked me to bring you the radio spots . . . I thought your husband would be here. I'll just leave them, then . . ."

"Don't make excuses, Father," said Rita, still swaying with the rhythm. "I was just dancing with our new Miss Sweet Cap!"

He smiled:

"Please don't stop for me! It doesn't bother me a bit. And that boogie-woogie! What rhythm, eh? I belong to the new generation, I love the modern dances."

"Is that right?"

Rita turned the volume up again.

"In that case, c'mon and dance!"

His resistance was brief. And there was this curious trio, Rita in her apron, Cécile as Miss Sweet Caporal, and Father Marquis, his soutane whirling and his heels flying, all of them hopping and swaying for all they were worth, as people did in 1949 thanks to boogie-woogie.

Ovide, surprised at the racket in his kitchen at half-past noon, blew in the door and stood astounded at the spectacle. Then he began to guffaw, and was unable to stop laughing even when he joined the prancing trio.

And why not? Weren't they right to laugh and dance and sing while there was still time?

Rita kept Cécile and Father Marquis there for lunch. They chatted good-humouredly and Ovide was especially brilliant after the priest had told him of Monsignor Folbèche's admiration for the courageous talk to be broadcast the following day. Rita, having discovered a new friend in Cécile, swore that they'd often go to the movies together. Then the party broke up. The weather was so fine! Ovide returned to the radio station with the priest's spot announcements, and went on, whistling, to the jewellery shop. His wife, who was still upstairs, was doing the dishes and packing Ovide's suitcase. He was leaving for Sept-Iles that evening.

And Ovide, light-hearted as he had not been for a long time, bounced into Pacifique Berthet's workshop, only to be greeted with a grim expression that acted as a cold shower on his exuberance.

"Well, Pacifique! How are things?"

"Hello," the other said.

"Something the matter?"

Pacifique expressed his dissatisfaction more clearly than usual:

"There certainly is something the matter. Another fifty dollars in radio spots for your Monsignor's ceremony!"

Ovide was furious.

"That is called institutional advertising. The most effective kind, I'd like you to know. It must be done. You can't profit from society's progress unless you help it develop."

"You can run yourself into the ground, too!" retorted Pacifique.

"Look, you're the one who told me I had to join the Knights of Columbus and other social organizations, remember!"

"I said nothing about throwing money out the window. I work my fingers to the bone ten hours a day in a closed-in box, repairing watches by lamplight, and you go around getting to be the local hero with your radio show. On which you talk a lot more about politics and music than you do about our watches."

The blow struck home. Ovide had felt this growing anger of Pacifique's for some time now. He pulled out his script:

"Listen here, what I say this week. 'Perfect and guaranteed repair and maintenance is done for YOU by a French expert of international repute, M. Pacifique Berthet of Grenoble!'"

Berthet shrugged.

"Blowing my horn a bit, eh? But we're not earning what we should. All these travel expenses. . . ."

Ovide's back was up:

"You think I haven't had enough of these trips out in the bush? You recall our agreement? You look after repairs and I look after sales. Let's see you do it! I'd be delighted! I'd far rather stay here with my wife and our little daughter than hang around those country hotels."

"Where the wine and scotch flow at every meal. You can sell watches without that."

Ovide, perturbed, stared at him for a long time. Was Pacifique trying to break off their partnership? The cripple read his mind.

"Don't worry, I'm not about to call off our agreement. It's too late. Your uncle from the Beauce suckered me first, and then your family, and then you. The business is you: Ovide Plouffe Incorporated. And you could easily find somebody else to do your repairs. It's not fair! I have forty-five per cent of the shares, just as you do, but your uncle with his ten per cent, he can decide everything and tip the balance your way. I hope I still have the right to say what I think and speak out against bad management?"

Suddenly Ovide felt ashamed. His shoulders slumped. He owed his prosperity to an idea that had come from a defenceless cripple whom he was now neglecting. The man had a right to complain.

"Look, Pacifique, if I've been unfair, I'm sorry. I'll try to be better and do things your way. All right?"

"All right," grumbled the other.

Ovide went out to the store and with a rapid glance checked the inventory of his stock. He felt sad and bitter at the same time. He, the great Ovide Plouffe, had been created by this cripple who now was jealous of him and hated him, of that he was sure. Without admitting it to himself, the former record clerk had begun of late to become detached from the business. His out-of-town trips were a nuisance. As an overworked travelling salesman he saw the history of Quebec developing without his help. In his radio program, the advertising element seemed to him increasingly ridiculous, taking away from the serious message that followed. Obliged to be frequently away from his family, he noticed their increasing distance from him. When he came back from his tours he would find his wife absent-minded, as if she were enfeebled by some profound boredom, an obvious lack of vivacity. And his daughter, Arlette, gave him a routine peck on the cheek at night and ran to bed. Ovide was grieved when he saw her happier on the knees of her little friends' fathers than on his own.

In a sense his life was moving ahead on crutches, like Pacifique on his. A vague anxiety invaded the very depths of his being. Wasn't everything going the way it should? No, not really.

At seven o'clock, carrying a suitcase filled with watches and cheap jewellery, he wearily boarded the plane that was to take him to Sept-Iles. He was going to make quick work of it this time, with no loitering in restaurants, and he'd get home just as fast as he could.

19

Next day Joséphine, casual as could be, made her daily visit to the shop. She disappeared for a moment into Berthet's workshop to leave him a maple sugar tart and quickly came out to the counter where Rita was putting price tags on watches. Joséphine jerked her head toward Pacifique's retreat and whispered:

"He's like a bear with a sore head today! You can spoil that one with all kinds of goodies, he'll barely give you a thank-you-ma'am. He's a tough one to soften up."

"Oh, him!" said Rita, shrugging. "Don't talk too loud. He's got ears like a cat."

Joséphine wasn't too critical of Berthet's unwillingness to be tamed. She knew very well that he saw through her kindness: she spoiled him so that he'd be useful to Ovide and help him earn piles of money. And wasn't he an ideal chaperone for Rita (certainly not dangerous, helpless as he was), making sure she behaved herself in the store?

"I hear you had a great time yesterday, you and Cécile. You dressed her up as Miss Sweet Caporal!"

"You bet we had fun, Mrs. Plouffe! Lord! We laughed for two solid hours."

Joséphine was plaintive:

"Next time give me a call. I'd like to have some fun with you some time. I'm not so old and narrow-minded after all, you know."

Eyes half closed, she was watching her daughter-in-law's sinuous movements. No wonder the men. . . .

"You're getting better lookin' all the time. That's the best age of all: thirty! You should have seen me at your age," she said, glancing around, keen-eyed. "I was just like a swallow. By the way, you keep this place ship-shape. Congratulations!"

Rita smirked:

"I always did like a little decorum." (Where did she get that word?)

"Decorum peccatorum," laughed Joséphine, who was a little short of comedy material but very anxious to find out what had gone on in that film her daughter had seen at a private showing, and about which she remained most evasive. "Well, I'll leave you now, it's your lunch time."

But she didn't go. Rita said:

"Oh, I think I'll skip lunch today. I have to watch my figure. I'll do the inventory instead. There's no problem, Arlette gets her meal at kindergarten."

Joséphine shook her head. What was this new craze, all the girls dieting and slimming, turning skinny as eels?

"Take care, my girl," said the mother-in-law, who seemed to know a lot about men's tastes, "don't ever forget that men like a woman with a bit of flesh on her bones. If you get too thin you might lose your husband."

"No danger of that, Mrs. Plouffe. I can lose weight without touching the capital, never worry!"

Joséphine smiled craftily:

"Well, a word to the wise, eh? You know Cécile's a shade on the thin side. Well, Major Bélanger, when he was still coming to our place, I had the impression he paid more attention

152

to me because I've got a little meat on my bones. But I never let on. Crazy, eh?"

"Mrs. Plouffe!" cried Rita, pretending to be scandalized.

Joséphine winked mischievously at her and the two women laughed heartily. Rita began to see new depths in her mother-in-law, who for years had been so cold and reserved to her.

"Well, now I'm really going," said Joséphine. "Cécile must be home. Oh! Speaking of Cécile! Did she tell you about her famous movie?"

Rita had been warned by Cécile, and gave the agreed-on version.

"Not very much. Boring, she said. Models, dancers parading around."

"Just what I thought. I haven't been to a movie for ten years. The radio's good enough for me," she said, going out with unslaked curiosity. "Now don't you starve yourself!"

Rita accompanied her to the sidewalk and watched the heavy form move off on its short legs. Eyes open, Rita turned her face up to the sun and let its light pour down on her. The day was perfect, there was a perfume of lilacs in the air and a slight breeze caressed the heart of the world, animate and inanimate. Rita, happy as a plant in springtime, heard all sorts of music in her flesh, the kinds of music that inhabit those who make life dance. She didn't see Stan Labrie's car appearing around the corner. Singing to herself, she went back into the store.

Stan parked. Putting on a burst of silent speed, he sneaked in behind her before the door had closed. Rita was examining a shelf when he caressed her waist with discreet admiration. She jumped and turned around, shocked.

"Hey!"

There he was, erect, elegant, tall and handsome, before her.

"Hello beautiful!"

"Stan! What're you doing here?"

"Long time no see, eh? But I don't see you fainting with joy when old Stan turns up. Huh? It's been months since we had a chat. Oh, I saw you all right, from a distance, just like that, in the Château. And you snubbed me. Sure! The great Ovide Plouffe's wife!"

On the defensive for a moment, she smiled and then relaxed. What could happen to her here?

"Well, how do you like the merchandise?" she asked, seeing how Stan's ferret eyes shifted here and there, checking out the watches, seeing what they cost.

Then he turned and stood straight in front of her.

"God damn, you look good! Better all the time! Like sin on wheels."

In the wall a hole slid open between two alarm clocks and Pacifique's hawk-like eye shone in the opening. He noticed that Rita was on the *qui-vive*, but that the visitor's compliment delighted her. What was that Stan Labrie doing here? The man was a well-known underworld pimp, and Pacifique had met him once in a gambling joint where a high-stakes poker game was in progress.

"Ovide's away?" asked Stan as if it didn't really matter.

"He's gone to Sept-Iles, but you know him. He could come back any minute."

"I don't blame him for bein' jealous. Anyway, nobody can say I was on your back since last fall. How's business?"

Rita, always talkative, told him what a success the business was, and how Ovide was away so much, and how she often got bored. She swore to Stan that she'd behaved like a saint for months, and stamped her foot when he looked incredulous.

"You never believe a thing I say!"

"Sure, I always believe you, except for little bits now and then. Listen, Rita, don't worry, I just came around to give you a hand. I need a stop-watch."

Relieved, she dug one out for him. He paid without asking for a discount.

"Beautiful day, eh?" he said, pocketing his change. "Wow! Noon already! Have you eaten lunch?"

"No, I think I'll skip a meal. I'm slimming."

He moved slowly toward the door.

"Well, okay, then. If you hadn't turned all goody-goody on me I'd ask you out for a little picnic beside the Montmorency. Such a great day. Nice to get a little fresh country air."

"Don't you try getting me mixed up in your tricks, there!"

Pacifique's eye was burning like a coal. Stan shrugged, and smiled sadly:

"Too bad! The little pleasures of life don't interest you any more. Just think, two old friends, sitting there on the grass like a couple of students, with a checkered table-cloth on the ground, and some Cokes and sandwiches, and the birds singing, and the river at our feet and the sound of the waterfall in the background. . . ."

"It's true it's a nice day." Rita was tempted.

Her gaze grew dreamy. She'd have nothing to fear from Stan. But suddenly she thought of Pacifique. She'd completely forgotten him.

"You're going to come?" asked Stan.

"Not so loud!" she hissed, placing her finger on his lips and glancing at the repair shop. She hesitated, then whispered, unable to resist:

"Okay. But I have to be back by three. Wait for me in front of the Paquet parking lot. I'll be there in ten minutes. I can't leave here with you. Everybody's keeping an eye on me. Three o'clock! You promise?"

"Sure as gun's iron!" he said, delighted.

He made his polite adieux and left. A second later she was sorry she'd accepted. Hadn't his eye had that well-known trouble-making look? She stuck her head in the repair shop at the back.

"Mr. Berthet, I'm closing from noon till three. I have to do some shopping at Paquet's."

He said nothing, his grey, pitiless gaze boring into her soul. She raised her voice:

"After all, I'm not your slave in this business, eh?"

"I didn't say a word," he said smoothly, with a little smile. "You don't have to make excuses to me!"

She turned on her heel, hung up the "Closed Till Three" sign on the door and jumped into her convertible. She left it in the parking lot of the big store, climbed in with Stan, and off they went! Off to the shores of the Montmorency! She was as happy as if she were twenty, and hummed "Le petit chemin," one of Mireille's songs, so well performed by Jean Sablon.

As they drew near the village of Boischatel, close to the Montmorency, some twelve kilometres from Quebec City, Stan, in a gaudy sports shirt brought back from Hawaii the previous winter, cleared his throat.

"Have you seen Bob?"

"No."

"You know he's got himself a real babe? One of the most beautiful women in Canada."

"Better than me?" she couldn't resist asking.

"Why, just the way you look today, I'd say you're still better.

155

Bob's crazy about her. He says she's the sexiest broad he ever met. But he forgets too easy, eh?''

Rita did not forget. Her memory, prodded by Stan, recalled how Bob, during her escapade, had told her she was the most extraordinary girl he'd ever known. Rita would just like to get a look at this supposed marvel! Stan said, all casual, ''You know, I wouldn't be a bit surprised if we ran into them having a picnic on the Montmorency!''

She turned on him in sudden anger:

''And you didn't tell me! I'd never have come if I'd known! But I felt there was something wrong. It's a trap!''

Stan tried to back out of his problem:

''Hey, you know, I was just sayin' that. Maybe they're not there at all! Anyway, if they are, you can see the girl, you can judge for yourself.''

Rita's heart beat faster with regret and chagrin. Her instinct told her to order Stan back to town. But maybe the couple wouldn't be there? She sat silent, listening to the car radio. Some cars there are that bear us irrevocably toward our fate!

As fate would have it, Stan and Rita, on arriving by the banks of the Montmorency, found Bob and his companion Maryse with their picnic cloth already spread on the grass a few metres farther on.

''What a surprise!'' Stan shouted, while Rita, stiff with anxiety, gave the superb brunette a close inspection. A Latin type, with one arm squeezing Bob's waist. Of course it would be too silly for such good friends to picnic separately. And so they made it a foursome. The atmosphere quickly grew familiar, with a tinge of licentiousness encouraged by the country setting. A first champagne bottle popped its cork. There were toasts. And the rivalry that is inevitable when two women are with one man raised its ugly head. Stan didn't count. With encouragement from the champagne, they even began to look around for a shady corner sheltered from curious eyes.

As often happens in Quebec in the month of May, a heatwave such as would not be seen in the summer lay over the land, leaving man and nature stunned and dazed. Three weeks earlier there had been heavy snow. And soon to come was June with the misdeeds of the great tides, bringing with them cold rain and a north wind to freeze your bones, fed by the ice of the glaciers floating from the North Pole toward Newfoundland. After long months of a Siberian winter, that Tuesday seemed to be a gift of the gods, a delicious respite accorded a population that enjoyed only a few days of spring each year.

The jolly picnic organized by Stan was turning out better than he had dared to hope. Sitting on red wool blankets spread on the young grass, the group was chatting away at a great rate. From time to time the ladies uttered small shrieks, turning to screams of laughter, all this triggered by the two bottles of champagne that had already been emptied in the process of washing down delicious wedges of toast with caviar. Stan had ferreted out this secret place on the shore of the Rivière Séchée* where it empties into the Montmorency, from which the couples were invisible, as they were from the bridge above the famous falls which Quebeckers say with pride is higher than Niagara. This heavenly corner provided absolute privacy in a picture-postcard setting. Nearby they could see the silhouette of Montmorency Manor, built in happier times by the Duke of Kent for his mistress, a lady called Saint-Laurent. To one side, on the east, the Royal Quebec Golf Club welcomed its bourgeois members. To the north, the oldest mountains in the world, the Laurentians, crouched with their time-worn humps; in the valley the sumptuous river made its noisy way, swarming with trout that had already left their lakes of origin.

Pow! Another bottled opened! Champagne, anybody? Bob, in a white shirt open over his hairy chest, filled the glasses with a steady hand, without creating too much foam. He splashed a few drops on Maryse's thigh. Maryse was squatting in a way that forced her skirt far above her knees. Bob then wiped up the drops with his index finger, and Maryse, a superb, long-legged creature in her thirties, her eyes half closed, said to Bob in the voice he described as "vaginal,"

"Oh, Bob, please go on! I hope it never dries!" But it was Rita's throat that grew dry, as she began to be excited.

Twice now she had heard the throb of an airplane motor, but it was not the DC3 that would be bringing Ovide back from Sept-Iles. She thought about the pornographic film that Cécile had described, and the unspeakable dream it had provoked last night, including a role for Father Marquis. Rita wet her whistle with another gulp of champagne. She was getting nervous.

---

* Rivière Ferrée

That Maryse, God, she could be provoking with her sexy airs! Rita regretted having worn her silk stockings. She should have come bare legged like Maryse . . . . It was so hot! Stan, getting worked up himself, read her like a book, and suggested:

"Undo your garters, honey, roll your stockings down and let the fresh air at your peachy skin."

She tossed back the rest of her champagne, defied all three of them with a look that sparkled as her drink had done, and replied:

"Well, why not? I'm going barefoot!"

In a trice she had undone her garters and slipped off her shoes and stockings. She sat with her legs to one side, her knees chastely together, but cleverly showing as much thigh as Maryse. Stan poured a drop of champagne on the exposed area.

"Oh! It's so cold! Don't give me the shivers!"

There was no more stopping this wave of languor that swept over her, stimulated by drink and Bob's way of caressing Maryse, while Stan stared at the spectacle with his strange, fascinated objectivity. Bob reached out a hand, but Rita half-heartedly pushed it away. He started again, very gently this time, until Rita, breathless, all resistance gone, let him stroke the skin still wet with champagne, just where her thigh took on the most sumptuous, curved proportions. Desire welled up in her and blurred her sight. There was no room in her thoughts for the jewellery shop, or Ovide, or virtue. Her whole body was on fire.

"It's only fair," said Bob's deep voice, "I dried one of you off, I've got to do the other."

"But not longer than you did me!" protested Maryse. "Ten seconds, no more!"

The laughter grew less open, as if muted by a dark obsession. Bob, the architect, just thirty-five, tall and slim, his chestnut hair slightly wavy, enjoyed in Quebec the reputation of an accomplished womanizer. Athletic, prosperous (he had snaffled some big contracts from the Duplessis government), he occasionally called on Stan's "escorts" to offer a treat to certain influential officials. He would have been too much of a gentleman to pass along his own conquests. He flashed a smile at Maryse's warning and went on caressing Rita's leg, creeping an inch or two higher. Rita, going wild, could barely resist attacking him. He guessed as much, and planted a burning kiss on the spot he had just been stroking. Rita waited, tense, her eyelids drooping, ardent. But Maryse made a stormy interruption, grasping Bob's head and pressing it to her own thigh, which was now entirely exposed.

"My skin's as soft as hers, isn't it honey?"

Stan Labrie, his eyes shining with a strange light, went down to the bed of the Rivière Séchée to make sure no stray group of geology students was about to appear. Reassured, he returned to the trio, where, in a crescendo impelled by alcohol, the two women were wrangling over the favours of the real male. Vibrant with passion, they were already showing signs of real jealousy and anger.

"I've got a great idea, kids!" said Stan, who felt the moment had arrived for his big move.

"Who needs ideas?" shouted Maryse.

"Come, come, you're going to love my idea. Just hold it a second there, my beauties, and listen to the old prof, Stan Labrie. Raise your hand when I'm finished."

Master of this little ceremony arranged that morning with Bob, he spoke with a pious calm, drawling as he looked up at the sky:

"We're alone in the wide world here! The farmers are farming, the kids are in school, the golfers are golfing, the women are into the soap suds and the priests are in the confessional. We're just like the birdies, free as the air, and our bodies are tingling with love. Now, I've been readin' a book lately, an amazing book, all about the ancient Hindu civilization. Their god, called Shiva I do believe, taught some lovemaking secrets to the Hindus, which we don't know about at all. We're underdeveloped."

A glance reassured him that the two women were hanging on his words, and he went on:

"Do you know the butterfly trick?"

He clucked his tongue at their ignorance.

"It takes two women and a very capable man, and a referee to apply the rules. Because this is a game we're talking about! The man goes from one to the other, like a butterfly from flower to flower. He makes love to each of them for twenty seconds at a time. Very Oriental, you see? And finally, because all good things come to an end, the cork gets blown. And the lady who receives the elixir is declared the champ and the more feminine of the two."

"Bob, you're to start with me!" ordered Maryse, a little high.

159

"Yes, go ahead," said Rita, who had grown somewhat pacified during Stan's explanation and was thinking vaguely that she could still refuse when her turn came.

"No, we're going to flip for it!" Stan insisted. "Fair play for all!"

Maryse clapped her hands:

"I'll take the King of England's head. That's my lucky side."

Deftly, Stan flipped his dime. It was the profile of George VI that came up.

"I knew it! And Stan, you're not to watch, eh?"

"I respect your modesty, my dear. I'm going to cross the Rivière Séchée and count the seconds. I'll be your fair and incorruptible referee."

He took out the stop-watch he had bought from Rita.

"Now, wait for my signal."

He ran across the dry river bed and leaned against a birch tree, watch in hand.

"Go!" he shouted.

The revels of the participants were reflected in his sunglasses. The spectacle would have floored Pacifique Berthet with a heart attack. The couple came together in a rush, and Rita, who had tried in vain to look away, felt all her desire surge up again. Breathless, she tore off her pink panties and hurled them as far as she could. This charming piece of lingerie, borne by the wind, fell into the Montmorency River and went over the falls.

"Stop, it's Rita's turn!" shouted Stan.

Bob and Rita flew to each other's arms, while Maryse, her eyes rolling in frustration, clutched the hips of the male. He, for his part, seemed amused by the hoarse little cries of his new partner. Bob proved a better lover than Ovide (that man she seemed to have known somewhere . . .), who was swift on the attack but too quickly sated. The architect lasted through his twenty seconds with Rita. Stan's shouted "Stop!" cracked like a whip through the spring air. Rita held back a sob, as she always did at the approach of an orgasm. Bob had returned to Maryse. Rita was panting as Bob, unvanquished, came back to her. After ten hectic seconds she emitted a loud cry of utter pleasure. Bob, overwhelmed, not daring to look at Maryse, who was in a rage, collapsed. And Rita leapt to her feet and placed one of them on Bob's nude torso. The triumphant amazon shouted to the heavens:

"Hurray! The winner! I'm the champ!"

And got a slap in the face from her rival.

Stan kept his word. Rita was back in the store at three, her hat askew, her throat burning, her heart in her boots. The vapours of alcohol and lust, as they evaporated, left behind the dregs of despair.

Her life would never, never be the same.

20

Pacifique's eye at the hole in the wall was observing Rita as she inspected her dishevelled appearance in the mirror. With trembling hands she tried to spruce up her wilted beauty. Making love when your conscience rebels makes you ugly, Ovide's wife was discovering. Like a robot Rita wandered from counter to shelf and back to the counter. Stan blew in the door holding her purse.

"Here, you left it in my car!"

Her eyes filled with tears, she took her handbag and scolded through clenched teeth:

"I'll never forgive you, Stan, never! I hate you! And I'm so ashamed!"

"Come on, baby!" he said, "that's an experience you'll never forget. You'll be one of the few women in Quebec ever to do the butterfly trick. Isn't that somethin'? You shoulda seen those pretty gams of yours sawing the air like a pair of scissors. And when you did the Tarzan with your foot on Bob's chest and shouted 'Hurray! I'm the champ,' I just thought, if I was to organize a butterfly number contest you'd be the winner for the whole country."

"Not so loud! Will you shut up?" she hissed, with a terrified look toward the back of the shop. "And get out of here, scram! I hate you so much!"

Persuaded at last of Rita's remorse, he fell silent, crestfallen, and left. Rita walked toward the back of the shop, opened the door a few inches and called in a voice meant to be almost casual:

"Not too many customers bumping their noses on the door, Mr. Berthet?"

161

"Come in, come in, dear little lady, I won't eat you up. You seem to be in better humour than this morning."

Pacifique's speech was thick and his eyes had a disturbing glint.

"Customers, customers! What about 'em? It's more important to make love, eh, Rita?"

She turned livid and could hardly breathe. The cripple must be drunk! But she'd had to warn Stan not to talk so loud. How much did Pacifique know? If he was on to all her thoughts and deeds, the whole city would soon get an earful. Or had already. Suffocating with panic, she felt her legs go weak and flights of butterflies take off in her stomach. The after-effects of the champagne, just wearing off, left her utterly defenceless. Pacifique, leering and bestial, held out a trembling hand:

"Come a little closer, Rita. Be nice, come, come!"

For the second time he had used her first name! Did he think she was at his mercy? But the fact that he was begging her was reassuring. Hesitantly she moved toward the sofa. He was smiling blissfully. After Rita had gone, at lunch-time, Pacifique, tortured with passion, had drunk a whole litre of De Kuyper gin. This was the first time he had allowed himself such a folly since they had opened shop.

"Closer, come closer, I won't hurt you!"

"You've been drinking, Mr. Berthet!" she whispered.

Like a frightened little bird, her feathers all ruffled, she stood before him, mesmerized by his falcon eye.

"And did you have a pleasant picnic? It must be pleasant making butterfly love on the shores of the Montmorency?"

She was rocked by this blow. He had obviously heard all that she and Stan had said. Or had he had them followed?

Her eyes staring wide, she managed to murmur:

"What's that you're making up? You must be drunk!"

"Come closer, come here, I'm a man, too! You have to understand. You drive me wild! I want you!"

She didn't notice his obscene gesture. In a dull, altered voice she repeated her question:

"What's all this about butterfly love?"

He still had his beatific smile, but was playing the sphinx.

"I have eyes and ears all over the city. All the taxi drivers in Quebec are friends of mine. So don't play the innocent, my dear. I know Stan Labrie the pimp and I know he saw a lot of you before you married Ovide. He is the one who created a whole network of prostitutes for the fine gentlemen of the world of politics and conventions. He's a dangerous man, stay away from him. I recognized his voice just now and heard what he said. He has a loud mouth and I have good ears, I can hear a fly sneeze. But don't worry, I'm not a tattle-tale. It'll all be our secret, just yours and mine."

Jerking his body, he caused the sofa to move toward her as she retreated. Would she give in, she wondered? Could she be a woman of easy virtue, loving Ovide as she did and making such sacrifices in order to be good? It was true, last year, out of frivolity, just for a laugh, just for fun, she had committed certain errors and regretted them still, but they had remained without follow-up. And today had been an accident, her will-power had been caught off guard. She had been trapped, made drunk. She felt a terrible desire to run to the church and pros-trate herself before the statue of the Virgin, asking her pardon. Then she would go and confess in another parish. Reaching out for her, Berthet was trembling now as if he had taken a chill. Seeing her there before him, desperate and defenceless, only spurred his desire.

"I won't tell anyone, I swear. I love you too much for that. I don't want you to be unhappy, Rita my darling."

"That's really nice of you," she murmured in a gust of total gratitude.

He grasped her hand.

"I love you, too!" he almost shouted. "Like any other man, more than any other man. You never noticed?"

Her freezing fingers could not escape from Pacifique's burn-ing grasp, which held them more and more tightly. He was talking very fast:

"I've been dying for love of you ever since I saw you in the hospital. That's why I wanted to be your husband's partner. Imagine what I go through, seeing you at the counter, in the front, flirting with other men all day long! I writhe with jealousy back here in my corner. And you never look at me once, it's as if I was some kind of filth."

Rita was astounded. What divine punishment was this, being able to unleash such feelings in most men? He still clung to her arm:

"Rita, give me a kiss?" he asked, almost in tears.

She tore loose from him, sprang back, pale as wax. How could he dare to ask that of her? She felt a wave of nausea at this Berthet with the wounded side and the stink of alcohol on his breath. A blackmailer, too; and one fine day he'd leak it all to Ovide and break up their marriage and ruin her reputation. But she'd never give herself to him just to keep his mouth shut. That would make her his prisoner forever. Where on earth could she take refuge, poor black sheep that she was? He was on his feet now, hobbling toward her at his top speed.

"I beg you, give me one kiss!"

She retreated toward the door, paralyzed with shame and horror. She could not hold back the cry that rose from her very depths:

"Never, you lousy cripple!"

What had she said! She saw him turn grey and stagger as if he had been struck by a volley of bullets. She was ruined. He'd tell Ovide! She fled to the counter, shouting:

"I'm sorry. I didn't mean that."

He fell full-length on the floor and crawled to his sofa, groaning like a wounded animal. His head buried in his arms, he wept at first to himself and then in a crescendo of despair that ended in a fit of rage. She went back to the doorway, which she had left open.

"Please forgive me, Mr. Berthet," she said weakly.

Watching this sick man weep, his shoulders heaving, racked by hoarse sobs that broke her heart, she thought she must be the cruellest woman in the world. She closed the door as one would leave the cell of a condemned man, and, her eyes staring, walked like a robot to the cash register and took out the German revolver that Guillaume had brought back from the war and recently given to Ovide, for every jewellery store should have one. She weighed it in her hand and turned it every way. No, she was not suicidal. She put it back in the drawer.

Desolate, holding her head in her hands, her arms resting on the counter, she wondered how this evil dream would end. Who could she tell? Stan? He'd want to do away with Berthet, and that would only lead to a more horrible situation. Not only would she lose Ovide, she'd ruin him as well. Oh, why had she driven him to make more money, to go into business? She could hardly wait for five o'clock when she'd run to the church, she'd be almost alone there, but maybe some old woman would see her and tell Joséphine . . . but at least she could talk there to the Virgin as she would to her own mother, begging her to take her into her ethereal arms and console and protect her and tell her what to do. Didn't Jesus pardon Mary Magdalen? She had half an hour to suffer this leaden presence of Pacifique Berthet, whose animal stare pierced the wall and burned the back of her neck.

Pacifique, somewhat sobered, was back on his sofa. In a few minutes he had changed drastically. His face looked grey, and his eyes had an icy glint. Rita, with her awful insult, had blown out his tiny flame of hope, which at best had burned precariously, carefully kept alive over the years and recently revived by the success of the shop and his passion for this woman. Now all that was over. What did he care for the profits he was unable to enjoy, generated by his talent and mostly squandered in senseless spending by Ovide Plouffe, who exploited him every day, every hour? Why go on living, rejected and despised by his beloved Rita, who had just spit on his love? Lousy cripple indeed! And all he'd wanted was a kiss!

His glass screwed into one eye, he was concentrating on an insurance policy with incredibly fine print, and re-reading one paragraph whose letters would not stay in place. They kept turning to fire and spelling the killing words, "Never, you lousy cripple!" From now on Pacifique would be nothing but a corpse that left its casket each night to feed on the blood of those who had made it swallow such humiliation.

His sight blurred. He folded up the insurance policy and slipped it back into the chest of drawers he used as a filing cabinet. Oh, he'd been very far-seeing, getting Ovide and Rita to take out this accident policy among them, under which the beneficiaries would receive a hundred or fifty thousand dollars, depending on the circumstances. Ovide was always on the go, by air, by ship, by land! And Rita drove so recklessly, often turning to look at a passerby who had whistled at her. One never knew! And if something happened to them? Pacifique would be a rich man! He remembered how reluctant Ovide had been to sign the policy: "I don't like making death into a transaction."

At five o'clock Rita left her counter and went across to the church, where Father Marquis was astonished to see her praying so fervently before the statue of the Virgin, and glancing sideways from time to time at the electric purgatory. How could he guess that she identified with the most desperate of the souls there? A few moments later, Pacifique left the shop and waited for the taxi.

When Ovide arrived at the Ancienne-Lorette airport aboard the Canadian Pacific DC3, he was assailed by Rita, who threw her arms around his neck and held him tight as if he had been away for years. She gave him a host of little kisses all over his face, until Ovide, submerged and surprised, made a smiling effort to escape from these effusions.

"Oh, I missed you, Ovide! How I missed you! I never want you to go away so long again."

"The plane was grounded two days on account of fog, can you imagine? What a way to make a living!" he sighed.

"Next time you take me along, right?"

"I promise."

"And you look so tired, my poor baby!"

At first surprised and delighted to see Rita meet his plane for the first time in seven months, his reason took control, and tried to imagine the motive for her sudden elation. With her little finger she traced the dark bags under his eyes.

"You're working too hard, darling. We don't want you to get sick, do we?"

He shrugged, resigned.

"It's never easy to earn a living, it's never a rest cure. But I'll admit that this life in country hotel rooms is starting to get on my nerves, always keeping an eye on a suitcase full of jewellery."

He began examining Rita more attentively.

"Hey, you look tired yourself! You're not the way you usually are. Our daughter isn't sick, is she? Is it the shop?"

No, everything was fine. Her denial was a shake of the head, and her hair flew left and right. The only conclusion was that life without Ovide simply had no meaning for her.

"What's in the parcel?"

He smiled:

"I brought you some wooden trinkets carved by the Indians, and a little buckskin skirt for Arlette."

Her lips tightened, she closed her eyes and pressed her head against his shoulder. While she was being stupidly unfaithful to him, he had been thinking of her and buying her presents. How could she ever forgive herself? They walked toward the white convertible.

"I'm really worried, Rita. You're not telling me everything. I can tell you're really upset. Something's the matter."

She had a mad desire to tell him everything. Today was

166

Friday. The last two days she had gone to the shop as if it were the gallows. And yet Pacifique behaved as if nothing had ever happened. She decided not to tell. You never knew. Maybe the Holy Virgin, whom she had prayed so hard to, would make everybody forget this bad dream, and she'd atone by having another baby and becoming a perfect wife to Ovide.

"You know, you really are worried about something," Ovide insisted. "You so cute and sprightly and bubbly as a rule!"

"The fact is, I don't want to work in the shop any more."

He was afraid for a moment that she was going back to her old urge to be a waitress. But that wasn't it. They didn't need money now. She sighed, hesitated, and then, opening the car door:

"It ties me down so, being at the store. And you're away so much. I want us to live our lives together."

A gentle balm enveloped Ovide's heart. He decided to drive, though he almost never did so, and he took off like a racing champ.

"Don't worry. We'll find somebody to take your place. In fact, I like the idea. You haven't had any problems with Pacifique Berthet, by any chance?" he asked, frowning.

She answered feebly, "No," with a forlorn look.

"You know, it makes a funny atmosphere for a woman my age to feel that there behind her back is this sick man lying on his sofa. He works twelve hours a day but he always seems to be spying on us with his x-ray eyes."

He laughed.

"I admit it's not exactly a scream working there. But at least you have the customers to chat with. Think of him, shut up there in the back. But what can we do about it? I'm getting a little fed up myself with the situation. But let's be patient for a while. We'll save up a little more money and I'll sell the business and we'll take a sabbatical in Paris. Then we'll see. Life is beautiful and can dream up better plots than a thousand Balzacs put together. So laugh! Shake off your troubles!"

Rita sighed a deep sigh full of faith in the future. Thanks to Ovide she was surfacing again, and he was the man she had deceived.

"You know, you're terrific," she said, dreamy and loving.

"And now let's change the subject. Did you hear my talk on the radio Tuesday?"

No, she'd completely forgotten about it. That was the day

167

she'd played butterfly in the grass, and Berthet had attacked her, and she'd called him a lousy cripple, and she'd run to the church. And the whole evening when Arlette was in bed she'd chewed her fingernails, weeping and despairing. Ovide was piqued. He made a face.

She saw it, and hastened to add:

"But Monsignor Folbèche came to talk to me about it. He was rubbing his hands together, he was so happy. The farther you go the better he likes you. Oh! I forgot! He's inviting you specially to a reception for Jean Marchand and Father Lévesque after high mass on Sunday."

"Why didn't you tell me!" cried Ovide, delighted and braking nervously. Rita was thrown forward.

"Sorry. My driving. . . . And so the big ceremony's shaping up?"

Rita, delivered of her obsession, had her tongue loosened as well:

"You should see it! The cars with the loud-speakers are all over town. People are talking about it on the radio. It even seems Monsignor Folbèche has become Duplessis' *bête noire*. Delegations of students, teachers, journalists and striking miners are going to come. It's just like the big parade in 1940 against conscription. Monsignor is a real general heading his troops."

Ovide smiled, his gaze dreaming of the future of Quebec. In his trips around its small towns and villages he could see that the traditional society was crumbling. And here was his own parish church at the centre of a major happening, a ceremonial symbol of the profound changes stirring in the community. This high mass organized by Monsignor Folbèche, with Jean Marchand taking the pulpit and preaching the word before the very altar – this seemed to him like a small tremor, precursor of greater sociological quakes. He thought of the three open letters in vitriolic style penned in hotel rooms on the North Shore and sent to the newspaper *Le Devoir*. In them he had tongue-lashed the Duplessis dictatorship and excoriated the flabbiness of the masses and their blind acceptance of the powers that be.

"You fix yourself up real nice," he said. "We're going to be at that historic mass, in the Plouffe pew. Oh, when I think Monsignor Folbèche is inviting me to meet those champions of our future! That's really great of him. Do you realize? I'm going

168

to shake the hands of Maurice Lamontagne, André Laurendeau, Marchand, Pelletier, maybe Pierre Elliott Trudeau!"

Saturday evening, to her husband's great surprise, Rita didn't
want to go dancing at the Château. She just wanted to rest and
stay home with him. She claimed to be tired, but she seemed
unable to get rid of some vague yearnings that were beginning
to worry Ovide. Hadn't she said she had a bad migraine as an
excuse for refusing the joys of love he had been waiting for all
week? No, she preferred to listen to him talk, cuddled close to
him like an unhappy little girl, her head on his shoulder.

21

That Sunday Monsignor Folbèche was to live through the most
stirring time of his priestly career. In his mind, this combination
mass and political meeting represented a kind of resurrection
of the parish and the Church in Quebec, which had been increasingly neglected in recent years. The sunlight, filtered through
the stained-glass windows of the temple, struck golden glints
from all the altar paraphernalia, and the tabernacle seemed to
be on fire. The sanctuary was packed with guests from neighbouring parishes: monsignors, canons, priests and vicars. The
whole church, filled to bursting, seemed to give off a strange
murmur, as if everyone felt that this high mass was going to
take an unexpected turn.

The parish Zouaves, commanded by Ephrem Bélanger in
dress uniform, provided the forces of order. Ephrem, domi-
nating his field of battle with a pontiff's gaze, kept an eye on
everything. He had never walked so fast, and his silver-trimmed
scabbard clacked on the stones of the church floor. Each time
he passed before the altar, he came to a halt, drew his sword,
held it to his lips in salute and made a slight genuflection toward
the tabernacle.

Monsignor Folbèche trotted here and there in the aisles, his
forehead sweating. An evil omen: his air-conditioning was out
of order. Bright eyed, his step agile despite his age, he took
good care that the special guests, the young intellectuals, the
reporters from Montreal and Quebec, the Dominicans and the

university men were seated to their satisfaction. Thus, he found it only polite to put the union leader Jean Marchand and his friends, the journalist Gérard Pelletier, the intellectual Pierre Elliott Trudeau and Father Lévesque's favourite student, Maurice Lamontagne (a protégé of Louis Saint-Laurent, who predicted a brilliant political career for him), in the most sought-after pew of the whole church: the front one, that of the Plouffes.

Monsignor Folbèche slapped his forehead. He'd forgotten to notify Mrs. Plouffe. Luckily she and her family had not showed up yet. And that in itself was surprising. But Joséphine would understand and give up her place. He noted with satisfaction that many eyes were fixed on his electric purgatory glowing red on its stand, the souls in pain executing a particularly brilliant ballet for the occasion.

Monsignor Folbèche went out on the platform in front of the church, and his breast swelled with a generous pride as he saw the large and restless crowd awaiting the speeches Monsignor and Marchand were to deliver in the church, after the mass. Then, as announced, Monsignor Folbèche would remove the eucharistic species so as not to embarrass or compromise Our Lord in this violent internal struggle among his children, for the clergy itself was divided as to the true meaning of this ceremony organized by the petulant pastor.

The old priest felt in himself the heart of a hero. This striking action, which he dimly guessed could damage the last days of his career – was he not performing it for five thousand miners on strike, those workers exploited by the foreigner secure in the protection of Duplessis? How could certain members of the higher clergy reproach him with using his church in the cause of all French-Canadian workers under the pretext of a collection for the miners? But had the Archbishop of Quebec not authorized, nay, recommended such a collection in every parish? And had not that good and wise prelate, who had been through the whole war as an army chaplain, phoned Monsignor only yesterday to suggest that he not overdo it, that he be prudent, because he himself was taking steps, as a special negotiator, to bring the antagonists together? This was not the time to light a match near the powder keg or fish in troubled waters out of simple vanity, when a discussion favourable to the workers' demands seemed on the verge of success.

The old priest felt that he was close to overriding the Archbishop's directive. He was worried. But he was driven by destiny itself.

The bells were ringing wildly, and the technicians were checking the loud-speaker system. Here and there in the crowd you could see officers of the provincial police and, in civilian garb, a few members of the Royal Canadian Mounted Police. Monsignor Folbèche smiled. Why the police, when this multitude had come here to show its generosity, its solidarity with workers fighting for more humane treatment? With satisfaction he noted the contingent of young girls, men and women by the great stairway, ready with their wooden bowls to begin the great collection as soon as the signal was given.

Suddenly he frowned. The Plouffe delegation, Joséphine at the head, came in the centre door. The mother was flanked by Cécile, dressed with a care entirely new; Napoléon followed, with Jeanne, then Ovide and Rita. They were late: just as Joséphine was ready, Rita had felt faint. They had put cool washcloths on her face. Ovide, as anxious as he was vexed by this hitch in their plans, had softly suggested that he take her home. Never mind, he'd give up this ceremony he had so looked forward to. But she had insisted, deciding to go to mass despite her spell. Ovide kissed her. It was to please him, even though she felt wretched, that she insisted. Dear Rita!

Monsignor Folbèche trotted behind them, but the group had already reached the front pew. Staring like a gendarme at these intruders on her property, for which she paid twenty dollars a year and had done for a long time, Joséphine, silent and stubborn, waited for these "squatters," these intruders, distinguished though they might be, to make way.

Ovide whispered, embarrassed, tugging at her sleeve:

"But that's Jean Marchand, that's Gérard Pelletier, that's Mr. Trudeau, there's Maurice Lamontagne and Gérard Picard and the abbé Pichette!"

"Mrs. Plouffe, Mrs. Plouffe!" whispered the Monsignor in Joséphine's ear when he had caught up with her, "these are special guests."

Neighbouring worshippers watched the huddled group. Those who knew Joséphine smiled and awaited the climax.

"Our pew is our pew," said Joséphine, intractable. "If we've been paying for thirty years, I think we should have it on special occasions. I'm sorry, they can go and sit somewhere else."

"Please, Mrs. Plouffe, don't do this to me today. Look, you can have a place in the chancel, with the canons and bishops," begged Monsignor Folbèche.

"Of course!" decided Ovide. "Come, mama, let's stop this idiotic scene!"

"Let's go, mama," Cécile agreed. "How often do women get to sit in the chancel? It's a real honour!"

Joséphine hesitated a second, then, with a sigh:

"Good thing it's for you, Father."

Relieved, Monsignor Folbèche escorted them to the chancel, where a few vicars had to be shuffled around. Joséphine looked haughtily over the congregation. It was the first time she had seen the church from the sanctuary.

Then the solemn high mass began, accompanied by the most beautiful hymns sung by the men's choir, which had been rehearsing all week. Cécile whispered to her mother that she found Rita mighty pale, they'd have to see to her. Napoléon laughed to himself, thinking that for such a revolutionary mass they could have hired a trumpet player! Ovide actually forgot about Rita, so avidly was he examining all the intellectuals he so admired. He could hardly wait for the reception in the presbytery, where he'd be shaking hands with all of them! Maybe they'd heard about him and his talks on the radio . . . .

When the mass was over and the communion species were put away, the crowd seemed to sigh with relief, as if the Good Lord's presence had been paralyzing them. Then Monsignor Folbèche climbed to the pulpit and took the microphone. He coughed. His stomach was chilled by stage fright. A strange thing: the normal tone of his sermons refused to come to him. He found himself converted into an impassioned political speaker, as he had been during the famous procession of the Sacred Heart in 1940, when he had harangued thousands of demonstrators. Over the microphone he gave the order to begin the collection outside the church. It had already been done inside. Dollar bills were said to abound. Then he welcomed all those who had come from all parts to this nationalist, pro-union rally, which made his church extremely proud, and which would be written in the history of the parish in letters of gold.

Major Ephrem Bélanger, obliged to join his Zouaves standing at attention along the wall, had to pass again within range of the tabernacle. Forgetting that the communion species had been removed, he persisted in kissing his sword and performing his

172

genuflection. His eyes met Joséphine's gaze, and she sent him a friendly wink. He blushed at that, then turned another shade of scarlet on noticing his error of form, which caused all the dignitaries in the chancel to smile. He fled to the ranks of his baggy-trousered troops. Ovide barely suppressed a laugh. He hid his mouth behind a hand and paid renewed attention to the homily of Monsignor Folbèche, who was waxing eloquent. But the priest suddenly broke off, staring at an individual who was feverishly writing everything down in a notebook. A gust of anger caused his face to turn purple:

"I know that spies have infiltrated this splendid assembly. Make yourselves at home! Go ahead, write, take notes, the truth has no secrets from you. It's time that the French-Canadian people showed its courage, refusing to let the energy it expends to defend its culture and religion be undermined by those who, in order to keep tranquil possession of their privilege and power, favour the exploitation of man by other men, by people who control our natural riches and treat us like oxen, like inferiors, just because we are a defenceless French minority. So be it! We shall counter-attack through our French and Catholic union movement! Because it is only within our patriotism and our religion, our two great sources of power, that our workers can defend themselves."

His voice grew fuller, vibrant with anger. Old frustrations, held in check too long, burst forth.

"Oh, I know that some bishops do not think as I do. Very well! It's not on their fingers that such bishops should wear their episcopal rings, it's in their noses! Yes, in their noses!"

An astonished murmur rose from the crowd. How daring! Those in the chancel and those in the front pews were perplexed, though grinning in embarrassment. What an incautious priest, but how admirable! From the back of the church a scattering of applause had the effect of loosening the orator's tongue:

"As priest of this fine parish of brave working-folk, I know the dilemma of those victims of the Asbestos mines who have been suffering now for three months, treated by the Hon. Maurice Duplessis as enemies of public order, of the nation and our economy. I'll admit it, I encouraged my parishioners to vote for him four years ago. Was he not then the champion of Quebec's autonomy? Had he not rallied all our patriots? We elected him to fight all the red Grits, all the boot-lickers of the British Crown. Hell is red, the sky is blue, I said at the time. But today, when I see the premier send in his troops of the provincial police against our hungry, defenceless French-Canadian miners, I must shout loud and clear, STOP! along with the Saint-Jean-Baptiste Society, the Faculty of Social Sciences and the Catholic Unions. The premier is a dangerous man, a perverse man, who has resorted to false pretences by using our nationalism just to get elected!"

Thundering applause shook the church. Napoléon was getting anxious. Was Duplessis going to be driven from power? What about his plumbing contracts? Joséphine said to Ovide, it was just as well Gédéon wasn't there, friend of Duplessis that he was. Ovide applauded ostentatiously, glancing proudly toward the Plouffe pew where Jean Marchand, like Jaurès, and Pierre Elliott Trudeau, the intellectual in the Chinese mask, son of a rich Montreal family, were sitting, their faces tense with a certain disapproval. Ovide was astonished at their attitude. Why this reserve? Father Folbèche shouted:

"And you, men and women militants outside the church, mix with the crowd, bring passion to your collection! Let the clink of quarters by the thousand sound a generous carillon for our brothers of the mines. Those who can do so, let them give a day's pay! I'm counting on you all!"

And, turning to the congregation:

"Yes, I know that great powers will be turned against me after this speech. But what does it matter? If I say the truth and all our clergy joins in a common front to defend the rights of French-Canadian Catholic workers, why, I will die contented!"

Father Folbèche was dripping with sweat, and trying to keep up the vibrant but exhausting level of his rhetoric. From the chancel came only faint applause. Father Lévesque was shaking his head apprehensively. Monsignor Folbèche was assailed by doubts. Had he gone too far? But it was time for the old priest, in his perplexity, to call upon Jean Marchand, secretary-general of the Catholic Unions, to speak to the assembly. Marchand, his mane shaking aggressively, ran rather than walked toward the pulpit.

Father Folbèche's speech had aroused in him all sorts of contradictory feelings along with a passionate eloquence he could not hold back. At first ill at ease in the pulpit, he soon recovered his nerve, and began to speak in his loud, persuasive voice:

"Dear friends!*

"Your mass participation in this gathering shows in an impressive way the interest you take in the cause of the Asbestos miners of the Eastern Townships, who are today the spearhead of the social struggle under way in Quebec.

"My thanks to the organizers, and to Monsignor Folbèche for making an exception and placing these sacred premises at our disposal – the place par excellence of reflection and meditation. Even though the sacremental species have been withdrawn, each of you must understand that the invitation to us to gather here is in itself a message of the highest importance!

"My friends, we are not faced by an ordinary conflict in which business and labour rival each other's claims for a share of the fruits of their common effort. This is a struggle that calls into question our greatest institutions, and is fought in the name of freedom and justice! The Asbestos strike is unsettling our old social structures and obliging our society to re-think its traditional values. On the one hand, the legitimate custodians of those values are becoming aware of the acuteness of the problem; and on the other, the manipulators of those same values are in a panic, and afraid that they will see the disappearance of the undue privileges they have enjoyed.

"It is a commonplace to say or write that we are at a turning point in our history, but this platitude in no way diminishes the gravity of the situation we are experiencing in Quebec today. For centuries we were content to constitute the agricultural and industrial proletariat, in order, as we thought, the better to safeguard our language and religion – and all this under the protective wing of the Church; but now French Canadians have decided to enter the twentieth century on an equal footing! Here's an end to our isolation, an end to the confusion between the spiritual and temporal; an end to the collusion among the powers that be which has allowed the shameless exploitation of workers and the poor! Here's an end to the period of obscurantism in which education was the preserve of a handful of bourgeois!" (Ovide Plouffe nearly shouted "Bravo!")

"We want to be recognized and respected! We want equality before the law and before the state, as well as equality of opportunity, to become basic principles and fundamental require-

---

* The complete text of Jean Marchand's speech follows.

175

ments of our society! We want to promote a system of social security that will ensure a decent minimum income and services for the disinherited of this earth!"

Joséphine approved with a decided nod. Some of the phrases were a little too much for her, but the idea of a decent minimum for the disinherited of the world suited her just fine. "He's got a lot of common sense, that boy," she whispered in Cécile's ear. Ovide was jubilant. He sought Rita's agreement. Twice she had clung tightly to his arm. She was pale and staring. She hadn't heard a word the speaker said. "That's normal," he thought. "She never did take an interest in politics." Cécile murmured to her mother, after several glances at Rita: "I'm telling you, mother, she's pregnant!"

Marchand was continuing with renewed ardour:

"My Lords Bishops, most of them, have understood the extent of the transformations taking place in the minds and hearts of our people. They have set up a Sacerdotal Commission of Social Studies, the purpose of which is to inform them on the increasingly numerous demands of the people. Prominent members of the clergy make up this group, which plays a considerable rôle. We find in it the names of Monsignor Leclaire, Father Jacques Cousineau, Father Gérard Dion, Canon Pichette and Father Bolté. Thus there is still hope, if we persevere and do not refuse to fight when fighting is necessary.

"The Duplessis government, which has made French-Canadian nationalism its favourite weapon, hastened, in the Asbestos strike, to support the American company, Johns-Manville. Do you not see the extent of this contradiction? This man, Mr. Duplessis, who boasted he had the Bishops eating out of his hand! When I spoke to you a few moments ago of the confusion of values, note here a striking example!"

Napoléon, his jaw set, whispered to Jeanne:

"What've they all got against Duplessis this morning? They might as well be communists, those guys."

Ovide shushed him imperiously, for Marchand was continuing:

"Sooner or later our unions will no longer be called 'Catholic' nor will they refer to the social doctrine of the Church! Not out of ideological opposition, but out of respect for those who do not share our beliefs, given the facts of our trade union system. So let us leave the sheep to the Saint-Jean-Baptiste Society and Church doctrine to the Catholic Action movements! Then we will be in a better position to tell the government to stop exploiting those values for election purposes!

"Going back to what was stated here a few moments ago, I would like now to make it clear that the concept of social security is not the prerogative of French Canadians, nor of their culture, language or religion. It is a concept universally recognized, and accepted by almost every nation. Many countries, like Sweden, Norway, Belgium, France and England have had systems of social security for a long time and are far ahead of us in this. Let us stop dreaming and look reality in the face!

"Let us go back to the Asbestos strike, the prime reason for this impressive gathering. The miners are calling for help. They are struggling for recognition of their union and for decent working conditions. Their working life is full of hidden dangers: landslides, explosions, lung disease and so forth. They deserve your support! I would even say that if we do not come victorious from this struggle, it is doubtful whether we shall be able to undertake the others I mentioned a moment ago which would lead our people to liberation from the bondage that has held them, up to this time, in a state of inferiority.

"I know that my remarks do not agree entirely with those you heard just previously, but I owed you the truth, even if it may hurt someone who, today of all days, has proven his great generosity toward us.

"I am convinced that when you give, today or in the future, toward the cause of the strikers, it will not be out of charity or pity, or even to ease your conscience, but to ensure your participation in a tangible way in the struggle we are undertaking.

"Let us shout together: Long live the Asbestos miners, long live freedom! United we shall overcome! Divided we die! And, in advance, I thank you for your understanding and support!"

Quickly the orator stepped down from the pulpit amid an ovation triggered by Father Lévesque standing up in the chancel. Almost all eyes converged on Monsignor Folbèche, whose face was flaming with humiliation. Jean Marchand had contradicted him in public, before his own parishioners! The union leader had spoken with moderation, while he, the priest, had come close to demagogy by letting himself go unduly. He would be reproached by his superiors, beyond a doubt. But Marchand had dared to promise that the unions he led would drop the word "Catholic" in their designation. The Monsignor, whose instinct seldom failed him, had seen this coming. Drop the word

"Catholic" as applied to French Canadians? The very idea! They could never live without religion and their clergy! And there'd be the money from the collection: that would count in his favour. The verger had just whispered in his ear that it came to almost five thousand dollars! Such a sum would outweigh any speech, and what was more the amount would be published in all the papers! Gradually the old priest recovered his equanimity. He stood up, shook some hands, and reminded his guests to come to the presbytery. While Ovide, in seventh heaven at seeing Jean Marchand, introduced himself and fell over himself congratulating the speaker, Joséphine, in front of the church, accepted her share of congratulations at having been admitted with her family to sit in the chancel. At the same time she tried to gather her clan for the Sunday dinner of potted mince of pork and *graisse de rôti*. How animated the crowd was, still milling about but slowly, noisily leaving the church grounds! The speech had unleashed violent arguments. The partisans of Duplessis were furious. Napoléon, taking a random sounding of the crowd, was trying to gauge the premier's popularity. Somewhat reassured, he made his way to where his mother was, with Ovide, Cécile, Jeanne and Rita.

"Well, are you coming or not?" said Joséphine.

Napoléon, still a little anxious, said timidly:

"We're not going to your place today, mother. I'm taking the kids for a picnic on the Montmorency River. I'll do a little fishing and the kids can play in the Rivière Séchée nearby. No danger they'll get drowned. There's no water in it. Why don't you come along, mother?"

Joséphine shook her head. She wasn't going to baby-sit those brats all afternoon. Napoléon turned to Rita and Ovide:

"I'll take your little Arlette along. Why don't you come, too? Get a bit of fresh air, that'll put colour in your cheeks."

Rita had turned even paler at the mention of the Rivière Séchée.

"No thanks, I'm going to lie down. My stomach's acting up."

Cécile, more affectionate than ever toward her sister-in-law, offered to keep her company. Ovide followed suit: he was ashamed to go celebrating in the presbytery while his little wife was ill. Rita refused. No, she wanted to be alone, just have a drink of pop and take a rest. What she could not say was that in her desperation she had decided to call Stan Labrie to tell him of her growing panic, her fear of Berthet and her concern that he might tell Ovide about her butterfly love adventure beside the Rivière Séchée.

Joséphine was put out:

"So! I'm left alone with Cécile! Napoléon's gang, you're off on a picnic. Ovide's invited to the presbytery, and me, I give up my pew and do I get invited? And Rita's going to bed. She's right. But the fact is family tradition's going down the drain. Come on, Cécile, we'll eat like a couple of orphans. Like two old, abandoned women. Oh, it's a hard world."

Everyone protested. Joséphine had always known how to make them feel guilty. Furious, she left them there, about to go home. But she glimpsed Major Bélanger who had just dismissed his troops.

"Ephrem! How are you? We don't see much of you these days!" she cried, beckoning to him.

"That's for sure, Major," said Cécile. "We were starting to miss you!"

He stammered, deeply moved and red faced with shyness:

"You mean . . . after what happened?"

Joséphine shrugged, and said firmly:

"You just forget about the chevrons and come along to our house. We'll have a bite like old folks, just the way we used to."

"Well, thanks a lot!" said Cécile.

Joséphine gave her a mocking wink:

"What I want most is to smoke a Sweet Caporal!"

22

That Sunday Pacifique Berthet, on crutches, was giving his row boat its spring coat of paint. It lay bottom up on two saw-horses beside his cottage on Lake St. Augustin. Nearby, the public beach and the camping grounds were loud with children's voices, some paddling up to their knees in the icy water, all infected with the excitement of summer visitors preparing for their yearly stay.

Rowing slowly on the lake near sundown, fishing for a few perch – these were the only amusements of this curious Pacifique Berthet, always deep in his private and mysterious reflections. A lone eagle! The neighbours never invited him for cards or bowling or a picnic at the marina. Though he had owned the cottage for several years, he remained a foreigner, a Frenchman, a cripple who never laughed and who occasionally had lady visitors wearing too much make-up, brought out there by taxi drivers.

He turned with a start. Someone had tapped him on the shoulder. He looked, and turned pale. It was Stan Labrie himself, whom Rita, in despair, had called on returning from mass. Stan's teeth were clenched and he had a nasty glint in his eye. Mockingly, he said:

"Why, it's Pacifique!"

Wary, guessing why Stan was there, the cripple waited.

"What an honour!" he said at last, laying down his brush.

"Right. And you know why. You heard something last Tuesday when I went to get Rita for a picnic. When she came back you went after her. True or false?"

Pacifique had been sleeping poorly ever since. He would wake up at night, his temples and his chest hammered by Rita's cry of "Never, you lousy cripple!" Now, cornered, Berthet's eyes shifted around in search of an escape route. Stan had one hand in his pocket. He could stab Pacifique this minute and no one would see. He stammered:

"Who . . . who the hell are you to talk? Sure I did, but I'd had one De Kuyper too many. You know how it is? And you didn't exactly whisper. You're not very discreet about the women you compromise."

Stan lost his temper at the insult:

"I'll tell you who's goin' to be discreet, you rotten son of a bitch. If ever you touch a hair of her head or try to blackmail her by threats to tell Ovide, something might go wrong with your other leg. D'ya hear?"

Stan's eyes were murderous, his nostrils pinched, almost white.

Berthet sighed with relief. Stan wasn't going to stab him now, at any rate. But he wasn't fooling, either. His odd trade of pimp brought him in friendly contact with professional strong-arm men who specialized in this kind of work.

"You don't need to worry about me," he said after a moment. "It's not in my interest to lose my partner. And I don't want to hurt Rita, on the contrary. The whole thing is buried and forgotten. I give you my word. And I'll keep it."

"We'll see if you do. And in the meantime I got my eye on you, see?"

Stan went off to his car whistling. It was parked on the dirt road behind. He was just as upset as Rita and Pacifique. And remorseful into the bargain. She had cried on the phone, all sobs and tears: "I hate you forever!" He bitterly regretted having dragged her into that adventure. But what was done couldn't be undone.

Berthet watched Stan's car disappear. He took up his brush again, but changed his position. A neuralgic pain shot down his healthy leg, as if it had been broken. . . .

Rita was still furious at herself. Why, at the peak of her panic, had she gone and phoned Stan? He'd promised to take care of Berthet if that individual ever talked. He had even gone to see him at his cottage. The guy was going to behave himself, or else. . . . But she should have waited it out, taking a chance on things settling down and being forgotten. And now here was Stan, whom she'd never wanted to see again, back on the scene. When would he disappear, and how?

Ovide came in humming "Rachel when from the Lord . . ." – the aria that came to his lips whenever he was very happy or uplifted by some great project.

"Dear Rita, don't hate me for being late. The reception at the presbytery just ended. Two hours! God, the time passes quickly when you're talking with interesting people! I found Jean Marchand very friendly, very open, very sensitive. He'd heard some of my radio talks and says I should keep it up. He says I'm a born editorial writer. He himself comes from a humble background. And Father Lévesque! A real prince! Gérard Pelletier seemed to me more distant and speaks very choice French. As for Pierre Elliott Trudeau, there's a real sphinx with slanty eyes. He smiles a lot and doesn't say much. You'd think he was looking at you from the top of a mountain in Tibet. He's bummed around all over the world. I don't know exactly what he thinks. But there's one thing I can say: I've been accepted in their group, and almost at their level. That's the life for me, that's my world, the world of ideas."

He stopped, suddenly remembering something, and said:

"Just imagine, Monsignor Folbèche – he didn't seem too happy, and I can understand that, after the lesson Jean Marchand read

181

him from the pulpit – but he took me into a corner and asked me the darnedest thing – you'll never guess!"

Ovide's words reached her like the echo of distant rapids. She envied him for being so happy and relaxed.

"How could I?"

"Do you know the Order of Jacques Cartier?"

"Is it like the Knights of Columbus?"

"It's a secret order, and a lot of important people in Quebec belong to it. Politicians, bishops, great intellectuals. Its aim is to protect our religion and culture. It has tremendous influence in every sphere. Well! Monsignor Folbèche wants to sponsor me and get me into it! What do you think now of your husband who was just an ordinary leather cutter when you met him, eh? A real Julien Sorel!"

"I knew when I married you that you were a somebody," she said faintly, wondering who Julien Sorel might be. "Did you accept?"

"I said I wanted to think it over. But I think I lean a little more toward pluralistic ideas, and the Order is against those. Anyway, I'll wait, I'll wait and make them want me. Two loves have I," he quoted, and laughed loudly.

"Why don't we move to Montreal," she asked, "and start a new life? Just shut the shop, and you could do the things you like, journalism and radio? I'm starting to get bored with Quebec. No friends. And my parents gone to Toronto. Let's get a change of air, Ovide?"

He looked at her quizzically.

"All in good time. We'll see. But honey, what's the matter with you these days? Something's eating you. And that fainting spell this morning. . . ."

He chucked her under the chin:

"You wouldn't be pregnant, by any chance?"

She shook her head, still sad.

"We're going to see the doctor tomorrow. You're always so bright and gay. . . . I hope you haven't gone and caught my 'psychological spasms'!"

Her eyes were brimming with tears:

"I haven't the heart to want anything."

Ovide felt that he was being a bad husband. All he talked about were his own problems and plans. He never wondered what went on inside his Rita. He took her hand and looked deep in her eyes. "Tell me, eh? I'm your husband and I love you."

Quickly she found an answer.

"I'm worried about Arlette out there by the river. What if Napoléon's boys don't look after her? She could fall in the water and get drowned!"

Her concern gave him a twinge of anxiety, but he laughed to reassure her.

"They're by the Rivière Séchée. There's no water in it. That's a terrific place. I went on a picnic with the Fathers there when I was in the monastery."

All these coincidences around the Rivière Séchée, which she had never heard of before her escapade, seemed like threatening portents to Rita. Ovide drew her up from the couch:

"Up! Off we go, we're going to get some fresh air. Hey, let's go and join Napoléon! That's a beautiful spot, you must see it. And we'll bring Arlette back with us."

She agreed to the ride in the convertible. But she'd rather not stop in at the Rivière Séchée. Couldn't they go toward Ste Anne de Beaupré and visit the Basilica? It was a famous place of pilgrimage. She had a favour to ask of Ste Anne. Ovide reflected that Rita was developing, and for the better. On the way they had a long discussion about starting a new life in the big city of Montreal.

It was the very next day, the Monday, that events began their headlong course. Sunday had held them back: now there was a runaway. First of all Monsignor Folbèche had a most serious phone call: he was urgently summoned to the Archbishop's palace. He realized at once what was waiting for him, and for an hour he prayed desperately like an aged child before the statue of the Virgin. From time to time he cast a blurred glance at his electric purgatory. The suffering souls therein were enduring a martyrdom that was nothing compared with the suffering in store for him, because he, unlike them, was a creature of flesh and bone. His gaze fell on the fourteenth of his modern Stations of the Cross. It was true, after all! Why had the painter equipped his Christ with such long feet? He, Monsignor Folbèche, felt his own feet to be very small inside his shoes! He asked the Holy Virgin to take him by the hand and guide him to the Archbishop's palace, both on foot and in the bus, for his sight grew blurred each time he looked long at any object, his eyes grew clouded and saw nothing more than indeterminate shadows.

He had been stubborn, he had wanted to deny the obvious. Of course it was true: society was in explosive change, and the more he reflected, the more Jean Marchand's words seemed right and his own seemed wrong. Yet the radio and newspapers gave great praise to his memorable high mass, impressed by the five thousand dollars collected for the miners. They talked much of the difference between the speeches but little about their virulence. Yet he was in danger, and he knew it. Finished, in fact. He had gone too far. He thought how men like himself, of too great integrity, always end up in a last ray of glory, like so many apostles, like so many great men, whose shining deeds the world can never pardon.

Then he roused himself and was humble again. He was only a country boy who had come to this presbytery by chance and circumstance. He would never have been sent to a well-to-do parish. "Little peasant priest, be satisfied with a worker's parish!" But it was through living among the poor that he had become a nationalist in revolt. And Marchand was right to demand the right of individuals to equality of opportunity. He was right!

He knew that it was too late, and that he would lose his kingdom. To the mediatrix, the Holy Virgin, he murmured his mother's name, his mother so long dead: "Oh, mama, help your child!"

It was a broken old man who walked toward the bus stop, turning several times to admire the belfry tower of his splendid church. Its clock stood at ten.

And in Ovide Plouffe's jewellery store all the watches and alarm clocks also stood at ten, for this was a craze of Berthet's, whose intelligence functioned with an implacable regularity, submitting all those movements to a single discipline: the time of day.

Ovide, at the counter, was struggling over his radio chat for Tuesday. The phrases for his ads refused to come. Only the resonant lines describing Sunday's ceremony came easily to his pen. What was more, Rita's behaviour troubled him. She had slept badly again last night, groaning and trembling. She had cried out, "The hawk is going to pick my eyes out!" He had caressed her gently, reassuring her and promising to take her on his next trip to Baie-Comeau, or maybe to Anticosti on the Jupiter River where they could visit with Guillaume and Ti'-Mé in a grandiose natural setting, and fish for salmon. He had cautiously suggested that she tell him her troubles, but if she preferred not to, that was her privilege (a pluralist notion), to keep her own secrets. In matters of that kind a woman should have to account to no one, he thought magnanimously. Ovide laid down his pen, thinking of Berthet, who was acting very strange this morning, almost as if he were frightened and was expecting a tongue-lashing or some kind of reproach. He went into Pacifique's repair shop. Berthet was tense. He removed his eyeglass. Ovide spoke curtly:

"I should tell you that my wife will not be serving at the counter from now on."

Pacifique managed to appear calm. Had Rita told?

"Oh? I see."

"She has to come off the pay roll. We'll get a male clerk this time."

"That's too bad. It was pleasant, Madame was always singing," said Pacifique, concentrating all his senses to catch the slightest intonation or gesture of Ovide's. Rita must have complained.

"You complained about her pay, but you will no doubt realize that she attracted customers and that our over-the-counter sales are going to suffer."

Pacifique was pacified. If Rita had talked, Ovide would be acting differently.

"I can be wrong, Mr. Plouffe. Your wife earned her money. I even understand that you have your 'public relations' expenditures that must be made. But I'm only human and I have my bad days, like everyone else."

Ovide frowned. He had not heard remarks like this from Berthet since they opened the store.

"Were you ever, perhaps, disagreeable to my wife?"

"I?" he asked, disconcerted. "I hardly ever saw her. I always treated her respectfully. You should ask her."

"My wife never says anything against anyone."

"Is she not well?" Pacifique asked timidly.

"She is going through a difficult time. She is close to a depression. And in any case I want her to spend more time with our daughter."

Berthet had recovered his self-assurance. He was not about

185

to lose his partner, and Stan Labrie would not undertake reprisals. He grew very objective:

"I can imagine she had enough of this place. She was bored to death in the store. And at times she was harassed by customers. All the more annoying."

"What's that? What do you mean? Harassed by customers? What customers?" Ovide's eyes were staring angrily.

Pacifique backed off prudently, choosing his words as he chose the tiny screws for his clockwork mechanisms.

"She is so pretty, it's quite understandable. But you must not imagine things. I felt this, though, at a distance, when my door was partly open. She is such a fine young woman. This may be one of the reasons impelling her to leave."

Ovide stretched toward him his innocent head:

"You're hiding something from me!"

"Why, no! If a person suggests the slightest thing to you, it starts taking on mountainous proportions. I was thinking of little Father Marquis, for example."

"Father Marquis? The new vicar?"

Amused, the cripple distilled his words with circumspection:

"He comes quite often. The presbytery is so near! I even believe he cherishes some feelings for your charming wife. But she behaves like a saint and gives him no encouragement. But that kind of thing, over a period of time, could explain her having had enough."

Ovide felt like guffawing. What next! Father Marquis, whom he had caught dancing the boogie-woogie with Rita and Cécile, the latter disguised as Miss Sweet Caporal? Come on! But what a kind little wife he had in Rita! She would rather suffer in silence than compromise a priest who might be posted to another parish if his feelings for her were known. And Rita was making herself sick over that? Surely it would take more to put her in such a state! But how could one tell, the way women were? Perhaps the poor little inexperienced thing had overdramatized this situation? He'd go up and see her shortly and play the husband jealous of a vicar, and afterwards they'd have a good laugh about it. Then she'd feel better. Ovide remained silent so long that Berthet thought he might have said too much.

"For goodness sake don't tell her I told you about this. She'd resent it, and I'd lose her friendship."

Ovide was thinking about how to raise the subject with Rita, and answered absent-mindedly:

186

"Don't worry, I'll tell her I got wind of gossip going around. . . ."

"Fool!" said Berthet to himself.

The hours go past quickly when fate makes them dance in her hand. It was almost noon, and Monsignor Folbèche, haggard and undone after his interview with the Archbishop, somehow made his way back to the presbytery. But he couldn't bear to go inside. Where could he go? Without thinking he took the street that led to the queen of his lady parishioners: Joséphine Plouffe.

Joséphine, alone with Cécile, who was home from the factory for lunch, was just dropping into her frying pan two thin slices of beefsteak hammered tender, which she was about to transform into shoe-leather. Cécile was drying her hands.

"Lord, do you never stop smoking, ma? The ash is going to fall in the potatoes!"

Joséphine found the ash tray and tapped off her ash.

"D'you think Major Bélanger was pleased to be here yesterday? He watched you walking around constantly. I wouldn't be surprised to see him pop the question one of these Sundays."

"Oh!" said Cécile, shrugging her shoulders. "He's just a little old guy. I'm not a hundred yet, eh? My body's still young and quite presentable."

Joséphine smiled.

"Would you believe it? Ever since you started going to movies in private houses you're all of a sudden interested in young fellows. Just think it over well, dear daughter. Good things are often wrapped in old paper."

"Talking about movies," said Cécile, "I want to take Rita out tonight. We're going out, just us two girls. She looks as if she needs a change these days."

"Her blood's changing, it's spring," said Joséphine, who had all her life had periods of languor in the month of May.

An old priest knocked at the screen door. Joséphine, seeing him, furtively stubbed out her cigarette like a kid caught in wrongdoing. She wiped her hands on her apron.

"Why, it's you, Father! Come on in! Sit down at the table, we'll talk about your beautiful sermon yesterday!"

He stood there, stock still, near the door. The two women realized at once that their priest had been through a terrible

187

ordeal. At last he was able to say a few words, in a quavering and almost inaudible voice:

"I often confessed you, Joséphine. For the last thirty years, I expect. Now it's my turn to confess to you today."

"Come, come, Father, are you sick?"

He let fall the axe.

"I am no longer your priest."

"What?"

They stood like pillars of salt before him. After thirty years, he wasn't their priest any longer? Monsignor Folbèche uttered his words one by one, like stones tossed into the boiling depths at the foot of Montmorency Falls.

"Carried away by vanity at church yesterday, I went too far, I acted like an irresponsible man. I did considerable harm to the Church in Quebec and to our Archbishop, who is now, behind the scenes, trying to reconcile the two parties in the conflict of the strike. Our Church cannot antagonize the government, for the two govern together still. But I fear that happy situation may also be near its end."

"Good Lord, it's complicated!" said Joséphine.

Cécile, distressed, thought how she would feel if her foreman fired her. Monsignor Folbèche remained standing there, still frozen in his tracks.

"And so they are punishing me for one year. They are sending me to take on the cure of souls in a new settlement-parish near Baie-Comeau. I must leave the day after tomorrow, in the morning."

Joséphine was marching up and down, shaken and livid.

"They could have sent you closer by, not that mosquito-ridden place! I can't believe we won't be seeing you! Well! I'm going to promise you one thing: your successor will never see my face in church. I'll go to mass in another parish."

These words were a breath of fresh air to the suffering priest. Briefly he managed to achieve a certain equilibrium.

"I appreciate your heartfelt thought, Joséphine, but don't do it. I beg you, keep going to our church. It needs your presence more than mine. I beg you to protect it by your submission and your presence. Don't try to avenge the grave error I committed. I accept my punishment. Again, I beg you, Joséphine, stay faithful to our parish."

The tone in which he pronounced these words was vibrant with such a desperate gravity that Joséphine instinctively took him by the arm and brought him face to face with Théophile's photo, beside that of the Monsignor himself.

"He was your best friend, I should say he *is* your best friend, because for me Théophile will never die. Well, Théophile and I, Monsignor, we're with you with all our hearts."

"Me too," interrupted Cécile, her eyes brimming.

The priest pointed to the photo of the deceased:

"Nationalism killed us, my poor friend."

Suddenly the Monsignor began to sob in a strange fashion, muffled, restrained, overwhelming. The two women were devastated. Joséphine signalled to Cécile to leave the room, out of deference to the weeping priest. Mrs. Plouffe had never seen such a thing as a priest who sobbed. As if he were a sick man, she helped him to the rocking chair.

"Let yourself go, have a good bawl, it'll do you good. Just see, life don't leave you alone. You think because you're old it's going to respect you. Not a bit of it."

He clung in despair to her plump arm.

"You'll be back with us in a few months! We'll get the Ladies of the Holy Family and the Children of Mary and the parish Zouaves to sign petitions. Ovide will back us up on the radio. We'll fill Napoléon's trucks with people and go visit you. You'd better believe it! Life's not over yet! We're going to fight!"

The priest's emotion subsided. A wan, wonderstruck smile lit up his face, still a little sad.

"What an amazing woman you are, Joséphine! It's a good thing I came to see you first. Through your lips it's a whole love song from all my parishioners I hear."

Joséphine bit her lower lip. She didn't want to show him her pain and disarray. Monsignor had become like a child to her, and she was a mother once again.

"Undo your Roman collar so you can breathe," she said, helping. "I'll make you a nice cup of coffee. You can come back, Cécile, the worst is over!" she cried.

He took courage and rose to his feet. He tried to make his voice sound firm.

"Thank you, Joséphine. But I have to go back to the presbytery. And you gave me the strength to go there."

Joséphine didn't try to change his mind. Faced with a trial, she had herself often taken a combative stance, and that had kept her alive.

"In that case, I'll see you home. In your state you most likely

189

don't see clear and you could get run down by those young fools in their cars. Look after your steak, Cécile."

23

What a moving sight: Joséphine, short and pudgy, holding the arm of this tottering, tall churchman, steering him toward the presbytery as if he were her husband! The old man halted from time to time to speak to women of the parish, all of them astonished to see him towed in this way by Joséphine. They took a roundabout way, as the presbytery had all the charm of a slaughter-house for the Monsignor. His pretext for the detour was that he wanted a last look at these familiar streets. He had organized so many religious processions and parades, and walked those streets so often! Every house-front reminded him of a death or a wedding or a birth! Thus it was that, impelled by a sudden intuition on his part, they headed for Ovide's shop.

Ovide, an amused smile on his lips, was just shaking hands with the latest customer, Father Marquis, who said:

"Your good wife is not here today?"

"Did you want to speak to her personally?"

"No, not especially. . . . But I'm so used to seeing her here, always on duty! I always say hello on the way past. So I just noticed that she wasn't here, just like that. . . ."

Ovide bore no grudge against the little vicar for having a crush on Rita. On the contrary, he was flattered. Had he not undergone the same temptations while he was in the monastery? With gentle amusement, he said:

"No, my wife won't be working in the store any more. She finds that too many customers are giving her the eye. But don't let that stop you dropping around to trip the light fantastic a bit – preferably when I'm there. Hmmm!"

The vicar blushed and searched for an excuse.

"Er. . . . Madame had sold me a watch for my father, but she forgot to give me the guarantee."

Ovide assumed the attitude of the Superior of the White Fathers of Africa when he had advised Ovide to renounce the religious life. His tone was slightly teasing:

"You know, if I was a priest, and the thought of women kept me awake or left me at a loss for words, I think I'd put my

190

soutane in mothballs and charge like a lion into the pleasures of the flesh."

Father Marquis, first astonished, then embarrassed, was beating his retreat toward the door, mumbling about the weather, when he bumped into Monsignor Folbèche. He took off like a young delinquent, under Ovide's mocking eye, which at first did not notice the long faces of the approaching newcomers.

"Mother! With Monsignor Folbèche!"

He smiled. The old priest was dragging in an ally to persuade him to join the Order of Jacques Cartier!

"Monsignor, let me say it again: you were marvellous yesterday!"

"Alas!" sighed the priest.

"Marvellous, maybe. But at what a price!" said Joséphine.

The priest lacked the courage to humiliate himself before this son of the Plouffe family. However, obeying an interior command that doubtless came from heaven, he said to Ovide, who was suddenly intrigued:

"I have bad news. Your mother will explain it all to you," he said. "I'm going to have a word with Mr. Berthet."

Ovide, wondering what unusual event had taken place, led the priest back to the cripple's quarters. Berthet started, his bushy eyebrows joining in a frown. Ovide left the two alone and closed the door behind him. Monsignor had come to see Pacifique once before, to sound out the degree of faith the man possessed. He had left in a state of shock: a perfect pagan! The priest stood there in total humility. The other, on the defensive, waited with cynical curiosity.

"I have come to ask you a favour," said the priest.

"If I can, gladly, but don't ask me to repair the clock on your church tower. I can't do it."

The Monsignor was invulnerable to this kind of sarcasm today. Never had he known such a state of dismay. Why was he coming to this Berthet, an atheist who, he was sure, was his worst enemy in the parish? He begged:

"No, it's not my belfry, not my clock. Not any more. I am going through a difficult ordeal. I have lost my cure of souls. For disciplinary reasons I am leaving my presbytery the day after tomorrow to be the curate in a settlement-parish near Baie-Comeau."

Berthet frowned again:

"Oh, that's most annoying for you, is it not? You have all

my sympathy. But . . . how on earth can I help you?"

Monsignor Folbèche, almost weeping again, stared deep into the other's steel-grey eyes.

"Make fun of me if you like, and I realize that what I am doing must seem odd to you, but . . . I wish that just once you would . . . pray for me."

Berthet had no desire to sneer. Intelligent as he was, and no stranger to suffering, he understood the pain the old priest was feeling. Is it not always our worst enemy who comes to our aid in bad times?

Pacifique remained silent for what seemed to the priest an interminable time.

"Yes," he said at last. "That means that you're in a real fix, if you ask me that. I, Pacifique Berthet, should pray for you? The world is upside down! You know that I have no faith, and if God did exist I would hate him for what he has done to me. So why me, Father?"

He had almost blushed as he spoke. Monsignor Folbèche wavered, seeing himself accused via God of Berthet's misfortuntes, and he felt guilty. The cripple spat out his bitterness:

"To cure me," Pacifique fumed, "they dragged me on pilgrimages to Ste Anne de Beaupré, and ordered novenas, and laid medals and beads on my wound. Nonsense, all of it. I don't give a curse for your religion. You're going through a difficult time, so you say, but you still have two legs to walk on, and don't know your luck! Do you know what it means to walk on two legs, Monsignor?"

Before the intensity of Berthet's withering gaze the priest retreated a step. This cry of despair burned and lacerated like a whip lash. How true! How petty it was, this ecclesiastical punishment of being exiled from his parish, compared to the suffering of this cripple, daily and irremediable.

He suddenly stood erect, marvelling at the mysteries of grace.

"Thank you, thank you, Monsieur Berthet. You just prayed for me."

"I did, did I? You're not hard to please."

Monsignor Folbèche was recovering his natural unction, as he began to feel his salvation.

"The ways of the Lord are unfathomable. I shall pray for you in my exile, whether that interests you or not."

"That's your business. Anyway, what's your new address? One never knows. . . ."

The cripple was politely sending him on his way. He wanted to be alone to reflect on things that mattered to him: Rita, Stan and Ovide. When Monsignor joined Joséphine at the counter with her son, he found Ovide ready for a holy war.

"I'm going to talk about this scandal on my program!"

Horrified, the priest begged him to do nothing of the kind, this would only hurt him more and he would never get back to his parish.

"But there's a limit! If we don't denounce injustice where we find it, there'll be no end to it!"

"Ovide, that'll do!" Joséphine cut in. "If we want to get our Monsignor back in a year's time, let's just shut up and bear it. For the time being he's like a child doing penance, he has to kneel for ten minutes. If he gets up too soon, he'll have to do worse next time."

Ovide shook his head. What a society! Monsignor Folbèche, before he left, said with a sad smile:

"About the Order of Jacques Cartier, I guess we'll just have to wait a little, won't we?"

"Don't worry about that. Let's just see if the Order can help you! Which I doubt. . . ."

On the home stretch to the presbytery, Monsignor Folbèche lost the momentary protection from despair that the cripple had given him. His teeth were almost chattering as he climbed the front steps. He rang, like a visitor. Joséphine looked quizzically at him. She could feel his panic in the arm she was still holding.

"Come now, Monsignor, get hold of yourself, for the love of God! I'll go in with you, it won't be so hard then."

The nun who was Father Folbèche's housekeeper opened the door and stared, surprised, at this couple. Then her stare turned icy. What a nerve this fat creature had! Coming inside hanging on to her priest! What was this all about? The sister was to find out soon enough, and burst into bitter tears. What genuine love reigns at times in the presbytery between the good sisters and their priests! Unspoken, unconfessed, transformed into blind devotion, these passions may take on dimensions rarely found in the lay world outside.

Rita was afraid to walk on the kitchen floor, as if she dreaded setting off the explosion that was building up against her down in the shop, where Ovide and Berthet were together. Stan had called again a half hour ago, just to reassure her. He had seen Pacifique the previous day and threatened him. The cripple had been terrified and had sworn to keep his mouth shut. And if he didn't, he'd lose his good leg as well. This phone call produced the opposite effect of that desired. Instead of settling the whole business as she had hoped, it began to take on dangerous proportions. She screamed at him not to do her any more favours, never to call her again, and never to try and see her. It was then that her panic took on proportions of near madness. She spotted the gin bottle standing in the little bar she had given Ovide for Christmas. She seized it and took two large swallows right from the bottle. Perhaps the alcohol would help her to find her old, light-hearted self! She wasn't made for tragedy, but it now seemed to her impossible to avoid it. For a few minutes she cherished an illusion of salvation, her eyes closed, her lips smiling almost blissfully for that brief moment of tipsiness. But the moment also led her to think of her sin beside the Rivière Séchée with Bob, the architect, after many glasses of champagne. Then, as the effects of the gin wore off, she relapsed into even greater despair. Ovide was bound to find out soon. She felt a chill as she heard him running up the stairs. And he'd been so good to her lately!

After the priest's departure Ovide succeeded in calming his excitement. He forced himself to think of more agreeable things, such as Rita – and Father Marquis. That was it, he should cheer his wife up, pretending he was jealous of the young vicar. He'd feign indignation and have a laugh immediately after. Cheered up himself, he went up the stairs two at a time, then put on a severe and worried expression. Rita, standing near the kitchen stove, was waiting for him, terrorized. She nearly hiccoughed with fear when she saw his face, tense and drawn. He began with the exile of the Monsignor, but she made no comment.

"Is that all it means to you? Our priest is unjustly fired and you have nothing to say? Heartless girl!"

"Sure, it's terrible for him," she murmured, shaken by his criticism.

Poor little thing! How sad and miserable she looked, with dark rings under her eyes. He'd better give her a laugh at once, shake her out of her melancholy, and then take off for a week in Montreal, where he could sniff out the possibilities of a journalistic career:

"Now, let's get down to brass tacks. Berthet's attitude surprised me a little this morning when he found out you weren't going to work in the shop any more."

She couldn't breathe, waiting for the blade to fall. Ovide seemed ferocious. He was setting up his act, simulating anger. Then it burst out, as if he couldn't hold back:

"Have I been hearing things!"

Rita's knees were shaking. Berthet had talked! Ovide, blind to his wife's terror, thought only of staging his little joke about Father Marquis and the laugh he'd have with Rita when he told her how he'd suggested to the young priest that he commend his soutane to the moth balls. He could barely keep a straight face.

"Yes sir, I've been hearing things," he went on theatrically. "We've got to come to a decision. This can't be put up with! You've been unmasked! Ungrateful woman!"

Rita tilted into utter terror.

"Ovide! I'll tell you everything!" she cried.

Stupefied, he saw her running toward him and falling at his feet, devastated, trembling with terror. What an actress! She was clinging to his jacket like a drowning woman. She'd tumbled to his idea and was acting out her side of it! What? What was that she was saying?

"Yes, it's true, Ovide, I was unfaithful to you, four times but no more."

Flabbergasted, thinking at first that he was taking part in a bad comedy in which he had an accidental role, he listened to this fantastic tale interrupted by sobs, told by his trembling, weeping wife. Led astray by Stan Labrie, she had been unfaithful to him three times last summer, out of vengeance, because Ovide had made her give up her Miss Sweet Caporal job, and also out of need for money – and her own foolishness. As for the last time, she was hardly at fault at all. It was last Tuesday, at the Rivière Séchée, and Stan had given her too much champagne. Ovide mechanically caressed the hair of his Mary Magdalen. But suddenly he withdrew his hand, as if it had received an electric shock. She went on, clinging tighter to him:

"And yet I love you! I admire you so much!" she swore, between sobs. "I just can't live any more, I am so sorry for what I did! I'm dying! Send me away, I deserve it! I wouldn't blame you, I deserve it. Oh, Ovide!"

Stunned, he didn't think of helping her up. He went to the kitchen sink and stared at the crockery with a baleful eye. The confession had been massive, complete. This was not a bad dream. It was a real disaster, and it was happening to him, Ovide Plouffe. He could feel the pain starting in his gut and spreading up through his veins, his heart, his head. He relived the operatic scene he had so often played and sung, where Pagliaccio stabs Colombina. He could never have believed that this atrocious experience of being cuckolded by a woman he loved, to whom he had been faithful, and who occupied the centre of his mind, could ever happen to him, of all people! He felt no urge to strangle or stab her. On the contrary, despite the hurt around his heart, he remembered his time in the monastery and the readings from the holy gospels where Christ defended the adulterous woman.

Rita lay curled miserably in a corner of the couch. Through her tears she admired and loved Ovide more than ever, this Ovide of the livid face, the man she had lost, this cuckolded husband who committed no act of violence, showed no anger, only an awful distress. Why didn't he say something? The silence was unbearable.

"Ovide! Say something, Ovide! Beat me, won't you?"

But he still said nothing, his hands going through useless motions, such as turning the tap on and off or straightening his tie. A veil had been torn, bringing him face to face with a reality that he had long repressed. The businessman who goes bankrupt knows for months that he will do so. Ovide had always KNOWN that Rita would be, or was, unfaithful to him. Was it not this certainty that had driven him to marry her in the first place, since his destiny condemned him to defeat in all he did? Or had he done it out of masochism, to punish himself for his sexual urge? He had made this woman, now heart-broken at his feet, into a terrible penance for himself. He was the guilty one, for having used Rita and married her out of egotism, subtly enslaving her to his own fantasies.

"Do something!" she groaned. "I can't stand it! Beat me, why don't you?"

He grimaced with pain. His whole being was on fire with carnal jealousy. It was true then, he couldn't look away from it, Rita, his wife, the mother of their child, had made love with other men. Whom should he kill? Her, or her lovers, or himself? Ovide was frightened by this flame that consumed him and would lead him, if it continued, to commit some irrevocable act.

"What's going to happen to us, Ovide?"

At last he broke into laughter, loud and terrible, and waved his long arms.

"Get yourself a steady lover. Some night when I've had one too many we'll be unfaithful to him together. Wouldn't that be charming?"

She was pale as death. Had he gone mad?

"Oh, don't talk like that, you scare me! Now I've lost you there's no more love for me."

That, coming from her? He ground his teeth. He imagined himself cuckolding Rita's lover. He felt a sudden, savage desire to possess her like an animal there on the linoleum floor. But that was impossible, everything was finished between them, forever. He wiped a hand across his sweating forehead, suddenly realizing how final the break was, and wanted to sob like a child. It was true! They were lost to each other! Her tears reminded him of her groans of pleasure, their embraces and her exultation, her eyes rolling as she cried out, "Oh, oh! I love you my darling, aaaah!" And she had cried out in the same way in other men's arms! It literally made him sick. He vomited into the kitchen sink. Ashamed and exhausted, he wiped away the mess with a rag that he afterwards found the courage to wring out under the tap. He splashed water on his face, glanced at his watch, and walked to the door without a backward look at the prostrate woman.

"It's four o'clock. Arlette will be home any time. At least you can look after her."

"Don't do anything crazy, Ovide! I'm scared!"

He replied as if she were a stranger:

"And not a word to the family or Berthet about this awful business! Keep it between us. Don't even tell the priest!" he shouted. "You've made your confession. And you get no absolution from me."

He slammed the door behind him. Rita got to her feet, and suddenly was struck by an intolerable realization: Berthet hadn't talked! Again she huddled in a corner of the couch and gnawed at her knuckles like an animal caged for life. Wherever she turned her way was blocked. Berthet had told Ovide nothing, and she had given in to a stupid moment of panic! But that wasn't the question either: her guilt had grown unbearable in any case. Might as well have it over with. As if her body was aching, she got up, and, pausing in front of the mirror, thought how old she looked. And another wave of terror broke over her.

Would Ovide, headstrong as he was, commit some irreparable folly? When two people lived together they began to be like each other, for better or for worse.

24

This extraordinary day in May, filled with tragedy and spring sunlight, made the little park called Parc des Braves, overhanging the Pente Douce, an ideal refuge for Ovide and his suffering. This grove of oak and maple trees, of linden, poplar and hawthorn, with its shaded corners and benches for the elderly or for children, lovers and poets, had been Ovide's oasis in his dream-filled adolescence. Napoléon, dragging little Guillaume by the hand, had often brought Ovide along to play Tarzan. They had tried to swing from branch to branch like chimpanzees. Ovide, not gifted at this sport, had often fallen. And when his brothers took off through the bushes to watch what lovers did (sometimes the young barbarians would pop up behind a busy couple and shout "Police!"), Ovide, alone on his bench, listening for nightingales, experienced the most marvellous times of his young life as he recited to himself poems by Verlaine, de Musset or Gérard de Nerval. Occasionally, a self-taught rhymer, retired civil servant or romantic intellectual who came to the park to convalesce from his consumption, would join him and read him home-made sonnets and give him suggestions for books he should read, opening up horizons of beauty unsuspected in his everyday life.

He found the bench where he used to be so happy and sat limply down, holding back his sobs. His soul, he felt, was dead, and he thought of the young poets of other years, could almost hear their voices as they recited their poems. Suddenly he thought of Sully Prud'homme's sonnet, "Le vase brisé." He, Ovide Plouffe, was that broken vase, the husband cuckolded by Rita

Toulouse. The pain came back with renewed violence. Why couldn't he have died in his adolescence, when he was happy? He could have been spared years of misery, not to mention their terrible culmination today!

He felt a sharp pang of yearning for his home, his little Arlette and even Rita. He was glad he had been restrained with her, that he hadn't heaped abuse on her. He thought of Othello, of Pagliaccio and the great aria of the sobs, which he was on the verge of singing. Men like that killed the women who deceived them. Strange, there was never a cheating husband killed by his wife. Two lovers went by, hand in hand. Stinging, intolerable images of Rita naked, caressed and penetrated by other men, Rita crying out her ecstasy as her orgasm convulsed her, triggered a murderous rage in him against those rivals so deserving of his revenge, starting with Stan Labrie, who was most at fault. How should he go about it? He thought of the .38 revolver lying in the drawer at the jewellery store. Suddenly he gave a start, shouting:

"What the. . . ."

"Dearie, you looked so lonesome!"

A man in his forties, his fly open, had emerged from the bushes and kissed the back of his neck. A homosexual like those to be found in all the parks in the world, hunting for company on a spring afternoon. He had been sure that Ovide, with his dreamy, tragic expression, must also be hoping for such an encounter. But Ovide leapt to his feet, fists up like a boxer.

"Get back, you swine, or I'll strangle you!"

"All right, all right, don't get worked up, bozo. I made a mistake, okay? But you don't know what you're missin'. Bye, sweetie, good luck, eh?"

The marauder disappeared back into the bushes. Ovide again felt like vomiting. Fate was overdoing it. Just when he'd discovered that he was being deceived by his wife, here he was attacked by a homo! As if Rita was still flouting his virility by means of this outdoor bum. Why did he attract men like that?

Disgusted, he sat down and wept scalding tears. Never, never could he tell anyone about this horrible incident. Above all, not his family. Exhausted, he dozed a little, then walked around the park, unsteady on his feet. He had no appetite, and no idea where he should go. In the Church of the Holy Martyrs he knelt and asked God for help He felt a wild urge to rush home and hug his child, shouting to Rita, "I forgive you!" He still felt nauseated. No, it was impossible. Everything was finished between them.

When night fell, around ten o'clock, he went back to the parish and prowled around the familiar streets, noted the light in his mother's window, in Napoléon's window, in his own. His behaviour was as erratic as that of Monsignor Folbèche that afternoon. He entered the jewellery shop and turned on the light.

He looked around with contempt at the trash that was his daily bread. Why go on? For whom? There was no sense in living. Even his passion for politics seemed shoddy now. He opened the till. There lay the revolver, black, shiny and menacing. Mechanically, he shoved it into his pocket. What for? His intention was vague, but Stan Labrie's mask was sneering in the back of his troubled mind. Ovide listened intently to catch any motion in his apartment upstairs. Nothing. Rita must be sleeping with Arlette, holding her tight and crying.

Furtively, like a burglar, he left his own shop. And his feet bore him almost unconsciously toward the restaurant Chez Gérard. There he might find Stan Labrie. But another shape was floating somewhere beyond his murderous fury: that of Marie, the waitress.

The week-night clientele at Chez Gérard was very different from the weekend crowd. American conventioneers and noisy beer-drinkers filled the place. Yet the star of Quebec City's radio, Claude Saint-Amant, from whom Ovide bought his five minutes' air-time, was there at the best table, in the company of a girl singer and two potential sponsors. It would be a good night for a quiet chat: the show consisted of Frédo Gardoni, a Frenchman of Italian origin whose prowess on the accordion brought him fame on Radio-Canada. Gérard Thibault, the owner, went from one group to another, greeting everyone, asking what was new. . . . On Mondays he lost money, but took advantage of the lull to make friends and smile. When Ovide came in, Claude Saint-Amant saw him at once and rose to meet him.

"Come and sit with us, Mr. Plouffe!" he said, taking his arm.

And, turning to his potential advertisers:

"Mr. Plouffe is the man to tell you how popular my program is. Tripled his turnover, didn't it, friend?"

Ovide's smile was ghastly. He nodded agreement. But declined the invitation.

"Please excuse me. I have to think over an important problem. I have to be alone. I hope you don't mind?"

He found a small corner table and ordered a whisky. With the cold stare of a hit-man he searched the place for Stan Labrie. Yet he was relieved not to find him: he was also looking for Marie. He spotted her, but she did not see him at once. Since Rita had played the jealous wife over his friendship with the waitress, Ovide had refrained from going to Chez Gérard. And all the while she'd been two-timing him! What was the use of being faithful to people who were ready to betray you? Ovide stared hungrily at Marie, following her every move. He clung to her presence as if she were his life-saver. She was lovely as ever, elegant, eminently desirable. The tune of "Les Chemins de l'amour" floated for a moment above his suffering. Then he frowned, shocked by what he saw at the next table: five drunks were telling dirty stories, laughing loudly and using blasphemous language. How ugly everything was in this world! Only Marie soared high over such vulgarity. He sighed and looked for a darker corner in which he could give way to his chagrin without interruption. Nothing was free. He began by sipping at his whisky, then downed it at a gulp. At Claude Saint-Amant's table the star was talking about Ovide, glancing toward him from time to time:

"Mr. Plouffe is an extraordinary fellow, quite exceptional and not easy to understand. He started out as a leather cutter, now he's an opera fan and knows all the arias by heart. And he's a brain: you'd be surprised the ideas he has. And he's a first-class writer. He has a jewellery business that takes in the whole eastern part of the province. In the five minutes he buys from me he doesn't talk much about his wares. He uses at least three to comment on current events. And sometimes he'll play a favourite record. A very original chap. And my listeners like him."

The chanteuse remarked:

"Take care! Maybe he's a Trojan horse. What if he was buying air time to get popular and take your place?"

Claude Saint-Amant laughed:

"That's been tried. But never by Ovide Plouffe. If you ever accused him of such a thing he'd never go on the air again.

He's so honest it hurts. He's all wool and a yard wide, but if you get him really mad, watch out! Funny guy, but basically okay. And what about this: in six months he's reached the 'third degree' in the Knights of Columbus! Look at him now, holding his head. That's no pose. He's really thinking about something. I'll bet it's the Asbestos strike."

Frédo Gardoni was doing his stuff. Neapolitan folk songs, "java" waltzes and South American music poured from his immense instrument, which rested against his belly, supported by a broad leather strap. His fat fingers flew over the keyboard with such agility, you'd think they had eyes and ears for avoiding each other among the black and white keys on the right hand and the rows of anonymous buttons on the left. Ovide loved music but had never learned to play an instrument. Napoléon, who knew nothing of musical theory, had become quite a respectable trumpeter. Maybe one didn't have to take an intellectual approach to achieve a performance that depended more on instinct than on reason. . . . Ovide reflected that a critical approach could nip in the bud any real urge toward creativity. Perhaps it was this kind of cold intelligence, the merciless clarity of mind that plagued him, which had frozen Rita and pushed her into the arms of other men who were more stupid but more reassuring and easier to get on with. Again his nausea welled up, and at every wave he took a slug of whisky. Again his gaze did its inventory of the guests. Still no Stan Labrie. Again he was relieved. The accordionist struck up "La Vie en rose," and the lubbers at the next table began to sing along loudly, roaring away out of tune and putting Ovide into an indescribable rage. Who would be the victim of this fury, powerful but restrained, that had built up inside him since Rita's confession? What an uncivilized place! Poor Marie! If she hadn't been there he would have left long ago. At last she saw him, and was coming toward his table with a happy smile. He stood up.

"Mr. Plouffe! Imagine! . . ."

She began to reproach him with a kind of gentle familiarity as if she had known him forever.

"I'm angry at you! You haven't been in a single time since the night when I had our Poulenc song dedicated to you. But I've seen your brothers. The big blond one, Guillaume's his name I believe, my he's good looking! But here you are at last."

202

"I've had a very busy winter. Always on the road," he apologized.

She smiled tenderly. Her eyes sparkled with sympathy.

"Oh, I know all about you. Your brothers told me everything. You own a flourishing jewellery business"–she touched an imaginary cap in salute–"and no more selling records? That's too bad. But I hear you on the radio, too. You say very original things, and your voice is deep and beautiful, it has remarkable harmonics."

At last a woman appreciated him at his true value and said what he needed to hear. Rita had never perceived these qualities in him. His eyes welled with tears.

"That's so good to hear," he sighed.

She noticed his emotion and looked at him with a new curiosity. She asked him to sit down, for people might think he was more than just a customer for her. The revellers at the next table, for example, had begun to make remarks of doubtful taste.

"Is something wrong, Mr. Plouffe?" she asked.

"Just a bit of a bother. But when I see you and talk to you, it all goes away. I still remember what you did for me in the music store, the time I fainted."

Hesitating, her splendid eyes flashing, she dared to say:

"Last time you were here your wife seemed furious at me. Is that why you never came back? I often wondered. . . ."

He was careful how he answered:

"Of course, my wife is a bit jealous of any pretty woman I meet. And you are so beautiful, Marie! So beautiful!"

He stared at her adoringly:

"Your intuition has told you everything."

And thinking of Rita, he added:

"But I won't have to put up with her moods for long. You're so different, Marie. I should have come to see you during all those long, winter months. Have you found a boy friend? I'm sure you must have."

Coyly, she shook her head in a charming denial.

"No. I'm still alone. That way I don't hurt anyone."

Ovide was astonished at his own audacity:

"I go for long walks on Sunday mornings. Could I come by your place some day and listen to your records? May I?"

There was a mischievous glint in her eye. Oh, those French

203

girls, thought Ovide, they're just made for the "games of luck and love." He was sure she'd say yes. But she was playing cautious.

"Take my phone number. Maybe. We'll see."

He wrote rapidly. She was immediately the waitress in a rush:

"Oh! I have to leave you. People are watching. Do come back, Mr. Plouffe!"

And she left him. Ovide remained with his solitude, now occupied by just a spark of hope. As Marie was going past the next table with its drunken roughnecks, the biggest of them grabbed her brutally and tried to kiss her. Indignant, she pulled away from him. And Ovide's pent-up fury was unleashed. Just as he had knocked out Brother Léopold at the monastery of the White Fathers, he leapt at the good-for-nothing and knocked him out with a powerful left hook to the chin. Ovide lacked his brothers' powerful, muscular build, but in his nerves and his very bones was a Herculean strength that could be triggered by a fit of anger. But the man's buddies rose to attack Ovide. They tried to take him from the rear and hold him so that their blows would connect. This was the first such brawl that had ever been seen in Chez Gérard. All the customers were on their feet. Marie, pale as a ghost, was watching the spectacle, wringing her hands. Someone shouted, "Call the cops!"

What bad publicity this would be for the club!

Ovide, his hair tousled, had already taken a few blows from his assailants, but he wrested himself free from the four of them, got his back to the wall and, to the stupefaction of the crowd, drew his .38 from his pocket, brandishing it like a d'Artagnan who had traded his sword for a pistol. Someone shouted, "Murder! He's a killer! Careful everybody! Help!"

The drunks retreated, their hands in the air.

"Hey! Take care, eh? We was only jokin'!"

All the customers were frozen where they stood, terrorized. Ovide looked like a dangerous maniac, his face streaming with blood. He felt as frightened as the others, and the pistol was trembling in his hands. He seemed to have grown a little more calm. Cautiously, Claude Saint-Amant approached. As a radio reporter he was known for his courage during a hostage-taking in which he had successfully intervened. He spoke quietly:

"Come, come, Mr. Plouffe! What's wrong? Give me your pistol, won't you?"

"These hooligans were insulting a woman!" Ovide was puffing. "It's unheard-of!"

Claude Saint-Amant quietly took the gun from his hands and checked the cylinder. He showed it to the crowd, smiling.

"See, it isn't even loaded. Don't call the police, Mr. Thibault. The incident is closed. I will answer for Mr. Plouffe. He's a respectable and well-known man. Now, sit down everyone and let the show go on. There's nothing wrong here, our fellow-citizen is a jeweller and has a right to carry a gun. And if certain clients don't carry on with the waitresses they would not attract the wrath of a chivalrous man like Mr. Plouffe. I'll take you home, my friend. Frédo, play us a java!"

The alert was over. The drunks, sobered somewhat, sat down again sheepishly. Ovide's dazed glance met that of Marie, who was upset and bewildered. Claude Saint-Amant asked his friends to wait for him and made his way toward the door with his protégé. Saint-Amant was very much aware of the harm it could do his popular program if the incident ever became public. His car took off like a rocket.

"Wow! Hey, what got into you, my poor friend? I knew I could expect surprises from you, but not a fist fight or pulling a gun. Incredible!"

Staring, still out of breath, his heart still racing, Ovide cherished in the depths of his being the look burning with gratitude that Marie had given him as he left the restaurant.

"Come on, tell me, Ovide? What got into you?"

Disgusted with himself, Ovide tried to answer:

"I was just as surprised as you were. But those scoundrels! Did you see? They were going to wipe the floor with me."

With his handkerchief he dabbed at the small stream of blood flowing from his split cheek. Claude Saint-Amant was driving jerkily.

"Luckily I was the only reporter there. Just imagine what it would do to your business if that got into the papers! And to your reputation, and mine, too, and me counting on you as a model customer! Wow! Was I worried! And two potential advertisers there! Shit!"

"I'm sorry," Ovide mumbled. "One should never carry a gun, even if it's unloaded."

"Is somebody out after you? Tell me, I'm your friend."

Ovide shook his head.

Saint-Amant went on:

"You really weren't yourself tonight. Got problems?"

"Like everybody else. Just a little family upset. But I'll get over it. And I worry about what's going on in Quebec, with that dictator, Duplessis."

Claude Saint-Amant interrupted:

"Don't give me that stuff again. I'm already worried about your talk tomorrow night. Duplessis is a powerful man, and he knows we're Grits."

"Don't I know it!" said Ovide with a sigh. "With all these compromises made at every level, how can a person live honestly or have any pride if he can't defend the truth against all kinds of censorship?"

Ovide's face was distorted with disgust. He was still dabbing at his wound with a shaky hand. Claude Saint-Amant dropped him abruptly at his door, as if glad to be rid of him. Claude was beginning to worry about his association with this unpredictable client of his, capable of stirring up a ruckus like that. Was Ovide crazy, perhaps?

Ovide went into his store, put the revolver back in the till, and thought about finding a male clerk to replace Rita. He had to leave shortly for a trip around the North Shore. He heaved a great sigh. Now he'd have to share his lodging with a woman who was no longer, biblically speaking, his wife.

It was one o'clock in the morning. Entering on tiptoe, he saw a small lamp burning above the folding bed. Two spotless pillows, inviting to his burning head, awaited him, along with covers turned back so that he could easily slide between the sheets. Of course: he had to sleep somewhere, and it couldn't be with Rita. He was not touched by the preparations. He turned out the light, as if to mark the beginning of a new life.

He failed to notice that Rita, through a crack in the door, spied on him anxiously, her lovely eyes filled with tears.

25

Month after month can go by, apparently quite uneventful. Then, like a swollen stream into quiet waters, tumultuous days burst into tranquil lives.

It was the smell of coffee that woke Ovide next morning. Rita, looking drawn after a sleepless night, was setting the table for breakfast. But her shaking hands couldn't quite bring order to the knives and forks and spoons and plates. Her motions were awkward because of the turbulence of her feelings, but she made a valiant effort not to give way to panic. Like a drowning soul she stared hopelessly at her husband, Ovide of the bloodied face, who had opened a bleak eye on the view from his divan. Plaintively, she asked:

"Did you hurt yourself?"

He had gone to bed fully dressed. He leapt to his feet without replying and rushed into the bathroom where he remained for half an hour, at least ten minutes of which were totally given over to deciding what attitude to adopt with Rita. Freshly shaved, his scratch almost cauterized by after-shave, he sat down to eat in silence.

"What are your plans?" he asked finally, without looking at her.

Her teeth were chattering, and a quaver hid somewhere in her voice, like the voice of an old woman.

"I don't know. Not any more. I lay awake all night."

He said curtly:

"The main thing, for the moment, is for this business to remain between us. The only favour I ask of you is absolute discretion, especially with my family. Even Cécile. Promise?"

"Promise."

She poured their coffee, splashing some into his saucer.

"I aged ten years in one night, Ovide. I deserve it. I want to pay. I'll never want to be a waitress again, or a model. I want to go back to the shoe factory, my old job. They'd take me in a minute."

Her eyes and voice were begging. Ovide's heart ached with a sudden rush of bitterness. To please Rita he had tried to climb the social ladder. His marriage was now broken in any case. And now she wanted to find a refuge for her remorse and pain in that factory he had fled from as a symbol of defeat. He succeeded in hiding his emotion.

"Too many people will ask questions. I think little Arlette needs you more than either the factory or I. She's spent more time with baby-sitters than with her parents. You should learn to be a real mother, even if. . . ."

"Even if I can't be a good wife."

207

He gave her a cold stare.

"Enough said. And for the next weeks – or maybe months – this is how it will be. Time will bring its own solutions. What is important for the moment is to shut up and lie low."

"Just as you like," she murmured.

He barely touched his toast, and drank his coffee while trying to read *Le Devoir*. They hadn't published his letter! Wearily he left the table, bored at the idea of meeting some young man who would replace Rita at the shop. Out of the corner of his eye he noticed that she walked like a sick woman, her back bent. She hadn't slept, she said. And Marie, after last night's fight, how had she slept?

At half-past eight, Cécile, just before leaving for work, was astonished at Rita's weary voice on the phone.

"Well! What's got into you today? Just wait till I see you, you'll change your mind. I'm goin' to drop in and see you on the way home for lunch. Have I got a surprise for you!"

She hung up and rubbed her hands. Joséphine peered at her suspiciously.

"What're you up to with her, will you tell me that?"

Cécile, avoiding her mother's eye, seemed disinclined to confide.

"Didn't you see her Sunday at mass? Our Rita's still in a bad way. I just want to give her a little fun. She's bored. And no wonder, with Ovide away the whole time."

Joséphine frowned and took a long, exasperated puff on her cigarette.

"All right, don't tell me!" she said. "I'll tell you one thing, Cécile, when there's a daughter-in-law problem in the family you don't just brush off the one that can help the most. And that's the mother-in-law."

Cécile shrugged:

"There she goes again. Lord, how you can be jealous of everything! Your sons, your daughter, even your priest!"

"Jealousy's a sign of love. And when I remind you I'm still around, just don't you forget it!"

Cécile smiled, after an affectionate silence in which she wrapped her mother.

"Very well, if you have to know everything. All the workers at the factory are goin' to have a little masquerade ball. I want Rita to come along. Give her a change."

"A dance? And a masquerade into the bargain? Just ask Ovide! And you didn't tell me a word about it. I'm fed up with your secret ways."

Suddenly straight as a ramrod, she added:

"I certainly hope you're not going to dress her up as Miss Sweet Caporal?"

Cécile frowned. How many secrets she had had since her childhood, and all for fear of her mother! She shook her head.

"No, she'll wear the wedding dress I had made up, the time I was thinking of marryin' Onésime."

Joséphine grew pale, and Cécile was sorry to have hurt her mother, whom she had often accused of having made her miss that chance.

"Mama, believe it or not, it's me who's goin' as Miss Sweet Cap."

Joséphine's eyes popped out.

"Are you crazy, girl, at your age? In that little bit of a skirt? You're fooling your mother. I can't believe it."

"No, I'm not fooling you. It fits me like a glove. And apparently I've got nice, straight thighs. Rita was real surprised when I tried it on the other day. And Ovide paid me a compliment. I'm not so old, you know! The world's changing. Look at you, starting to smoke and you're almost seventy!"

Joséphine, sulking, replied with a shrug. Cécile's dreamy, almost languorous eyes showed that she already saw herself at the dance as Miss Sweet Caporal, and all the men were looking at her, especially the new assistant foreman who had just arrived from Montreal, a tall, handsome, dark-haired man with broad shoulders and eyes that burned like coals when he talked to the girls. Maybe if he saw her dressed up that way he'd desire her too . . . but of course she'd put up a certain resistance if he tried to make a pass – but not too much. She'd experience "it" at least once in her lifetime, and she'd never again look at her body in the bath the same way.

Joséphine smiled mysteriously.

"I have a confession. I've got my secrets, too. To prove that I keep nothing from you, I had a call from the major today. He wants to see us both at noon."

Cécile's hand fell from the doorknob and she moved back into the kitchen. Her face lit up.

"Did he sound serious?"

"He did."

"This is it," Cécile concluded, more amused than excited. "He's going to pop the question. That means I'm still on the marriage market. That's a good sign."

Joséphine's words came out sliced thin as salami.

"If you're right, I might as well get used to living alone again. That won't be a big change. Now you're almost a stranger to me anyway."

Cécile's shoulders slouched in discouragement.

"Who says I'm going to say yes? I'd like to have a real husband. Not an old fogey decorated with stripes and medals."

"Think about your old age, Cécile!" said Joséphine thoughtfully. "In the normal way of things he'd die first."

Torn between her crush on the handsome assistant foreman and her weakness for money, Cécile hesitated, indecisive, then said irritably:

"Well, if ever I do marry the major, you're going to stay with us! We won't need much privacy."

"I don't want any eternal triangles!" said Joséphine flatly.

"What do you mean, triangles?" Cécile exclaimed. "Are you off your rocker, mama? You've been seeing too many movies. Really!"

Tension was rising.

"Sure, I'm just an old woman, I've no charm left, eh? I'll show you, my girl, that I'm not dead yet and I haven't got a tumour any more. And I know my men! None of these triangles, I tell you. Not for me."

"Poor mama!" sighed Cécile.

"Go on, get back to your work, you're going to be late. They'll dock you an hour's pay. I have to get on with this sweater I'm knitting for the Monsignor. He goes into exile in the North tomorrow. You know, it's so cold up there, the earth never thaws. And full of mosquitoes, too. They're cruel, those Church bigwigs. Sending him away for a year, and at his age, to that awful country up there! A year's too long, I'm going to get your Uncle Gédéon to do something about it."

"My Uncle Gédéon don't know the Archbishop of Quebec," said Cécile.

"You'd be surprised, my dear. Now go to work."

Since the death of Onésime, Cécile never took the bus. Walking quickly, she reflected: if she married the Zouave, little Nicolas could count on another protector. She shivered at the notion of sexual contact with the major. No, he would have to be satisfied with reincarnating Onésime and being a "man around the house" on long, winter nights. They'd have to teach him how to do the dishes. Cécile thought of the handsome assistant foreman. Maybe she could two-time a bit on the old Zouave: what would be the harm? Life owed her so much, Cécile thought. And what was making her mother so cranky? Cécile could still hear Rita's voice on the phone, low and anxious. That was strange. Perhaps if Rita was in that kind of mood she wouldn't want to go to the dance that evening.

When Ovide went to the back of the shop to say good morning to Pacifique Berthet that day, the Frenchman greeted him with an apprehensive look.

"Are you all right, Ovide?"

Ovide wondered if Berthet knew something. What an odd tone in his voice as he asked the question! Had he heard about the scandal at Chez Gérard? Was he aware of Rita's infidelities and the scene upstairs the day before?

"Why do you ask?"

Berthet's anxiety vanished. Ovide knew nothing. Rita hadn't talked.

"Oh . . . just . . . you looked as if something was wrong."

"Is that all?" said Ovide, wearily. "I have to fill the new clerk in on what he has to do. He's waiting for me out front. I hate doing that."

His eyes ringed with shadows (Berthet had noticed), Ovide was explaining to Rita's young replacement all the tasks for which he would be responsible. He spoke in jerky phrases, with nervous gestures, of the inventory, sales, the cash register, how to sweet-talk a customer, sales figures in the repair department, politeness and respect toward the customer, how to get on with Berthet, etc. Suddenly the door flew open and Napoléon barged in as if he was reporting a fire.

"Ovide, I got to talk to you. Right now."

Dear God, he knows something! thought Ovide, his stomach turning over. With a glance at the clerk he said to Napoléon:

"Well, let's go sit on the church steps. We'll be quieter there. Oh, by the way, meet our new employee."

Napoléon hadn't the heart to meet anyone. They went out. The plumber didn't want to start in on his reasons for this urgent visit until they were solidly seated in front of the church. This was serious business.

"So Rita's not working in the shop any more? Good for you! Jeanne and me found her pale as a ghost last Sunday. She must be either sick or pregnant. That'd give you only two kids. A little brother for Arlette, eh? That wouldn't be too bad. Might be a good thing."

"No, she's not pregnant," said Ovide, grimacing at the sudden ache he felt around his heart whenever Rita was mentioned. "I've found her depressed myself lately. So she's going to take sort of a sabbatical year, just to think things over."

Napoléon shrugged.

"But it's easy enough to get pregnant, isn't it? Look at Jeanne, I'm doin' my level best not to give her another one. A sabbatical year, eh? The sabbath. Are you two goin' to lay off entirely?"

"Something like that."

Napoléon didn't push any further. He had been accustomed all his life to Ovide's laconic answers, which came from a world he didn't understand. But never mind Rita and her pale face. Napoléon's problem was more crucial than that. They were seated now, side by side. Talking out of the side of his mouth, looking far away, Napoléon asked:

"Ovide, what's it all about, the fight and the business with the revolver at Chez Gérard last night? I couldn't believe it. One of my hands was there, he's the one told me."

Ovide had trouble believing it himself, but it was true. He took his time answering.

"I didn't think much about it, I'd just stuck the gun in my pocket. I'm getting threats, you know, because of my editorials on the radio. And I dropped in at Chez Gérard all by myself, just like that, to kill time and think over my next radio talk in a corner of the bar. And I had one too many scotches, without even noticing."

Napoléon was fussing nervously, anxiously. He seized his brother by the arm:

"Listen, Ovide, think about me a bit, you've got to stop your attacks on Duplessis and the Blues' party. They're the ones who keep my business going. Those government contracts, they're the bread and butter of Napoléon and Sons. Are you going to see me go broke because of you?"

"Have you been threatened, too?" Ovide was concerned.

"People have dropped a word here and there. You've got to protect me, Ovide, I'm up to my neck with the bank, and I

212

have five kids and ten workers. Don't do it to me, Ovide, I'm scared. There's no sense to it."

Ovide was sad. Napoléon was reacting like Claude Saint-Amant and so many others: he was scared. He, Ovide, couldn't defend his ideas, his own truth, without compromising the family, which would be penalized for his frankness. Napoléon was afraid Ovide would reject his plea. His voice grew louder:

"Do ya see what they did to Monsignor Folbèche? Out! Maybe they can't chase you away, you're an independent operator, you talk on the radio and sell watches all over the province. But even at that, who knows what they could do to you? But me, now, I've no education, just a big shop to keep goin' and it's those guys keep me alive!"

Ovide was staring down at the steps. What was the use of being courageous and chivalrous if your deeds of derring-do resulted in misfortune for your loved ones? Napoléon was right: he was in danger because of Ovide, his brother!

"Very well. You can sleep in peace," sighed Ovide. "For three weeks I'll have nothing but music on my show. My favourite composers, especially Poulenc. And I'll make a few remarks on musical subjects. It'll all be recorded in advance."

Napoléon was calmed, Ovide had promised.

"Don't go too classical," he said, with the air of a connoisseur. "Stick in a trumpet piece here and there. People love it, you know."

What he wanted to say was, "What a relief!"

Ovide, still pensive, hoping his brother would forget the incident at Chez Gérard, pulled a letter from his pocket.

"You don't need to worry for the next few weeks, I'm off on the grand tour of all my territories. I'm even going to Anticosti Island. Read this. It's from Guillaume."

"You lucky bum," Napoléon sighed when he had read it.

Ovide took back the letter, saying:

"Yes, our two madmen are inviting me. They're waiting for the sport fishermen to come, and building their famous log cabin, hidden in the woods near the seaside, a place for their old age or in case of atomic war or any kind of disaster. It's on my way, so I'll drop in on them. At last I'll see that famous Jupiter River!"

For the first time Napoléon felt bitter at being tied to his business and his beloved family. The more his Jeanne and the kids loved him, the more surely was he imprisoned by his responsibilities. What a dream, fishing for salmon with Guillaume, shooting the rapids in a canoe, felling trees, going to bed drunk with exhaustion and waking up at five next morning, stretching and blowing a salute to the rising sun with a great blatt from his trumpet! Impossible, he wasn't a free man. But he missed Guillaume this very minute, remembering their boyhood days when they were thick as thieves, excelling in every sport and winning every time. He heaved a great sigh.

"You're really lucky."

"Don't say that, you never know what's over the wall. And, by the way, I'm not too keen on wading up to my knees in the Jupiter's icy waters."

But Napoléon hadn't completely shot his bolt. A little embarrassed and hesitant, he told Ovide about his greatest worry.

"You know, that bit of trouble last night at Chez Gérard, er . . . it didn't make the papers, but there's a lot of people know about it. Seems you were a terrible sight. I'd never have thought you'd get into a mess like that. Now if I'd been there, you'd never have needed a revolver."

Ovide got up angrily.

"Could we forget about that? Sure, it was crazy. But those bums had insulted Marie, the poor kid, and I stood up for her. In my place you'd have done the same thing, wouldn't you?"

His voice was trembling, but he sat down again.

Napoléon swore he'd have done as much if not more. He didn't want to insist, because he saw that Ovide had other cares burdening him. But still, he had to inform his brother of a great injustice committed because of Ovide.

"But it's a sorry business. Just between us, our little Marie is too good-looking. And the more popular she gets, the more problems it makes for Gérard Thibault. Gérard feels bad about it, but Marie thought she'd better quit. She's unemployed right now. And to tell the truth, she's been fired."

Ovide turned pale. He jumped to his feet again.

"Marie's been fired? And it was my fault?"

He was dumbfounded. The plumber went on:

"Poor kid, she gets the boot because she was honest and pretty. And it all goes to prove what I was saying: you're trying to be straight and generous and help somebody, and you end up hurting the ones you wanted to help!"

Ovide wiped his forehead with his hand.

"Dear God, what have I gone and done?"

But Napoléon was used to his brother's histrionics.

"Don't take all the guilt in the world on your shoulders, now. It was bound to happen one of these days. She couldn't have stood it much longer. Nor Gérard either. She's too good-lookin', I tell you."

Ovide insisted that he was the sole author of this misfortune, secretly yearning to run to where she was and beg her pardon on his knees.

"It's all my fault. I was the last straw. Do you realize what I've done to her? If she was a Canadian it would be different. But she's French, she's an orphan, and nobody to protect her, unless it's the Consulate, I suppose. And you know how some of us hate the French and their snobby accent. She may have to leave the country, and I don't want that to happen on my account. Hell, no! That mustn't happen! I'll have to think of something. And quick."

Napoléon, silent, was walking beside Ovide. He tried to come up with a way to help.

"Yes, if only you could do something. Maybe I could put a word in with the Party, eh?"

"Not on your life!" Ovide broke in. "Deliver Marie up bound hand and foot to those political swine? No, I did the damage, I'll make it up to her."

In his little leather-bound pocket phone book he had written down her number. He'd call her at once and make an appointment to see her. The plumber was thinking back to the good old days.

"Remember how happy we were, Ovide, back when nothin' much was happening to us? Sport, baseball, chicken pox, the war, a bit of unemployment? Eh?"

Ovide didn't answer in this vein, but reassured Napoléon that any injustice he had caused would be redressed. The moment he was alone he rushed to a telephone. Marie, touched and confused, agreed to see him.

26

Marie Jourdan lived in a neat little furnished two-and-a-half, thirty dollars a month, near the St. Charles River. Nothing belonged to her except a few personal effects: clothes, souvenirs and photos. Furnished flats were a novelty, part of a revolution in housing concepts for the city of the future.

Still suffering from the shock of her conversation with Gérard Thibault, Marie was wandering aimlessly around her apartment, from the kitchen to the living room, and from there to a wall where she would straighten a picture or pause to wipe away a tear. She felt as lonely as she had on the day of her mother's death, alone as a bird abandoned in its cage. What was to become of her? She felt flashes of resentment. She was being penalized because she was too pretty, had good manners and some education and a Parisian accent – and didn't let people take liberties or act vulgarly with her. They'd told her she'd find a real paradise in Quebec. But what kind of paradise was this, where people hated those with a certain style of life, as if everybody was supposed to join the mob, at the bottom of the ladder! Her buzzer sounded and she opened the door to find Ovide, over-excited but restrained. His burning eyes seemed to consume the girl's sweet face, now pale and drawn by her distress.

"Oh, Marie! This is awful!"

There was a long silence. Then, as if it were inevitable, decreed by fate, he held out his arms and she ran to lay her head on his chest and sob. He stroked her hair, holding her close. Only last night, in the cabaret, he had hoped that their first meeting would be a romantic one, and here they were in the throes of a painful panic, clinging to each other like two lost children. The words of the *Berceuse from Jocelyn* came to Ovide's mind: "Hidden in this refuge where God has led us, united by misfortune for so many long nights . . . ." He tried to tell himself that he would always act like an older brother, always protect her. He was entering the sacred sphere of an amazing friendship, a passion he had never experienced, which intensified his rapture. At last his life was enriched by a profound and exceptional feeling. Pressed close to the body of this man whom she barely knew, Marie guessed that he was at that moment the only person in the world she could depend on, as if he were that father she had never known. She didn't dare lift her head from his thin and bony chest, the seat of his love for music and a furiously beating heart. He spoke, saying anything that came into his mind.

"Come, let's be calm, let's talk, I'll think of something. . . ."

They sat down on the little sofa. Her hands crossed, her expression already more relaxed, she began to show signs of hope. He smiled.

"Fine, that's better," he said. "Was it that stupid business yesterday that lost you your job? It was, wasn't it?"

"No, no, it would have happened anyway. It's not the first time customers have misbehaved toward me. It had grown unbearable for Mr. Thibault–and for me."

Ovide refused to have his responsibility played down. He wanted to be totally guilty of Marie's misfortune.

"I don't believe it. It was me pulling that revolver," he said, and slapped his head angrily. "What on earth came over me? Fool that I was! Idiot! But that's in the past, let's forget it. We're young–I mean, you are–I have a few white hairs already, alas! But let's take a cool look at the situation," he said, taking her hands. "Are your parents in France? In Paris? Please, tell me about them, won't you?"

She looked down as if ashamed of what she must reply:

"Only an aunt. I never knew my father, and my mother was murdered by the Resistance at the end of the war."

Ovide held back the question that was on the tip of his tongue: had she been a collaborator? But now Marie related the tragic events that had brought her to Quebec. Her mother, an actress in a variety theatre, had been a great beauty. Marie, who never learned her father's name, was raised as an unwanted child in a luxurious apartment in Neuilly, where the actress threw wild parties, mainly for the Parisian theatrical world. Otto Abetz, the Nazi spy who created the Fifth Column in France by converting a number of intellectuals to Hitler's doctrines, had frequented her mother's circle of friends just before 1940. Sacha Guitry and Yvonne Printemps had come to one of the parties. The famous performer had sung "Les Chemins de l'amour." The memory of that party had marked the thirteen-year-old girl. She had admired and spied on the great Yvonne from

217

behind a curtain. Then came the war, and the girl lived through a strange period during which the actress continued her extravagant life in the same apartment, where her former guests were replaced by senior German officers. Marie was seventeen by then, more in the way than ever, and her mother sent her to live with an aunt in a Paris suburb. Then tragedy struck: her mother, because of her German contacts, had her head shaved and was shot by Resistance forces in 1944.

Marie had moved back into Paris to continue her studies. But she resembled her mother, the former collaborator, and found herself the target of intolerable harassment. People used Marie's beauty to besmirch her dead mother's memory, and life became a nightmare. It was then that she fled to Quebec, where friends of Pétain assured her that she would be warmly welcomed.

"And that's my story," she said, close to tears. "Not very brilliant, is it? When I arrived here I had introductions to some very kind and influential people. But . . . I'd never worked in an office. You know, I was brought up in a soft world and never learned anything very useful. But I had to earn a living, and I took the job with Chez Gérard as a stop-gap. And now I don't know what to do."

"We'll find out," said Ovide, trying to surface.

During the girl's narration he had been borne off to pre-war Paris. Comparing her tragic fate to his own life, he was ashamed of his petty misfortunes. With their wars and their dead, the Europeans showed a maturity in suffering that he, Ovide Plouffe, spoiled French Canadian that he was, could barely imagine. He went over to the wall and examined the panoply of photos – stars and writers and the actress herself, her beauty the image of her daughter's. Ovide wondered how Marie had managed to preserve the purity, the impression of immaculateness that emanated from her. In such frivolous circles, how had she managed to preserve her sterling qualities?

Marie was anxious: why didn't Ovide say something? She regretted having told him so much.

"You're disappointed by my past, aren't you, Mr. Plouffe?"

Calm now, he turned toward her.

"On the contrary, I'm very moved. You've had a rotten time. But I'm thinking of something positive!" he said with a smile, taking her hands again.

"I need a secretary," he announced. "And it's going to be you."

She shrugged and said softly:

"But I told you. I can't type or do shorthand."

His gesture brushed away such petty objections:

"You'll come with me when I travel and arrange my itineraries for meetings all over the province. You'll come to my business lunches and help me keep my paperwork in order. I'm very untidy. It won't be a sinecure. I really need someone. And I'll show you some extraordinary places in Quebec."

He was talking too fast, stumbling over his words. Seeing her surprised, almost unbelieving, he insisted as if to convince himself:

"Here in town you can work at home. Nobody will know. I really need your help. Try it for a month or two, you'll see if you like it or not."

She smiled sadly, shaking her head:

"You're just doing this to get me out of a jam," she said. His proposal seemed too fantastic to her, almost naive.

But he was growing enthusiastic about it himself, and had already worked out a whole plan.

"Of course you'd have your own room in hotels. And you can be sure that my conduct toward you will be irreproachable."

"Oh, I don't doubt that for a moment. But I'm . . . thinking about your wife. Your plan just doesn't work."

He was suddenly ashamed. She was better than he was. And he had dared to offer her such an empty, unjustified job! Nobly, she had thought of Rita, while he was busily exploiting the dismay of the prettiest girl in the world in order to make her his travelling companion. Separate rooms, indeed! From the bottom of his heart he despised Ovide Plouffe. But there was no turning back. It was his fault Marie had lost her place.

"The salary, by the way, will be slightly higher than what you got at Chez Gérard," he added.

Marie was still hesitant. He smiled timidly.

"I can't give you tips, after all!"

She went to the window and absent-mindedly adjusted the curtains.

"You didn't answer my question about your wife's reaction. She seemed very jealous to me! I mentioned that to you last night."

He wrung his hands. He didn't dare shout, "Because I don't owe her any more explanations! Because you are my salvation!" He went on in a broken voice:

"Come and sit down. Please."

She came hesitantly toward the sofa, as if she were approaching a grave and unknown danger. When she was sitting beside him he hesitated and, unable to restrain himself, blurted out:

"Marie, an awful thing has happened to me. My marriage is ruined!"

It was her turn, at this agonized admission, to take his hand. He drew her to him and, with tears in his eyes, told her of his misfortune and the break with Rita.

"Let's not leave each other, Marie, let's help each other, shall we?" he said clinging to her like a drowning man.

Her brimming eyes looked up at him and she murmured:

"I'll not leave you, Ovide."

The bond that was beginning to form between them caused a tragic heaviness to hang in the room. Was Fate trying to tie irrevocably the lives of Ovide Plouffe and Marie Jourdan?

27

It was a quarter to twelve that same day. Cécile was walking homeward, the Miss Sweet Caporal uniform rolled under her arm. She had just left Rita and frankly didn't understand her any more, didn't recognize her either. Hair parted down the middle and tied in a bun at the back, Cécile's sister-in-law was wearing a black convent dress and low-heeled shoes. To Cécile's amazement Rita explained her decision to change her life. She was going to renounce the world and its pleasures to devote herself full-time to little Arlette, her home and Ovide. That very morning she had sold her convertible back to the garage. And of course there was no question of her going with Cécile to the much-anticipated dance. How stupid life was! Just when Cécile was beginning to enjoy the fevers of her Indian summer, Rita, in the flower of youth and with rich experience behind her, was taking up austerity and sacrifice, as if she had decided to enter a convent. A completely different woman from the one who a few weeks before had dressed Cécile up as Miss Sweet Caporal and danced the boogie-woogie with Ovide and the moon-struck priest! Cécile was disappointed and bitter. Without the collaboration of Rita the flashy, Cécile would never dare to go to the dance alone as Miss Sweet Cap, to be admired and perhaps desired for her lovely legs by the young assistant foreman from Montreal! She gnashed her teeth and frowned. Something serious must have happened to transform Rita into a kind of zombie. Could Ovide have given her formal orders to act this way? But Rita had denied it stubbornly. The decision had sprung from the depths of her being. A kind of illumination, a miracle, like Paul's on the road to Damascus!

Damn men anyway! Cécile was striding angrily and swiftly down the street. Ovide was behind this somehow, she was sure. Rita had dropped the hint: "I'm doing this mainly for my husband's happiness." Ah! How many women in misfortune find in themselves the powers of salvation, while men, sapped of their energy and robbed of all their dreams, melt like clouds in tears and lamentations! Cécile thought about women she had worked with who had given in to the slavery of the kitchen. What courage and endurance it took to overcome the loneliness of a home full of egotistical brats, while the husbands, eternal boyish rascals, continued their irresponsible high jinks! That was it: the man sacrificed his wife, and put her to the test so that she would be armoured against the day when serious disaster threatened.

Well! It surely wouldn't be Major Bélanger who'd alienate the rights and liberties of Cécile Plouffe! Rights and liberties? Come, come, she wasn't going to arrive home in a state like this. . . .

Major Ephrem, in his dress uniform with sword, sparkling with medals, had come in with such pomp and circumstance that Joséphine had given him the rocker to relax in, slipping beneath his legs the footstool she herself used to relieve her varicose veins. He accepted a cup of tea and sipped it slowly. Joséphine smiled to herself at his shyness and imagined herself a porcupine, flicking from time to time one of her barbed quills at this traitor who wanted to steal her daughter. They'd had such fun before, the three of them, with no talk of marriage. Life had run smoothly by in tasty dinners, card games, harmless stories and Zouave parades of which Cécile and Joséphine were faithful spectators, always admiring and ready to applaud. And here was the major wanting to marry her daughter!

"What time does she get here?" he asked, after some hemming and hawing.

"In about ten minutes, just like always. Are you in such a rush to see her?"

The question gave him a moment's respite, and he protested only feebly. Joséphine grinned.

"Come on, say what you have to say. I'm still a friend of yours. Do you want to marry her?"

"Well, er. . . ."

"You don't have to ask my permission, you know. She's been of age for a while."

"Do you think it would be wise? I'm nearly seventy. She's not even fifty."

Joséphine couldn't quite resist being cutting.

"You'll make the perfect couple! Best of luck! She'll never say I stood in her way."

The major pushed away the footstool and began rocking rapidly.

"I really wonder, Mrs. Plouffe, if it wouldn't be unwise. It's a big decision. You know, up to a point. . . . Do you think I would be her first man?"

Joséphine was indignant. What an insulting question!

"Yes, my Cécile's a virgin. My family always married in white."

He sighed, more anxious than ever.

"In that case, she'll be very energetic. It could call for great energy, good health and sustained effort. I'm no longer the man I was forty years ago."

Joséphine saw before her the incarnation of indecisive man in this be-medalled major.

"What's the use of commanding three thousand men and shouting orders the livelong day and then shy away from a little decision like this?"

Just at this moment Cécile came in, mincing and primping, and exclaimed:

"Well, I declare! It's our fine general! How nice! There, a little peck on the cheek just to congratulate him."

He turned pink and huddled down in the rocker.

"Well," said Josephine, "my meal's ready in five minutes. Sit down, Ephrem, before my spuds stick to the pot. Come, don't hold back, let's hear your big question, the answer will be yes, and we'll have a celebration. Why wait? Life's too short for that."

"Yes, Ephrem, it's not so hard," added Cécile impatiently. "You always did know how to talk to women."

He stood up, almost to attention, took a deep breath, and said without a pause:

"Very well Cécile would you have any objection if I asked for your mother's hand in marriage."

If all the elements had attacked the house at once the two women would not have been more thunder-struck. Then Joséphine repressed a little smile of triumph. Cécile was trying to recover from the blow, while the major's eye switched from one to the other as if they had been playing Ping-Pong.

"See that, Cécile? I told you I'm not dead yet!"

"Congratulations, mama, you'll make a nice old couple!" said Cécile, still staggered.

Joséphine smiled, her eyes squinting maliciously.

"Can't be that old if I'm still getting proposals, my girl!"

This comical situation was so far beyond Cécile that she began to pace up and down in the kitchen, trying to imagine her mother in bed with Ephrem. And a burst of laughter began to find its way to the surface, like a haemorrhage of hilarity. It finally broke from her lips as she passed her father's photo on the wall and tipped her ancestor a wink.

"I'll have to get out," Cécile hiccoughed. "None of these eternal triangles for me."

Her laugh overturned all in its path, except Joséphine herself, a formidable barrier of menacing vexation.

"Am I so fat and ugly and old that you die laughing at the thought? You don't have to split your face from one ear to the other!"

Cécile was out of control, bent double, tears in her eyes. Strangely enough, she was thinking of Rita.

"You were always so beautiful and tempting with your pretty curves, I don't know why you weren't snapped up long ago," she said.

Shocked, Joséphine thought of her youth when she was such a fine bit of a girl, and of her white wedding, on Théophile's arm – such a fine figure of a man – and the family celebrations afterwards, when she had sung with Gédéon the Alsatian song, "The Three Ribbons": "When I was eighteen and came out of the church, on the very first day of my Hymen. . . ."

It was the major who brought her back to reality.

"You're the prettiest woman your age in the parish, Joséphine."

Cécile was still breaking up.

"Now, that's the truth!" she managed to interject.

"Well, is it yes, Joséphine?" said the major, begging to be put out of his misery.

But before saying yes to anything Joséphine wanted to collect herself and think. In turn she winked at Théophile's portrait and finally joined in the hilarity of her daughter. The major looked at one, then the other, losing courage fast. Then he too burst out laughing, completing the chorus. When things grew calm again they all wiped their eyes, and Joséphine, quite out of breath, said softly to the major:

"I'm very flattered by your proposal, Ephrem. And I thank you for it. But . . . talking about marriage in the summertime – it's a little too warm, don't you think? Let's put it all off until fall, say, when the cold comes again. And till then let's just go on as before, eh?"

The major beat a strategic retreat.

"Oh, a month here or there, you know . . . we have time. Yes, let's do that, let's wait a while."

Cécile loved and admired her mother. How splendidly she was able to handle any situation, just by her strength and simplicity! After a moment's hesitation she shouted,

"Dinner's on! Who's hungry? Step-father to be?"

Ephrem, in high spirits, and rather relieved, thought he had been very noble in asking to marry at least one of them. Now he could go on seeing both as a friend without having to perform in bed with either. Cécile had broken the ice, now Joséphine pursued the good work:

"You know, Ephrem, our priest is taking the plane to fly up North tomorrow morning. A lot of parishioners are going to turn out and wish him well. It'd be nice if you could be there with your Zouaves to give him a 'present arms'!"

The major slapped his forehead:

"And I never once thought of it!"

"Cécile," said Joséphine, "you're not going to the factory tomorrow, we have to be at the airport. Napoléon's car and trucks are going to be there packed with friends. So don't get home too late from your dance, you and Rita."

"We're not going," said Cécile, suddenly saddened. Embar-

224

rassed, she fled to her room and stuffed the Miss Sweet Caporal costume at the back of a drawer.

On Wednesday, a crowd of grieving parishioners were at the Ancienne-Lorette airport to bid farewell to their dear Monsignor Folbèche, exiled for a year. The plane stood on the tarmac, its propellers whirling, and the other passengers were growing impatient. The ceremony in progress in the departure area just in front of the airport building was dragging on.

In his Sunday best, Pacifique Berthet leaned on his crutches as he stood in the bay window that looked out on the runway, listening to the motors and studying the shape of the plane. He cast a final glance at the ticket counter and the baggage area, then went outside: the Zouaves' band, commanded by Ephrem Bélanger, was striking up the "present arms."

The crowd stood motionless in the hot sun, many of them wiping their eyes. Joséphine, Cécile, Rita and Napoléon with all his family were there in a group. Monsignor Folbèche, straight as a fence post, listened, pale and fragile. Was he not being chased from this parish he had cherished for the last thirty years, from these children, these faithful friends of whom so many had given up a half-day's pay to come and demonstrate their love and sorrow? Through the mist of his tears he caught sight of Pacifique on his crutches. A strange feeling mingled with his grief. Berthet, the atheist, had come, too! Was God not making him, Folbèche, pay for the conversion of the cripple? He was surprised at the remark that flashed through his mind: "Converting a Frenchman is an expensive joy!" The band stopped playing and a cry rose from the crowd:

"Speech, Father! A speech!"

The nun who served as his housekeeper came close to him, pale and trembling, and took his freezing fingers in her fat hands. He shouted:

"You have all my love! Thank you, thank you!"

He ran inside the airport building, his small suitcase flapping, rattling with his pills, his breviary and a handful of cash.

The crowd sniffled collectively and did not move away. Suddenly they all felt like orphans. Joséphine murmured to Rita, on her right:

"I'm sorry Ovide didn't come. He's in town, too. Look there, even Berthet, the foreigner, came out!"

"Ovide has so much work. He's at it night and day, our Ovide is, Mrs. Plouffe."

"Our Ovide." An unexpected gust of affection invaded Joséphine's heart, affection for Rita, her daughter-in-law.

28

Joséphine was wrong to reproach Ovide for avoiding the ceremony. Walled up in his solitude, he had not told his mother that at nine o'clock that morning he had paid a visit to Monsignor Folbèche to say good-bye and to promise that during his next visit to the North Shore he would visit the priest in his new parish. He had done even more for the old man. Without too much difficulty he had, to his great surprise, persuaded Pacifique Berthet to go to the airport in his stead. It was bound to touch the exile, for he took a special interest in the cripple. This interest was not only reciprocated: Berthet would give the priest a splendid present.

It was this present that Ovide now held in his arms, as he walked quickly toward the jewellery store: an awkward package that looked like a child's coffin – a statue of St. Christopher, bought at Paquet's store, to be sent by Pacifique to Folbèche for the Fourteenth of July, the great French holiday. Ovide began to feel a soft spot for Berthet that he had never previously experienced. They were thoughtful, those French, when they put their minds to it.

Ovide had noticed the change some time ago: Pacifique had grown all soft and charitable and full of consideration for Ovide. Had his intelligence ferreted out the great pain Ovide was afflicted with, while unable to identify it? Oh, the damned package was getting heavy!

It was a statue of St. Christopher to protect Monsignor Folbèche from accidents. What an odd idea of Berthet's! Ovide thought of the words of Ecclesiastes: "Time and chance happeneth to them all. For man also knoweth not his time."

Ovide's thoughts turned to Marie again, and his pace grew more rapid. How deep this feeling was that he had for her! She had accepted his proposal that she accompany him on his trip as far as Anticosti Island. Guillaume and Ti'-Mé would know enough to keep their mouths shut. Ovide smiled, and his package grew lighter. He imagined with delight how those three dream-weeks would be. He and Marie, walking along the strand or through the fields. He would pick daisies for her and make wreaths and necklaces of them. In the evening, before they went to their separate rooms, he would kiss her hand. And he'd see her again at breakfast, happier every day, lovelier and blossoming. And he tried to think coldly of Rita, as of a kind of hired foster-mother who would look after Arlette for the next few years, no more. But this was more difficult, and he succeeded only sporadically, as the old pain came back. Strange: he was no longer resentful of Rita: as if he, Ovide, had been responsible for the whole affair. Ovide wondered how he would go about explaining his new temporary secretary to Berthet.

Pacifique Berthet, back from the airport, was whistling as he bent over his work bench. His wound was barely festering, and he had had no pain in his hip for several days. He passed his time correcting the defective works of watches of all kinds. At times he would stop and listen for Rita's footsteps in the apartment upstairs. Waves of desire submerged him, the floor above dissolved, and he stared with devouring eyes at the progress of this woman walking in the heavens. His desire would then give way to acute frustration and then to ferocious hatred as he remembered her insult: "lousy cripple" – it had buried itself so deeply in him that it echoed with every heart beat. Maybe he could be calm if he saw her in the shop from time to time. Oh, only ten seconds! The other day as he had emerged from his taxi he had met her face to face as she left the house. She had retreated quickly behind the door. And that morning he had been unable to repair a single watch, but had drowned his misery in gin.

Then, to escape his martyrdom, he found an amusement to fill the breaks he allowed himself between repair jobs. The man who could barely walk had become fascinated by champion runners, racing car drivers, airplanes and anything else that ran or flew.

His grey eyes were scrutinizing the fuselage plan of an airplane – a DC3 like the one that had carried off Monsignor Folbèche. If ever Pacifique was cured he would become a pilot.

And he'd learn fast! He calmly rolled up the diagram that he had torn out of a magazine, as Ovide came in and laid his heavy parcel on the work bench.

"There," he said. "I found your statue for you at Paquet's. Awkward thing to handle. And it seems they usually sell statues only to nuns, old women and priests."

Berthet showed the hint of a sardonic smile.

"Could it be that we have the souls of apostles and don't know it?"

Ovide avoided his gaze and thought of the monastery where he should, perhaps, have stayed.

"It cost thirty-five dollars. Here's your fifteen dollars change and the bill."

Berthet tore up the bill without looking at it and tossed the pieces into the waste basket.

"Everything went well at the send-off?" Ovide asked.

"Very moving. Many people were crying. It made one sorry to see Monsignor Folbèche. But he's only leaving for a year, after all."

Ovide was trying to understand his peculiar partner.

"Thanks for going. And I always thought you hated priests! Yet here you are preparing a delightful surprise for him, a touching gift to console him in his little backwoods parish."

Berthet was evasive.

"Oh, you know! He came in person to ask me to think about him and pray for his salvation. And I promised. To think about him, yes. Not to pray. After all, eh? But the statue's to take the place of praying. I'm a man of my word, and I think logically, that's all."

Ovide reflected that there must be endless reserves of goodness and nobility in this cripple with the hard, grey eyes. As Berthet seemed in good humour, Ovide dropped a word about his temporary secretary. Pacifique frowned. Had his partner taken a mistress? Surely Ovide had found out something about his wife.

"Now, don't go imagining things," said Ovide. "I'll be paying her out of my own pocket. I need a lot of help for my big summer trip. I'm getting swamped. She can look after appointments and keep my billings in order. And who knows? Our business is growing. She might be able to replace me in many ways in the future, if we keep her on."

"So why pay her yourself, if she has to be hired? I'll accept the cost if you say so."

Ovide was a poor liar. He stammered:

"No, no, not for the moment. It's just a crazy idea of mine, a trial, maybe I could get along without her. I insist on paying her myself, I'll feel better about it."

"Good-looking, is she?" said Berthet with a cynical edge to his voice.

"Not bad," said Ovide, non-committally. "But of course it's a purely business relationship. And I'd appreciate you keeping it to yourself. People are so ready to gossip. . . ."

Ovide caught himself just in time. He musn't tell Pacifique that Marie, too, was French and that the anti-Pétain people had their eye on her, poor old Pétain, in his way he'd done his best to protect the French. . . . In any case she was never to come to the store, and he'd pay her cash. Berthet was still thinking, his bushy eyebrows frowning.

"But why don't you use your wife? It wouldn't cost you a cent!"

Ovide was categorical:

"Never. It's always bad business to hire family. No, she and I have decided she'll just keep house for the time being."

Berthet said innocently:

"Madame Rita must find that a bore. She likes company so much. I even heard she's sold her car. Are you sure this is best for her? I hear her walking up and down the whole day long. As if she had something awful on her mind."

"She's getting used to it, she's adapting," said Ovide hastily, anxious to get off the topic. "Well, we agree about the secretary, right? And not a word!"

The cripple replied solemnly:

"A professional secret is sacred for me."

Taking advantage of Ovide's vulnerability, he suggested, with false timidity:

"Tell your wife to drop in at the store sometimes. I could have a chat with her. I can talk of many things, you know, but I never see a soul! Nobody speaks to me and I haven't a friend in the world. I had grown quite used to having the little lady down here."

Ovide thought how isolated this man must really be. Of course he'd make a tactful suggestion to Rita. For that matter

229

she seemed to be going through a tardy but acute phase of noble sentiments. Pacifique knew very well that Rita wouldn't come. But he had an important request for Ovide, one that he had been thinking about for some days now.

"You're a lucky guy," he said. "Going off on a three-week trip with a pretty secretary. Sometimes I envy you. But that's not your fault, nor anybody's. You wouldn't guess it, but I must admit I miss your company when you're away a few days. I count on my chats with you, you're so understanding and friendly."

Ovide was touched. What had got into Pacifique today?

"This fall we'll close the repair shop and you'll come around with me all over our sales territory."

Berthet considered this blissful possibility for a moment. But then he shook his head. He wasn't going to be the handicapped person that had to be dragged around out of pity.

"Oh, I'm big enough to put up with my pain alone," he said, staring downward. "Luckily I have my cottage on Lake St. Augustin. I do find a certain calm there. I have many projects there for the summer. I'd like to do a little gardening, but my land is covered with tree stumps and rocks as big as a car. It would take tractors and horses and workers to get rid of them."

Ovide was afraid Berthet was going to ask for his help, and he detested manual labour. Perhaps he'd ask for assistance from Napoléon and his workers too. . . .

"Look," he said, "you're making money now. Sell your cottage and buy another one where the ground's been cleared."

Pacifique had a far-away look.

"I thought of that. But I've grown attached to my little plot of ground that I paid for with pain and privation. No. But I could clear the land if I had some dynamite."

"Of course," said Ovide, relieved. "But take care. It's dangerous stuff, dynamite. There are lots of accidents."

Pacifique rolled a cigarette and licked the paper with deep concentration. Then he lit it.

"I have another little favour to ask."

"Don't hesitate. This is my day for good deeds."

"You're going away Monday for three weeks. But tomorrow, on your way back from the radio station, could you drop in at Samson and Filion's hardware and pick up about fifty sticks of dynamite and a few detonators? I'd appreciate it. I'll have all my stumps out by the end of the month."

Ovide stared. He had never bought dynamite in his life.

"Don't you need a permit?"

Pacifique waved a hand.

"Not at all. The only thing is, they don't sell it to just any-body. Nobody's ever heard of me. But you! You're Ovide Plouffe, the radio personality, the watch man, the Knights of Columbus man!"

That seemed logical, Ovide thought. It was true, he had a certain celebrity.

"You only have to say it's for a cottage, for blasting stumps and boulders," suggested Pacifique.

Ovide glanced at his watch. He was in such a hurry to leave with Marie on this tour that he was clearing up his minor chores (such as buying fifty sticks of dynamite) with the greatest non-chalance.

"I have a great many details to look after before I leave," he said, "so I'll get it for you right away. If there's any other little thing I can do, tell me now, I'll tidy everything up at once."

"No, that will be all. I'm most obliged," said Pacifique.

Ovide went off briskly, happy to be able to please his partner. Pacifique relit his cigarette, then opened a folder showing a superb 1949 Chevrolet with automatic transmission. The sales-man had assured him that the braking and acceleration controls could be transferred from the floor to the steering column by an expert mechanic. Maybe he'd buy a car like that. Hey! Why not the convertible Rita had sold back to the garage! And why hadn't he thought of it before?

Ovide returned from Samson and Filion's hardware carrying a heavy brown paper bag containing the fifty sticks of dynamite, and, in his right jacket pocket, an envelope with the detonators. Prudently he kept these explosive accomplices at a distance from each other. He walked with slow and ginger steps, as if he were carrying a viaticum. After all, he didn't want to go blowing himself into a thousand pieces just before the trip of a lifetime!

People greeted him as they passed. It was true, he noticed it more and more: he was becoming a celebrity. He smiled with satisfaction. The hardware clerk had raised no objection. More-over, the man was a Liberal who liked his radio pieces and shared his taste in music. Ovide had gone on quite a bit about Alfred Nobel's prize, which had rewarded so many scientists and writers thanks to the invention of dynamite. He hadn't even had to mention Pacifique Berthet. The explosives were for blowing up stumps at a cottage in the mountains. The salesman had merely insisted that elementary measures of caution be observed, and had described at some length how to place the sticks and detonators.

"You're a precious asset to Quebec, Mr. Plouffe. We don't want to lose you!"

"Oh, no," Ovide protested, "don't worry about that."

He was asked to sign a receipt and the dynamite was handed over to him as if it were a hammer or a saw.

Ovide, having laid the bag and envelope on Pacifique's work bench, rubbed his hands, as if he had finished a hard day's work.

"Well, that was fast!" said Berthet, astonished. "They didn't give you any trouble?"

"Just like posting a letter. I said it was for a cottage."

"Did you say it was for me?" said the cripple, with feigned indifference.

"Didn't have to. I said it was for *a* cottage, so I wasn't lying. But please take care of that stuff."

"I know how to handle it, and I have no wish to die. Sleep easy."

"You should have seen the clerk's face when I started talking about the Nobel Prize. Unfortunately the prize didn't exist in Stendhal's day. He'd have been a winner. No, I was in a hurry, so they just had me sign for it and away we go with the loot. I'm going to leave you now before you ask me to go and fetch you an atom bomb."

They both laughed at this far-fetched idea. Ovide went upstairs to his apartment, fearfully, like a guilty man. Since his wife's confession he always looked at her sideways, and if he spoke to her the words came from the corner of his mouth. He noted that Rita was wearing a black convent-school dress and low-heeled patent leather shoes, and that she was tossing all kinds of vegetables together in a double boiler. She turned her head toward him with a pale smile.

"That farewell ceremony for the Monsignor really upset me," she said. "It was so sad! And your mother was disappointed that you weren't there."

"I know. Tonight I'll tell her why."

How she suffered from these merciless, brief exchanges!

"I'm just making you some Chinese food. You like it so much."

He made no reply. But she expected none, as she had decided to accept everything as a punishment.

"Did you notice, this is my convent dress? I want to start my life all over again, as if I'd just got out of convent school. My car's sold, and I don't miss it a bit. Cécile wanted me to go with her to the dance yesterday, but I said no. Did you know Major Bélanger asked your mother to marry him? Isn't that crazy? Cécile was shocked."

"Yes, I know about that," said Ovide, trying not to smile.

"You're being awful hard, Ovide," she complained.

Her voice tugged at his heart strings, and he rushed into his bedroom in order not to show his emotion. He opened the wardrobe where Rita held his clothing hostage (he was still sleeping on the couch). He decided on the summer suit he would pack for the trip, and put his camera in the suitcase so as not to forget it. He'd take lots of pictures of Marie, and if she left he'd at least have them to remember her by. For his visit to the wilds, Guillaume had written that he'd fit him out from head to foot Jupiter River style. Having overcome his agitation, he went back to the kitchen where he caught Rita wiping her eyes. With a certain friendliness in his voice he said:

"Berthet complained that he never sees you in the shop any more. He lives such a boring life. It would be a real act of charity if you went down from time to time. You haven't fallen out with him? Just because you're wearing your convent dress you don't have to act like a shut-in, do you? You worked at the counter for eight months and all of a sudden you won't set foot there. My partner is starting to ask questions, and I'm starting to appreciate his qualities."

Rita's drawn face was contorted by sadness and regret. How stupid she had been to admit her sins to Ovide, and break their marriage up for nothing. Berthet had never talked, showing himself more reliable than she had thought he could be. In a weak, submissive voice she replied:

"I don't know why, Ovide, that man scares me."

"You're wrong," he cut her short. "In your place I'd be afraid of handsome men with hungry eyes. Anyway, I don't give a damn!" he shouted.

There was silence for a moment. Ovide regretted what he had said and how he had said it. He was not made to be cruel. Her face had turned ashen, and she was trying not to cry.

233

"I don't blame you for getting at me any time you can. If you want me to, I'll go and chat with Berthet."

It was hot in the room. Ovide, looking out, realized he had forgotten to take off the storm windows. This damned business was putting him off balance. Behind him Rita got up the courage to say:

"I talked to Cécile. They'll take me back at the factory. I could put the money aside for Arlette. Jeanne would be glad to look after her for me."

Ovide was on the point of protesting, but he held his tongue in time. She was free, after all. What strange turnabouts there were in life. Rita would go back to the factory she never should have left! He suddenly had an acute certainty that they were being much discussed in the family.

"I hope you said nothing at home about what's happening with us."

"I swear I didn't. But they can see there's a change."

He grew as sad and upset as she was.

"Let's not decide right away. Let's both think it over for the next three weeks, while I'm away. We'll see when I get back."

"Oh, you can be sure I'll pray the good Lord you'll start to forgive me."

"What's dead is dead," he mumbled.

She sat down in the rocker and laid a hand over her brimming eyes.

"My, you're hard!"

From Ovide's heart surged the cry: I forgive you, I've already forgiven you! But he choked back the cry. If it had become audible he wouldn't have been able to leave with Marie. Suddenly he felt ashamed, and said:

"Maybe time will patch things up. Try to be brave, like me."

Rita returned to the stove, where she went on preparing the vegetables in the double boiler. As the days slipped by she was able to measure the extent of her disaster. She was made for an easy life and butterfly pleasures, but she saw her horizon growing ever darker.

29

Guillaume and Ti'-Mé, on Anticosti Island, were enjoying a quieter life. It was only the first of June, and the tourists were not yet out in force. But already a few salmon had begun to go up the Jupiter toward their freshwater spawning grounds. During the first days of the cousins' early appearance on the Island they had joined the head guides repairing trucks and canoes and clearing out the forest roads, replacing culverts washed out by the spring floods. But these chores didn't take long. The employees of the fishing camp had their best times while they were waiting for the customers to arrive. They played cards, made slippers, handbags, dagger sheaths, wallets, all of fine deerskin, and then took them a hundred kilometres west, to the general store in Port Menier, the place where the sporting gentry arrived from outside. These sport fishermen, transported by truck over a narrow, washboard dirt road that skirted lakes, marshes and *raspoutitsas*,* arrived dog tired at Camp Number Twelve right on the banks of the Jupiter. On every trip the trucks, rounding the curves, ran down two or three deer that had crossed the road in panic. These casualties were not even brought back to the cook: they were tossed into the forest where they were soon devoured.

Guillaume and Ti'-Mé had not wasted their time doing crafts or playing cards. They would disappear for days at a time, their sleeping bags on their backs, pretending they wanted to explore good hunting areas for the fall, or discover new rivers – trout streams, no less – where they could take the tourists for a picnic encounter with the speckled beauties. This would give them a rest from the eight- and ten-kilo salmon that put up such a fierce fight they gave you lumbago for the rest of the day. They were allowed to leave without too many questions asked. After an absence of four or five days they would come back with fifty or so lobsters, some of them weighing five pounds. They were

---

* Russian word for pot-holed, thawing road with glutinous mud. Adopted into the French language in 1925.

quizzed as to what corner of the seashore had yielded up this treasure, but they always replied: "Just eat them. We can say no more."

In fact they had devoted their time during these absences to building their cabin, of spruce logs hastily stripped of their bark, located one kilometre from the Jupiter and two hundred metres from the sea. Splashing around in the puddles of slush from slow-melting snow, they had been busy as bees for the last three weeks. Up at dawn, smeared with spruce gum, they would crouch by their wood fire, eating enormous breakfasts of eggs, pork-and-beans and bacon and smelling the absolute, authentic and voluptuous odour of coffee in the Island's pure air. They were very proud of this monument to happiness they were building, eight by six metres, and admired it as they listened to the morning's concert, orchestrated from the chirping of insects, the song of birds and the roar of the sea nearby. Then they would plan their day's work in monosyllables, rise to their feet like sated giants and go lift the tarpaulin from the truck where they had hidden axes, cross-cut saws, sundry tools, tow, putty, nails and all sorts of odds and ends. A friend of theirs, captain of a coaster vessel, brought it all in by boat, after anchoring his ship in deep water. This sea route for deliveries was used only by initiates. Port Menier was for greenhorns. In return the seaman had the right to deer and salmon. Poachers often get more enjoyment than others from the good things of the forest.

That day Guillaume and Ti'-Mé stood with arms akimbo admiring their masterpiece.

"I can't believe it! It's our cabin! And we built it ourselves," said Guillaume softly. "It's the nicest one I ever saw."

Ti'-Mé tried to say something grand:

"You know, Guillaume, it's just like it was my baby, that cabin."

They grinned blissfully, astonished at their own good fortune: a paradise surrounded by trees, fresh and salt water, fish and game; and to top it all off, they had only to walk down to the sea, a stone's throw away, to get to the little cove inexhaustably stocked with lobster. Up to their knees in water, they had fun driving the crustaceans from their cover beneath the rocks and catching them in a net. Happier than millionaires, they were sure they had found here a kind of total security. No one could spot their refuge from a passing ship, because it was built in a hollow and surrounded by ferns and spruce and birch. This location also protected them from the terrible winter gales as well, blowing from all corners of the earth.

"Hear them buggers cry, would you!" said Ti'-Mé, cocking an ear.

Above the muffled roar of the Gulf waves you could hear the barking and yelping of a herd of five thousand seals that had gathered on the shore of the Island three kilometres farther north. But the ears of our two chums had grown used to this cacophony. It was another sound they had picked up: the howl of a ship's horn.

"It's our coaster!" shouted Guillaume. "Our furniture, Ti'-Mé!"

They ran inside their empty cabin. Guillaume was the planner:

"Don't forget, Ti'-Mé, the stove goes here, the sink goes in the corner, the table here, the bunk beds there, the rockers and chairs in the middle, the firewood gets piled to the ceiling, there'll be oil lamps, we'll fill the cellar with fish and dried meat and potatoes and flour and butter and caribou and nuts and acorns and a barrel of salt pork and pork and beans to boot! Yahooo!"

"Are we goin' to risk the winter up here, cousin?"

"Might be a bit long, eh?"

"Yeah. What we'll miss up here is the women."

Guillaume grew severe:

"Forget about the women. It's not even summer yet and we're stuck here for three months. And right now we have to unload that furniture."

They ran to the shore and waved a frantic welcome to the approaching boat piled high with goods. The captain replied in kind. Guillaume was jubilant:

"I can hardly wait for Ovide to see our cabin, Ti'-Mé! Jeesus!"

"Yeah, it's goin' to do him good," said the other, laughing. "He's green as grass. But wait till he sees our mystery guest. That'll be a laugh, eh, Guillaume?"

It was the same captain and the same coaster that were to bring Ovide and Marie a few days later.

Ovide had started out on his trip accompanied by his superb secretary. Marie, uneasy at first, had quickly recovered her calm good humour, thanks to her companion's deference and friendly

237

tenderness. This trip, punctuated by the unexpected, by detours and stopovers in Quebec's north country, seemed to her like the most fascinating voyage in the world. At last she was getting an inkling of this Canada, about whose grandeur and wonders she had been told so much. For months she had lived a mole's life in a night club, up until the small hours of the morning serving customers the worse for wear. Then she'd sleep till noon. She had wandered around the city a lot and strolled over the Plains of Abraham. She had even ventured, one Sunday, to take the ferry to Lévis. And here she was discovering the fabulous Baie St-Paul, Les Eboulements, Petite Rivière Saint-François, Saint-Irénée, La Malbaie, the Saguenay. She felt at the same time small and exultant in this rough land of mountains, lakes, rivers and sea, a land for fishermen and hunters, made for giants, but inhabited by warm-hearted people clustered around their churches, living off its forests, its fishing boats and nets. A population transplanted out of seventeenth-century France that had managed to adapt to this immense wilderness, this peninsula that was the province of Quebec, the "head" of North America that looks toward the Gulf, Newfoundland, the Atlantic and – Europe!

On the deck of the coaster that was carrying them toward the mouth of the Jupiter, where Guillaume and Ti'-Mé were to meet them with a rowboat, the couple, arm in arm at the stern of the boat, turned their faces toward the spray and grew brown in the June sunlight. Marie was smiling with a happiness that knew no clouds. The wonder of the days she had lived through floated through her memory like an unforgettable film.

But what fun it had been, all those lunches with the jewellery salesmen, whom they had met one by one in the various centres. The guest, sizing her up, would make admiring grimaces and wink at Ovide, as if to say: "Not a bad little bird you've got there, boss." But Ovide would quickly put the indiscreet ones in their place, with a brutal frankness that left no room for doubt. Marie was delighted that her presence sold watches: the sales gents, asking for bigger consignments, tried to make themselves look more important to her. What a fascinating job! And what a friendly population! All these people, men and women alike, made her think of the country folk of France, with their acumen in business, their harsh, singsong speech.

She smiled under the fine spray, recalling the delicacy with which Ovide had, in every inn they stayed at, seen her to the door of her room. He always left her quickly, without ever allowing her to feel his desire to be invited in.

She remembered the "hop" at the Ile-aux-Coudres, where they had danced with the villagers to the jigging rhythm of frenzied fiddles. She re-lived their long walks on the shore of the Escoumains, where Ovide had discovered some agates. He had promised to have them made into earrings and a ring for her. Some day she would go back to France with these talismans, which would remind her of a Canadian called Ovide, now lonely again, and sad.

She would never forget that rural excursion that had "just happened" near Hauterive. They had spread a checkered cloth on the ground, and Ovide, with a magician's grandiloquent gestures, had produced from a wicker basket a supply of red wine, cheese, cold cuts and home-made bread still hot from the oven. They had laughed, they'd had their picture taken by a young Nimrod passing by who snapped them with Ovide's camera. She must have posed a hundred times for Ovide during the trip. Excited by the red wine, they had run through the fields picking flowers. He had woven her a tiara of daisies, sticking their stems through the links of a golden chain, and had crowned her with it. She looked like an Indian princess with the little golden pendant hanging on her forehead. Then they came to a stream teeming with trout and waded barefoot in it. When they returned to their picnic they opened a second bottle of red wine, and he softly sang the first verse of Baudelaire's "L'Invitation au voyage": "My sister, my child, dream with me the wild, sweet beauty we'll find in that far land. . . ." Marie remembered that her caressing fingers had pushed back Ovide's unruly locks. He had taken her hand and covered it with burning kisses. And then they had gone to sleep in the sun, remaining as chaste as Paul and Virginie in the famous novel. They had the feeling that day of spending the sweetest hours of their whole lives.

Ovide was still in the midst of this ethereal, idyllic adventure, as yet untroubled by any thought of Rita. Yet his romantic nirvana was beginning to wear a little thin. Standing on the tacky deck, frowning, he watched Anticosti Island loom up in the distance. He clenched his fists and made a face. He had forgotten to visit Monsignor Folbèche in his new parish! And he had promised his mother he would. He could not admit to himself that his flight from reality was about to end. But the bliss he had experienced was fading slowly, as his impossible situation grew clearer in his mind. Perhaps Marie had been so kind to him only to cure the hurt of his conjugal misfortune! And what was Guillaume going to say when he saw Marie? Ovide banished these inconvenient thoughts and clung to his illusions, which were, however, already on their way out the door.

"Is something wrong?" she asked, gently squeezing his arm.

"On the contrary, Marie, it seems everything is going as I wanted. Even the Asbestos strike is almost settled. It's a union victory, just as I had been preaching. We must never betray our deepest convictions, nor those we love."

He couldn't help thinking of Rita's tear-filled eyes as he was leaving.

"I know you'll never betray me, anyway," murmured Marie, her dreamy eyes gazing far across the water, toward Europe, as she thought of her mother, lovely France, the plane trees and the chestnut trees in bloom.

He winced with fear. She wasn't saying so, but he was sure she dreamed of going home to Europe soon. Quebec and Canada were not made for her. She would never adapt to them. But in defiance of this intolerable notion he started spinning fantasies:

"Now that we've made such a success out of this trip to the shores and forests of Quebec, we could try the same thing in France! Why not?"

She looked up at him, beaming. Ovide the magician. The man was ready to undertake anything!

"Why not?" he repeated. "It's logical. We have to look up the sources of watch-making: Switzerland and France! I simply must keep on top of the latest developments in the industry so that I can plan for them. Without you, Marie, I could never do all that."

His optimism was contagious. She began to dream aloud.

"Oh, I'd love to take you through Paris, the Paris I love . . . in spite of everything I suffered there. . . . But perhaps it would be better not to. . . . Maybe you'd never want to go home after that!"

"So what! We'll stay there! We'll wander up the Champs-Elysées, hand in hand. At last I'll see the Paris Opera. And we'll listen to the great organ of Notre Dame at the Sunday mass. And then go across to the Boulevard Saint-Germain, stop at the Brasserie Lipp, across from the Café de Flore, where Jean-Paul Sartre and Simone de Beauvoir hold court, near the church of Saint-Germain-des-Prés, with its little park and the bust of Apollinaire by Picasso!"

"My goodness! Anyone would think you'd been there already!" she exclaimed, astonished.

He was going into raptures.

"I've spent my life reading and dreaming of the City of Lights. I know its history, its topography and all the principal monuments. At my finger tips!"

They talked for a long time about Paris, the symbol of paradise for escapists, poetry lovers and those in search of culture and beauty. But the sea was getting rough and they had to break off their conversation to grip the railing. They were in the open Gulf waters. How were Guillaume and Ti'-Mé going to handle their frail rowboat in these high seas? A tiny helicopter flew overhead toward the Island. Ovide reflected that it would have been a more enjoyable vehicle than the coaster. They were sailing parallel to the Anticosti coast now. Gulls circled the ship, and Marie was fascinated by the rough shore eroded by the sea, where fierce looters had once lurked on the lookout for wrecks. How many ships had been lost off Anticosti!

An hour later the Captain tapped Ovide on the shoulder.

"Get your things ready, we're getting near the mouth of the Jupiter! In case Guillaume stays ashore, tell him I'll pick you up in three days' time, at four in the afternoon. And I'll be bringing his four propane lamps and the little gas bottle. Woops! Never mind! Here they come. Look! I can tell them myself."

Ovide's eye was not sharp enough to pick out the two long figures waving from the beach, then jumping into a boat, which they rowed swiftly into the waves.

What a faithful accomplice and ally the Plouffe cousins had in that old sea-dog! He shared their secret about the hidden cabin, and in return went poaching with them when his ship left him free time for a stop. He had picked up Marie and Ovide in Sept-Iles, weary from their bus travel through the most isolated spots. He had wondered about the couple, but this blue-eyed, white-whiskered captain, who only took off his cap to go to bed, asked no questions. He bore a strange name: Louis-Quinze Ferguson. He was the descendant of a Scottish soldier who had taken part in the British conquest, acquired roots and a wife in Quebec and adorned his eldest son with the name

241

Louis-Quinze. Thus the Fergusons marked their entry into a French Quebec through the front door. Louis-Quinze the ship's captain, tenth in the Ferguson dynasty, accustomed to solitude and discretion, didn't even ask Ovide by what happy chance the brother of Guillaume Plouffe the trapper happened to be travelling with such a pretty Parisian secretary. When the two passengers embarked they had left their bags in the pilot's cabin and stood dreaming for hours at the coaster's stern. Guillaume hadn't said his brother would have anyone with him.

Ovide and Marie, their suitcases at their feet, watched anxiously as the two cousins rowed closer to the ship. The captain had anchored and was lowering a rope ladder.

"Hi, Louis-Quinze! Did you bring our lamps? Hi Ovide!" shouted Guillaume.

"No! Next trip," cried the captain, shouting between his hands, as Ovide said proudly to Marie:

"That's my brother Guillaume and our cousin Aimé. Aimé's quite a guy, you'll see. And I think you met Guillaume last winter at Chez Gérard, didn't you say? Oh, we're going to have three marvellous days here. A royal feast, with Louis-Quinze to bring us here!"

The rowboat waltzed on the waves, and Guillaume turned to Ti'-Mé:

"Good God! Don't tell me Ovide's brought Rita?"

"No," said Ti'-Mé, who had eyes like binoculars. "It's not Rita. Rita's a blonde and this one's dark. Rita's taller, too. Guillaume, get ready for this one, she's a knock-out. If my eyes don't lie, she may be the prettiest critter ever seen up here. A little super-deluxe squirrely, hey!"

"What the heck's going on?" mumbled Guillaume, who had recognized Marie. "God, that guy Ovide! You never know what he's up to."

"Do you know her?" asked Ti'-Mé.

"Yep. Come on, Ti'-Mé, one last heave. Row your heart out and we'll see what's up."

They rowed like madmen, with gigantic grunts, and managed to come alongside the coaster. Marie looked so clumsy as she came down the ladder that Guillaume caught her by the waist and set her gently on the centre seat.

"Hello, Marie!"

Ovide followed the baggage into the boat and shouted:

"Ho, you lubbers! Steady as you go for Plouffe Island!"

The two partners tossed three smoked salmon up to the captain, hoisted up a cardboard box of lobster with a list of necessities for the cabin, then received in their turn a bottle of rum from Louis-Quinze, who shouted:

"Good day, then! Don't stoke your stove too full, you can see the smoke. You can drink that good Barbancourt rum to my health. Have fun. I'll be back in three days. Between four and five o'clock. Be sure you're ready!"

The coaster, its anchor raised, made off into the gulf. Ti'-Mé and Guillaume laid to with the heavy oars.

"How about a knock-down to your relative," said Ti'-Mé to Ovide, his eyes stripping Marie to the bone.

What knees, what legs, what breasts, what lovely hair, eyes, lips – what a charming little squirrely! But Marie, for her part, was contemplating Guillaume. How handsome he was! Even handsomer than she remembered him at Chez Gérard when he'd been there with Napoléon and Jeanne. Guillaume, spellbound, captivated, was rowing like a robot. The furies were tearing at all his senses. He was so young, so strong, and deprived of women for so long!

"Marie," he said, caressing as only Guillaume Plouffe could be, "you're lovelier than ever."

"You're handsome, too, Guillaume," she answered, blushing.

First names? Ovide was astonished. Did these two know each other better than they let on? Marie, of course, was extraordinary. A true European, a unique beauty, a miracle of the old civilizations. Guillaume was forgetting his boat, the sea, the cabin. . . . Ovide grumbled:

"God, I'll be glad to get on land!"

Salt water slapped against their tiny bark, spraying their faces and soaking their clothes, which made Ti'-Mé laugh, and provided a cover for his amusement at something going on between Marie and Guillaume. Ovide was pale and stiff, gripping the board seat with both hands. He felt a wave of nausea. Was he going to be seasick now, after being spared on the coaster?

Ti'-Mé fumbled in his pocket and took out a handful of leaves, which he handed to Marie.

"Chew some sorrel. It's good for the scares and the upset stomach."

"Oh, with you two I'm not scared," she interrupted gaily.

She had been sailing so often as a girl, when her mother took her aboard the yacht of one of her rich lovers, in the port, at Cannes.

"Marie!" shouted the cousin, "my name's Ti'-Mé Plouffe. What's yours?"

She shouted back in the same friendly way, against the sound of the waves and wind:

"I'm Marie Jourdan. I think you're nice, Ti'-Mé!"

Ovide started again at the first-name intimacy. Ti'-Mé too?

Ti'-Mé put his back into his rowing. Despite the roar of the sea the two trappers began to exchange fraternal exclamations with Marie that were rich in friendship and camaraderie, but which also managed to establish some romantic complicity. A tiny thorn of jealousy pricked Ovide's heart. Between Marie and himself there had been an ethereal relationship, politely distant as became this Eden inaccessible to ordinary folk. Now, suddenly, she was deserting him, descending with obvious joy and relief to the warm and rustic simplicity of the two woodsmen. He thought, wearily, that he would never achieve the common tone of this direct and contagious communication that came so easily to Guillaume and Ti'-Mé. For that matter, he understood, albeit unwillingly, that Marie might well be attracted by his brother, the magnificent male. He was at the same time proud and put out at the fact. But he banished these preposterous ideas. They were nearing land. He took Marie's hand to help her leap to the beach littered with driftwood and seaweed. The two guides hauled their boat out of the water and pulled it up on the shingle to tie it to a tree. Guillaume and Ti'-Mé stood there with the luggage, timid now, as if *terra firma* had changed them somehow.

"Miss Marie Jourdan is my secretary, and only that," said Ovide seriously. "I'll explain to you later, little brother! But there's no mystery about it. Marie, this is my cousin, Ti'-Mé, the greatest hunter in all Quebec."

Aimé lifted his hat and bowed.

"In person, at your service. And I'll tell you something, little Marie. If my father, old Gédéon, could see you, his eyes would look two ways at once!"

He held out his arms to lift her up.

"Come, I'll carry you to the cabin. Mustn't hurt your pretty little feet on the rocks and sticks."

"Take it easy, Ti'-Mé," Guillaume broke in. He had caught Ovide's angry glance. "Let's go, forward march!"

Three minutes later they emerged before a tangle of giant

244

ferns, which Guillaume held open with his long arms. They stood looking down at the cousins' precious lair, its varnished logs shining in the sunlight.

"There's our cabin!" cried Ti'-Mé, fishing for compliments.

"Superb!" murmured Ovide, and, humming a line from Mignon's song: "'. . . there would I live forever!'"

Marie clapped her hands.

"My Canadian cabin! You're wonderful, both of you! Oh, congratulations."

"Come on," said Guillaume, leading the way. "It's not a luxury hotel, not very big but it's neat and tidy."

Ti'-Mé cut ahead to open the door and bowed ceremoniously, holding his felt hat to his stomach. An odour of roasting meat, with a touch of resin, filled the room. A leg of venison was sizzling in its own juice in the oven of the iron stove. The table was set, and a bottle of red wine stood ready. "How happy you must be here!" murmured Marie, almost moved to tears. At the same moment, Ovide was thinking how wonderful it would be to live there, far from the world, with her. He flushed darkly. But there was Rita, along with Arlette and all the other bonds that tied him to family and society.

"You know, Ovide," said Guillaume gravely, "this cabin is our insurance. Just in case, you never know. We're sure to be protected here. Atom bomb? The cabin. Unemployment? The cabin. Unlucky in love? The cabin. The army trying to call you up? The cabin."

Ti'-Mé lifted a pompous finger:

"The police on your heels? The cabin! The cellar's stocked to the ceiling. You could hold out here for months. And she'll take more than two!" he said, with an elaborate wink as he turned his head to the right and pointed his resin-blackened index finger at the two double bunks.

"You mean we're going to sleep here?" Ovide asked.

"Sure," said Ti'-Mé, gently mocking. "You two won't mind a little privacy, will you? The two of us, we go up to the camp after supper. We leave our guests in peace."

He added:

"We're not party-poopers, eh?"

Ovide, embarrassed, turned to Marie:

"Is that all right with you?"

"What's the harm in it?" she cried gaily. "You know I trust you, Ovide."

Suddenly a strident fanfare sounded. A trap door opened in

245

the floor and Napoléon emerged, his trumpet to his lips. He wiped off the mouthpiece, observing the flabbergasted expressions of Marie and Ovide.

"Greetings, kiddies!" shouted the apparition.

"Don't tell me!" gasped Ovide.

"Yeah! We had him flown in by helicopter to give you a surprise. So we'd have the three Plouffe brothers together on Anticosti, in our cabin!" Guillaume was exultant.

"Am I dreaming this?" murmured Marie.

"Hi there, pretty Marie! I couldn't believe it when I heard your voice, when I was down cellar, there. Talk about surprises, that's a real one!"

Ovide gave a little cough.

"I'll explain everything, just among the family, after supper, Napoléon. Marie's acting as my secretary for a month."

Marie apologized:

"Oh, this is too bad! I'm afraid I'm butting into a nice family reunion!"

She was embarrassed by Napoléon's gaze, switching from her to Ovide and seeming to say, "Does Rita know about this?" But Napoléon was a good sport and realized he musn't ask that question before the girl. He gave her his toothiest smile:

"Marie with the gang of us! That's even better! What a beautiful life!"

Ovide was thinking, what's the use of running away? The family always beat him to his destination.

"Cost me a fortune, this trip," said Napoléon. "I flew to Sept-Iles and took the helicopter here. Here's to life! The bank can never seize the trips we take!"

Guillaume didn't like dramatics and endless palaver. A woodsman, used to quick decisions, he insisted that everyone sit down at the table. Marie offered to watch the roast, but Guillaume protested that she was their guest. He was the commander-in-chief. Ti'-Mé was looking after the stove, stoking it with logs, while Guillaume served the pea soup. Ovide poured the wine and Napoléon set the table. A kind of childish gaiety set in as the aroma of the roast grew stronger. Napoléon and Guillaume stole many a glance at Marie and Ovide in turn, wondering how badly things were really going between their brother and Rita. For Marie this unusual picnic was one of the high points of her life. Obviously Ovide's family was not aware of his tragedy. That bothered her at times, but the cordial atmosphere and her own youth soon dispelled her embarrassment. It took nothing at all to make her laugh, she thought Ti'-Mé was just a scream, and, in the innocent delight of her convent girl's heart, seemed unaware of the desires she ignited in the stares of these surrounding males. It was Guillaume, though, who captured most of her enchanted attention. Ovide picked at his food, unable to join in the mood of common festivity. He realized that his exceptional idyll with Marie was coming to an end with this meal, where they were somehow celebrating Rita's victory. At dessert Guillaume announced the plan of action for their three-day vacation:

"Listen! Beddy-bye at nine tonight! And everybody up at five in the morning! Salmon fishing in the best pools, we'll get the first crack of the season at them. Then we'll have lunch, as civilized people call it," he smiled tenderly at Marie, "on a young salmon, beside the Jupiter, at noon on the dot. At two o'clock we go to the lobster inlet and catch ourselves a score of them. And have a supper fit for a king! Tomorrow it's a big holiday for the Anticosti guides. No tourists tomorrow. Everybody's busy getting ready for the Governor General and his guests from London. They're arriving by sea tomorrow in a navy corvette, and then they'll haul them upriver in a big wagon called Cleopatra, drawn by three teams of horses. They're taking them up to Camp Number Twelve, just like in Henri Menier's time. That's really a sight. And Ovide, no trying to sell watches to the guides. For one thing, you're on holiday, and for another, we don't want our hide-out discovered. We're poachers, we're poaching a little happiness from life and from Anticosti. We're free men!" cried Guillaume.

"Free men and poachers!" shouted Napoléon and Ti'-Mé even louder, excited by the red wine.

"Hey, Ti'-Mé! Easy on the wine, eh? And no rum! Yeah. We've got fishing gear and clothes for everybody. Ti'-Mé is goin' to act as guide for Ovide and Napoléon, and I'll look after Marie," he said, smiling at her. "Beautiful, Guillaume Plouffe is about to show you how to catch your first Canadian salmon!"

After coffee, Napoléon suddenly stood up, and with a wink to Ti'-Mé said to Marie:

"You're one of the gang now, my girl. That means you get to wash the dishes. With Ti'-Mé. Us three brothers, we've got family problems to talk over. We're going down to the shore

247

and light a little bonfire where we can sit around like the Indians."

Ti'-Mé's mouth made a capital O, and he took Marie by the hands:

"Little French squirrely! Your hands are too nice for dishwashing. I'll wash, you dry. I won't hurt you. But maybe I could give you a kiss while they're gone, eh?"

She gave him a friendly shove. She had adopted him as the big brother she never had. With Ovide it was different. And as for Guillaume, that was very different. Ovide was vexed and reluctant as he followed his brothers outside. He was bracing himself to resist them, not to reveal his secret, to protect the honour of his household and Rita's reputation. On the shore Guillaume and Napoléon were laying the fire. Silence reigned until the first sparks died down. Then the flame rose. Anticosti nights are cold. Ovide, shivering, chewed nervously on a salty blade of grass.

Napoléon was the first to speak:

"I can't get over it," he said. "A family as close as ours is, and three brothers brought up together and thick as the fingers on my hand, and we don't tell each other any more than this about our problems."

"Yeah," said Guillaume. "You know, Ovide, I think this business with Marie, it doesn't smell so good."

The distant seals kept up their racket. Ovide bit his lip:

"Marie lost her job at Chez Gérard and it was my fault. You know, Napoléon. She was desperate, alone, broke, or almost. All I did was take her on as secretary for a few weeks. So she gets a few dollars ahead to tide her over."

"But she must have family in France?" Guillaume objected.

Ovide looked sad:

"She was practically hounded out of her own country. Her mother was an actress. During the Liberation the Resistance people shaved her head and executed her."

"Well!" said Guillaume.

The story upset him. He had tried to forget his visions of the war. In 1944 he had witnessed revolting scenes in which pretty girls who had had German friends were dragged by the hair before joking or vociferating crowds, then to have their heads shaved in public. He remembered how the captor in one case had waved the cut hair in the air like a scalp.

"A collaborator, eh?" said Guillaume, frowning.

"Not Marie, her mother," Napoléon reminded him. "It's not the kid's fault her mother was like that."

Guillaume was lost in thought. Suddenly:

"Napoléon told me about the ruckus in the restaurant. And the revolver. Was it the same one I gave you when you opened the store?"

Ovide nodded. Guillaume had a strange sensation. This was the gun he had used to kill the German girl, the whore who looked like Rita. Was fate going to see the weapon used again? And against whom this time? What a crazy idea! He shivered and roused himself from his daydream:

"And Rita doesn't know Marie is on this trip with you?"

Ovide shook his head. Napoléon, feeling his distress, came to his aid.

"Just as well she don't," he said. "Rita's awful jealous. And Jeanne and Cécile find she's pale these days. Won't go out, dresses like a nun. She's just not herself lately, that wife of yours."

Silence fell among the three of them again, as if acknowledging defeat by the din from those five thousand seals who filled the night with their cries. Guillaume seized Ovide's arm in an iron grip.

"Yes or no: are you in love with Marie?"

Ovide lost his patience.

"Come on! What do you guys think you are? Detectives? The answer is no. I'm not. In love."

Napoléon was contorting his face in signals to Guillaume: "Don't push him too far!" But Guillaume was launched. He shook Ovide like a rag doll.

"Talk, will you? We're your brothers, we know you, we love you and we won't let you down. Talk, it'll do you good. Talk, will you?"

For a second Ovide was on the point of telling them his whole tale, crying on their shoulders, how he had been two-timed, how he was suffering. But he revolted at the thought that his brothers were taking advantage of his distress to pierce the protective armour of his inner world where not even his family was admitted.

"Will you guys let me alone? What is this? Mind your business, will you?"

He walked with a rapid stride toward the camp, repressing a sob. Guillaume slowly got to his feet.

"We've got to do something, Napoléon. Marie doesn't love him, and he doesn't love Marie. He says! In any case, I'm worried. The whole thing just doesn't seem right, it's heading for trouble. We have to protect the two of them."

"And I thought we were here for a treat, to fish some salmon!" Guillaume almost smiled.

"We will, don't worry. But it's right now that we have to look after Ovide. I don't like that business with the revolver, and Rita wearing a black dress and never leaving the house. I just don't know our brother any more, Napoléon. He scares me."

Napoléon, growing worried too, added:

"Yeah, he's not the same Ovide. And my Jeanne is wondering about a lot of things."

Guillaume slapped him on the shoulder:

"Don't worry. Go to bed now. Ti'-Mé and me's got twelve miles to paddle yet."

They took a long leak on the fire, which was thus extinguished, and walked back toward the hut. Guillaume was thinking aloud:

"The Plouffes, you know, it's like a chain. Every link counts. If one breaks the whole chain goes to hell. And that's the end of a great family, our family, the Plouffes!"

Napoléon was easily moved.

"No use talkin', Guillaume, you're a real man now. I guess the war makes a fellow older."

"Ovide, there, we've got to do an operation on him," said Guillaume with a wry smile.

30

As Ovide came back to the cabin, Ti'-Mé was putting away the last plates, while Marie, who had put on her dressing gown (she had made Ti'-Mé swear he wouldn't peek), was making her bed. It was only nine o'clock, but the pure air, the voyage on the coaster and the heavy meal had made her irresistibly drowsy. She slipped between the covers.

"Good night, gentlemen!"

"Don't bang the pots around too much, Ti'-Mé. I'm for bed myself."

He disappeared outside and came back in pyjamas. Shivering, he saw that Marie was already asleep and that Ti'-Mé, standing at the foot of her bunk, was contemplating her with tender admiration.

"It does a guy good to see a beautiful girl like that in our cabin. If she wanted to work in the main camp for the summer she'd make a fortune in tips. I'd protect her and they'd treat her like a queen."

Ovide pouted. He hated tips. Rita had made him a cuckold for fifty-dollar tips. And now Ti'-Mé dared to mention tips in connection with this "pure and radiant angel"! It was his turn to slip between the covers, in the bunk that was no more than a metre away from where Marie was sleeping.

"Don't even suggest it to her, Ti'-Mé. She's made for better things. Turn down the lantern, will you? It hurts my eyes."

Napoléon and Guillaume came in and glanced around.

"That's good, everybody have a good sleep now. We'll be here at a quarter to five tomorrow. Come on, Ti'-Mé, let's go. The canoe's waiting."

Guillaume, with a burning glance at the sleeping girl, again smiled his almost imperceptible smile. Ti'-Mé blew her a kiss, was pushed outside by Guillaume, and the two disappeared. Napoléon stoked the fire with dry wood, frost was expected that night. Then he looked at the upper bunk above Ovide's. Slowly, reflectively, he undressed. He was a sound sleeper. Could it be that things might happen during the night without his hearing? A woman half-awake has so little resistance! And Ovide was impulsive. He shook his brother.

"Come on, get in the top bunk. I've got to get up and stoke the fire a few times. If I don't Marie's going to freeze."

Ovide knew exactly what his brother was thinking, and it shocked him. But what was the use? He got up, grumbling, and climbed up top. Napoléon went to sleep at once and his noisy snoring filled the cabin. Ovide, preoccupied by the conversation with his two brothers, was slow in dropping off again. Then he succumbed to the heat of the cabin and slept, just as Marie, too warm under her heavy blankets, shoved them off with her foot, revealing her long, full thighs with their graceful lines. Napoléon, choking on an unusually violent snore, woke

251

with a start and saw them. He was possessed by a ferocious desire to touch them, just with a finger tip. He took a deep breath, thinking of Jeanne, whom he mostly caressed in daytime – at night she was too tired – and then, gritting his teeth, he turned on his side with his back to Marie, his body curled tight and tense, his fists clenched like a boxer's. Two hours later the fire was out and he awoke shivering. With tender respect he tucked Marie in her covers, and re-lit the fire. As he waited for the flames to rise he thought again of Guillaume's strange smile as he promised to operate on the very quick of this abscess called Ovide-Marie.

The early morning sun was just beginning to warm the breeze that was making thousands of delicate white caps on the crystalline surface of the Jupiter River. Ti'-Mé, on the bank, arms akimbo and hat pulled down over his eyes, was guiding Ovide and Napoléon through their hesitant first steps toward catching their first *salmo salar*. Their casts were clumsy, especially Ovide's, but they were going to get their fish: ten metres away, just in front of them, Ti'-Mé had spotted a group of a dozen or so. He was able to point out to them the very place.

Ovide was fussing and trying to cast elegantly, but got no farther than two or three metres, and the hook kept catching in his hat or in his red wool windbreaker. The fishermen, wearing rubber hip waders, went over their knees in icy water trying to reach the pool, which lay in front of a limestone cliff thirty feet high. The Jupiter is famous as one of the easiest salmon rivers in the world, because one can not only travel it by canoe or truck or on horseback, one can walk its length on the pebbled bottom, and make long casts without fear of entanglements behind.

A hundred metres upstream Guillaume, at Marie's side, tirelessly tried to guide her wrist so that she would be the first of the guests to make a catch.

"There, on the left, there's twenty of them!" he said.

She was all tense and already enthusiastic about this extraordinary sport. In the distance they heard Napoléon shout:

"Got a bite!"

It seemed as if the scratches left by these little artificial dry flies were waking the water of the river. A six-kilo salmon had just slapped Napoléon's line with his tail and made off. Another one jumped near Ovide's line, as if to taunt him. Silvery backs fluted the water.

"We're goin' to catch a bunch today!" exulted Ti'-Mé.

Guillaume put one arm around Marie's waist, brushed her neck with his lips and again grasped her wrist for a cast. An eight-kilo *salmo salar* broke out of the water and dove straight at the fly Guillaume had chosen.

"Oh, my God! I've got him!" she cried.

"Yes, my lovely, you've got him. Give him a good jerk, like this!"

She exclaimed, with a sweet, childish pout:

"Oh, no! I've lost him!"

"Not a bit of it, he's playing dead. The fight's just starting. Quick, turn the reel this way, see? And keep your line tight by reeling in slowly. When he jumps, give it some play. If you don't he'll rip out the hook."

Just then the splendid creature leapt three metres out of the water, twisting head, body and tail in such a rage you could imagine him scolding. Guillaume listened with delight to the happy little laugh that cooed in Marie's throat, and he thought she would be a matchless lover. The two other fishermen, feverish and nervous, cast erratically, trying to imitate Marie. They glanced continually from Marie's fish and its frantic leaps to their own flies drifting with the current at the foot of the high rock. Ovide was the next to have his reward, then Napoléon. Now there were three salmon leaping in a prodigious ballet, and the lines pulled taut, then relaxed, grew taut again, the fishing rods bent almost double as Guillaume and Ti'-Mé kept a watchful eye on the scene, landing net at the ready, waiting for the *salmo salar* to grow weary after twenty minutes of epic struggle, to be drawn toward the shore and fall into their nets. Then they would kill the salmon with a rock energetically applied to its head. For the group these were such intensely thrilling moments that they no longer thought of love or fate, for man's strongest instincts are those of the hunter and fisherman.

By eight o'clock in the morning they counted a catch of fifteen. The guests realized they were exhausted: their arms were numb from the struggles and their stomach muscles were hurting from the pressure of the rod. The picnic beside the river was quickly organized around a fireplace of round stones laid one on the other. Ovide, humming softly, poured some Pouilly-Fuissé (a gift from the blonde American girl to Guillaume) into the belly of the two-kilo young salmon they were about to grill in foil. Marie squeezed some lemon juice on it, Ti'-Mé added a few rashers of bacon, and Napoléon brought up the rear with his chopped onions. Water for tea was boiling in a blackened saucepan, and while the fish was roasting, the happy companions, squatting like Indians, drank their soup straight from the can. Ovide, bubbling over with joy, uncorked another bottle. "Bless, O Lord, this food to our use and us to Thy service. . . ." Full glasses were raised and Ovide declared, raising his the highest:

"To the Jupiter, to Canada, to France!"

"To Marie!" joined in the others.

Then they set to and consumed great servings of the parr that only an hour before had been alive in the river, and now, seasoned by experts, was giving off an extraordinary aroma. They all swore that no one on earth could really deserve the delights it offered to the palate. And all agreed to dream of living forever on Anticosti; and Marie, accepted and desired by the four men, declared in the heat of the wine:

"With lovely men like you I could live here my whole life, as long as there was no other woman!"

"What would we do with another one?" they protested.

"For that you all get a kiss!"

Warm-hearted, sweet, holding their heads, she kissed them one after the other on both cheeks. Ovide, to his surprise, wasn't jealous. Why shouldn't such a jewel of a woman have a harem of men? The tranquil joy he felt was so much more restful than the pangs of jealousy! He raised his glass in a daring toast:

"To Marie's male harem! And I get to choose her choicest days!"

"What? Me with a male harem?" she said, laughing heartily. "Ovide, I didn't think you were so broad-minded!"

Ti'-Mé declared with comic gravity:

"I'll settle for her worst days. And I'll guarantee to make them better."

Napoléon, bemused, said:

"I don't think my Jeanne would go for that."

Guillaume said nothing, but glanced at his older brother. Marie had conquered their hearts. She was their sister, their friend, perhaps their mistress. Napoléon wanted to fetch his trumpet to salute the Jupiter, divine river that had given them this day of great happiness. They convinced him that it was not a good idea. Some guide on a poaching spree miles up the river might hear the music and might imagine the Governor General was arriving two days early! Dead-tired, relaxed by the fresh air, they stretched out on the warm boulders and went to sleep to the gentle murmur of the Jupiter, where for centuries the salmon had made their breeding ground.

"Marie," said Ovide softly, "do you remember our song, 'Les Chemins de l'amour'?"

Their siesta ended, they returned to the cabin and decided to put off till the next day their excursion to the lobster inlet. Ovide, unused to such strenuous exercise, seemed tired out. He asked the others to look after Marie, excused himself to her and climbed into his bunk, where he fell fast asleep. The three men exchanged significant glances. They suggested a game of cards, but Marie wanted to wander around the cabin to pick wild flowers.

"Well, this time I'm your guide!" Ti'-Mé exclaimed. "I'll show you flowers and animals like you never saw, little French squirrel!"

She clapped her hands.

"Agreed!"

Holding hands like romantic school kids, they went off together, but Guillaume had time to catch his cousin's eye and order:

"Take the third path down to the river. That's where you'll find all kinds of flowers, and plenty of them."

Napoléon put on his severe face, as if Marie were his own daughter.

Ti'-Mé would never forget that walk with Marie down the path that led to the river. He talked and talked, more than in all the rest of his life. Hearing the tale of his loneliness and his fear of his father, Marie was at first surprised, then saddened. She nibbled on a blade of grass and stooped with him to examine mushrooms she had never seen. A fox, a deer, a hare leapt away at their approach.

"You're not like other girls," he told her as they made a halt on the pretext of a rest for Marie. He stared at her long and tenderly, as if she were a work of art. "All the women I ever knew were kind of heavy. My mother, my sisters, my cousins and aunts. But you're like an actress in the movies. For me it's a great honour to walk with you. Thank you, Marie, thank you!"

Playfully she pushed his felt hat down over his eyes. She liked Ti'-Mé very much, but realized that the slightest encouragement from her would cause this good and simple fellow to fall deeply in love with her.

"I never had a big brother. But if I'd ever had one I'd have liked him to be like you – tall and sensitive and strong and ready to protect me."

He seemed embarrassed and crestfallen.

"Like Guillaume, too, eh?"

She laughed, looking straight ahead toward the river.

"Oh, Guillaume! I couldn't think of him as a brother."

His head hung down and his face was sad, but she didn't notice, she was already fascinated by the river. He put a hand to his ear. He had heard the cry of an osprey.

In a tone of mixed vexation and concern he said:

"Stand here on this rock and wait for me. I heard a strange noise, let me have a look."

"Not a bear, I hope!" she exclaimed.

He had disappeared into the forest for no more than two minutes when a loop of rope, a lasso, sailed through the air, hesitated like a halo over Marie's head, then tightened around her arms.

Terrified, she cried, "Ti'-Mé!"

In answer came a loud laugh.

"It's me, the Lone Ranger!"

"Guillaume!"

He freed her from his rope and took advantage of the chance to kiss her swiftly, but with passion. She blushed.

"Guillaume, really! And where is Ti'-Mé?"

"I sent him back to camp. I want to see you alone. Let's sit down on the big flat rock over there. It's still warm from the sun."

She obeyed with perfect confidence. Suddenly Guillaume's voice was so serious! He didn't mince words.

"Nothing happened between you and Ovide?"

"Why, no! He was a perfect gentleman with me."

"Do you love him?"

"Not the way you mean. But I have great admiration and respect for him."

"And my brother Ovide, does he love you?"

Guillaume saw that she was weighing the question honestly.

"No, it's more like a tender kind of friendship. He loves his wife, you know. He's a very loyal person."

That was all that Guillaume's conscience wanted: no formal obstacles! Would Marie tell him about Ovide's and Rita's problem? Did she know more than the family did? She remained silent. He moved closer to her, and, as if they had been lying in the dark, whispered to her:

"You know, Marie, I wanted you from the first time I ever saw you."

"Yes, I know," she murmured.

He was playing with her fingers.

"I don't know what it is, I got used to European girls. And when I saw you! . . . I feel so good with you."

She was toying with his blond curls, rolling them around her finger.

"I feel good with you, too, Guillaume!"

Why think about the pretty German girls Guillaume had possessed, and who cared that Marie's mother was a collaborator? He was a young god, she was a goddess, somehow they had both strayed to Anticosti, beside the Jupiter, lying close to each other. And they made love with a passion never before attained on that island.

Meanwhile Ovide, awakened, saw Ti'-Mé come into the cabin hanging his head, his teeth clenched. But Ti'-Mé's moods were of little interest to Ovide.

"Where's Marie?"

Ti'-Mé turned his back on Ovide. He had seen the embraces of the happy couple as he peeked through the branches. What torture for him! He stammered:

"They're chattin' down by the Jupiter."

"B-but . . . we mustn't leave them alone. You know Guillaume! And I'm responsible for Marie! I promised to protect her. I'm her guardian!"

"Oh, let them be! They're young," said Napoléon, who couldn't wait to see his wife.

Ovide ran out and took the path to the river. He was, of course, too late. Guillaume and Marie were throwing stones at the surface of the water and counting the skips. He would never know that his brother Guillaume had played him the same trick with Marie as he had with Rita while she was still single. But this time the motive was a good one. Guillaume was almost convinced that he was acting to protect his brother's marriage, which he had almost prevented years before. Seeing his brother, he shouted:

"Come on, old uncle! Come and skip stones!"

There was some pity in his voice. Marie, after they made love, had told him the tragedy of Rita and Ovide. She made him promise to keep it a secret. No, Guillaume would never tell.

31

While the Plouffe brothers were enjoying such a marvellous holiday, Rita heard by phone from Stan Labrie that Ovide had left accompanied by his secretary, Miss Jourdan. Everybody knew about it at Chez Gérard. So, said Stan, why should she eat her heart out over a husband who used her little peccadillo as an excuse to trollop around with a waitress? Rita answered coldly and cut the conversation short. Her heart was torn with grief and jealousy and anger. Was this Ovide's revenge? But with Marie, of all people! Her rival! And he'd probably only held her hand and sung classical arias with her! Once his bitterness was past it would be his turn for remorse, and he'd come slowly back to her. And she'd become beautiful again, her face touched by melancholy, perhaps, and her lovely fingernails would grow again, as soon as she stopped biting them all day long. The Plouffe women hadn't given her up. Almost every evening Jeanne, Cécile and Joséphine played whist with her. They weren't trying to make her talk, they just smothered her with affection. Had Ovide fallen for another woman, or was it Rita who'd been unfaithful? The Plouffe ladies weighed these possibilities and Joséphine opted for some grave fault on Rita's part, for otherwise her son Ovide would never have done such a thing. Cécile shrugged, sceptically, and Jeanne defended Rita, who, fortified by this support from the women of the family, felt a resurgence of her will to fight. If this was war, she'd go to the front, but in her own way.

Ovide, before he left, had advised her to chat with Pacifique Berthet. She would do that this afternoon, despite the terror this disquieting man inspired in her. When she arrived during lunch hour he was absent-mindedly eating an egg sandwich and carefully re-reading the hundred-thousand-dollar insurance policy that covered Rita, Ovide and himself. If one of the three died accidentally, the other two got fifty thousand each. If two of the three died the survivor pocketed the whole bundle. Pacifique smiled cynically to himself. He remembered Ovide's surprise and his hesitation before signing the document, as the premium was so high. But if Pacifique insisted! Maybe the cripple was right: one never knew, did one? Rita coughed politely, in the doorway. When he saw her he dropped the policy on his bench. Her little blue suit clung to her superb figure. She stared at the cripple with a new look, in which there was a hint of her old flirtatiousness.

"Hello!" she said, smiling, despite the shivers that afflicted her at the very sight of Pacifique.

He felt her reserve, remained on his guard, and invited her to sit down.

"Well! This is a surprise! Fancy you dropping in! Have you decided to end your fit of the sulks?"

She was aware of the beginnings of aggression in Berthet and tried to forestall it. She needed an ally as strong and intelligent as he was.

"Yes," she said. "I've been through a bad time. I needed to come to terms with myself all alone, away from here."

He ground his teeth. Of course she wouldn't want to awaken his memory of the scene where she had called him a "lousy cripple." She was going on with her little game.

"I'm so grateful to you for not saying anything to my husband after that awful afternoon – awful for us both. Thank you for that."

Pacifique's eyes glittered. Just as he had loved and desired her before, he detested her now. "The little slut," he said to himself. "Now she's insulting me." He shrugged.

"I have my faults but I'm not a tattler. I respect other people's secrets and keep my own."

"Did you know," said Rita bluntly, "that Ovide's travelling with a secretary?"

He laughed aloud at such innocence.

"If you know it, I guess I do, too. But it's only for the summer, part time. He really needed her. Sales are booming. He just called me from Sept-Iles. Seems they had a terrific time at Anticosti. Lobster, salmon, canoeing." Rita paled. She imagined Ovide and Marie on the banks of the Jupiter indulging in the same kind of antics she had with Bob, the architect, by the Montmorency. Only Ovide would never admit it. Pacifique saw her suffering and rejoiced at it. His contempt for her was growing. Berthet reflected that with two good legs one could without scruples enjoy the kind of adventures Ovide was doubtless having. Suddenly he hated his partner, as if Ovide had robbed him. What a pity: if he had been normal this Rita might have fallen into his arms to avenge herself on her husband, or just to console herself. Then a glint came into his eyes. Why hadn't he thought of this before? At once he became jovial:

"Listen, little lady, this trouble between you and Ovide has been going on too long now. It's bad for you, bad for him, bad for business and bad for me. If you can put an end to it you'll be his only travelling secretary. You'll get together again and the past will be forgotten."

"Oh, I'd be so happy!" she cried. "Then I'd really get him selling watches! Do you think he'd agree?"

She couldn't believe it, Ovide had seemed so hard.

"I could try to put a bug in his ear," he said, thinking of something else. "We'd save money, and you'd be happy!"

"If you can do that, you get two big kisses from me!" she promised. "Oh, if only we could live like before!"

Still lost in his speculations, he didn't say what was on the tip of his tongue: "Have you any idea what love is anyway?" He was counting days:

"Is this the twenty-first of June? July fourteenth is the big French holiday, my holiday. That's the day Ovide goes to Baie-Comeau to bring some stock to our dealer there. Could you go with him?"

"Oh, I'd say yes right away! I'll talk to Mrs. Plouffe and Cécile and Jeanne to help look after our daughter."

He had to hold her back.

"Better wait till I see your husband. You know him, he's not to be rushed. You have to know how to get around him."

She sighed:

"I used to. And I have a feeling it's coming back to me!"

He smiled with imperceptible cruelty.

"Maybe you could take the opportunity to go visit Monsignor Folbèche! Seems he's so bored there he's getting depressed. He'd love to see you. Who knows? You and Ovide could both go to confession and get absolution from the Monsignor, and his blessing. You'd be making a new start, just like honeymooners!"

She heard him with delight.

"Oh, I should have talked to you before, Mr. Berthet. My goodness, we misjudge other people sometimes, don't we?"

"You couldn't stand me, could you?"

"Oh! Don't say that! You get the darnedest ideas!"

The compliment pleased him.

"Yes, from time to time. Tell me," he said, staring at her, "if Ovide hadn't asked you to make this little visit, would you have come on your own?"

"Well . . . Ovide told me you complained you never saw me."

What a fool he was! In his mind he railed at this intolerable pity that the whole world lavished on him since his accident. She left him, light of heart and hopeful, promising to come back and leaving him with his burden of bitterness. Should he buy the convertible or not?

Ovide returned from his trip, and in the taxi that took them toward the parish Napoléon noticed that his brother looked more worried than he had on landing at Anticosti. They let Marie off at her apartment. She seemed in a hurry to leave them and shook hands hastily, like a stranger. Napoléon was not offended, for this was a sign that Guillaume's offensive had been successful. Ovide gave all his salmon to his brother and took home only his suitcase and his briefcase.

Hunched in a corner of the rear seat, Ovide was trying to fathom the slow but sure reversal in Marie's attitude toward him, from the moment when, on the bank of the Jupiter, he had caught Guillaume and Marie skipping stones on the water like two lovers on vacation. After that Marie had seemed more distant, as if she had been caught up by the attention she received from Napoléon and Ti'-Mé, and hypnotized by Guillaume, the blond giant. Just as Rita had been before her. Had she not cautiously given him to understand in the plane that she intended to become a model as soon as possible? He asked the driver to make an about-face and go back to Marie's apartment, she'd left something in the cab. He asked the taxi to wait and rushed up the stairs. Sick at heart, he rang once, twice, three times. No answer. Slowly he went back down the stairs, swallowing his bitterness. Marie was there, no doubt of it, but she refused to let him in. Why?

He supposed she had her reasons. Their romance made no sense. His brothers had interfered. Obvious! It was all over. The happiness hunter was heading home with an empty game bag.

Jeanne had just called Rita. Her Napoléon was back! And so happy! They'd freeze the salmon and lobster and have enough for a whole year. Ovide had given up his whole catch to Napoléon. Rita could take all she wanted from it, help herself. What? Ovide wasn't home yet? Oh! Rita could hear him now, coming up the stairs. She'd have to hang up. Her heart beating fast, she ran to open the door, for she was all dressed up for him.

"Hello!"

His eyes vague, he was just emerging from his abyss of misery.

"Hello. Is the baby in bed?"

"Sure! It's almost ten o'clock, Ovide!"

He had snapped out of it now, he realized where he was. She had prepared the sofa for him. Had anything happened while he was away? He dropped his bags and scrutinized his wife's face.

He noted with surprise that Rita had recovered her gaiety and her expansive nature and was talking a blue streak. Others were able, then, to raise their heads after the storm? She told him about card games with the women of his family, the fine afternoons she'd spent in the park with Arlette, the Parc des Braves, and her visit to Berthet. He had really been quite nice. She had misjudged him. Wasn't Ovide going to Baie-Comeau on July fourteenth?

From this question he realized that she knew Marie had been with him on his trip.

"Did you know Marie Jourdan acted as my secretary on this trip?"

She smiled.

"Sure. So what?"

"Was it Berthet told you?"

She shrugged.

"News travels fast. Everybody knows about it at Chez Gérard. Quebec's a small town. You did the right thing. You have too much work. I have confidence in you. Are you hungry?"

Mechanically, he opened his suitcase. The maddest ideas were racing through his head. His heart was beating slowly, as if deadened by contradictory feelings. Thousands of eyes were fixed on him, following his slightest moves, all of them incoherent, in this solitude from which he was trying in vain to flee. He saw no way out. He made sure that Rita did not see the rolls of film on which Marie appeared so often. How he longed to have them developed! He transferred them to his briefcase. No thanks, he wasn't hungry. He spoke almost tenderly to her. She could go to bed. He was very tired. He went to Arlette's bed and his eyes grew misty as he looked down at her. On his return to the kitchen their bedroom door opened and Rita came out, beaming.

Ovide's eyes opened wide. Could this be? Rita had nothing on but her red high-heeled shoes, her black stockings with the lace garter-belt, pink panties and a flimsy black bra.

"This still do somethin' for you?"

He succeeded in not shouting "yes!" but sighed a long sigh and turned away. He went to bed and had trouble sleeping. But Rita closed her eyes and, with a smile on her lips, fell into a deep sleep. She was beginning to be happy again.

The following day Ovide was very busy putting his accounts in order, which Pacifique went over and approved with his stamped signature. Three times Ovide got up and dialled a number. No answer. This was it, then. Marie didn't want to talk to him any more! Pacifique Berthet watched him, guessing that his romance with Marie was on the rocks. In a friendly voice, as he pushed away the invoices, he said:

"Your wife Rita came to see me the day before yesterday. She was charming. I hope I didn't commit an indiscretion, but I mentioned that you were travelling to Baie-Comeau on July the fourteenth, and that I would be delighted if she went along."

"You said that?" said Ovide, annoyed.

The cripple shrugged.

"She's your wife, isn't she? I had a feeling that something serious had come between you. Try to put an end to it, it's very bad for the company. Your family is worried. They all know that the French waitress went with you to Anticosti. Even people in town are aware of it. You didn't tell me about that when you talked about a secretary. But if you travelled with Rita the gossip would be silenced."

"I'll think about it," Ovide replied, less curtly this time. He was shaken.

"Would you be so kind as to take along my gift for Monsignor Folbèche, the statue of St. Christopher?"

At this moment Napoléon appeared.

"Hey, Ovide! I was just over seeing our mum. She says you never come to see her. She's really upset!"

Ovide felt guilty. He hadn't gone to see Joséphine since his dust-up with Rita because he was afraid: he was sure that, like a midwife, his mother would make him deliver the truth.

"I'll go, I'll go. Tonight after supper."

"Okay, then. I took a smoked salmon to Marie just now. My, she was pleased!" said Napoléon, watching for Ovide's reaction. Ovide didn't flinch.

Disappointed, Napoléon suddenly turned toward Berthet.

"Mr. Berthet, you're a friend of the family. I thought I'd make you a present of a nice piece of fresh salmon."

"That's very kind. Lay it on the work bench," said the cripple, surprised at the sudden friendliness of the plumber, who as a rule ignored him completely.

Napoléon had his reasons. The whole family was already aware of the project launched by Berthet to reunite Rita and Ovide. This ally deserved good treatment. Napoléon exclaimed:

"Tell me how you like it. If it's good, there'll be more where that came from."

Suddenly Napoléon did something very unexpected: he took one of the crutches, hefted it on a finger, then carefully measured it with a rule he took from his overalls. The cripple grimaced: he was hurt because the crutches were part of his most private life.

Napoléon saw this and winked:

"I'm doing this for your own good. You'll be glad of it very soon. You'll see. People who are good to my family get rewarded. And now, Ovide, I'll just run up and give your wife a kiss and leave her the salmon. Jeanne's crazy about your Rita. I want to tell her about our trip, I don't suppose you've told her much yet, eh?"

As soon as Napoléon disappeared, Ovide invented an errand and went to the nearest pay phone. What was going on? Napoléon could get through to Marie with no trouble at all, whereas Ovide. . . . Hurt and angry at the same time, he dialled the number. He jumped when he heard the girl's voice.

"Well! At last!" he exclaimed, relieved. "It's me! I was trying to get you. Something must have been wrong with your phone."

But as the conversation went on his face became drawn. He realized that everything was finished but didn't want to believe it. Yes, she had refused to open the door for him last evening. No, there was nothing wrong with the phone. She knew now how close the family was, she had realized in Anticosti that her affection for Ovide and his for her could end in serious trouble. She was too young, he was married, he should get back together with his wife and forgive her.

"I see it all now. Napoléon and Guillaume have done a real job on you!" he said, his voice strangely altered. "I'm going to Baie-Comeau on the fourteenth of July. I beg you, come with me, just one last time. Say yes, Marie!"

"I'm telling you it's all over, Ovide, it's too dangerous. Anyway, I'm invited to a party at the French consulate on the fourteenth."

He insisted, desperate as a drowning man:

"Can I come and show you the pictures when they're developed?"

"No, Ovide, please send them by mail."

He was livid now and lost.

"Then come for one last walk on the Plains of Abraham. We can have one last talk – it's so awful on the phone. If you come, I'll say good-bye and you'll never see me again. The thing is, Marie . . . I think I love you! Alas!"

There was a pause.

"It's precisely because of that, Ovide, and because I'm very, very fond of you. Good-bye!"

"Marie!" he wailed.

But she had hung up. He was stunned. Of course she was right. But he was suffering so. After his call he went through hours of misery. He only picked at his dinner, feeling that Rita's stare was almost triumphant. He even pushed away little Arlette, who was hanging on his neck and trying to kiss him. At eight o'clock he decided to visit his mother, and Rita encouraged him to do so.

In the street Ovide began to think he was the victim of a general conspiracy, that he was being pushed around like a pawn. He rebelled and walked toward the park of the Champs de Bataille. There, alone in the gathering shadows, sitting on a bench, he would imagine that Marie was by his side, telling him the secrets of her soul by way of farewell.

On that July evening, its sky sparkling with stars, the voluptuously warm air bathing nature, man and objects, Ovide could be seen strolling along the cape where the famous park ended beside the St. Lawrence River. This was where France had lost Canada to the English in 1759. Ovide, similarly vanquished, collapsed on the bench where he had sat on several occasions with Rita before their marriage. Behind him stretched the great field where the two armies had faced each other and where the two generals, Montcalm and Wolfe, had bitten the dust. Before him lay the Quebec Museum and the jail. He heard steps and jumped to his feet, fearing a repetition of the assault he had suffered in the Parc des Braves. But no, it was two lovers who had thought the bench was free. Cyclists pedalled continuously toward Gray Terrace, on super-nickel-plated bikes decorated with little flags and sophisticated bells and horns. Gaudy as fireworks, he thought. . . . He could see the heads of a few prisoners who were whistling at the girls from behind bars. How unhappy those men must be, locked in on such a lovely night! Napoléon often told him their sad stories, Napoléon who was so proud of his contract to maintain the eavestroughs, roof and plumbing of this morbid dungeon. Ovide felt himself as much a prisoner as these poor devils, but at least he could come and go as he pleased. He saw himself sawing through all the bars, releasing the captives and fleeing with them across Abraham's Field.* Perhaps their race toward freedom would cure him of all his troubles!

He tried to re-create Marie's presence beside him. The effort required enormous concentration. But just as he was about to succeed Marie would turn into Rita in high heels and black stockings. Then he mumbled, like a rosary, all the avowals he had prepared for Marie; the heart-breaking farewell scene he had envisaged evaporated like a ghostly Amen. He was shocked that he was unable to call up Marie's image as precisely as that of Rita, but he imagined that when he had her photos, which were to be ready tomorrow, the magic would return.

Weary, disgusted with himself, he walked toward home as

---

* Owner of the land in 1759

if it were a punishment to go there. It was half-past ten. As he laid his hand on the doorknob he failed to see Joséphine marching up and down. Her sharp voice broke into his daydream.

"Ovide!"

In a fright, he replied:

"Mama! At this time of night!"

Upstairs, behind the venetian blind, Rita, along with Napoléon, Jeanne and Cécile, peeked out at the confrontation. There had been a great family council this evening. They feared the worst for Ovide in his condition.

Arms akimbo, the boss lady held her son in thrall.

"Yes, me, at this hour of the night. Me, your mother. You haven't been to see me in a month. Tonight I was promised you'd be there at seven. No Ovide! You had us worried sick, my boy. I call, I call, the gentleman is still out, as if I'd been dead for years. Now you come back with me to my kitchen. I have things to talk about with you. And I'm in a hurry."

He walked silently at her side, just like in the days when she'd come to drag the dreamy boy from his bench in the Parc des Braves. But he was already building up resistance. She made him sit down at the table and sat across from him, her elbows on the table.

"So I don't even exist any more, is that right?"

"Mama," he stammered, "I'm thirty-six years old, I have my own life and I'm a busy man!"

"How is Monsignor Folbèche? Did you go and see him like I asked you to?"

He shut up like an oyster. That was it. Napoléon had talked. Or someone else? The unexpected severity of Joséphine's expression showed that she knew about his adventure with Marie. A raging impatience rose from somewhere below his stomach. Why not leave it all behind and slam the door, go and give French lessons to the Anticosti guides! Joséphine felt the danger. She now spoke gently, nodding her head and touching his hand.

"I knew you hadn't been to see the Monsignor. It seems when you got to Anticosti you smelled like good French perfume."

"Just as I thought. Napoléon blabbed."

"Don't flatter yourself. Lots of people know about you and the little French girl. Passionate love is a dangerous thing, Ovide.

267

Rita has her faults, but she's improved. Now we appreciate her, we love her. I want you to come back to her a hundred per cent, like a good husband, like before."

Ovide was utterly desolate, plunged into an uncontrollable panic. This super-woman, Joséphine, was beating him to his knees. And the supreme confession burst from his lips, despite his efforts, in a great cry:

"I can imagine you, mama, if someone had been unfaithful to you!"

As if he had struck this fat woman with a fist in the throat, she sat with her mouth open for a long moment. She came and sat beside him and laid her hand on the back of his head. This Ovide, her child, still breathing so hard. Gravely, but relieved, she said:

"So that was it! Aha! I thought as much. Or you'd never have done such a thing! Now I understand, now it's all clear!"

It was too late. He couldn't run. She had penetrated his defences. Softened in defeat, he dropped his head on her shoulder as she talked in a monotonous voice:

"I know how much you suffered. I've been through that. Your father did it to me with a certain Ramona."

She felt him give a little jump.

"Yes, my dear, but I didn't say a word. I cried alone in my corner for a long time. But I stuck it out, and your father never guessed that I knew everything. What good would that have done? Break everything up? There'd be no more family. And as for you, Ovide, remember our Lord's words: 'Let him that is without sin cast the first stone.' "

Emotions were racing and colliding throughout his whole being. His father had deceived Joséphine! Then he began searching for all the sins he had committed, which would prevent him from throwing the first stone at Rita. He started up, horrified.

"Let this be a secret between us for all eternity, mama! You must swear it!"

"I swear, Ovide."

Then she went on, her hand in Ovide's hair.

"Men can't imagine it, but it hurts a woman just as much to be deceived, you know. When I think about it my heart still smarts, but I've forgiven him. It's never as bad if the man jumps the fence. But a woman! That's the end of the world!"

He had a profound admiration for Joséphine. But he, weak

as he was, would he have the strength to follow her advice? He couldn't imagine himself going home and waking Rita to tell her solemnly, "All is forgiven, let bygones be bygones." He shook his head feebly. But his mother went on reading his mind.

"Oh, you don't get there by saying Jack Robinson. It comes slowly. And in the meantime, if you have a good heart – and I think you have – give it a try. One drop of forgiveness per day. Later, when the glass is filled with all those drops, you'll start enjoying life again and you'll love each other more than ever because you went through suffering together."

Ovide shuddered. He had never suspected that Joséphine could express sentiments that were so delicate and profound. He whined, like the little boy he still was:

"It's hard, mama, it's going to be hard!"

She made as if she would hold him tight.

"I know, child, I know. Look, I've an idea how you could start: your trip to Baie-Comeau on July the fourteenth. I hear somebody suggested you take Rita along."

He sighed:

"Are you in the plot as well?"

"There's no plot. The whole family wants to save you and Rita. The idea even came from your partner, and he's a very wise man."

He stood up. He wanted to get to sleep. He had never in his life felt so tired.

"Very well, I'll take her, if that's what you want."

Joséphine cried happily:

"At last! That's my old Ovide again! Good boy!"

Ovide, arriving home, found Cécile, Napoléon, Jeanne and Rita playing whist. They stopped playing and all gave him the same oblique and searching look.

"All right, you win. I'm taking Rita along to Baie-Comeau on the fourteenth. If she wants to come."

All four stood up. Rita's eyes filled with tears, and she ran into the bedroom, while Jeanne and Cécile broke into smiles. Napoléon muttered, with intense feeling:

"That's fine of you, Ovide."

Rita came back with a card in her hand.

"I don't know if this is going to upset our trip. We're invited to a party at the French consulate on the fourteenth, the same day."

Ovide took the card and put it in his pocket.

"I'll answer it. We aren't going. We leave for Baie-Comeau and that's final."

The visitors were yawning. They broke up the game, in their innocence imagining that the conjugal bed would shortly be the scene of a very special reunion. But nothing of the sort took place. Rita knew her Ovide. She prepared his sofa with even more care than usual.

"Good night," she said, "sleep well." And she smiled to herself in the dark.

32

In the days that followed, Ovide was increasingly irritated by the importance his family attached to the Baie-Comeau trip. The women nattered on about what Rita should wear, Jeanne was delighted to look after little Arlette, and Joséphine was preparing a bulletin of good advice and encouraging news for Monsignor Folbèche. "Good Lord!" said Ovide, "do they think it's my honeymoon?" What he found most perplexing was that his partner, Pacifique Berthet, was happier about the whole thing than anyone else and full of pride at this initiative that had turned him into a great family friend. He had even authorized an astonishing allocation for Ovide's restaurant bills during the trip.

They had all underestimated Ovide. He refused to allow his fate to depend on a family conspiracy. It was bad enough that they had already blocked his only view of the dreamland he needed for his salvation. Since making that promise to his mother he had thought the whole thing over and come to an honourable compromise. When he came home around ten he found Rita all spruced up and happy, trying on the sky-blue suit she intended to wear for her first plane trip. He bit his lip. God, she was good-looking! Even better than on their wedding day. He said softly:

"Come and sit down, I want to ask you something."

Without knowing why, she shivered with apprehension. She had never seen him so calm and serious.

"D'you like my suit?"

"Of course, you're very pretty, very nice. You're quite popular in the family just now."

"They've been so good to me!"

He gave a little cough, his closed hand to his mouth.

"Rita, do you think you can behave like a big grown-up girl?"

"Don't you think I've proven that in the last while?"

She was worried now, prepared for the worst.

"This trip with you," he said in a toneless voice, "I've been stuck with it by the whole family and even my partner. I want you to know that my state of mind is just not ready for that trip. Can you understand that?"

She turned pale:

"We're not going? I just brought Arlette over to Jeanne. Everybody's so pleased. My bag is packed. I've spent the whole week getting ready."

He was ashamed of himself.

"You're going, but alone. Nobody needs to know. I'll take you to the airport and disappear for three days, just while you're away. Then I'll pick you up when you come back. You know how to do things, you can deliver the stock to our dealer in Baie-Comeau and visit Monsignor Folbèche. I'm just not ready to see him with you."

He said all that looking at the floor, knowing she was on the verge of tears. Oh, she had so hoped to win him back on this trip! How dearly she was paying for her sin! But she was not protesting, merely weeping softly.

"You know very well, Rita, that what happened to us is much more awful than the others would believe. Mama wants me to forgive everything – for I told her about it. She thinks she can flip my wound over like a pancake and let the whole family feed on our reconciliation. This business is just between the two of us. I understand how disappointed you are, but, Rita, I'm not ready, it still hurts too much. You'll go alone, won't you?"

He touched her hand, as if to console her. She was overwhelmed. The fact that Ovide would talk so openly to her renewed her courage and made her disappointment easier to take.

Heavy-hearted, she said:

"All right. I'll behave like a big girl. I'll go alone."

He admired her, rewarding her with a pale smile.

"Thanks. I knew I could rely on you."

After a long silence she dared to say, with humility:

"Does that mean that for three days . . . Marie . . .?"

He cut her off brusquely:

"There'll be no Marie, there is no Marie any more. Where I'm going I'll be quite alone with myself. I'm going on retreat to the monastery of the White Fathers of Africa, to my old cell. After those three days I hope to see a little light."

Rita could have danced and shouted for joy. No Marie, never again! And at the monastery God would tell Ovide to forgive her. During this trip, which she was now to take alone, she would get her husband back. Staring down at the sofa she seemed to murmur to it, "Say good-bye to Ovide. He'll soon be in my bed again."

She said aloud, with happy little sobs:

"Oh, that makes me so happy! I'll do whatever you please. And I'll pray so hard with Monsignor Folbèche that I'll be sure to win your forgiveness and your love."

Too moved to continue the conversation, they went to their separate beds, convinced that this episode in their lives was about to end.

Berthet drove up at seven A.M. on July fourteenth, at the wheel of Rita's former car. He parked the white convertible with the red leather seats at the door of the jewellery shop. Making sure that no one was watching, he succeeded with some effort in extracting a long parcel from the trunk and carried it in to his workshop. A few minutes later he went through the same business in reverse. Closing the car trunk, he heaved a sigh of relief. No one had seen him. Then he settled on the edge of his chair, sitting almost straight, as if his ability to drive had left him less infirm. He unfolded a map and with one finger traced the track of the plane that would carry Ovide and Rita. It would be over St-Joachim at twenty past ten and flying over the river ten minutes later. Perfect. Canadian Pacific Airlines was known for its punctuality.

At ten to nine the couple came downstairs with their luggage and saw the car.

"Why, that's my car!" exclaimed Rita.

"I thought you said you sold it!" said Ovide, frowning.

"But I did!"

"And I bought it," said Berthet, smiling, leaning on his crutches

272

in the doorway. He was enjoying their surprise and showed unusual good humour on this splendid summer morning.

"I drive it myself!"

He said it triumphantly, as he might have said, "I can walk now!" Yes, he'd bought it as a Fourteenth of July present for himself, celebrating the date and the couple's happy trip at the same time.

"My, you're lovely today! A real July bride!"

Ovide nodded agreement.

"The main thing," he said, "is that this car should bring you good humour and happiness. You've worked hard. Congratulations, you've done well. You deserve it."

Berthet was hobbling around the car, which Rita gazed at nostalgically. He said:

"I have a hand control to replace the gas pedal. And my left leg is fine for the brake, no problem at all. Can I take you to the airport?"

"No, no thanks," said Ovide prudently. "I've called a taxi. We have to hurry now, I must take along the stock of watches."

"Ovide, don't forget the statue! Ovide!" said Berthet. "The St. Christopher for Monsignor Folbèche! On the work bench!"

Ovide made a face. That damned statue! He ran to the shop and came out at once with the parcel. The driver took the long package from Ovide and was going to toss it on his front seat.

Pacifique shouted in terror:

"Careful! That's a plaster statue!"

Ovide took the parcel from the driver.

"We'll lay it across our knees. Oh, Pacifique! I almost forgot. Would you just write a little note to the Monsignor. That would be normal, it's such a splendid present for him."

Berthet, annoyed, hesitated, then disappeared into the shop, from which he emerged a few minutes later with a sealed envelope duly addressed to Monsignor Folbèche. Ovide slipped it into his inside coat pocket, and Pacifique smiled a strange smile.

"I wrote him a brief message from a repentant sinner. The priests always go for that."

The taxi moved off.

"Have a good trip, you two lovebirds!" cried Pacifique from the sidewalk, with an almost solemn wave.

The cripple's eyes were so intent on following the taxi which bore off Ovide and Rita with the statue, that he at first failed to notice Napoléon, standing at attention in front of him and carrying on his shoulders, like two rifles, two crutches made of aluminum tubing.

"Long live France, and happy Fourteenth of July, Pacifique!"

And before Berthet's astonished eyes he lowered the crutches to the sidewalk:

"Stand at – ease!"

Pacifique's face grew hard. This ass, Napoléon, was always tactless, drawing attention to his infirmity. Napoléon, proud of himself, was jubilant:

"That's what I was measuring for the other day. I was wondering what I could give you for the Fourteenth of July. Lift one, just lift it! Lighter than wood! And looks better. Silver grey."

Disconcerted, Pacifique lifted the crutches, incredulous. Napoléon was exultant:

"Made 'em myself in the shop, evenings. And that's not all! Above the grips I installed two flashlights. See the little lenses? Great for walking at night. You're never going to trip. Just push the button and pop! – the light goes on! Seeing-eye crutches!"

Pacifique, overwhelmed, tried the buttons.

"The batteries are in the tubing!" Napoléon added. "Simple as can be, I'd like to patent it. And that's still not all!"

He took a crutch and removed the upper part above the grip:

"Just like a trombone. You go to the movies, take 'em apart. They take up less room. Try them, why don't you?"

Pacifique was smiling now. Mockingly, he said:

"All I need now is paddles on the ends."

Napoléon slapped himself on the forehead, then put the parts together again.

"Damn, I never thought of that! Come on, let's see you go, give 'em a try, eh? I gotta see this."

Pacifique tucked them under his arms and moved toward his convertible, appearing very satisfied.

"Thank you, Mr. Napoléon Plouffe. It's true, they're extremely light. I'll have them with me when I go for a Sunday drive."

"But that's Rita's car!" the plumber exclaimed.

During the drive to the airport Ovide and Rita found little to say. The box with the statue still lay across their knees. Rita complained:

"Am I going to have to cart that box around all the time till I get to see the Monsignor?"

Ovide was apologetic:

"I have to act as if I was going with you. And I'd promised to bring the package. But never mind, I'll ask the baggage people to have it delivered by truck. You just go to the hotel I mentioned. They're expecting you and they'll give you a great welcome. Our dealer's going to meet you at the airport, what's more. You can give him the watches, and don't forget to ask for the receipt. Tonight he and his wife are having you over for dinner. Hauterive is a charming town, right nearby. Very lively."

"It would have been nice if you were there," she sighed. "But I'll get along."

At the Ancienne-Lorette airport the DC3 that had carried off Father Folbèche a short time ago was waiting for passengers. Ovide cancelled his ticket, got Rita her boarding pass and took the parcel to the baggage counter, where the clerk on duty greeted him as he took the package.

"Our great traveller, Ovide Plouffe! What's this, a grand-father clock?"

"It's a statue of St. Christopher. A present from my partner for Monsignor Folbèche. A plaster statue: Fragile! See – in big letters. So take it easy. Be sure it's stowed someplace where it won't get bashed around."

The employee, having weighed the package, laid it carefully on the baggage wagon.

"That your wife?" he asked, jerking his head toward Rita. "She's a real going concern. If I was you, I'd never let her out of my sight."

Nervously, Rita was waiting for Ovide and thinking about the terror of taking off. She was also just managing to disregard the insistent eye of one of the crew. What a pretty uniform he had, this flyer! For his part, he swore to himself that he'd pay special attention to this passenger during the flight. What could she want in Baie-Comeau? Rita always projected this aura that set her off from other women. Ovide was there again, giving her the ticket and boarding pass.

"Nervous?"

"Yes, a little. Are you sure I won't be sick?"

He answered kindly:

"Why, no, dear child. The DC3 is an excellent plane. Flies like a kite. And the weather is heavenly."

An announcement was coming over the speakers:

"Take-off for Baie-Comeau and Sept-Iles is delayed by ten minutes. We are waiting for the iron-mine management. Their plane has just landed."

This would have been bad news for Pacifique if he had heard it. He was so punctilious about timing. Ovide strolled down the waiting-room hall and bought Rita a Coca-Cola. Three businessmen burst into the hall, obviously in a hurry. Veritable giants, cigars clamped in their teeth.

Ovide, noticing these mastodons, murmured:

"You'd swear these big companies insisted on their people being six foot four. And weighing at least two hundred pounds."

"They're not too heavy for the plane, are they?" asked Rita, getting worried.

"No, no," he laughed, "a DC3 can carry a big load. It floats on the air as if it were on a cushion."

The passengers were pouring into the passage that led to the plane. As their separation approached the couple grew clumsy, embarrassed and hesitant. Oh, if only Ovide would give her a little peck, how happy she'd be!

"Have a good trip," he said awkwardly. "You're really behaving like a big girl!"

"Cheerio, Ovide, dear. Take care of yourself, eh? And have three good days with the Fathers. I'll be praying, too."

She joined the line of passengers, in one hand holding Madame Plouffe's bag of presents and in the other the suitcase with the jewellery. She turned back, smiled at him in a last good-bye. Ovide was overcome by a strange sensation. How serious this was, just for a small farewell! He was on the point of calling her back and cancelling the trip. But she had disappeared. He listened for the throbbing of the engines, then, stoop-shouldered, hailed a taxi to go to the monastery.

In the cloister Ovide was awaited like the prodigal son. As he pushed open the enormous door he had the impression of escaping from the naughty world he had been living in. It was Brother Léopold who met him at the door. The lay brother's usually mocking smile was illuminated by a touch of other-worldliness and much genuine joy.

"I'm very happy to see you again, brother . . . I mean to see you, Ovide. Oh, we haven't forgotten you! We follow your talks on the radio, just marvellous! We're most proud of you. But we'll talk about all that tonight in the refectory. The Father Superior is waiting for you. You've forgiven me for torturing you in the old days, hm?"

Ovide clapped him fraternally on the shoulder. He shut his eyes, breathed in the atmosphere and listened to the calm of the corridors. He smiled and said, very gently:

"I'm happy, too. What an oasis! I must say, as soon as I set foot in this place I feel an immense serenity and peace. And I need that."

His hand still lay on Brother Léopold's shoulder.

"Just to think I once beat you like a savage. I'm so violent!"

Suddenly Ovide was struck by a coincidence. It was because of Rita that he had left the priesthood, and because of her that he was seeking retreat here now. Brother Lépold laughed good-naturedly:

"That punch in the nose? I had it coming. At any rate, Ovide, I must admit I missed you for a long time. You should have come back to see us sometimes!"

Ovide did not reply. A phrase was dancing in his mind: "When I burn my bridges they stay burned." But he didn't really believe it. He was here to burn a bridge called Marie or the other called Rita, but he despaired of succeeding, ever. At the same time his eyes drank in the spectacle of a thousand objects, statues, portraits of churchmen, stained glass, white-washed walls and holy-water fonts, things that for months had been the mute witnesses of his botched vocation. Brother Léopold saw him into the Father Superior's office and waited at the door. The monk opened his arms to Ovide.

"Oh, my dear son!"

Even Ovide's own father, Théophile, resurrected and embracing him affectionately, would not have aroused a richer or more intense emotion than the one he felt that moment. He stammered:

"I've been very daring, haven't I, and brazen, asking you to offer me a retreat here for three days? I don't want to cause anyone the slightest inconvenience."

The superior shook his head, his face lit up by a joy Ovide had not seen for a long time on the masks of those involved in the bustle of the world outside. The monk played the part of the gruff authoritarian:

"Ovide! I order you to hold your tongue! When one of our children returns to spend a while with us, our hearts are full of joy. I have many questions to ask you, and I suppose you have some things to confide in me, because you are suffering greatly, is that not so? But don't talk now. Your old cell is waiting for you. Pray and meditate there as much as you wish. In three days, maybe less, if God wills that you confide in me, remember that I am your father in our Lord and you are my son."

Ovide choked with emotion. Brother Léopold led him to the very cell where he had spent so many nights in the throes of temptation and his love for Rita. The bare little room was furnished simply with a cot (where Ovide laid down his briefcase), a chair, a chest of drawers and a small work table in front of the window.

"You will notice, Brother Ovide," teased Brother Léopold, "that there are no more bars on the windows! Things are much freer here nowadays. There have been many changes. If one of the brothers wants to sleep out, who is going to know? If he takes a notion to fly away leaving no address, too humiliated to confess a failed vocation to the superior, the window is wide open."

Left to himself (my, how oppressive total solitude could be!), Ovide stared idly out the window. It was reassuring to be on the ground floor. He straightened the crucifix on the wall, checked the stability of the table and chair legs and felt as if he had been cast off by life, sidetracked and forgotten. He had hoped to find an oasis here, designed for meditation, where his soul might find the calm and detachment necessary for making decisions worthy of the upright man he was. He sat down on his bed, got up again and began pacing up and down the little room, his hands behind his back. He was agitated by a host of thoughts racing through his mind: Marie, France, Rita, sexuality, family, business, his editorials on the political situation. Instead of falling into place, all these problems and people which intertwined with each other flew apart and grew distorted. His own father, unfaithful to Joséphine! That was really something! How could his vision of Théophile have been so simple: a nationalist typographer, fanatical cyclist and beer drinker.

Ovide shook his head to rid himself of this confusion, then opened his briefcase and sat down at the little table. In a secret compartment his hand caressed the packet of photos from his trip with Marie. No, he would be strong: he'd resist looking at them for the tenth time. Wasn't he here for a cure, after all? Then his invitation to the consul's party – for Frenchmen in Quebec City and their friends – turned up among his papers. He had forgotten to reply. But wasn't the ceremony at noon today, July the fourteenth? He must be in a real mess these days to be getting so forgetful, when he was normally so punctual and efficient! His hand wandered to his jacket pocket. Good lord! Berthet's note to Father Folbèche! He'd forgotten to give it to Rita! He must post it today, even if it arrived after the statue. He took out a clean sheet of paper and started scribbling words, meaningless numbers and doodles on it. Then he made two columns, one with Marie's name at the top, the other with Rita's. He'd draw up a kind of moral balance sheet, as accountants did: debits, credits, losses, profits, pros and cons. He chewed nervously on his pencil. His glance fell on a picture of Ste-Anne hanging on the wall, but he quickly looked away from her: Ste-Anne, whose basilica stood a few kilometres away, receiving pilgrims from all over America come to ask for a special favour or a miraculous cure. He sighed impatiently. What the devil could Ste-Anne do for him? He pressed too hard on the paper with his pencil. Rita and Marie, two superb women! He thought of the crystalline waters of the Jupiter. Guillaume had possessed Marie, he was sure of it. But no! Not Marie! And Rita, being ogled by that crew member at the airport. So persistently, too! He had a flashing vision of her in her red shoes and black stockings. Then the memory of the Montmorency River floated back in front of his eyes, incomplete because Rita had not included in her confession the subtleties of the butterfly procedure (she had been sparing with details). The pathways of love! *Les chemins de l'amour*! The "river" theme was multiplied in his imagination until his mind was filled with waterfalls. Ovide imagined himself lying between Marie and Rita, naked on the banks of the Jupiter, while five thousand seals barked and roared, and giant salmon leapt arching from the water. He surfaced unwillingly from his daydream and found himself in

279

a sweat. What evil spell inhabited this monastery – and this cell in particular? As soon as he set foot in it the Beelzebub of sex attacked him mercilessly. Furious at himself, he began again to pace in a rage from one wall to the other; then he lay down on his bed, trying to think of the dead or of a locomotive running howling toward their naked bodies. It was no use. He was no St. Anthony. All this simply made his temples throb harder. He kissed Rita's breasts, Marie's breasts, and grovelled like a snake between their paradisiac thighs. His breathing grew faster. Quick! The window! He leapt out onto the grass, briefcase in hand, and fled like a burglar. Of course, he had to find a letter box where he could mail Berthet's missive to Monsignor Folbèche! Didn't he?

33

As Ovide in his tortured mood sat facing the blank sheet of paper and preparing his flight from the monastery, Dufferin Terrace, overlooking Quebec harbour, was swarming with people. A French frigate flying the tricolour lay grey and graceful along the quay. Hundreds of curious onlookers leaning on the parapet were admiring its elegance, while the young French sailors wearing their berets with the red pompons combed the famous promenade in search of pretty Quebec City girls. Their harvest promised to be a sumptuous one. The telephone operators and secretaries held out for officers and NCOs, while the working girls, just as pretty and charming, were the joy of the other ranks. A river seaport, Quebec City turned loose its festive maidens every time foreign sailors came to town. The fact that these were French made the celebration ten times as joyous. But, alas! there were always a few silly geese left holding the bag nine months later!

On the part of Dufferin Terrace from which the Ile d'Orléans can be seen, as well as the Beaupré coast and Cap Tourmente, Pacifique Berthet, leaning on his new crutches, wearing a driving cap and sunglasses, was scanning the horizon in a state of increasing anxiety. Nervously he looked at his watch. Ten minutes late already! That was odd! Twenty to eleven? Were his calculations wrong? Yet as a rule he was never a minute out, not even a second. In this fine weather eyes as good as his should have been able to see a plane in the sky, even fifty kilometres away! Could it be that his July fourteenth was going to be a flop? And if it was . . . Berthet began to panic. Where could he go? Certainly not to the shop on his national holiday! With his aluminum crutches lying on the back seat he drove aimlessly through the narrow streets, turned on his radio and made his way to the road that leads to Sainte-Anne de Beaupré, not realizing he was speeding. From time to time he wiped drops of sweat from his forehead that the July sun and his overwhelming anxiety caused to ooze from every pore.

He would have been surprised to learn that at ten-thirty in the DC3 over Saint-Joachim the handsome officer was leaning over Rita's seat. Ever since take-off he had shown her the most tender care. She started at every air pocket.

"There's no danger," the young man assured her. "Just relax with the plane. Do the way it does, float with the wind. Coffee or tea?"

She shook her head, tensed for the next bump. Not far from where she sat the American businessmen seemed quite at ease, sipping their whiskies calmly as they studied the documents on their knees, ignoring the cries of the babies in the rear of the plane.

"See?" said the young officer. "Except for the babies turning on the waterworks, everybody's happy as a porker."

"It's just the way I am," Rita apologized, giving him her defenceless-lamb look. "I'm scared anyway."

"Hold my hand for a minute. Then you'll never be scared in a plane again."

She grasped his hand without hesitation and gave him a long look filled with gratitude.

That was Rita Toulouse's last look.

A frightful explosion ripped open the fuselage. Ovide Plouffe's wife had just died, along with twenty-two other passengers. On the ground below, in a field at Saint-Joachim, a farmer heard the explosion and looked up to see the airplane's belly torn away and its fuselage in pieces. It went into a vertical dive and crashed in a swamp. If it had not taken off ten minutes late it would have fallen farther on, into the water, as fate had intended. But Rita's pathways, unlike Ovide's, never went down to the sea.

At twelve-thirty Ovide was skirting the gardens of the French consulate, where a great tent had been pitched to house the hors-d'oeuvres, the wine and the champagne. A *bal musette* orchestra dominated by the accordion played music for the occasion. The two hundred guests, among them the officers of the training ship berthed in the harbour, their uniforms bright spots in the crowd, were hopping, dancing and singing "Oh, the little white wine!" Curious passers-by in the street tried to peer through the hedge surrounding the grounds. Ovide Plouffe pushed past them. He hesitated, then made resolutely for the entry, where the consul was welcoming his guests. Ovide, fearing he might be taken for a free-loader, said hastily:

"Here is my invitation. My name is Ovide Plouffe, I do editorials on the radio and I'm a great friend of France."

"Of course! Mr. Plouffe! A great friend of my country! Please, do join the party and enjoy yourself!"

Others were coming in behind him. Ovide set down his briefcase beside the hedge and examined the groups and couples. He recognized a few political personalities here and there, but most of the guests were strangers to him. Perhaps Marie was somewhere in this crowd. Would she come? He saw Claude Saint-Amant from the radio station and rushed over to him.

"Well! Fancy seeing you here!" said Saint-Amant. "Come to think of it, it's not surprising either. You say such pretty things about General de Gaulle. You're such an ardent supporter of his you defend French maidens in peril. You'll get your Legion of Honour yet! By the way, I just saw a pretty Parisian lady I believe you know. There she is, dancing with a young officer."

Ovide blushed. Marie. Mischievous and happy, just as she had been with Guillaume and Ti'-Mé and Napoléon on Anticosti, doing a java in the arms of a Navy lieutenant. Ovide was suddenly ashamed of himself and wanted to flee. What on earth was he doing here? She had asked him never to attempt to see her again. Marie caught sight of him. Astonished, she came toward him, dragging the officer by the hand.

"Ovide! What a surprise! I thought you'd left on a trip with. . . ."

So she knew, too! He stammered:

"Yes, I'm leaving, I'm leaving, I just dropped in to pay my respects to the consul."

Marie did the introductions. She described Ovide as an extraordinary music lover, a kind French Canadian who had been very helpful to her. The officer, who was less than fascinated, wanted to dance again, but Claude Saint-Amant asked them not to move. A zealous photographer was making the rounds in search of interesting groups. Thus Ovide, at the very moment when a team of rescuers was extracting the bodies, including Rita's, from the DC3, was being photographed, with his broadest smile, along with Claude Saint-Amant, Marie Jourdan and the naval officer.

Marie went off to dance with another partner, as if her meeting with Ovide was of no importance. Despite this fact, Ovide, wine glass in hand, felt a sweet kind of bliss creep over him, accompanied by a touch of acid bitterness: the bliss that was triggered by the Parisian accents of the conversations that caught fire around him. After all, he was a Frenchman himself, uprooted these three hundred years, lost in this Siberian Quebec, but a Frenchman who in the emanations of his distant origins caught the true odour of his identity. Yes, he was French, and he repeated this with such pride that it suggested he might be renouncing his Canadian citizenship. Claude Saint-Amant, called away to the phone, left the group where Ovide was holding forth.

At the phone, Saint-Amant was frowning. The senior news editor on the radio station had given him an unwelcome report. It concerned Ovide Plouffe, the best known and most important of his customers. A Canadian Pacific Airlines DC3 had just crashed at Saint-Joachim. Among the victims the jeweller's wife was one they had been able to identify.

Stunned, Claude Saint-Amant stood cracking his knuckles, then returned to the garden and took Ovide aside.

"I just had a call from the station."

"Oh!" cried Ovide, still on the crest of his July fourteenth enthusiasm, "I could improvise an editorial for you on this splendid occasion in about five seconds. On ten minutes' notice! Hey! What's the matter?"

He had noticed how pale Saint-Amant was.

"A call from the station? Have they cancelled my contract?"

Claude Saint-Amant wished he had never taken the call.

"No, Ovide, no. But leave here this minute. It's urgent that you go straight home. Hurry. That's all I can say."

"But nobody knows I'm here!" said Ovide in a toneless voice.

"Never mind. I repeat, you must go home. It's urgent."

This last phrase filled his whole being with anxiety, his eyes clouded over and he saw the things around him as in a mist. Was this calamity knocking? But for whom? Arlette? His mother? Rita? An accident?

Mechanically he picked up his briefcase, pushed his way past groups of guests and, his ears still ringing with *La Margoton*, ran down hills and staircases and three times just missed being hit by cars. Despite his haste it seemed he'd never reach home, where some frightful misfortune was surely waiting for him.

Pacifique Berthet was still driving along in his convertible, the radio on full blast. Impatiently he bit with rage at the hot dog he had bought at the service station where he had just filled up. Suddenly the music was interrupted for a special bulletin. He hurled away the piece of bun dripping with mustard. There was a long pause. Its five seconds seemed interminable to him. Finally, a funereal voice came through:

"This is a special bulletin. At ten-thirty this morning a Canadian Pacific Airlines DC3 crashed at Saint-Joachim after a powerful mid-air explosion. The tragedy has claimed twenty-three lives, including the crew and three American executives of the Iron Ore Corporation. Among the other victims, not all of whom have yet been identified, we find the name of Mrs. Ovide Plouffe, wife of the Quebec City jeweller and radio editorialist. Mrs. Plouffe, née Rita Toulouse, was last spring chosen Miss Sweet Caporal. A special rescue team was sent to the scene to recover and identify the bodies. Experts from Canadian Pacific Airlines are examining the wreckage of the plane, which is said to give off a strong odour of dynamite."

Petrified, Pacifique Berthet turned off his radio. And so they would soon have identified Ovide. Ten-thirty! The plane must obviously have taken off late, since it exploded over land at Saint-Joachim! It was in the river, farther downstream, that it was supposed to crash!

A frightful panic overcame Berthet. He clung to the accelerator lever as if to a lifeline. The siren of a police car wailed behind him. Pacifique slowed to a stop.

"Hey! Are you crazy?" said the officer.

"I'm sorry. I just heard that my partner Ovide Plouffe and his wife were killed in a plane crash! It's frightful!" he added in a trembling voice.

"Take it easy. No use killing other people into the bargain," said the policeman, flustered. He had forgotten to ask for Pacifique's permit, which, by the way, he did not yet possess.

"A plane crash, did you say?"

The policeman was beginning to get the message.

"It's all over the dial. Twenty-three dead!"

Leaving the officer in a state of shock, Pacifique now drove very slowly. He finally reached the jewellery store and hobbled inside. He didn't even notice that the new clerk had left for lunch without locking up. In a few hops Pacifique was in his work shop. Feverishly he bundled together his maps and aviation magazines. Hurrying as if the devil were at his heels, he upset objects in his way, cursing:

"Son of a bitch of a life!"

When Ovide appeared in the doorway, pale as death and out of breath, Pacifique, his back turned, was closing a suitcase in which he had stuffed his papers pell-mell.

"Pacifique, what's going on?"

Berthet whirled around like a top. In his terrified surprise he was managing to stand up without crutches, his eyes popping out at the sight of this ghost.

"You? You?"

"Yes, me! Me!" puffed Ovide, exasperated and mad with anxiety.

Pacifique spoke as if in a nightmare.

"You didn't take the plane with Madame?"

"No! No! Will you tell me what's going on, damn it!" cried Ovide, at the end of his rope.

Pacifique, dazed, overcome by a sudden pain in his hip, subsided onto his cot and, hanging his head, told Ovide what he had heard on the radio.

Ovide listened, struck with consternation, silent, as if, in his mad race from the consulate to the shop, his frightful anguish had prepared him for this catastrophe that now had a name. He felt a strange relief, which soon turned to a state of grace in which suffering, unmeasurable suffering, could find its place. He did not weep, not right away, but murmured disconsolate bits of phrases:

"God didn't let me go with her! . . . I never had time to pardon her! I'll never go to France! The store, the store is finished. Rita, my love, you knew it would happen, didn't you? Poor little Arlette! My dear child! God has punished me enough now."

He dropped onto a stool and began to weep. Then, as if propelled by a spring he rushed out of the shop and ran to his mother. Immediately afterward, Berthet tossed the suitcase into the convertible and drove off like a whirlwind in the direction of his cottage.

The news of the accident was all over town and caused great agitation. When an airplane crashes close to home people react more strongly to the tragedy, they feel its impact more deeply, then try to imagine the victims' last moments, they are horrified by the thought they might have been among them.

Misfortune struck the Plouffes like a whiplash. Cécile had fled the factory, weeping like a lunatic. Napoléon and Jeanne had hurried to their mother's side, for she too knew the story now, and sat collapsed in her rocking chair, refusing to listen to her children's comforting words, groaning:

"It's my fault! I forced them to go on the trip! Ovide didn't want to go!"

"No, no, mama," sobbed Cécile. "We all wanted it too! I pushed for it, so did Napoléon, and you did only at the last minute."

"We all killed our Ovide!" howled Joséphine. "It's all over for me now."

Ovide was in the doorway. On seeing him they froze, dumbfounded. He said in a toneless voice:

"No, I was not on board. At the last moment I decided to let Rita go alone, and I went to the White Fathers to go into retreat."

Joséphine rose slowly to her feet, transfigured:

"The Good Lord has saved you!"

"But Rita is dead, mama! Dead! Dead!"

In the street a crowd was gathering. They were moved by the groans of those good people, the Plouffes.

Part Three

34

There was a strange effervescence in the parish on the day of Rita Toulouse's funeral. She was the wife of Ovide Plouffe, she was the prettiest woman in that part of town, and there she was, dead in a most unusual airplane accident that all the papers were starting to talk about, harping on the smell of dynamite that hung over the wrecked plane. Rumours were running wild. Russian sabotage? After all, there'd been those three top executives of the American company that was about to start extracting the immense deposits of iron ore on the North Shore. In 1949 people didn't hesitate to blame all the misfortunes of the Western World on the communists.

On the other hand, could it be a crime of passion, or a foully motivated murder? That Ovide Plouffe, for example, had escaped death by cancelling his flight at the last minute and letting his wife go alone to Baie-Comeau. . . . A conceited pup, sometimes he'd stare you up and down or pretend not even to see you – did he have something to do with this tragedy? His wife, Rita, had been so pretty and such a flirt! Jealousy? The mystery promised to be a spicy one! But then people rejected their suspicions. That would have been too awful. And he spoke so well on the radio! It wasn't possible that Ovide, son of that good woman Joséphine Plouffe, was mixed up in this affair. What's more, he was a child of the parish, a neighbour!

When they saw his grief at the undertaker's the insinuations stopped cold. Haggard, distracted, his eyes red from weeping, he was despair incarnate. The neighbours were shattered after seeing him. They left the funeral parlour shaking their heads sadly, which did not escape the hundreds of curious visitors lining up outside, kept under control by a police officer.

Quebec City was ill at ease, people were waiting for some extraordinary development. The shadow of the DC3 hung like a vulture over the town. Premier Duplessis, very upset, humiliated in the eyes of the barons of American high finance, to whom he liked to present a favourable image both of himself and his Quebec, had his Attorney General launch the most massive police investigation the government had ever undertaken. But for the first three days it remained underground.

The face that appeared in close-up in this frightful tragedy was that of Rita Toulouse. Her photo had been in every paper. You saw her there, sitting in her seat among the wreckage, intact, seeming sound asleep, while the other victims were torn to pieces or unrecognizable. She was beauty in death incarnate. At last Rita was getting the kind of publicity of which she'd always dreamed, the kind normally reserved for movie actresses.

Those struck directly by Rita's death – Ovide, his family and Rita's – barely had time to experience their own bereavement. Caught up and numbed by this mass invasion of sympathetic curiosity, they stood in the funeral parlour like robots, continually repeating the same phrases and gestures, kneeling to say a rosary each time a priest came in. The coffin (closed as Ovide had decided, to the disappointment of the curious who had admired Rita's beauty in the newspaper picture) lay against the back wall. There were no wreaths, just a single red rose lying on the cover. On the card attached you could read: "From your adoring husband, who will never forget you!" It was one of Rita's favourite roses, like the one she had stuck in her hair the day she had first worn her white dress to attract Ovide.

Standing at the entry, Ovide was shaking hands, but had trouble recognizing the visitors and barely noticed the suffocating heat or the floral tributes lined up along the wall. Ti'-Mé, Cécile, Guillaume and Napoléon didn't take their eyes off him for a moment. Ovide saw them as dark phantoms, aware only of the ubiquity of his mother Joséphine, who was also watching his behaviour with anxiety. Like a trip-hammer his guilt resounded in his head. Monster! Monster! Why did you take so long to pardon Rita? He discovered that he had always loved her and, now that she was dead, loved her even more.

He was surrounded by all these people, but felt so far from them! A great and deep river separated him from them. The visitors, at a loss for words, asked what he thought about the castastrophe. Did he believe in sabotage? The smell of dynamite, etc. etc. . . . A touch of horror was thus added to his pain and remorse. In vain he tried to efface a memory that, he kept telling himself, had nothing to do with the accident. The scene when he had bought the sticks of dynamite and the detonators, and his remarks on Nobel and universal culture played back a hundred times in his imagination, and beads of cold sweat stood out on his forehead.

For two days now he had not slept, broken with grief and increasingly haunted by that word "dynamite." He would have been even more apprehensive had he known what was afoot. Who were these sinister-looking strangers hanging around the funeral parlour, going from group to group, scrutinizing every visitor, listening to conversations? Guillaume and Napoléon, annoyed, watched them with frustration. Things were happening that Ovide did not understand. Marie Jourdan, Claude Saint-Amant, his former boss at the Royaume du Disque – none of them had appeared at the parlour, nor had the White Fathers of Africa, nor the officials of the Knights of Columbus. Why? And Pacifique had stayed only a few moments and hadn't said a single word. Even his uncle Gédéon had spent most of his time with Rita's parents and had barely offered his sympathy to Ovide. Not one of his North Shore dealers had turned up. All these minor clues added up to more anxiety for Ovide. He thought no one liked him any more except his immediate family.

Guillaume, who often went outside for a breath of fresh air, noticed Stan Labrie prowling around on the opposite sidewalk.

He ran over to him, took him by the throat and said in a frightful voice:

"I hope you've at least got the decency not to go in there!"

Terrorized, in a shaky voice, Stan begged him:

"I'm awful sorry, Guillaume. You know, Rita was the woman I loved, too. You gotta understand that!"

"We know all about that. In a way you killed her. You got her into trouble. Get out of my sight before I strangle you. You make me sick."

Stan had taken to his heels. The giant of the Plouffe family had used the phrase that pounded in his brain ever since the accident, against which he found less and less defence: "You got her into trouble. You killed Rita!" Did Guillaume know the whole story? Stan thought his life might be in danger from this day on.

Guillaume, panting with rage, went back in the funeral parlour thinking about the Jupiter. And about Marie, who, after making love, had explained the reasons for Ovide's distress. And Guillaume felt that he, too, was responsible. What if he and Napoléon hadn't interfered to break up Ovide's romance with Marie? Would Rita not be alive today? He didn't mention his encounter with the pimp outside. And as for the secret Marie had confided to him, he would keep it for the remainder of his days.

Stan Labrie, behind a pillar at the rear of the packed church, was at the solemn mass being celebrated by Monsignor Folbèche, who had the Archbishopric's permission to return for the occasion. As Joséphine had predicted, her former priest's face was pigmented with red spots, resulting from being bitten by those North Shore mosquitoes. The Monsignor was most touched to hear that Rita had been bringing him a fine St. Christopher statue, a gift from Pacifique Berthet. He had thanked Pacifique profusely: "Even though I never saw it, I appreciate your intentions, my son!" he had exclaimed to the embarrassed cripple.

The inquisitive public, who had flocked to the church from all parts of town, were standing in the aisles or jammed in the back of the church. Plainclothes detectives circulated in the crowd. One had the impression of taking part in a funeral rally in which the Plouffes had only an involuntary part. Hymns were sung by the fine voices of the Children of Mary, which Rita had joined just before her marriage. Uncle Gédéon was there, too, beside his son Aimé. With tears in his eyes he dreamed of the orange pie Rita had made for him a few months earlier.

And what a day for Monsignor Folbèche! For just one morning and to the great vexation of his successor in the post, he had re-occupied the church and parish from which he had been removed. He had never sung mass with so much pomp, authority and love. He climbed to the pulpit and began his sermon for the occasion. When he cried in his vibrant voice: "How sad it is for a woman so lovely and so young to die in the midst of summer!" there were sobs here and there, tears ran down many cheeks, and especially down those of Father Marquis, deacon for the day. Stan thought his heart would break. He pushed his way outside and wondered if he would ever live at peace with himself.

Sitting in his car, sunglasses on his nose, he watched the hearse move off followed by the widower, his family and about a thousand mourners. The church bells sang their noisy farewell to Rita. The procession was to go on foot to the St. Charles cemetery, where the Plouffes had their plot, and where Ovide's wife would come to rest beside the late Théophile. His teeth clenched, Stan watched with hatred in his heart as Pacifique Berthet hoisted himself into the white convertible. For the occasion he had put up the top. The cripple allowed the crowd to pass and then drove slowly behind it, bringing up the rear. Stan waited a moment, took a detour and arrived early at the graveyard, where he hid behind a tombstone. From here he would be able to take part in the ceremony, for it was his very own Rita that they were going to bury, the only woman he had ever loved, and the only one who had ever understood him without making fun of him.

The procession arrived. People gathered around the grave. Stan gazed intently at the scene, imagining himself in Ovide's place. Ovide, in a daze, watched glassy eyed as the coffin slowly descended into the earth, supported by green straps operated by an electric winch of sophisticated design. When the mechanism came to a halt Joséphine moved forward, gave her son a handful of the stony earth, which he tossed down on the varnished hickory, then seemed to listen for the patter of the pebbles on the coffin lid. Ovide's shoulders were heaving, as were Stan Labrie's. Then the family gathered around the widower, supporting him. Suddenly he stiffened, and with a kind of surprising fury, as if he had remembered that his family was as responsible as he was for his wife's death, he pushed them aside, leaving them to their consternation, and went off down the path at his rapid walk. He was running away from the Plouffes, from Rita, from his pain, and even from himself. It was then that Stan, from his observation post, witnessed an even more dramatic event, for (ah, Destiny!) as if this had always been in the cards, Ovide in his flight stumbled into two men of considerable size, who came one on either side of him and, seizing him under the arms, almost lifted him in the air. Their tone allowed for no argument:

"Police. Come along now, no nonsense!"

They dragged him so swiftly to the police car that the stunned observers didn't at once realize what was going on. Napoléon and Guillaume, the first to react, started in pursuit, but the car had already driven away, bearing off an Ovide who was flabbergasted and semi-conscious. In the days to come he was to find himself sinking into depths more profound than the abyss into which Rita had descended.

293

The family remained rooted to the spot, like a freeze frame at the end of a film. Pacifique Berthet, who had remained to one side of the group, understood at once. The anxiety that had gripped him since the accident now turned to panic. His aluminum crutches propelled him forward in great bounds. Like a desperate kangaroo he zigzagged among the mausoleums, the gravestones and the humble crosses, the whiteness of his face rivalling that of the marble monuments. Suddenly the members of the family emerged from their horrified surprise.

"My Ovide! He's being kidnapped! Run, why don't you! Catch them!" bawled Joséphine in terror.

With the spontaneous gesture of the pastor leading his flock, Monsignor Folbèche, with Gédéon's help, held Joséphine erect and led the clan away.

"Let us first go home," he said soberly, "and have confidence in Our Lord! Without him, I assure you, we are nothing."

Only Stan Labrie had seen Pacifique in flight. Despite his emotion he managed to keep an eye on the cripple, who seemed literally to have taken flight as he left the graveyard. Ovide arrested? So Bob the architect had been right yesterday on the phone when he said the police were looking very closely at Ovide's activities! Bob had warned him to stay away from the Plouffes: Caution! But the pimp's curiosity got the better of him. He left his hiding place behind the gravestone, ran to the deserted grave, tossed his own handful of dust on the tomb and crossed himself, murmuring, "Rita, I'll always love you!" Then, following his scoundrel's instinct, he walked rapidly in the direction Berthet had taken. Stan arrived at the road where the cars were parked in time to see the man toss his crutches into the convertible and drive off in a rush. Stan thought Berthet's behaviour highly suspicious, especially following hard on his partner's arrest.

Certain that Pacifique could only be going to his cottage on Lake St. Augustin, Stan took his time as he got into his own car and drove off in the same direction. During the few kilometres to his goal, he thought again of the frightening scene of Ovide's arrest and Bob's anxious phone call the evening before. What if Stan had to testify some day? It was awful how he was drawn to these Plouffes, as if by a magnet. And Berthet intrigued and obsessed him. What kind of a microbe was he, anyway? Stan had the odd certainty that in following the cripple in his car he was taking part in Rita's vengeance and proving his courage to her. To hell with Bob the architect and his petty fears!

Driving slowly along the winding road that followed the shore of Lake St. Augustin with its scattering of frame cottages painted in bright colours, Stan quickly located the cripple's hut where, a month earlier, he had threatened Berthet with reprisals if he ever whispered a word of Rita's escapade on the Montmorency River. He saw from some distance the white convertible, parked in the entry to his lot, which was fenced in with sheets of rusted metal. The pimp left his car a hundred metres away, near the public beach, where he could hear the shouts of children swimming. Looking frequently behind him and hugging the hedges, he finally reached Berthet's land and managed silently to take up a position between a thick bush and the hole left where a section of fence had been half detached by the wind. He saw no one in front of the shanty, where a little vegetable garden invaded by couch grass bore tomatoes on the point of ripening and ears of corn ready for picking. All kinds of rubbish was strewn on the ground, bits of board, rusty pails, empty cans, shards of beer or gin bottles. Beside the tin fence, at the back of the yard, lay the row boat, partly painted, upside down on sawhorses, showing that Pacifique had other pastimes than rowing in the gloaming. Stan cocked an ear. From inside the hut came the sound of drawers being quickly opened and shut, chairs pushed around, cupboard doors being pulled at and slammed. It seemed, indeed, that Pacifique in his feverish haste, was banging into chairs and furniture. This stir of activity must indicate a rapid inventory.

Berthet appeared at last on the veranda, this time on his old wooden crutches. He locked the door and cast a searching look around. Reassured, he went around behind his shanty to the rear of his property, and stood pensively over a square of freshly turned earth. A few empty beer cases were piled at the very rear. Limping rapidly, Pacifique returned to the cabin and took a shovel from beneath the veranda. He held it for a moment, glancing furtively around, then tossed it back where it had come from. Now he was hobbling swiftly over to the square of earth. He picked up the garden spade that lay there and started nervously breaking up the lumps of humus and manure. He shook them and spread them about. Again he cast his furtive glance around and went back to work, as if to give this patch of ground the look of a future garden. He had to work awkwardly, with only one hand, his powerful right, while the left one grasped his crutch as it sank into the loose earth. Then, sweating like a horse, he traced a few furrows. At every sound of a car driving by on the road he would turn with a start, stop for a second, then continue. At last he was satisfied with the result. He threw down the spade and went exhausted to the veranda where he managed to sit and rest.

Stan, behind his bush, wondered how Berthet could have the courage to do his gardening on such a steaming day. He was just about to leave his observation post when he saw a police car whirl into Pacifique's driveway. Two policemen emerged. The conversation was brief. Then Berthet, having picked up a jacket, followed them to their car and was directed to the back seat. The police car drove off at once.

Stan's heart was beating so fast that he could barely breathe. Wow! If the cops had caught him here! Bob was right. It was best to keep away from the whole business.

35

It was like a bad melodrama. Ovide Plouffe, limp as a rag, found himself being dragged from one office to the next at Provincial Police headquarters with a brutality, anger and hatred that revealed the conviction of the police: Ovide Plouffe had blown up the DC3. He kept repeating hoarsely:

"This is an outrage! Let me go! It's a nightmare! Wake me up! There's been a monstrous misunderstanding, call my family, reassure them, please! What on earth have I done? Are you crazy?"

The policemen sneered fiercely:

"Yeah, that's what they all say. So shut your mouth, eh? You'll find out what's going to happen to you in due time."

They had searched him, emptied his pockets and taken his finger prints. Reporters that they hadn't been able to keep out of the headquarters corridors had managed to get pictures of him as he arrived, dazed, between two detectives. Where were they going to take him? Merciless orders came down from the Attorney General: to the preliminary hearing, on the double!

And speed up the process! It was urgent that the investigation, the charge of murder and the trial should follow at record speed, skipping the thousand and one complications that so often slow these procedures. The defence lawyer would be informed of this as well. From now on, the world would be watching Quebec, and they would see with what a firm hand order was maintained there and how strictly justice was made to triumph.

Ovide was shoved onto a straight-backed chair facing a bare table, in a room at jungle temperature. Big enough to hide the door, a massive policeman, his right hand resting on his pistol butt, was mopping his brow with his left. Yet Ovide felt a chill. Assailed on all sides by emotions out of control, he reacted by fits and starts without rhyme or reason, or fell into a glacial apathy. His mind was working in slow motion, as if it were saving its strength to encounter the forces of fate converging on him. Still shattered by the loss of his wife, he was at sea, defenceless against this latest frightful blow of destiny. What appalling combination of circumstances had brought him here? Why was he being pushed around? This must surely be a nightmare – or had he died with Rita in the DC3? And was this his purgatory, where his torture consisted of his present suffering? Passing through all the stages of fear, he felt no urge to cry out or weep: only a violent desire to wake up. As through a fog, he saw two giant plainclothes cops sit down at the table across from him and dump on it a briefcaseful of documents. The cutting, icy words of the one who seemed to be in charge came to Ovide as through a wall. This was pure Kafka! The man's first, frightful words left him stunned:

"Ovide Plouffe, you are being held as a material witness in the case of the crash of the Canadian Pacific's DC3 aircraft. Twenty-three people were killed, among them your wife, Rita Toulouse. We have ample evidence that this is murder."

Ovide, his voice quavering, his brain function at the level of a lower primate, stammered:

"Murder? Material witness? But I witnessed nothing! This is all a mistake! Let me go home, please! This is a bad joke!"

The two men shrugged and smiled knowingly.

"Wouldya listen to that!" said the senior cop. "We all knew you were a good actor, but that beats all!" Then, in a steely tone: "We're going to ask you a few questions. You have the right to a lawyer of your choice or we can supply you with one."

"A lawyer? But I'm only a material witness, not a murderer. A lawyer!" floundered Ovide, horrified, beginning to see the shape of the threat hanging over him: they were getting ready to accuse him of murder!

His long arms fluttered like wings.

"I tell you I don't want a lawyer! It's stupid! I don't need to be defended! You're making a terrible mistake. Ask me your questions, any questions, I'll answer them openly, sincerely, straight from the heart. And after that you can make your apologies!"

The senior officer gave a meaningful glance at his assistant.

"As you wish. That'll save time. And as if it really made any difference. . . ."

The chief inquisitor stood up. Standing, his arms crossed, this man assumed gigantic proportions in Ovide's eyes, who felt himself shrink to the size of a fetus.

"Ovide Plouffe, is it true that in the spring of 1940 you were expelled from the monastery of the White Fathers of Africa for having delivered a knock-out blow to the man in the neighbouring cell, Brother Léopold?"

He almost smiled. At last, here was the proof that he was having a nightmare.

"Yes, but for very special reasons. In my place you'd have knocked him out twice."

He tried to answer brilliantly so that when he woke up he wouldn't have to be ashamed of Ovide Plouffe's behaviour in his dreams.

"Nobody asked you to comment!" snapped the torturer. "Just answer yes or no."

"Yes," he said, daunted and pitiful.

"When you were fifteen did you not try to choke another boy in your class, whom you would have strangled if you had not been prevented in time?"

Ovide stared at him, astounded. These policemen were real wizards! He had completely forgotten the incident. But now it all came back to him.

"Yes, but he'd called me a sissy. That's the worst insult for a man like me."

The senior cop smiled cruelly:

"Right, you're too fond of the ladies for that! But nobody can say you're a softy. You're pretty fast with your fists or a revolver or a stranglehold, eh? The rest follows from that, of course."

Horrified, Ovide realized that his past had been investigated in detail. They must have checked with all his friends. No wonder they hadn't turned up at the funeral parlour! A net had been cast over the sleeping gladiator! Luckily, this was only a dream. What next? A lawyer! Come, come! No lawyer for him! He'd explain everything, they'd apologize and he'd be set free at once.

"Have you ever been under psychiatric care?"

That set him off. He spoke in a flood, because the policeman had touched on one of his favourite subjects.

"Psychiatrists? Those quacks who take advantage of poor depressed victims? Never in your life. Freud? Thank you very much from Ovide Plouffe. I may be different from other people, I've been told that often enough, but I'm in full possession of my moral and intellectual faculties!"

The two men examined Ovide as if he had been some exotic animal. This strange material witness, who was, after all, responsible for the death of twenty-three people, was beginning to impress them. The assistant said, warily:

"We hear you're kind of a walking encyclopaedia, that you know everything, even the future, you understand everything, and you can learn in three months what another man would learn in a year."

"Let's not exaggerate," said Ovide, almost embarrassed and rather flattered, feeling that perhaps the wind might turn in his favour. These policemen actually seemed capable of appreciating his intellectual powers!

The assistant grew more daring, his tone grew confident:

"They say your late wife was very pretty. It is true you were jealous and made her give up the Miss Sweet Caporal title?"

That made Ovide angry. He said curtly:

"That wasn't jealousy, that was principle! And that was our business anyway, between her and me. It's true, I didn't agree to the Miss Sweet Caporal business, and Rita obeyed me. Would you like to see your wife. . . ."

"I'm not married. Is it true that in recent years she had some little flirtations, or maybe not so little, and that made you wild?"

Ovide stiffened at this odious insinuation.

"I'm not here to soil my wife's memory! I always loved and respected her."

The officers observed his reactions avidly.

"Come on, everybody knows about it, don't play dumb."

Again Ovide felt a wave of panic. Did they know about the adventures Stan had set up for Rita, or were they just fishing? Ovide remembered his wife's face in the morgue when he had gone there to identify her. In that moment he had forgiven her everything and had wept like a child. He moaned:

"Please, stop this torture! You know very well that a woman as pretty as my wife attracts men. Every husband has to put up with that. I admit, there were times when I was furious and unhappy. But I aways got over it, I knew she meant no harm. She loved being admired. But all that wasn't serious."

"Did you ever beat her?"

"Never! Never in the world!"

The tone of his questioners, following a planned crescendo, hardened again:

"On December the second, 1948, you did sign an insurance policy, did you not, which stated that if one of the partners died an accidental death, the two others would receive fifty thousand dollars each?"

Ovide was nauseated. What an unspeakable idea! He was supposed to have killed his Rita for fifty thousand dollars! He wished that he too could die. Oh, why had he not boarded the plane with her? He managed to pull himself together and speak, but wearily, as after a long effort:

"Insurance! The insurance! I'd completely forgotten it. Shortly after we started the business last fall, my partner Pacifique Berthet suggested we be insured. I found that a normal precaution. I often had to travel on business. But, gentlemen, this suspicion you seem to have, it's unheard of!"

"Yes, sickening, indeed!" the policeman said sarcastically. "But it's a little strange, isn't it, that when it came to the fatal trip you weren't on board!"

"Stop this, you're monsters!" cried Ovide, horrified.

They didn't react. He was sobbing in rebellion and frustration. How could God allow so many trials to descend on one man! Broken, he went on:

"And on top of everything else, you arrested me barely a minute after I threw the earth on her grave, in front of my mother, my family, my friends, everybody!"

And as if finally awakening from his nightmare, he straightened up, remembering:

"But they must be going mad with anxiety! Call them, tell

them it's nothing serious, I'll be home shortly. Napoléon will pick me up. Call my mother, for heaven's sake! And what about my little daughter, little Arlette!"

Astonished and slightly shaken, they looked him up and down. The chief's voice was softer, but still cutting:

"Maybe you should think a little about the other twenty-two funerals!"

His eyes staring, he slumped on the chair, livid.

"You don't mean you think I blew up the plane!"

The silence grew unbearable.

"Indeed, that seems very likely to us."

Before them they saw a broken man who now replied in a lifeless voice, from the depths of his despair. This was what they had been waiting for.

"On June the sixth last you were in the Chez Gérard restaurant. A fight started and you pulled a .38 revolver. True?"

"Yes. The waitress had been insulted by some hooligans. I took her part. There are things a gentleman cannot tolerate. I was attacked by four brutes who could have torn me to pieces. I wanted to frighten them. It was legitimate self-defence, wasn't it?"

"Do you always go around like that, with a .38 in your pocket?"

"As a jeweller I have a permit. The gun wasn't loaded. I don't know why, but I picked it up in the store that night and stuck it in my pocket. Probably thinking about the dangerous streets near the club."

"Absent-minded are you? Well I guess!" said the officer gently.

Ovide's mouth was dry. He was seized by panic. He had just told a small lie. He had not said that after Rita's awful confession he had felt a physical necessity to kill Stan, and then hadn't killed him, of course. But he was no criminal. The proof of that was, he had forgotten the shells. Yet Stan had been his reason for going to Chez Gérard. That and the desire to see Marie again and to get her phone number.

The police continued to unroll their carpet of questions before him. He was sure they were leading him on to further terrors.

"This young French girl, Marie Jourdan, you like her, do you?"

He started, tried to swallow.

"She is a very beautiful girl, cultivated, sensitive, alone and defenceless."

"You know her background?"

"Of course I do. No fault of hers, poor child! I hope you didn't go pestering her with questions about me?"

"Yesterday. She was actually getting ready to leave Canada in a few days. We're keeping her here. Right now she's under the protection of the French consulate."

Ovide was floundering like a chicken with its head cut off. His stupefaction could go no further. Marie, mixed up in this shameful business!

"You recently went on a three-week trip to the North Shore and Anticosti, right?"

Ovide shuddered. To think he had wanted to relieve Marie in her solitude and disarray! And all he had done was drag her into his own tragic wake.

"I beg you, leave Miss Jourdan out of this distressing affair. Because of her beauty and good upbringing, and because of myself and the fight I started in Chez Gérard to protect her, she lost her job. As she had nothing to fall back on, I thought it only fair to hire her as a temporary secretary for a trip around my territories on the North Shore. That's plain enough, isn't it?"

They were having a good laugh.

"I guess you had a piece or two. She's a bombshell, all right, the little French girl. Yes siree! Come on, get a load of this, friend!"

They tossed down the photos he had taken during the trip. They had seized them at Marie's place. There was the couple, barefoot in the water, hair blowing in the wind, hand in hand on the shore, picnicking beside a checkered tablecloth, in a field. Photographed alone on several occasions, Marie looked like the actress Viviane Romance. Ovide remembered how he had desired her as he was making the camera settings. Other pictures showed them eating in a hotel, swimming by a waterfall, canoeing on the Jupiter.

"All right, out with it. Does she do a good job for her country, the French kid? Tell us all about it."

They were laughing again. Ovide found them hateful. Joking this way while he was floundering in an immense sump of despair and death! But he still had the strength to raise his voice to defend Marie's honour as he had that of Rita.

"I forbid you to make any vulgar insinuations about that young woman! She is a pure and honest person, and our relationship was one of the noblest kind of friendship. We talked together about music, poetry, literature and France."

"Oh yeah?!!"

The cops were impressed. What a performer!

Cold rage hardened Ovide's heart. He would have liked to pepper them both with a tommy gun. Perhaps he did have criminal tendencies! The torturers, more and more sure of themselves, continued their interrogation with the gentleness of a bulldog holding a dead cat in his mouth. They offered him a glass of water.

"Ovide Plouffe, on the morning of June 12 you bought a statue of St. Christopher two feet high at Paquet's store, for which statue you paid thirty-five dollars."

"Yes, that was an errand I ran for my partner, who wanted to make a present of it to Monsignor Folbèche. As you know, the Monsignor was exiled to a settlement parish above Baie-Comeau after he attacked Duplessis and some of the clergy from the pulpit during the Asbestos strike. Monsignor Folbèche loves statues."

"Yeah, yeah, we know all that. And didn't you, on June 12"—they showed him a clipping—"refer to Mr. Duplessis as a potentate, a dictator and an enemy of democracy? With a four-column headline?"

"It's a free country, isn't it? I'll say it right here and now: Duplessis is a dictator!"

Ovide was thinking. Suddenly he sat up straight. Aha! Now the cat was out of the bag! This vile persecution was all politics! He thought of Garcia Lorca. The government was using the plane crash as a stick with which to beat Ovide Plouffe! At that moment he decided to consider this interrogation to be a detective film of which he would now act as the sceptical and well-informed spectator. But he did not reckon with the next question, which had been cleverly prepared and timed:

"You're against everything, against the government, against authority and law and order. You can't allow anything to stand in your way, or in the way of your opinions! Ovide Plouffe, on that same twelfth of June last, you went to Samson and Filion's hardware store and you bought fifty sticks of dynamite and detonators. True or false?"

The question came to Ovide like a blow in the solar plexus. The word dynamite had been putting him in a cold sweat for the last three days. He bleated:

"Yes, yes indeed. I even told the salesman the history of the Nobel Prize. I bought those sticks of dynamite at the request of my partner, Pacifique Berthet. As I told you, he is crippled and has trouble getting around. He needed the dynamite to blast some stumps at his cottage on Lake St. Augustin. Ask him. He'll confirm it."

"He's got to have broad shoulders, that partner of yours. We've thought of everything. We just arrested him. He'll be questioned, too."

"Pacifique arrested!" Ovide exclaimed. "But who's going to run our jewellery store? We'll be ruined! And look at the reputation you're giving the two of us!"

The police couldn't believe such simplicity in a criminal, in this arch-psychopath.

"I'm afraid, you know, your career as a jeweller may be over. By the way, it might interest you to know: your partner Berthet didn't blast any stumps at his cottage because there are no stumps there!"

Ovide sucked his cheeks to keep his teeth from chattering. The net was tightening around the gladiator, he could see the two policemen through the mesh. His brain had lost all control of the kaleidoscope that flashed there. Among other images he saw Pacifique Berthet at the hospital, starting his radio at a particular time with the aid of wires attached to his alarm clock. But he was not about to blow the whistle on Pacifique just to save his own skin! In a toneless voice he murmured:

"Gentlemen, excuse me, but don't you think you're putting together some sort of detective story here?"

"Yeah, and it's going to sell!" said one, while the other held up a Big Ben alarm clock, one of Ovide's most popular items.

"Do you know this kind of gadget?"

"Yes, of course! It's a Big Ben. We sell a lot of them in our store. It's a cheap alarm clock. Most of our clientele are workers and have to get up early. An alarm clock for a worker is almost as important as bread."

"Ovide Plouffe, on July 14 last, you personally took a parcel about two feet long out of your jewellery store and brought it to the airport in the taxi you rode in with your wife. All through the trip you reminded the driver to avoid the bumps and drive slowly because the package on your knees was very fragile."

"Of course, it was the statue, the gift from my partner to

Monsignor Folbèche, the one I bought for him at Paquet's store. I told you that already!"

"And at the airport did you not insist that the baggage clerk handle your parcel with special care?"

"Of course! A plaster statue is a fragile thing!"

Ovide was suffocating. Could the box have been stuffed with dynamite by Pacifique? The two policemen, measuring the progress of Ovide's panic, began to strike home with cruel precision.

"Your family thought you were going with your wife on this trip. How does it come that at the last moment you let her go alone? She'd never even been on a trip by plane with you! This was her first flight!"

Ovide's hesitation was occasioned by terror.

"We'd been on bad terms for a while. She knew I wasn't going with her, and she agreed. But I didn't want my family, my mother especially, to know I wasn't accompanying her, they thought the trip would bring us together again. It was a personal problem between Rita and me."

"What was the problem?"

"Surely a couple can be on bad terms without its being cause for crime! Can't they? We'd just had a spat, that's all."

"Did your wife know you'd been on a trip for three weeks with Marie Jourdan as your secretary?"

"Yes. And it certainly made her sad. But I swore that nothing went on between us."

They laughed.

"And she believed you?"

A desperate rage strangled Ovide.

"Yes, she believed me, because she knew me, damn it!"

They remained unmoved.

"Too bad that St. Christopher in the parcel couldn't help out against the explosion. Was your wife Rita supposed to carry it all by herself in her arms, right to Monsignor Folbèche?"

Disgusted by so much cruelty and cynicism, Ovide spat out his reply:

"I had made arrangements for it to be delivered by parcel service truck in Baie-Comeau."

"The plane took off late?"

"Yes, ten minutes or so. We were waiting for some Americans, directors of Iron Ore."

"Our witnesses say you seemed very nervous."

Ovide shrugged.

"I'm always in a bit of a fuss. And especially that morning, I saw Rita was anxious and I almost changed my mind. I nearly went with her. But I had an appointment elsewhere."

The senior officer attacked suddenly:

"If the plane had taken off on time it would have crashed right in the middle of the river. Then there'd have been no dynamite smell, the evidence would have been drowned in the sea, carried off by the current. It was the perfect crime, eh, Mr. Ovide Plouffe?"

He leapt to his feet, shouting:

"What? Will you stop this torture? Say it was murder, tell me why you suspect me?"

"Didn't we say enough? You don't catch on very fast. Go on, sit down, cool off, Mr. Innocent, the great actor. Let's continue this charming conversation. Your appointment elsewhere was at the monastery of the White Fathers of Africa, wasn't it? Eh?"

Ovide, exhausted, like a scarecrow without a crosspiece, his mouth twisted in a sob that refused to come, mumbled wearily:

"Yes. In the cell I'd lived in for a year some time ago as a lay brother. I wanted to find peace again, put some order in my life. I was going for a three-day retreat."

The policemen were smiling again.

"It sure didn't last that long. Barely two hours after you got there you took off out the window. But first you drew this."

They showed him the crude sketch he had left on the little desk before he fled. It showed Ovide cornered between two women with opulent breasts, lying nude beside a river. Humiliated, feeling unable to communicate his intimate life to these brutes, Ovide, who detested all kinds of confession, stammered:

"How can I explain it to you? I should never have gone back to the monastery. In that cell the past overwhelmed me and made the atmosphere of the place intolerable. I didn't know what I was doing. I wrote and scribbled automatically. I heard voices accusing me for letting Rita leave alone. The devil himself bombarded me with obscene images. I felt like Flaubert's St. Anthony. Oh! You don't know Flaubert? He's a great novelist, he wrote *Madame Bovary*."

The policemen could not believe their ears. This Ovide Plouffe was a character.

"You didn't know what you were doing, but you ran to the French consulate anyway. And celebrated the Fourteenth of July!"

"I suddenly found the invitation in my pocket. I was upset, where else should I go?"

"And right away you got together with Marie Jourdan! Just by chance she was there, too!"

"Nothing strange about that. She is French, and I'm the most ardent Francophile in Quebec!"

"I suppose this is you in the photo, with a big grin on your face and your arm around her waist?"

"Yes," he said, stupefied.

The voice of the senior policeman, sharpened with anger, indignation and disgust, tortured his ears and his mind:

"And while you were dancing the java and laughing your head off with your mistress, your wife was dead and sitting in the wreckage of the plane. You son of a bitch."

Ovide buried his head in his hands and wept. Every move he made was laid open to public opinion – he who was so jealous of his privacy. Why did this happen to him and not to others? The assistant, pitiless, took advantage of Ovide's despair to try for a confession.

"On July the thirteenth you went to a travel agency and asked how much it would cost for two people to fly to Paris and stay there six months. True or false?"

"I was tired out. I wanted a change from my country and the people I see all the time. I've been dreaming of Paris ever since I was a child, the Champs-Elysées, Notre-Dame, French culture, the Opera."

"Was your companion on this trip to have been your wife or Marie Jourdan?"

He would gladly have died to put an end to the torture. He stammered:

"M . . . my wife, I swear it!"

Ovide's replies had such an air of sincerity about them that the policemen, perplexed, were wondering if they hadn't stumbled on the greatest actor in the world, or a madman capable of ignoring the accumulation of circumstantial evidence that pointed to his guilt. They were silent for a while, then suddenly:

307

"Where were you when you learned of your wife's death?"

"At the French consulate. Claude Saint-Amant, from the radio station, had a phone call, and told me I should go home at once, that it was very serious. I ran to the jewellery store. My partner told me the news. He almost fainted when he saw me. He thought I was on the plane, he thought I must have died with my wife."

The inquisitors frowned:

"He thought you were dead? Oh yes. Of course. By the way, what do you think of Pacifique Berthet?"

"Don't ask me to point the finger at him. He's a conscientious craftsman, very competent. He is rather taciturn but that's understandable. It's his handicap that makes him that way."

"Is he a straightforward character?"

"Oh, I'm sure of that."

The next remark dropped like a ton of bricks:

"He maintains, and swears up and down, that he never asked you to get him the dynamite."

Ovide, taken by surprise, leapt to his feet:

"But that's a lie! A dirty lie! I got it for him, for blasting tree stumps! I could buy explosives because people knew me, he couldn't. What should I do, for God's sake, with fifty sticks of dynamite?"

"Blow up a plane and kill twenty-three people. And get rid of your wife!"

Ovide shouted:

"Pacifique would never say a thing like that! Impossible! You're lying! You're fooling me, that's it, you never even questioned him."

Berthet couldn't have denied it! Ovide thought he was going mad. Or else . . . Pacifique was guilty! The policemen were working up to their final attack. From a brown paper bag they took the twisted remains of an alarm clock.

The detective's voice took on a tragic tone for the finishing blow:

"Ovide Plouffe, dynamiting the DC3 is a heinous crime, committed by exploding a home-made bomb consisting of some thirty sticks of dynamite connected to an alarm clock, trademark Big Ben, the remains of which you see here. The mechanism was set to cause the plane to explode above the St. Lawrence River. As the plane was ten minutes late it exploded over land. The device was in the baggage bay in the left-hand corner. You are the one who bought the dynamite, you brought the package containing the statue and the bomb. You wanted to get rid of your wife so as to cash in the insurance money and live in Paris with Marie Jourdan. This was a horrible murder, the first of its kind in our aviation history. You planned your crime with diabolical cleverness and all we know about you indicates that you are an amoral person and a danger to society. Behind your frank and open appearance and your taste for culture is a man who stops at nothing to satisfy his whims. You are a low scoundrel endowed with a superior intelligence. Come now, confess, Ovide Plouffe! We've got you where we want you. If you confess you'll save a lot of time for a lot of people. Confess and you shorten the sufferings of your family, which you have dishonoured. The sooner you swing on the gallows, the sooner we'll be rid of a monster with a human mask!"

Ovide's jaws gaped. He saw himself dangling on a rope, just like in the westerns. For a moment he dreamed he had eagles' wings, to fly from this frightful world; then he became the invisible man who could evaporate in their faces and disappear through the door, only to reappear when the true villain was found. Again he leapt to his feet as if propelled by a gun:

"I admit nothing, do you hear? You're insane! I'm innocent! Make a bomb? Make a bomb? I could never do it. Ask Berthet, he'd know how. Look, at the hospital where I got to know him his radio came on at seven every morning. He had it wired to an alarm clock! And he talked me into going on that trip with my wife, my whole family backed him up! And he got me to buy the dynamite! And the statue!"

Ovide fainted, was unconscious for a few moments. They picked him up. In a daze, he heard the senior inquisitioner say:

"Your partner Berthet will be interrogated in a few minutes."

They dragged Ovide out. The officer gave a curt order:

"To the Quebec jail, fast. No bail. The Attorney General has enough evidence for a charge of premeditated murder in the first degree!"

Ovide's teeth were chattering. Was he still asleep? The nightmare was never-ending. Dragged along by two officers toward the exit, where a police van was waiting, as well as a crowd of photographers, the unfortunate Ovide met Pacifique in the corridor, accompanied by a single guard. He shouted to him:

"Tell the truth, Pacifique! Tell them I bought the dynamite for you!"

Pacifique's steely gaze stared him up and down, but there was no other reaction.

The two torturers who had just left Ovide in such a sorry state made Pacifique take the same chair, which he sat on as best he could, holding on to one crutch. They made him take the oath, but made no mention of a lawyer. The two detectives took their time, shuffling their documents. Everything pointed to Ovide, but his extraordinary frankness under questioning had impressed them, and they were still upset by it. They refused to admit they were impressionable, preferring to cling to their convictions. But Pacifique could have been an accomplice. If he was, they'd have to cover themselves. Pacifique also profited by Rita's death. Fifty thousand dollars! And he was the one who had suggested the insurance. They expected a different sort of performance from this cripple with the eagle eye. He would certainly be less emotional than Ovide.

"Pacifique Berthet, you were born in Grenoble, France, in a working-class family. Your father was a drunkard and your mother died of consumption when you were four. You're quite right to stick your jaw out like that, my friend, because your record in Grenoble, checked out by Interpol at our request, shows us that at the age of fourteen after several charges of breaking and entering you were put in a correctional school for eighteen months. That was where you learned your trade as a watchmaker. You arrived in Quebec in 1932 and at once found work in the jewellery store called La Canadienne. In 1935 you had a serious fall, which developed into tubercular coxalgia. From that time until one year ago, you lived from hand to mouth, first repairing watches at your domicile and then receiving stolen goods on occasion as well as committing other minor crimes. But nothing serious. Right?"

They had been doing their homework. But Pacifique didn't blink.

"Correct!" he barked.

"Apart from your little visits to the bordello at 33 Saint-Roch, no women in your life?"

"No!"

He stared at them with hatred, and his answers snapped back, short and cutting, as if he did not want to give them an opportunity to prolong the torture of interrogation. He was so sure that they couldn't touch him!

"I have to pay for that. In my state I've never found a woman ready to do it for nothing. The only woman who comes to my place is a cleaner, seventy years old."

"You're a Frenchman. Do you like it here in the province of Quebec?"

"Not today."

"The fourteenth of July: is that your favourite day for giving gifts, especially statues?"

"I promised it to Monsignor Folbèche when he left the parish. He seemed depressed."

"Ovide Plouffe bought it for you at your request on June the twelfth. Where did you keep it?"

"On the work bench in my repair shop."

"Ovide Plouffe lives upstairs above the jewellery store?"

"As if you didn't know."

"So he could come down in the evening?"

"He often does, in fact. Does his books."

"And you?"

"I leave at about six and come in at eight next morning. When I leave the place I have no desire to go back there at night."

"You bought a white convertible that had been Madame Ovide Plouffe's?"

"I paid seven hundred dollars for it. We're making money with the business and I thought I'd give myself a treat. I had the garage put in a hand control for the accelerator."

The two were sizing him up, the pause grew long. Interpol's report indicated that Pacifique Berthet was endowed with an above-average intelligence. Suddenly they moved in:

"Ovide Plouffe assures us that not only did he buy the St. Christopher statue for you, he also, at your request, acquired fifty sticks of dynamite and detonators at Samson and Filion's, in order, it seems, to blast some stumps at your cottage on Lake St. Augustin."

Pacifique knew that Ovide had not mentioned his name to the clerk at the hardware store, but had said only, " . . . for a cottage." His reply cracked like a whiplash:

"He lied. He lied. I know nothing about this business of buying dynamite. Look, he's got a nerve! What the hell would I do with dynamite? There's not a single stump at my cottage. Or are you pulling my leg? I can't believe he would make up such a story about me! That's too much! My own partner!"

Berthet's replies got the detectives nowhere. He had learned early at the correctional school to deal with interrogations. Pacifique tried to shift his position and grimaced with pain. The senior officer asked:

"What do you think of Ovide Plouffe?"

"He's a funny guy. He'd have to be, if he's my partner. That takes an oddball. He's power mad, was coddled and spoiled by his broody mother, is considered a little god in his family and lives in a dream world, non-stop. Those Plouffes are a family of profiteers. They want to grab everything. When we started the business that old farmer, Uncle Gédéon, demanded fifty-five per cent of the shares for Ovide, with forty-five left for me, just because he loaned us ten thousand dollars. We paid him back in four months. It'd make you sick."

"Do you resent Ovide Plouffe?"

"If what you're telling me about the dynamite is true, yes, sirs! In capital letters! That son of a bitch! I never thought that boy, whom I helped to success, would get me into this kind of mess and have me suspected of a crime!"

"Did you know his wife well? Rita Toulouse?"

"Yes. She worked behind the counter until June. A good salesgirl, very friendly. A bit of a flirt. Towards the end things weren't going too well between her and her husband."

"Do you know why?"

"No. I've got used to minding my own business."

The detectives had been baffled by Ovide's explanations. Now they were coldly weighing the cripple's replies – a tougher adversary. The senior man said casually:

"It was you who insisted Ovide take his wife with him in the plane on July the fourteenth? And his family afterwards encouraged the project?"

Berthet shrugged. These Quebec cops were really not up to scratch.

"In the first place, Ovide's trip had been on the books for that day for a long time. I was afraid their spat was going to be bad for business, and I hoped they might patch it up on the trip. And at the same time they could take my present to Monsignor Folbèche, the St. Christopher statue. Nothing funny about that."

"When did you hear about the accident?"

"On my car radio. For a Frenchman who can't walk, the best way to celebrate the Fourteenth of July is to drive."

"Do you think the sticks of dynamite were in the box Ovide Plouffe took to the airport? The one with the statue?"

"I repeat, I knew nothing about that dynamite, I didn't even know it existed. My parcel was ready to go a month ago, on the back of my work bench, addressed and all."

They took another tack:

"Ovide Plouffe says when he got to know you in the hospital you'd put together a device that connected your radio to your alarm clock, and you could have your radio turned on at seven on the dot. Is that true?"

Pacifique had a second's consternation. But he stood firm.

"Pretty elementary. Simple as hell. I even told him how it worked."

"So Ovide Plouffe, during the night of the thirteenth and fourteenth of July, could have gone down to the work shop, opened the parcel, inserted the dynamite, the detonators and the alarm clock set for the fatal hour, re-wrapped the parcel and gone to sleep again without a care in the world?"

"You're the one who said it. But I don't understand. Ovide Plouffe, doing a trick like that? I can't imagine it! Never."

"You knew about his three-week trip to the North Shore with the young French girl, Marie Jourdan, acting as his secretary?"

"Yes, but he was paying her out of his share of the profits. It was his business."

"Do you know her?"

"No, but I think it was because of Marie Jourdan that Rita and Ovide were estranged."

They showed him the wreck of the alarm clock.

"Does this mean anything to you?"

He hesitated, then, imperturbably:

"If I'm not mistaken it's what's left of a Big Ben. We sell them in the shop."

Their steely eyes met his. But he didn't flinch.

"Can you take this alarm clock and use it to explode a home-made bomb at a precise time?"

"You're repeating yourself. You said just now that it could be done. I suppose it can, with a little skill. But it so happens I never made one."

"Is Ovide Plouffe skilful enough to make such a device?"

"I can't answer for him. Ask him yourself."

The two officers, tired of ramming their heads against this granite block, concluded:

"You are aware that a parcel containing a home-made bomb caused the DC3 to explode over Saint-Joachim?"

"After all your questions I'm beginning to suspect it."

"Did you know that Ovide Plouffe was going to cancel his flight and let his wife fly alone?"

"No. I was sure he'd take the plane. I repeat, I was the first one to insist that his wife go with him."

"If he had gone, and the plane had crashed in the river, leaving no clues, you'd have been a hundred thousand dollars richer! Nice work!"

His mind was churning with superhuman intensity:

"Indeed," he said, clearing his throat. "One would have to prove first that the bomb was in the parcel. If it was, and Ovide Plouffe made it, it's logical that he wouldn't take the plane. I doubt very much that Ovide Plouffe would have got himself killed along with his wife just to make me a present of a hundred thousand dollars insurance money."

There was a long silence. The two officers realized that at this rate they were getting nowhere. They had searched Berthet's apartment, his cabin and his workshop, but had found nothing incriminating. And he had no friend or confidant they could have questioned concerning him. There was as yet nothing against him. Yet a doubt persisted. They'd have to keep an eye on this over-intelligent Frenchman who had an answer for everything. They stood up:

"For the moment, Berthet, you're a free man. But stay available. We're going to need you before, during and after Ovide Plouffe's trial."

"Our fine business! It's dead!" he sighed.

His hands less sure than usual, Pacifique swung heavily on his crutches, exhausted, grimacing with pain: his hip was hurting. To be sure, he was glad to be free, but now it was Ovide's word against his. And maybe he'd be suspected of being an accessory to this murder. In the last two days his anxiety had caused him more suffering than his hip.

36

Ovide was propelled brutally into a medieval cell three metres by four in the Quebec jail, where he slumped onto a wretched cot. The July heat was suffocating here. In his desperate abasement he tried to brush aside and reject the terrible truth: he was now in isolation, deprived of the society of others, robbed of his freedom and the happy outside world where birds were singing in the trees a stone's throw away. In fact, a branch cast on the floor of his dark cell the lovely shadow of its twigs and leaves. The shouts of children playing ball rose from the park below, where Wolfe snatched Quebec from the hands of Montcalm in 1759. Reeling, Ovide took the few steps toward the three black bars of his window, which stood as stripes against the blue sky. He could see the bench where, a few days ago, he had taken refuge after breaking with Marie Jourdan. Then he had vainly tried to imagine her at his side as he told her of his life and his aspirations. On that same bench, in the month before his marriage, he had spent long evenings with Rita punctuated by hot kisses and timid caresses on her breasts and thighs. Again on this same bench, just a week ago, he had thrilled at the thought of a mass escape from what was now his own prison; he had dreamed of sawing away the bars and running with the fugitives toward a new freedom.

Past the point of the cape, the St. Lawrence bore the liner *Empress of France* toward the Atlantic and its destination in Europe. Small sailboats and motor launches downstream greeted the giant as it passed, and bathers on the beach at l'Anse-aux-Foulons hurled themselves into the waves of its wake. Their splashing came as a duller sound right to Ovide's ears.

But he was inside. A prisoner! It couldn't be true! This nightmare was really too persistent! Perhaps he would never wake up! He wept without shedding tears, with small, hacking sobs that broke from him with an animal violence. He, Ovide Plouffe, imprisoned and soon to be accused of murder! A long cry of horror surged up from within him and came out in a heartbroken wail. Then he rushed head-first at the stone wall and fell to the floor unconscious. A guard came running and called the medical attendant.

After Ovide's arrest the family had gone at once to Joséphine's place. But Rita's parents had coldly declined to come along. They would not go to this post-burial snack with the Plouffes. Others who were invited followed suit. The clan was beginning to feel its isolation.

Among the Plouffes assembled in the kitchen reigned a tragic quiet broken only by long sighs and snatches of sentences filled with unbearable distress. Guillaume, Napoléon and Ti'-Mé were pacing up and down, hands behind their backs, silent, stopping at times near Joséphine, who sat, a veritable heap of misery slumped in her rocking-chair, gazing bleakly out the window. They would pat her shoulder and whisper with slight conviction:

"Don't worry, it's all a mistake, it'll be ironed out before long. We have to look at the bright side."

Her only reply was a gentle wailing. Her Ovide, arrested like a bandit right in the cemetery, just after tossing his handful of earth on Rita's coffin! Beside Joséphine, Cécile, in a straight-backed chair, was holding back her tears and rubbing Joséphine's hands.

"You know, mama, life isn't fair. Ovide's going to come back to us, though. It's a mistake. They'll soon see that he didn't do it. It's only jealous gossip!"

Jeanne, Napoléon's wife, drew up a chair on the other side and took one of Joséphine's icy hands.

"Cécile is right. A misfortune like that can't go on forever. And till it's all over, we've got to stick together, close as close."

Standing, his arms folded and his head bowed, Monsignor Folbèche was praying. On the seat near the screen door Major Bélanger sat silent and abashed. This kind of misfortune was too much for him, it made him want to run away. Beside the wall telephone Gédéon, his fists clenched nervously, was waiting for a call that might not come.

"Nothing, nothing, we can't find out a thing," complained Guillaume. "It's been three hours now."

Napoléon came face to face with Gédéon and bawled:

"What the hell's she doing, that Auréa of yours? Your famous Duplessis secretary! You're supposed to have so much drag . . . ."

Mumbling, humiliated, in the grip of the tragedy, Gédéon had never felt so helpless. It was two hours since he had called the premier's secretary. And she hadn't called him back! And Ovide was already enclosed in a dungeon of silence built around him by society. Gédéon was trying to judge how serious the whole situation was. There was no help for Ovide just now except the prayers of his loved ones. The old farmer was astonished and intimidated by a Napoléon he had never seen, made fierce by his suffering, his eyes bulging, supplicating:

316

"We just have to wait," Gédéon protested. "If Miss Auréa doesn't call back it's because she's got no news herself, right?"

"What if we turned the radio on?" Major Bélanger said timidly. "We might find out what's going on."

"No!" cried Joséphine. "No radio!"

And no one wanted the radio on. They were sure it would bring bad news. Ti'-Mé, standing at the screen door, was looking out toward the street.

"There's a little crowd gatherin' down there."

"Oh, Lord!" murmured the three women.

"I'm going out to see what's happening," said the major, glad of an excuse to flee.

Napoléon and Guillaume joined Ti'-Mé to have a look, and their dissatisfaction was expressed by a contemptuous snort. Napoléon looked at Jeanne, who understood, and again kissed Joséphine's plump hand. Then the phone rang and everyone jumped as if it had been a thunderclap. Gédéon pounced. "Well! Miss Auréa?" Then his face fell. For the benefit of the Plouffes, who were hanging on his words, he shook his head. It wasn't Miss Auréa. But as he listened his face turned pale and his moustache trembled. Then he hung up. They didn't even shout: "Well?" Was Gédéon going to shirk his duty? Would he let them learn the truth from another? His gaze fell on the photo of his brother Théophile, who seemed to be saying, "You're my older brother, Gédéon. Don't wait. Do what you have to do! Out with it, and do what you can to help!"

Gédéon thought this was something Monsignor Folbèche should take on. But Folbèche said nothing. Gédéon cleared his throat.

"You can charge a man, you know, and still be wrong. It happens all the time. Then they free the accused."

"Charged with what?" shouted Guillaume.

"Well, that was the neighbour's wife. She called to tell us they're saying on the radio Ovide is going to be charged with murdering Rita and the other twenty-two passengers on the plane. With a bomb. Ovide's been taken to the Quebec jail. It's all crazy!"

Not a sound was heard in the kitchen, as if the aftermath of the bomb extended to this place.

"It's not true, it can't be true!" wailed Joséphine.

They all rushed to her, clustered around her despairing lament. But she stood up and burst free of them, she rushed at Gédéon.

"Gédéon, call Maurice Duplessis himself! I want to see him right away!"

Gédéon made her sit down again.

"Let's wait till tomorrow, Joséphine. We can't do anything today. We've all got to settle our nerves. And you know what radio's like. They say he'll be charged, but that's a long way from doing it. Let's not be faint hearted!"

Monsignor Folbèche, who had been quietly praying all this time, came over to Joséphine and made the sign of the cross on her forehead. He said firmly:

"Joséphine, I say to you that Ovide is not guilty of this monstrous crime. Therefore, he will be freed."

Exhausted, she wept against the hand that had blessed her. She grieved aloud:

"He's in a cell, all alone, wishing he was dead, I know it. And I can't be with him! Take me to the prison, let me talk to him and console him and tell him we're all on his side! All of us!"

The old priest looked at them, one after the other. He saw a family so dazed that it could no longer react. He felt a warm light glowing in his heart. He was once more the shepherd of his flock, fearless and blameless, as if the Plouffes had represented the whole of his former parish. He stood tall and shook them awake with his vibrant voice:

"I'm staying here with you until this stupid judicial mistake has been corrected. And I'm not staying at the presbytery, either! The new priest treats me like an interloper, I undermine his authority! If you'll allow me, Joséphine, it's in this very house I'll stay, downstairs, in Guillaume's quarters. I will say mass every morning. It will be easy to get permission from the archbishopric. My vicar can look after my new parish alone for a while. What do you think, Joséphine?"

Joséphine, breathless, was coming back to life. The Good Lord would be in her very house! It would become a chapel! Ovide was as good as saved! Her voice trembled:

"Oh, yes! Yes, Monsignor! You're so good to us! Cécile! We have to get his room ready!"

"Ti'-Mé," said Guillaume, "you better go back to Anticosti alone. I can't go. Have to stay here."

Gédéon was pacing the room as if he had the itch.

318

"I've got to dig up a good criminal lawyer. To hell with the cost!"

"We can share the expenses," said Napoléon, looking at Jeanne, who nodded.

"Of course," said Cécile. "Even if it's expensive I'll pay my share."

"They'll never see a family stick together like us," Napoléon went on. "You go on home, Jeanne, and see to the kids, take any messages from customers. The rest, the family here, we've got to talk."

"Ain't I family?" she said softly.

Sadly, he shook his head.

"Don't say things like that, honey! We're in for some bad times, and everybody has to do his bit and protect whatever progress we make. It's Ovide we have to save. In the next while you're goin' to have to help me more than ever and look after me. Look after the kids. Keep the business going. It won't be easy, Jeanne!"

She held him close for a moment, kissed Joséphine and left.

"The major never came back up. We'll never see him again," Cécile said softly.

She was thinking of little Nicolas and the high lawyer's fees. The future looked difficult, with little prospect of joy for her. Absurd ideas kept racing through her mind: gone was the hope of landing the young assistant foreman. Tomorrow she would go down to the harbour and throw the Miss Sweet Caporal uniform into the river, along with the wedding dress she'd made for herself long ago and never used.

No one was talking, everybody was trying to evaluate the fallout of this disaster on his own life. Gédéon imagined his influence with Duplessis would be finished. And he was afraid no criminal lawyer of consequence would agree to defend a man charged with such a hideous crime. Napoléon knew that his business would suffer and perhaps go under. Good-bye government contracts! Already Napoléon was coming to terms courageously with these misfortunes, as long as the main cause was won: freedom for Ovide. Guillaume was thinking he would never be able to follow through on the romance he'd started with Marie on the banks of the Jupiter. What use was his strength if he couldn't help Ovide? In the war he had killed the enemy, taken prisoners, performed extraordinary feats. And here at home in peacetime he couldn't do a thing to save his own brother! And then, what if Ovide was really guilty! He shivered, thinking of the German girl he had killed over there. Could Ovide, betrayed by his wife, have done the same thing? He thought of their cabin on Anticosti, where Ti'-Mé and he had intended to have a fine time until the fall. And how his mother was suffering from all this!

Joséphine was rocking, eyes closed, moaning gently to herself, monotonously, spasmodically, as if she had gone to sleep holding a child in her arms. Ti'-Mé quietly opened the oven and took out two pork pies that had been put in to heat for after the funeral. Noiselessly he put them on the table.

"Ketchup is in the cupboard," said Joséphine weakly.

Guillaume shook Napoléon by the shoulder.

"We'll come to our senses, we'll come around!" he growled quietly. "We have to get our brother out of this. We have to!"

In fact, each of them was trying to keep burning in himself the tiny flame of courage without which nothing can be saved.

37

Despite Uncle Gédéon's efforts in the premier's office and those of Monsignor Folbèche at the Archbishop's palace, it was forbidden during the next two days for anyone to see Ovide. And he – his head throbbing from its encounter with his cell wall – saw himself tossed like a rag from one interrogation to the next. His constant suffering came close to a kind of hallucination and left him floating half-conscious, repeating defiantly, "I'm innocent! I'm innocent!"

Then news of the charge of premeditated murder against Ovide Plouffe burst like an apocalyptic thunderclap over Quebec and at once spread around the world. For the first time in history a criminal had blown up an airplane with a delayed-action bomb, to get rid of his wife and to collect the fifty-thousand dollars' worth of insurance that would permit him to set up housekeeping in Paris with a waitress. In every family, at every level of society, people talked only of the fabulous murder, plotted by this young man of modest background, with quiet manners, self-taught, a jeweller, opera buff and radio commentator. The photos of Ovide in handcuffs, of Rita as

Miss Sweet Caporal, of Marie Jourdan, said to be his mistress, of the accused and his wife on their wedding day, made all the front pages. Hundreds of curiosity-seekers came to gawk at the store – closed until further notice – then passed by and stared at Joséphine's house. Street urchins even threw stones at the windows. Guillaume replaced the glass as required. The city became world famous and was the focus of the news: a foul deed had made Quebec renowned. In the four corners of the earth excited reporters had packed their bags and were converging on the provincial capital. There were already twenty-odd combing the city and the parish, on the look out for juicy new details. Some even had the impudence to show up at Joséphine's house, but Guillaume sent them packing. And of course they went after Pacifique Berthet and all others who had had the slightest contact with Ovide Plouffe and Rita Toulouse.

The most anxious and nervous of all these journalists turned up from New York at Ancienne-Lorette airport. This tall, elegant young man, trim in a grey pin-stripe, was Denis Boucher, born in Quebec City and formerly a neighbour of the Plouffes and a great friend of Ovide's. He had had his baptism of fire as a war correspondent and was now working for the big American magazines, *Time* and *Life*. He filled his lungs with the good Quebec air he had not breathed for four years and glanced at his watch. His appointment with the premier, arranged by *Time*'s top management, was set for noon. Two hours to wait. That meant Denis had time to drop in on the Plouffes. What a scoop! His friends would tell him stuff that they'd never reveal to others! Denis knew the neighbourhood like the back of his hand. And he'd insist that the premier allow him to see the accused. When it was all over he would leave Quebec City a famous man. In New York he'd be a somebody! His friend Ovide Plouffe, guilty of a crime like that! Wow! What a thrilling adventure! He jumped into a taxi.

The Plouffe home was as thoroughly in quarantine as if it had been a place of the plague. Neighbours and friends often went the long way around to avoid it, for fear of meeting Joséphine, Cécile or the sons. What devotion Monsignor Folbèche showed, living downstairs in Guillaume's flat and saying mass every morning for the accused and his family or – as evil tongues would have it – exorcising the house of Ovide's diabolical genius! The Plouffes, haggard and confused, tried to pull themselves together, collect the remains of their shattered courage, make a common front against despair and organize – though in the dark – the groping struggle that might save Ovide.

At first Joséphine was told that she couldn't see her son before the following Sunday. The authorities, focus of the whole world's attention, were in a state of fury and zeal: here generosity had no place. Ovide had become an abject creature unworthy of even his family's affection. What a monster! The photo in the newspaper showing him with his mistress at the French consulate inspired universal disgust. He was grinning broadly, a glass in one hand and the other arm around Marie's waist, while his wife was dying along with twenty-two other people, including several children.

Ti'-Mé had gone back to Anticosti. Before his departure Napoléon and Guillaume had had a long chat with him – the three musketeers! There'd be some action. They weren't going to just sit still and take it. At the crucial moment they'd send him a telegram at Port Menier with the single word: "Matane." That meant Ti'-Mé should go at once to Matane on the Gaspé coast and phone Guillaume. Ti'-Mé didn't like the looks of Guillaume these days, his eyes had become like burning coals, and Ti'-Mé was worried. Guillaume, the crack shot: was he going to let fly a 270FM bullet at the executioner who was about to kill his brother? Taking Guillaume aside, he had said to him:

"Look, you, don't do anything crazy. If you kill, you hang. And no more cabin in the woods. Ever!"

That morning, while Monsignor Folbèche was pacing off the kitchen in his temporary lodging as he read his breviary, the two brothers, their elbows on the upstairs kitchen table, faced each other, their teeth clenched. They were waiting for news of their mother. By brute force, or almost, she had dragged Gédéon toward the parliament buildings, where no guard was going to stop her from throwing herself at the premier's feet. Gédéon hadn't been able to arrange the meeting? Joséphine wasn't to be stopped by that. On she marched like a frantic creature. Guillaume, incredulous, shook his head.

"What chance has she got of seein' him?"

"Don't you know her yet? I tell you, Guillaume, she'll get through."

Guillaume got up and paced the kitchen up and down, then sat again.

"This lawyer Uncle Gédéon hired – nobody knows him. Some young guy, no experience."

"He did everything he could to get the best, but they wouldn't touch it. And anyway, what's the difference? Even if Ovide defended himself it'd come to the same thing. Because he's innocent!" Napoléon protested.

Guillaume didn't pursue the point. He was afraid his scepticism would sap the will to win that was keeping Napoléon, Joséphine and Cécile from discouragement and despair. Cécile! He felt a growing admiration for this sister, who, despite the hell it meant to her, kept going to the factory, where her fellow workers barely spoke to her these days, whether out of embarrassment, pity or a kind of condemnation of the whole tribe: anything named Plouffe was now dishonoured and rejected.

"Our Cécile is mighty brave," Guillaume said, sighing.

Napoléon nodded.

"I'm really proud of her. She's facing the music, even with nobody speakin' to her. The fact that she's there in her place, working as if nothing was wrong, means 'My brother's innocent.' You know how stingy she is. But she'll help pay a lawyer. You're the only one that looks dubious to me. And that pisses me off!"

"Just the same, think about it: you can't imagine all the evidence they've collected against him. It's terrible!"

Napoléon's face flushed with anger.

"There you go again! I tell you, it's all craziness. The guilty man is Pacifique Berthet, his partner. I never did like his face, that son of a gun. And to think I spent three nights making him a pair of aluminum crutches!"

Guillaume was incapable of grasping any given idea and clinging to it, as Napoléon could do. His days in Europe and on the battlefield, the things he had seen and experienced, had developed the virus of doubt in him, doubt about everything, anything at all.

Tortured by his secret about Rita's infidelity, unknown, as he thought, to the rest of the family, an infidelity she had confessed to Ovide, Guillaume went too far:

"Napoléon, did you ever think that . . . you never know . . . Ovide being so crazy about Marie that . . . he'd have planted the bomb?"

323

Napoléon's eyes looked as if they would pop bloodshot from his head. He leapt at Guillaume, kicking his own chair backwards, and shook his brother like a rat.

"Just never say that to me again, do you hear? It's as if you were stringing a rope up to hang him! Ovide, our little brother, did nothing of the kind. And cut out your damned suspicions, see? Don't let me hear that again!"

He let go of his brother, who, leaning again on the table with his head between his hands, failed to see the tears in Napoléon's eyes.

"The world's changed so much," sighed Guillaume. "Nothing's like it was before."

"Well, we haven't changed, have we," said Napoléon, still out of breath.

But Guillaume's thoughts were far away.

"That's what we say. Just take you, a little plumber. Now you're a businessman. You make deals with politicians to get contracts. You even pay them commissions."

Napoléon made a face.

"Yeah. Let me tell you! The contracts are getting slimmer, that goes for all my customers. And I'm about to lose the biggest ones, the government ones – especially the one for the jail. My competition's busy as hell, trying to edge me out. I'm on the edge of going broke, but I'll defend Ovide to the bitter end!"

He was shouting to cover the sob rising in his throat.

Guillaume reflected, then remarked:

"I've often thought about it: close up or far away, whether you want to or not, you're always responsible for somebody's death. Did you ever think, for example, that if we'd minded our damn business in Anticosti, if we hadn't broken up the romance between Ovide and Marie, Rita might still be alive?"

Napoléon paled at these words:

"Now it was us killed Rita! That's right, go to it, now you're started. Are you crazy? You're like Ovide, you think too much. In any case, I'm warning you: doubt if you want to, be a sucker, feel guilty as you please, but don't demoralize the rest of us! We're makin' an honest effort, and if we had it to do again I wouldn't hesitate a minute. Get that through your thick skull!"

"See? It's got you worried, too!"

Napoléon had to hold himself back from jumping at Guillaume again.

"What's got me worried is getting Ovide freed. Nothing else.

And we're going to do it. If you don't want to help, stay in your corner. There's a limit, eh?"

Suddenly Guillaume was ashamed of upsetting Napoléon this way: he was so good, so simple, but so determined.

"If you only knew," Guillaume said, "how I'd like to be the way I was before the war! I had no worries, I laughed a lot, we did crazy things, remember?"

Napoléon jaw muscles tightened again.

"Never mind our little memories. Think about Ovide! Think what he's going through. I'd like to give him a great big hug, a rib cracker, and tell him over and over, 'Don't give up, we're with you, we love you and we're going to save you! The Plouffes can do anything!' Oh boy, I hope mother can get to see the premier!"

A tall figure carrying two suitcases appeared behind the screen door:

"Hey, you guys!"

They turned swiftly, ready to chase away any intruding reporter. Guillaume was the first to recognize him.

"Denis Boucher!"

"Our Denis!" exclaimed Napoléon, jumping for the door. "Come on in!"

There was a great deal of back slapping. Denis Boucher, Ovide's best friend, had come back from the ends of the earth! His presence gave them renewed hope. They came to the point at once:

"You've come to help Ovide! You must have!" Napoléon triumphed.

Denis corrected him gently:

"As a friend, yes. But I'm really here as a reporter, and I have to establish facts. I specially asked the editor in New York to give me the job of covering the trial. The fact that I know the surroundings and Ovide and the family should help. You can tell ten million readers the truth about Ovide and give me anecdotes no other reporter will have. Will you give me a hand?"

"You bet we'll help. A hundred per cent!"

They moved in on him now, implicitly begging with all their hearts for a particular word of encouragement. Denis understood. He had to come right out with it.

"I know Ovide by heart, and I'm sure he's not guilty!" he said firmly.

"What did I tell you, Guillaume?" roared Napoléon.

Gédéon, filled with misgivings, followed Joséphine straight down the corridor that led to the premier's office. He knew very well that her attempt would be in vain. But how could he refuse the wish of a desperate mother? Gédéon no longer wore the air of supreme confidence he had had last fall when he marched down this same corridor to get Ti'-Mé out of trouble. Maurice Duplessis, his power more firmly established than ever after the end of the Asbestos strike, had since grown more distant with his rural organizers. At least, that was what Gédéon was trying to believe, refusing to admit that his influence with Dear Maurice had been terminated by the explosion of the plane caused by his nephew, Ovide Plouffe. Duplessis was said to be furious. The damage to him had been worse than a lost election! The Americans no longer respected him, as the tragedy had deprived them of three of their most important steel executives. His "Belle Province" had become a place of shame. Joséphine was slowing her pace. Where on earth was this dratted office? Some reporters, unable to get to the inner sanctum, were just emerging. Auréa, the secretary, frowned as she saw this plump matron, puffing along with Gédéon at her heels. Now he had overtaken Joséphine:

"Good day, Miss Auréa. As you can see, I came, even though you didn't call back. This is my sister-in-law Joséphine, the mother of Ovide Plouffe."

"He's innocent, Mademoiselle! I have to see Mr. Duplessis!" exclaimed Joséphine.

The secretary, embarrassed, shook her head at Gédéon:

"You shouldn't have come, Mr. Plouffe. The boss isn't going to like that at all."

"Do it for me, Miss Auréa! I want to see him, just for one minute!" begged the farmer.

She hesitated, then moved toward the premier's door and opened it. Gédéon could barely hold back Joséphine, who had rushed after the secretary. Auréa came back a moment later and said to Gédéon:

"He'll see you, but alone. I warn you, he's like a bear with a sore head."

Gédéon finally persuaded Joséphine to sit down near Auréa's desk. She was still protesting, tearful:

"But I'm his mother, Ovide's mother! It's me he should let in. He must have had a mother, too, Mr. Duplessis! He should understand me!"

Gédéon insisted:

"Just be patient, let me smooth the way. Be reasonable, Joséphine. Talk to Auréa. Look, at least I get to see him! Be a good girl and simmer down."

With a sinking feeling he left Joséphine to the secretary and felt as if he was entering a predator's lair: the lair of the Chief!

What was said between the two men remained a secret forever, as Gédéon refused to open his mouth about it. But he was humiliated, broken and ashamed to be the uncle of that little degenerate, Ovide Plouffe, the killer who, moreover, had already dared to write open letters to the papers calling Duplessis a potentate, dictator and enemy of all progress.

Joséphine waited and waited. The longer the interview lasted, the more she clung to her hope. She said to the secretary, who offered her a coffee:

"No thanks. But oh, Lord! you seem to me like a woman with a heart. You know what I mean, eh? It's an awful thing to see your child accused of a murder he never committed. Oh, Miss, I'm so discouraged! Try to say something good about our family to Mr. Duplessis? I'm sure you have a lot of influence over him, eh? You'll try?"

Then she talked about Ovide, such a good boy, so exceptional. The secretary promised to tell the premier what she had said, but she cautioned her just the same:

"It's true, Mr. Duplessis is a good and sensitive man. They say he's all-powerful. But he can't do a thing against the normal course of justice, especially in a case like this."

"But if he wants to, he can be all-powerful against injustice, too! That's all I ask! I swear Ovide is innocent, Miss. Oh, I swear it!"

Then she began to cry, realizing the futility of her plea. She had just arrived at this certainty when a violent sound of voices was heard from the inner office.

"Are you clean crazy, Gédéon? Anybody would think all Ovide Plouffe did was slash down a few telephone poles, like your son Ti'-Mé! He's a killer! He killed twenty-three people!"

Coming in from the corridor, a young man appeared suddenly behind Joséphine. The secretary shook her head.

"The premier isn't seeing any reporters, sorry!"

He held out the copy of a telegram:

"I'm Denis Boucher, from *Time* in New York. I have an appointment for noon."

She bit her lip.

"Oh, excuse me. He's expecting you, that's right. Would you wait just a moment, please?"

Joséphine turned her head slowly, incredulous:

"But you're my Denis! My good Denis!"

"Madame Plouffe!"

"You've come about Ovide, your very best friend!" enthused Joséphine, hugging and kissing him.

"I'm coming to your place tonight, dear Mrs. Plouffe. We'll talk about everything then. Be brave, there's still hope!" he said, extricating himself.

"Hope! There's more than hope!" she corrected. "And put in a word for our Ovide!"

The secretary picked up the phone and notified her boss that the reporter from *Time* was there. A few seconds later Gédéon, almost ejected from the room, appeared in the antechamber, pale but holding an envelope. The secretary led Denis Boucher into the premier's office.

"He won't see me!" cried Joséphine.

Gédéon grasped her arm and dragged her like a buoy into the corridor.

"Not today. Better without it. But I've got this letter. We can visit Ovide, the whole family, at two o'clock. Personal permission from the Chief himself, signed by his hand. And Napoléon won't lose his contract for the jail."

She would see Ovide! Joséphine forgot about Duplessis. Denis, such a smart boy, come all the way from New York, would be a better one to plead her boy's case than she herself. The two wretched oldsters made their way home to gather the clan for the great visit, and Napoléon interpreted the preservation of his contract as a hopeful sign. The sudden arrival of Denis Boucher was another sign of divine intervention.

In fact, Duplessis was keen on the interview with Denis Boucher. He read *Time* and *Life* every week and was aware of their world-wide reach. He was wary and at the same time friendly with this young man who had lived in Quebec City and could make the most of the good qualities of the people of "La Belle Province," would dispense intelligent flattery of Duplessis' good government and the province's natural resources, its excellent manpower at reasonable wages. This plane explosion, a heinous crime, was incomprehensible in such a conservative environment, a province that so admired and liked the Americans! Of course, Denis understood perfectly. He also turned on his charm and promised Duplessis that his article would not be hostile. He received a special pass. He would be the only reporter to meet the famous prisoner in absolute privacy, starting the next day. But he mustn't spread the word about that.

38

Huddled on the cot in his narrow cell, Ovide had barely touched his food for three days. Glassy eyed, feverish, he jumped at the slightest sound – the rattle of the guard's keys or the footsteps of prisoners passing in front of his cell: he could even see them through a wicket no larger than a port hole. And as the inmates returned from their exercise in the prison yard they often thrust their grimacing faces into this opening to curse him and draw a finger across their throats to show him where the rope would go, gasping in imitation of his death throes.

He touched himself on the throat and with his soiled handkerchief wiped away the yellowish matter that came from a long scratch he had made there. The repeated gesture made by the prisoners had triggered a nervous gesture of clawing at his throat with his nails, even while he was sleeping.

How many times had he heard their imitation gasps in the last three days! It reminded him of the squawking of stolen hens as Guillaume would wring their necks before plucking them, back in the depression days. With horror he realized that all the boarders in the prison – shoplifters, swindlers, fences – despised and detested him. They shouted through his port hole that he should leave for the gallows as soon as possible as they didn't want to be in the same jail with such a monster. Hour after hour their "last gasps" became more enraged and the hanging gesture grew more precise, slower, more sustained and vengeful. God, how they hated him!

The notion of suicide crossed his mind. But how would he do it? There was no mirror in his cell, and he could not measure his wound, but from touching it he knew it was growing. On a smaller scale it reminded him of the suppurating wound he had seen on Pacifique Berthet's hip, that time in the hospital.

He dragged himself to the barred window. How dare the birds sing in his presence? How lonely he was. Abandoned by everyone! No news of his family or any outside events. Yet the Plouffes must have been trying to get in touch. Especially his mother. He hoped that they at least did not suspect him and accuse him as everyone else was doing.

These three days had been a constant martyrdom for him, a preview of Hell. Like a grim leit-motif the interrogation by the two policemen turned in his mind, a scratchy record that refused to stop. Why was Pacifique denying that he asked him to buy the dynamite? He could still see his partner putting away those murderous sticks in the larger drawer of his work bench. If there was a bomb in the statue of St. Christopher, Pacifique must have put it there! But there was no witness to Pacifique's request that Ovide buy the explosives! Had they arrested the cripple? He remembered now Berthet's consternation when he, Ovide, suddenly turned up from the consulate, very much alive. But the police had nothing on Pacifique, whereas Ovide was caught in an impressive web of circumstantial evidence. He groaned with pain and a feeling of revulsion, but only guttural, inarticulate sounds emerged. Then he would turn on his cot until he faced the wall, sure that he was going mad. He even wished he could. Maybe he was guilty, he'd been for so long split into a double personality: the Ovide who acted and the other who watched him act. Maybe he had had an attack of sleepwalking and stuck the dynamite in the hollow arms of the Christopher statue, crowning it with that Big Ben alarm clock connected to the dynamite by copper wires! Was there not in all of us, hidden away, a sleeping criminal? How often had he dreamed of killing those who insulted or humiliated or made a fool of him? Stan Labrie, for example. Maybe the legal world was not far wrong in suspecting Ovide Plouffe! Oh, God, he should have pardoned Rita!

Then, in a mood of desperate revolt against the beastliness of the world, and in order to declare the purity of his sentiments and the loftiness of his ideals, he had demanded paper and a pen. Like Caryl Chessman he would explain himself, tell his life story, his frustrations, and his loneliness in a world that was not made for him. His request was refused. If he was going to write a confession, he would have to have a witness. He started: keys were rattling. He hid his wound with one hand as the guard's face appeared at the wicket. The door opened.

"Follow me to the visiting room. Somebody to see you."

"The lawyer?"

There was no answer. With a policeman in front and behind and handcuffs on his wrists (they were taking no chances with this monster), Ovide stopped dead on seeing the whole family – and then some – in their Sunday best: there were Joséphine, Cécile, Napoléon, Guillaume, Monsignor Folbèche and Uncle Gédéon.

At first there was a heavy silence, during which Ovide examined them like a family photo, frozen in the pose. They were flabbergasted: this was not their son, their brother, their friend, he was a legendary Ovide loaned to them by the world of shades to which he would soon return. Joséphine was the first to speak:

"Handcuffs! There's no need for handcuffs!"

"What's the difference? I've always been in chains!" he muttered.

Seeing Monsignor Folbèche, the policeman removed the bracelets. As soon as his hands were free he ran to his mother. "Oh, mama!" "Son, son!" Cécile came close to the two and repeated idiotically: "Everybody knows you're innocent, innocent, innocent. At the factory everybody sticks up for you. You won't have long to suffer now." Then it was Guillaume and Napoléon who hugged him, the two of them squeezing so hard he thought he would suffocate. "Don't give up! Don't give up! You'll be acquitted. Never fear!"

"And how's Arlette?" stammered Ovide.

Of course it was best she shouldn't see him here in such a pitiful state. Skinny, feverish, his hair stringy and greasy, his face decorated with razor-cuts, he had forgotten the wound on his neck. Joséphine saw it first:

"And what's that now? What have they done to you?"

"I scratched myself in my sleep. Just nerves, you know. It became automatic. . . ."

"And they're so cruel they wouldn't even put iodine on it? You there, officer, tell the warden! You must have an infirmary here someplace?"

She took Ovide by the hands, pushing the others back. She was gazing at him with such intensity that you'd have said she wanted to re-absorb him whole into her being. And then they'd flee together. Ovide felt the same desire to melt into her in an impossible transubstantiation. With the gentle simplicity of an

331

unjustly scolded child he murmured: "I'm innocent, mama, this is a terrible mistake."

Joséphine would have liked to say something special, something reassuring, capable of wrapping up her Ovide as in warm diapers reeking of love and comfort. All she could say was:

"Of course you're innocent! Is your cell comfortable, at least?"

"All cells are the same, mama. This isn't my first one."

"You got out of the monastery, you'll get out of jail, too," said Cécile.

It took Napoléon to chase the nightmare and bring them all back to reality.

"Ovide, don't go soft on us. Your friend Denis Boucher just blew in from New York and he'll write the truth regardless of what the whole world says. He's starting his investigation today and we're going to help him."

"Denis!" cried Ovide. "Is that right!"

This was the only piece of news that gave him a little encouragement. The fact that Monsignor Folbèche was saying mass for him every morning at Guillaume's place impressed him less; and Napoléon's toss of the head and promises of liberation also failed to convince him. All these people seemed not to realize that he was accused of murder and overwhelmed with glaring circumstantial evidence! But Denis Boucher, with his pen, his fine intelligence and his friendship for Ovide, that was something!

"Would you like to make your confession?" asked Monsignor Folbèche softly.

"Confession of what?" he said, resisting.

"Just confide in me, if you like. It would do you good."

"Say yes!" said Joséphine gently.

"Later, later, thanks," he whispered, fearing a reproach from his mother.

Then Gédéon got up the courage to speak:

"We just hired a lawyer for you this mornin'. Very bright little fella. He's coming to see you this afternoon. You have to trust him, now. Tell him everything."

Ovide hiccoughed.

"Yes, I've been told. And I know in advance he's going to want me to plead psychological problems or even insanity."

His legs were trembling. He sat down on a stool that was pushed his way, then, head in his hands, began to cry.

332

"Stop that, now," said Napoléon, grasping his shoulders. "The proof that you're not guilty is, Duplessis isn't going to cancel my contract for the jail. Eh, uncle? That was decided this morning."

Not a muscle moved in Gédéon's face.

"You said it."

But ever since his nephew Ovide had come into the room he had seen him dangling at the end of a rope. Guillaume, in a nervous state, ran after the prisoner as they took him off to his cell.

"Listen, don't stand in front of your window. Somebody might take a pot-shot at you! Ovide, we love you, eh?"

Then Guillaume had to turn back to his mother, who had fainted.

On her return to the factory Cécile was advised to take a few weeks off to rest. In vain she protested that she had to earn money to help pay the lawyer's fee. Her mere presence, she argued, in this factory where she worked like a horse, indicated her faith in her brother's innocence and her confidence that her fellow workers shared that faith. Her superiors were charitable, they explained that the sight of her grief-stricken face eight hours a day was demoralizing her co-workers and slowing down production and, in short, creating a bad atmosphere in her department. She hadn't the courage to announce the sad news to her mother and went off to bed, supposedly with a migraine.

Napoléon had a difficult conversation with his bank manager, who was afraid the plumber was going to lose customers because of the nasty business with Ovide. It was urgent, he said, that Napoléon collect outstanding accounts and reduce his inventory in case his line of credit was cut. If that happened it would be the end of Napoléon and Sons. Guillaume, sitting on the corner of Napoléon's grease-stained metal desk piled high with invoices, saw that his brother was in a sweat.

"That bank manager won't let up. He's sure I'm going broke. What a life! Ever since Ovide got arrested I can't even work. Jeanne does her best, but we're slipping, we're slipping. It's true, you know! We hardly get any calls from customers, just as if all of a sudden we'd turned into lousy plumbers, shabby workers or like we had measles. And the kids, there's no putting up with them any more!"

Guillaume stood up, his fists clenched, full of an impotent fury.

"Son of a son of a bitch! We're big, we're strong, we're honest and we can't do a damn thing!"

He pounded the wall with his fist as if to knock down all barriers.

"I'd just like to take my rifle and kill, kill, kill! But who? In wartime you run, you charge, you scream, you know you're going to meet the enemy and take out a few of them. And get a ribbon for it into the bargain! But what's the use of knowing how to shoot if you've got no target? The whole world is against us, Napoléon. I can't even bear to read the papers any more. Pictures all over them of Ovide Plouffe, the monster! Our brother, Poléon! It's got so bad I'm startin' to believe it myself."

"Shut your mouth!"

Napoléon's shout had come like a whiplash. Guillaume's anger was deflated.

"I'm sorry, Poléon. I just don't know any more. I don't understand anything."

Napoléon's fist hammered gently on Guillaume's chest.

"This is no time for giving up, no time to go crazy. Ovide is innocent, that's all goin' to come out. In the meantime we're responsible for the whole family. If you want to kill somebody that bad go shoot a crow. There's lots in the trees. That'll cool you off, you nervous little bugger. The bankers, the plumbing business and the gossip and the newspapers – that's all temporary. Look at our mother: this is worse for her than anybody, and yet she. . . ."

"Do you think Denis Boucher can really do anything?" asked Guillaume, suddenly sheepish.

Napoléon reflected for a moment:

"I would expect a lot of that guy. He's a bit tricky but he's tough. And he's Ovide's friend."

With all this drama bubbling around him, Denis Boucher was striding happily toward Joséphine's house carrying his suitcase and his portable typewriter. To be sure, the terrible tragedy that had overtaken Ovide alarmed him, but at the same time he felt a strange elation: here he was an almost anonymous reporter employed by an enormous news factory and lost in the great city of New York, who suddenly discovers a sensational subject that might make his whole career.

It was during the war that he had encountered some *Time* correspondents. He impressed them so much with his charm, intelligence and impulsive, spontaneous nature that after the war they had helped him find a job in the magazine's head office, in the arts and letters department. But there he was a mere scribbler like so many others. What nerve it had taken to ask to be sent to cover Ovide Plouffe's trial! He wasn't going to disappoint his editors: on the contrary, he'd really show them! *Time*, thanks to its special correspondent Denis Boucher, would beat by several lengths the staid *Le Monde*, *Le Figaro*, the London *Times*, *The New York Times* and all the Canadian papers. They'd see what he could do!

What an amazing interview Duplessis had given him! The celebrated premier's impassioned words on the mineral, forest and hydro-electric wealth of Quebec, his hatred of the pluralist intellectuals and enemies of tradition who dared to denounce his nationalism and his political authority, had taken Denis back to the ardent enthusiasms of his youth. Denis, when younger, had denounced nationalism and preached socialism, to the great despair of Monsignor Folbèche. Fine old priest!

But poor Ovide! What a jam he was in! Denis remembered an evening when his friend, desperate, had admitted to him that he couldn't fit into any group or profession. Was Ovide the type to turn murderer? It was true that odd-ball dreamers and maladjusted people did sometimes end up as criminals. . . . All that presumptive evidence against Ovide! Incredible! Had Ovide re-lived in his own way the life of Pagliaccio, with the dagger in Colombina's breast transmuted into a time-bomb in a plane? For that to have happened, Rita would have had to be unfaithful. To be checked out. Ovide a criminal? Oh, not Ovide, the sensitive kid who used to tell Denis Boucher as a child the plots of all the great operas. And read him famous French novels, like *Fantomas* or *Les Misérables*, giving his keen, young intelligence a thirst for the rudiments of culture and opening to him the paths of intellectual adventure!

A novelist suddenly obsessed by a grand theme could not have been more excited than Denis Boucher when he set foot in the parish where he had grown up and which he had left so many years before. Nothing had changed, though he felt that the population had somehow been transformed: witness this frightful murder. Big cities sap your energy and crush you, your mind can't master them. Here, in Quebec City's lower town, Denis felt suddenly powerful and in control. He held this working-class neighbourhood in the palm of his hand – a neighbourhood which, because of Ovide, had become the focus of the whole world!

He couldn't wait to see Mrs. Plouffe again. Her ravaged face had shocked him in the premier's antechamber. What hell for her! If only he, Denis, could convince himself of Ovide's innocence! In that case, in his very first despatch, after meeting the accused in jail, he would drop a hint about judicial error; and obviously, in the same piece, he'd please the premier with a little flattery for his province, helping to restore some lustre to its escutcheon!

His face darkened and his pace grew slower. This afternoon at the Press Club, as well as in a bar and even in encounters on the street, he had found the same hatred of Ovide and the universal conviction that he would be sent up the long ladder and down the short rope. He passed by the jewellery shop with its sign in the window, then the church, which reminded him again of Monsignor Folbèche. How at home he felt here in these narrow streets, compared to Fifth Avenue! Adults, girls, old friends had recognized him: "Denis! Denis Boucher! I'll be darned! What are you doing here? Are you back to stay?"

"Not for good. Just in from New York for a little holiday!"

Now he had to persuade Joséphine to keep him at her place until the trial was over. He ran upstairs two steps at a time and burst into the kitchen as he used to do. Joséphine, her eyes red, sniffling, was preparing a basket of provisions for Ovide. Monsignor Folbèche was comforting Cécile, who, with a long preface of tears, had just confessed that she had been fired from the factory.

"There are times," said the Monsignor, "when we have as many troubles as there are beads on a rosary and we still have to cling to hope."

"Hi there!" cried Denis.

"Denis, my boy!" exclaimed the priest.

39

That night Joséphine finally got some sleep. She began her state of siege against the attacks of fate supported by two powerful allies: the Good Lord himself and Denis Boucher at the head of an army of ten million readers. In her very house, on the ground floor, the monstrance stood guard, along with the sacred host and Monsignor Folbèche: nearby, on her own floor, Denis Boucher was brandishing his weapon, his typewriter with its brand-new ribbon. The reporter had no trouble in getting accepted as a boarder. Joséphine, delighted, had put him in Guillaume's old room, where Guillaume joined him, embarrassed by the proximity of the tabernacle and the priest. Denis would write his reports at the kitchen table under her very eyes. He thought the atmosphere of this house and its tearful inhabitants would put him in the right mood and give his stories a real, human touch. What was more, it was here, on the battlefield itself, that he would find out the most essential things: why Ovide had become mixed up in such a business and how to prove his innocence.

It was midnight, and this end-of-July evening was so beautiful that the reporter went out on the balcony and sat there, one knee clasped in his hands, on the streetcar seat that Onésime had once given Cécile. In his mind he ran over the events as he knew them, remembering the hatred against Ovide and the overwhelming circumstantial evidence against him. He caught himself murmuring: "I wouldn't give two cents for his chances." He shuddered. In the first hours after his arrival in Quebec Denis had been exhilarated as he rediscovered old friends and familiar places. But now, in the still of the night, he realized the gulf that separated him from his acquaintances, who had remained unchanged in an existence without a future. He had to admit it: he was a stranger to them now. He tried to deny this bitter observation: if he grew cynical his reports would lack warmth. And these Plouffes who were counting on him as a last chance at salvation! Twice before Joséphine had gone to bed she had asked him why he wasn't already at his typewriter proclaiming her son's innocence. That had irritated him.

The night was growing cooler. He buttoned his pyjama top. A faint noise made him turn. Cécile was there behind the screen door, motionless, in her nightshirt, barefoot.

"Come and sit down, Cécile. Come and have a chat."

Without a word she sat down beside him. After a long silence he said:

"It's just as well that you aren't going to work for a while, Cécile."

Sadly, but trying not to show her emotion, Cécile sighed:

"I don't know anymore what's good or bad. You know, I used to have a lot of laughs with Rita, I felt young, I'd forget I was just an old maid with no prospects."

Denis should have protested and consoled her. But his impatience prevented him, and he asked:

"So you got along well with Rita?"

Of course! And she told him, with all the details, how she had begun to appreciate her sister-in-law this spring when Ovide was being so cold to her.

"Cold? Did they have a fight?"

Cécile had often wondered:

"Maybe he was thinking too much about his radio talks and politics. And there was that waitress, Marie Jourdan. A French girl, that was really something for Ovide. Or maybe because Rita didn't want to work in the jewellery store any more. Ovide never found out why, but I did. Rita told me."

"Oh? Why was it, then?"

"Rita," she said after a moment's hesitation, "made me promise never to tell. And even if I do, there was no witness. It wouldn't help much. I'm sure of that."

"How can I help you people if you don't tell me things? I want to know everything."

"You're right," she sighed. "While Ovide was away on a trip, just imagine, his partner had been hitting the bottle. He went on his knees to Rita, telling her he loved her. At first she was scared, then she got mad and called him a lousy cripple!"

"Whaat!"

"Yeah, but she was sorry afterwards. And she never wanted to go back and work in the shop. She was scared of him, and I don't blame her. She didn't say anything to Ovide about it, she didn't want to make trouble in the business, things were going so well. So Ovide replaced her with a clerk, but he wasn't as good behind the counter as she was."

Denis interrupted:

"She called him a lousy cripple, did you say? And you didn't want to tell me that? Why, it's extremely important."

"I know. That's why I decided to tell you about it. I was waiting until mama went to sleep. But as I told you, there were no witnesses. And I'm Ovide's sister. They might accuse me of making up a story to protect my brother. Don't go writing that down!"

Suddenly Denis was excited.

"In the first place, Cécile, you can be sure nobody's going

to accuse you of anything. But you've given me a fantastic lead. Thanks to you I'll know where to start looking!"

"'Oh, lord," she sighed. "I just wonder. . . ."

She broke off. Guillaume was coming upstairs carrying a box of plumber's tools. "Not in bed yet, you two?" and disappeared furtively inside the interior of the house.

Denis and Cécile went on chatting for a few minutes. She even managed a smile as she told him about the wild dance when she was dressed as Miss Sweet Caporal and boogie-woo-gied with Father Marquis. Then she went inside. Denis at once began planning his next day's activities. First thing, he'd see Pacifique Berthet. When Denis joined Guillaume in their shared room he caught him taking a Winchester 270FM rifle out of the tool box. But Guillaume merely looked up.

"Been hunting crows?" asked Denis.

The other shrugged.

"Don't you read the papers?"

"Mostly the one I write for."

"The day after Ovide was arrested, the sixteen-year-old son of one of the American executives killed in the accident arrived in Quebec, armed and ready to kill Ovide. The police picked him up near the jail on the Plains of Abraham and sent him back to the States. But those millionaires could afford a professional killer! So I patrol a bit around there, especially below Ovide's cell. That's why I made him promise never to show himself at the window. You never know."

Denis was disturbed by the hard, intense glint in Guillaume's eyes, the glint that recalled the battlefields of Europe.

"Come on, the war's over, Guillaume. This is no time for doing some crazy thing that would work against your brother. Think about it, and take it easy," he said, increasingly worried about Ovide.

The only reply was a grunt, as Guillaume stretched naked on top of the covers, his hands behind his head. Just as Denis was dropping off, he said:

"There's a guy I keep thinkin' about and nobody ever mentions him."

Denis raised his head.

"Eh?"

"Yeah," said Guillaume. "Remember Stan Labrie?"

"Sure I remember him! The guy who couldn't get it up! He still around?"

Guillaume thought before he answered. How could he draw

the reporter's attention to Stan Labrie without telling him all about how that bum had dragged Rita into minor orgies ending in the setback to Ovide's marriage?

"You know," he said evasively, "after the war Stan Labrie built up a network of 'escorts' for conventioneers visiting Quebec City. Know what I mean? In spite of Rita's marriage he kept hangin' around. He was the son of a bitch got her that Miss Sweet Caporal title. But Ovide saw through him and Rita didn't get caught."

"So why are you telling me about Stan Labrie?" asked Denis, feeling that Guillaume was holding something back.

"Because on the day of the funeral, just after Ovide got arrested, I saw him running after Berthet, who was hustling away among the gravestones. I was a long way off, but I have good eyes. There's somethin' funny about all that. But I don't dare go near those two. I'd have their guts out before they could say please."

Denis Boucher wasn't tired anymore. He sat up on the edge of his bed.

"Look, everything's homing in on this cripple! Guillaume, for god's sake, what does Stan have to do with it? We're trying to save your brother's life! Out with it, whatever you know!"

But Guillaume held back. If he talked about Rita's misbehaviour and how she was used by Stan Labrie, it could look bad for Ovide, giving him a motive that could put the rope around his neck. He shrugged.

"I just mentioned that because it's been gettin' my goat. Stan must know something about the cripple. Stan's a guy that's been doggin' our tracks for years. What more can I tell you?" he complained. "I spend five months a year on Anticosti!"

Denis was back in bed, convinced that Guillaume knew more than he was telling.

"All right. Tomorrow I'll see Berthet. And Marie Jourdan. And Stan Labrie and Ovide. I'll sniff out whatever it is you're holding back."

"Leave Marie Jourdan out of it! Poor kid, she's suffered enough as it is. She has nothin' to do with it."

Denis frowned.

"Hey! Are you sweet on Marie, too?"

"None of your beeswax," grunted Guillaume, and turned his back. "If you like, I can take you to the cripple's place in Napoléon's car."

"No thanks. I'll go alone. You'd upset Berthet and ruin my plan. Anyway *Time* pays my expenses."

Denis was starting to be annoyed at Guillaume's discretion. He was like a clam – and maybe on the point of some foolishness with that rifle. The reporter lay awake for a long time. He had always thought of the Plouffes as being direct and open, but they knew something about Ovide and Rita that they were keeping fiercely to themselves. The tribe really stuck together! Many ideas jostled each other in his mind: *Stan Labrie . . . a stable of escorts . . . Miss Sweet Caporal . . . lousy cripple . . .* At last he fell asleep, and with the strong conviction that Rita had two-timed her husband and that her husband had known it.

Next morning Denis, as in his boyhood, was altar boy for the mass celebrated with moving fervour by Monsignor Folbèche, who used the kitchen table as his altar. The good priest saw in Denis Boucher's arrival a message of hope sent by the Lord Himself, and he was almost happy. When Denis was an adolescent he had been an incorrigible radical, at the same time the priest's nightmare and his favourite parishioner, for he loved him like a son. He smiled indulgently on hearing him recite the *Suscipeat* with a slight American accent. Napoléon, Jeanne, Cécile and Joséphine remained kneeling all through the ceremony, mumbling prayers. Guillaume, kneeling, seemed made of marble. At the Elevation – a strange omen – one of the windows shattered. The stone thrown by a young boy skimmed by Napoléon's head, but he didn't flinch. Denis was relieved to get out of this overheated atmosphere and jump in his taxi. Joséphine and Napoléon followed him downstairs. From the doorway they harrassed him:

"Better get started writing today, Denis. It's urgent!" Joséphine repeated.

And Napoléon:

"Drop around and see my shop today. You'll see, I got modern equipment. Just like New York."

"Yeah, yeah," said Denis impatiently.

The taxi took off. The Plouffes were starting to get on his nerves. But he mustn't let them see it: he had to understand them. He checked his address book. A good reporter can dig up addresses with a celerity astounding to ordinary mortals. He stopped directly in front of Pacifique Berthet's cottage on Lake St. Augustin and found the man watering geraniums at the back of his lot.

Pacifique's hearing was as keen as his sight. He felt that someone was there and whirled around on his crutches. Like a dog showing his teeth he faced up to this nonchalant young man with his hands in his pockets, staring at him so insistently.

"Hello! My name is Denis Boucher, I'm from *Time* magazine in New York."

"I have nothing to say, so get going. I've had enough reporters here."

"You're French, are you?"

"And you?" croaked Pacifique.

"Yes, my dear compatriot."

A taste for verbal trickery, his weakness and also his strength, took over. His eyes sparkled. He had to strike now or go home defeated.

"I've just been here one day. Everyone is talking about you in town. I understand you, too, are a beneficiary of the insurance on Madame Rita Plouffe."

Touché! Pacifique had grown pale.

"Think what you please! I've nothing to do with it."

"Take it easy," said Denis, carelessly. "Too bad for you, all this publicity. Just think, I write for ten million readers. That's a lot. With a stroke of the pen, if you help me, I can wipe out the suspicion that threatens you, just as easily as others can blow up a plane."

Pacifique was examining Denis intently, as he would have examined the mechanism of a sophisticated watch. He saw his fine features, the shape of his mouth and hands, and the gleam of intelligence, of amusement almost, in his eyes. A smart young fellow. Careful!

"What can I tell you? Haven't I enough to live with – as you see me – without suspecting me of a murder done by a madman?"

"Ovide Plouffe?" suggested Denis.

"I didn't say it," Berthet corrected him curtly.

Sensing that Berthet was ready to talk, Denis sat down on the little veranda floor, his legs dangling. Pacifique grew more talkative and told how he and Ovide had met. Seeing the reporter's rapt attention, he concluded:

"And do you know why he was interested in me? Because my name is Pacifique Berthet and I come from Grenoble. He told me there was a great writer, a certain Stendhal, who had been inspired by a murder committed by a man called Berthet, and used it in his novel."

"I hope you're not a second Berthet," Denis joked ponderously.

"Now that's a dull piece of wit for you," said Berthet.

"Sorry!" said Denis, biting his lip. Then he remembered. "Of course! *The Red and the Black* by Stendhal! Now I recall it—that's Ovide all over!"

There was a pause. Berthet was withdrawing, suspicious again. Denis could have kicked himself for his imprudent remark.

"You know Ovide?" said Berthet, nervously scratching the earth with the tip of his crutch.

Denis shrugged.

"Everybody's talking about him. It's easy to dream up his psychological portrait. Fascinating. A really exceptional criminal."

"Show me your press card," interrupted Berthet, thinking he should have asked before.

Denis showed it to him. Half reassured, Pacifique again scrutinized the reporter's face, and added:

"Yeah, he's a funny number, he is."

Then he cast a furtive glance at his geraniums.

From then on Denis was up against a stone wall. He was furious at himself for his clumsiness. He'd get no more out of this man who now was on his guard and had been immersed for so long in the bitterness of his handicap. He said good-day to Pacifique and gave him a cynical wink:

"I'm sure we'll meet again."

"Not if I can help it," said Berthet.

Denis waved to the taxi driver that he would be leaving, but took the time to throw a final dart:

"I heard by the grapevine that the police found a diary in Rita Toulouse-Plouffe's handbag, it was intact in the wreckage. Seems she wrote about you. She even hinted you liked her a lot."

Pacifique turned ashen, but accepted the blow without flinching or saying a word. Denis felt that he had made his point and left with a mocking salute:

"See you soon, Mr. Berthet!"

On his way to see Marie Jourdan, the reporter felt sure that Berthet had had a hand in the famous crime. His almost im-

343

perceptible reaction to the invention of the diary confirmed Cécile's story: Berthet had been in love with Rita!

Denis rubbed his hands with glee, thinking that a lie was like a stone tossed into calm water: it made rings, but you never knew how many. There was no doubt about it, his rock in Berthet's pond had made waves! He must be biting his nails now! Just wait, just wait! And in the meantime Denis had things to do. Berthet was a possible candidate, but Denis couldn't chase away the question mark hanging over his friend Ovide. Could it not be that those great names with which he and Ovide had identified years ago – Stendhal, Berthet, Julien Sorel – had begun to whirl around in the vulnerable mind of the hyper-sensitive Ovide, creating a maelstrom that drew this self-taught genius close to madness? Like the policemen, Denis found himself plucking petals from a sinister daisy: Berthet, Ovide, Berthet. Who was the real criminal? Till now appearances were overwhelmingly against the accused. Denis was anxious to meet him that afternoon so that he could form his own opinion. He'd been sent to Quebec City, after all, to report on facts and serve reliable information to ten million readers. He swore to himself that he'd give up his tendency to be subjective, to give truth a push in the right direction. But wasn't a good reporter also a sleuth-hound?

When the door of Marie Jourdan's apartment opened he found himself face to face with a stalwart woman with a Parisian accent, no doubt a matron in the Intelligence branch. Marie was now under the protection of the French consulate, for which the murder had become a very delicate affair. In Paris they were anxiously following developments in this odious case of murder, in which the daughter of an actress liquidated by the *maquis* was implicated – at the very time when a great effort was being made to heal the wounds of the national division between followers of Pétain and those of de Gaulle. The guardian was no doubt assigned to keep Marie away from intruders, particularly reporters.

"I repeat, sir, Miss Jourdan is seeing no reporters. Do you hear me? I am extremely sorry."

Denis realized that it was useless to insist. Even the prestigious name of *Time* made no impression on this woman, who doubtless was accountable to high places. Over the shoulder of this skirted gendarme Denis could see Marie, standing against the wall and casting anguished glances in his direction, wringing her hands. God, she was beautiful! He understood Ovide's (and Guillaume's?) infatuation. From his distance he smiled to her and shouted:

"Keep your chin up! I'm a friend of Ovide's, too! He's not guilty! I'm going to help him!"

The door was slammed in his face. Neither surprised nor too disappointed, he was satisfied at having seen this Marie Jourdan. He'd gladly have taken her off on a voyage to the ends of the earth. . . .

"Now! Stan Labrie!" he said to himself with a grim smile.

Around eleven o'clock that morning Stan Labrie was out on the rear balcony of his bachelor apartment watering his flowers.

Ever since Rita's death he had been living in grief, tempered by anxiety and remorse. Every day Bob, the architect, kept calling him up, terrified that the investigation might reveal his adventure with Ovide's wife. If ever the architect was called to the witness stand it would mean the end of his marriage and his prosperous career in Quebec City. Each time he phoned, Stan stammered some vaguely reassuring story. No, he'd heard nothing that concerned himself or Bob. And what could the explosion of the plane have to do with Bob's escapades with lovely ladies? But each time Bob would hang up more tormented than ever.

Stan couldn't get interested in anything but the newspapers, which he devoured the moment they came out. He was neglecting his network of "escorts." The beauties in his stable, scattered all over the city, often called him in search of lucrative and pleasant occupations. They called him a piker when he explained that in summertime he felt less like working, content to water his petunias and do a little recruiting on the beaches. He asked them to be patient and reasonable, customers were more interested now in trout fishing or boating in the shade of willow trees than in amorous efforts that led to panting and perspiration.

To tell the truth, he was thinking hard about giving up this trade of procurer, which Rita's death had turned sour for him. His only excursions were in the early morning, to buy the papers. Every time his doorbell rang he jumped, fearing the worst: the cops.

Languidly he filled his watering can. He missed Rita, and

his depression grew deeper day by day. The more firmly the city's rumours doomed Ovide to the gallows, the more horrified he became. But what could he do if Rita's husband were guilty? It was obvious, it all added up. But as he concluded that the murderer must be punished, the vision of Berthet on his crutches came to Ovide's rescue, superimposed obsessively, and would not be chased away.

Then he noticed his cat, emerging backwards from a brown paper bag in which she had been playing. The sight turned for him into an evil omen: in this affair he was the cat, and if he was let out of the bag. . . . His confused mind now began to go adrift, because immediately after his vision of the cat he saw Rita as she had been the previous summer, at the time of the orange-coloured fifty-dollar bills, when she came to his place and helped him water his flowers. Brandishing the empty kettle she had sung, with her comic talent: "Next day she was smiling, to her window came beguiling, and watered her little climbing flowers with her little watering can!"

How they had laughed! And now she was dead. He'd never again hear her lilting, girlish laugh, never again see Rita who incarnated for him all the women he would never possess!

With a heavy heart he finished his chore and went inside. The furnishings and decoration, almost feminine in their delicacy, were punctuated here and there by a virile touch. His quarters reflected the ambivalence of his physiology.

The strident sound of his door buzzer made him jump. This must be the police! He laid his hand on his heart, trying to still its beating. Good God, he must be sick, he had palpitations at the least upset. . . . If all the innocent people on earth began digging in their past they would discover, as he was discovering, zones of darkness in which they had unwittingly participated in someone's murder. And the more they thought about it the more likely they would be to leap in the air at the sound of a doorbell. Rasping, the cruel sound came again and tore at his soul. He put on dark glasses (the ones he had worn on the fatal day of the butterfly sport on the Montmorency) and slowly opened the door. He staggered back.

"Stanislas, old fellow! May I come in?"

40

Stan wasn't dreaming. This ghost was indeed that much-hated little son of a bitch Denis Boucher, Ovide's friend, the guy who years ago, during his engagement to Rita, had informed her parents about Stan's impotence, putting an end to their love story. Shortly afterward, she had married Ovide. And Stan had never recovered.

"It's been a long time, eh? Almost ten years!"

"What are you doing here?" said the procurer, on the defensive.

This visitor boded ill for Stan. As Denis cast an eye around the apartment, he noted his host's anxious reaction.

"Nice place you've got. Very nice. How's business? So far as I can see you're a post-war success. Mahogany furniture, eh? And silk cushions! Congratulations!"

"If that's all you have to say you can bugger off!"

Denis smiled. He was a good angler and intended to hook his prey.

"I'm hurt! You don't even ask what I'm doing these days."

"You think I care? Get out. I've seen enough of you."

He tried to push Denis toward the door, but Denis raised his finger as if he were in school.

"Not before telling you that after five years of war I was decorated three times for exceptional bravery. I am a reporter for Time-Life, New York, and I'm here to cover Ovide Plouffe's trial. Heard of it?"

"Reporter for *Time*?" exclaimed Stan, suddenly chilled with fear, his arms hanging down, his mouth agape.

"Right! So you can congratulate me," added Denis, very relaxed, choosing an armchair and caressing its pink and blue cushion. "I'm the guy who's going to tell the whole world about Rita Toulouse's murder and that of the other passengers. It's great fun, you know. And I know you all so well, Ovide, Rita, the Plouffes and you, Stanislas, it's bound to make great copy."

Stan felt his limbs turn to jelly. His hopes of being left out of the affair crumbled. The crime was grasping him in its tentacles. He could no longer play the ostrich. He stammered:

"I . . . I've nothing to do with it. I don't know a thing about it."

Denis, his face hard now, spoke in a bantering tone:

"Nothing to do with it? We'll see. What about your network of 'escorts'? No doubt you tried to get Rita into it, maybe you even succeeded. To get your revenge on Ovide you tried to break up his marriage. And today he's accused of murder!"

"What do you mean get Rita into it?" asked Stan tonelessly.

Denis grew evasive. He didn't want to repeat the trick of the diary that he'd used on Berthet.

"There are people who know certain things," he said evasively. "In any case I'm going to make you sweat."

Stan tried not to tremble. His voice was almost inaudible.

"What do you want me to do?" he whined, terrified. "I never killed anybody."

"But you could provide some interesting testimony. Couldn't you?"

Interesting testimony. That was what Stan dreaded more than anything in the world. And Bob would have heart failure. Stan was sorry he hadn't listened to the architect, who had begged him to take a six-month cruise. In his panic he fell into the trap Denis had set for him. He said with vibrant feeling:

"That's it. You'd like me to soil Rita's memory, and some high-class people, professional people!"

Denis was triumphant:

"So! She did two-time Ovide!"

Stan could have bitten his tongue.

"That's why I can't testify. It would make Ovide look even more guilty. See? It could have been in revenge that he blew up the plane."

It was a good point. It would indeed be better if this bit of evidence remained unknown to the jury and the public. That would explain why the Plouffes didn't want to talk about Rita's escapades.

"Did Ovide know?"

"Yeah. She confessed to him. She never should have. But she cracked. She was so honest, poor kid."

"Damn!" muttered the reporter.

A sad business, he reflected. Ovide must have been through hell. Stan gave a little cough. He was relieved. Slowly he was rising out of the abyss.

"Do you think Ovide's guilty?" Denis hazarded.

"If all the two-timed husbands in the world blew up planes to get rid of their wives there'd be an awful slaughter. Women are flighty by nature, you wouldn't believe it," the pimp declared.

"I asked you if you thought Ovide was guilty."

"To tell you the truth, I wonder. You know, you can believe me, I never hated Ovide Plouffe. He's a funny guy. He stole Rita on me, but I never bore a grudge. But I wanted her to have some fun, because she never was a real wife for him, he was a story-book husband, he never got off the pages."

He's not so dumb, the bastard, Denis thought; but he was still suspicious and didn't let go.

"So you're not convinced Ovide's guilty."

Stan hated this question because it could drag him into close participation with Denis in his investigation, and he would surely end up on the witness stand. He answered warily:

"There's so much evidence against him, poor guy. How can anybody not believe it?"

"But you doubt it just the same. I can feel it, Stan. Now, be a good fellow and be honest for once in your life. It would be great if you could help me prove his innocence. You'd be forgiven everything, and you could be at peace with yourself."

"I'd like that," murmured Stan, unsettled. "But how?"

Denis half closed his eyes, and allowed only a glint to flash toward the pander's dark glasses.

"Don't you think the real criminal is Pacifique Berthet?"

Stan did, in fact, think just that.

"That bastard, I never could stand the looks of him."

"Did Rita tell you that Berthet got drunk and made advances to her? That she fought him off and called him a lousy cripple?"

Again terror gripped Stan's heart. Of course she had told him. But admitting it now would lead him straight to the witness box. In spite of his trepidation, he managed to look surprised.

"I never heard about that. If it's true she'd have told me. I'd have fixed Berthet's clock for him."

Denis felt that Stan was lying.

"At the funeral, Rita's funeral, you were seen running after the cripple, who took off as soon as Ovide was arrested."

He was close on Stan's heels, but the fellow felt safe and was getting cagey.

"Well, I thought it was sort of funny. Berthet intrigues me.

I wondered why he was taking off that way. But he jumped in his car and I lost him."

Denis stood up. The pimp was too skilful in his role of innocent blackguard. He hadn't hooked him properly, and Stan had got away. When exactly? And now he'd keep to himself any detail that would help Ovide, for fear of being called as a witness. Instinctively, still sure of himself, Denis loosed a random shot:

"Tell me what you're hiding. I need it for my investigation. I promise in the name of professional secrecy that I won't name my sources and nobody will bother you. Okay?"

Stan came close to caving in. But what did he really know? The game isn't worth the candle, he thought. And why should he help his worst enemy, Denis Boucher? It was up to the police to find out the truth. Not this little reporter. Never!

"I tell you, I don't know a thing. If I find out anything I'll call you right away, I swear."

"Very well." Denis sighed. "I'll give you until the trial to tell me what you're hiding. For my money Berthet's guilty, and you think the same. So take care! If Ovide's convicted and I find out you could have saved him, I'll write up your whole story and explain how you were involved in the murder."

Stan turned pale.

"And I suppose you're going to write about my health problem."

"Of course! That explains a lot of things."

Broken, Stan buried his head in his hands.

"Oh, Jesus, Jesus! But I tell you I don't know any more! If I knew how, I'd split myself three ways to help!"

Denis laid his hand on the doorknob.

"You found men for Rita. You should be able to find me some evidence to save her husband. I warn you, if Ovide is convicted, you've had it, chum! And don't you forget it. Guillaume Plouffe is in town, and he's got his finger on his rifle trigger, and I'm all ready to type up your obituary. A word to the wise, eh?"

The door slammed shut. Stan wanted to rush over to Bob's place and alert him to this new threat. He phoned him and recounted the conversation. He told him of his temptation to help catch the guilty man. "Stay out of it!" shouted the architect, horrified. If Ovide was innocent, the truth would come out, with or without the help of Stan Labrie, and their honour

350

would be saved. The architect urgently begged him to send away any reporters that came, and even ordered him to leave on a trip for anywhere as long as it was a thousand miles from home; because Stan had grown too emotional and vulnerable, he was on the point of making a terrible mistake. Stan packed his bag and decided to run to Old Orchard, Maine, by the ocean. Denis would never find him there and Guillaume wouldn't be able to shoot him down.

Denis, in his taxi on the way to the Quebec jail, almost forgot to stop at Joséphine's place and pick up the basket of provisions for the prisoner. Armed with a pass signed by the premier himself, Denis could give him the parcel directly. The reporter, still confused, was trying to clarify his impressions of the distressing encounter he had just had. This Stan Labrie was nothing but a small-time rat, incapable of being involved in a murder. Was he really hiding something important? The energy Denis had expended in his search for the truth had so far been wasted. He shook himself awake. He mustn't let his enthusiasm flag, corroded by this immense misfortune. Ovide's safety was at stake, first and foremost, but his correspondent's career was on the line as well. His despatches had to sparkle with life, suspense, intelligence and human interest. He was anxious to greet his unfortunate friend.

Gédéon Plouffe, puffing his pipe, was pacing up and down in front of the Quebec jail. He spat frequently. Was the name of the Plouffes, which he had made so glorious in the Beauce, about to go down in ignominy, and for ever? Ovide was only his brother's son, after all. But he was Gédéon's nephew! In the mind of the public Ovide's fate was sealed. He was the guilty party, and the trial would last only a few days. The doubt that afflicted Guillaume and the Plouffes' friends, and was beginning even to attack Denis Boucher, had already vanquished Gédéon. Now he would try simply to avoid the worst: a hanging. Poor Joséphine, she was all wrapped up in the presence of Monsignor Folbèche, living in *her* house, and seemed to cherish a blind and stubborn hope! Understandable, for a mother. But Gédéon, for his part, knew Ovide was a goner. All the money the rich farmer offered had attracted not a single high-class lawyer to the case. The young attorney, this greenhorn, who was now inside talking to the accused: could he persuade

him to plead insanity? Yes, madness would do the trick. He'd
not be hanged, he'd just disappear in an asylum. He must be
crazy anyway, attacking Duplessis like that in his letters to the
papers. Bad enough to have a lunatic in the family, but it was
better than a hanged man. And Ovide was demented, no doubt
about it. The late Théophile had often said to him, "My Ovide,
he's an odd one. I don't understand him. He's like a stranger."
Gédéon ground his teeth and spat on the grass again. His spit
was so bitter, the grass where it fell would never grow again.
How he regretted helping Ovide to get started in the jewellery
business! But Rita had begged so prettily, poor child! Gédéon
glanced up at the fourth-floor windows, behind which, he hoped,
Ovide was in the process of agreeing to plead insanity. At the
same moment Denis Boucher emerged from his taxi. Carrying
the picnic basket, he walked swiftly into the prison building.

Standing near his cot, a bandage on his neck, an irate Ovide
was looking daggers at his lawyer, who was leaning against
the metal door. Ovide's eyes were staring widely and he flung
wide his long arms as he declaimed:

"Me? Plead insanity? Why, you're the one with the addled
brain!"

Intimidated, the lawyer was driven to stammering by this
unlikely client who, despite the danger he was in, talked down
to a learned defender!

"It's the only way you're ever going to walk out of here, my
friend, even if you maintain you're innocent. There's enough
evidence against you to hang you ten times, let alone once."

"And you call yourself my defender!" yelled Ovide. "Me,
passing myself off for a loony? Never! I'd rather be hanged like
a proud man, clear headed and innocent, than put away for
life in an asylum! If I'm the only one left to defend my integrity,
all right! I'll do it alone! And you'll see what you will see! I'll
plead innocent with such sincerity the jury will have to believe
me!"

"How can I defend you, then?"

Ovide shouted:

"You'll never be able to defend me. You're sure I'm guilty.
And you are therefore useless."

Ovide gulped in despair. He seemed to be choking.

The lawyer flattened himself against the door, sure that this
fanatic was going to strangle him. Hearing the shouting, a
guard looked in through the grille.

"Get out!" Ovide screamed at his defender.

The attorney rapped on the door, requesting that it be opened at once.

"Your Uncle Gédéon is going to be very disappointed, and your family, too. But if you want to hang, it's your business," he said in farewell.

"My family knows I'm innocent and perfectly sane! But you can tell my Uncle Gédéon, his nasty sly peasant tricks aren't going to get me out of this crazy situation! If God wills that injustice should triumph and I should be hanged, hanged I'll be!" he shouted, and burst into sobs.

When the lawyer was gone Ovide, exhausted, sank down on his cot. What was the use of living? Before, when he'd had his bad times, he used to faint, and unconsciousness had created a healing pause. Now, despite his orders to his heart to stop beating, it kept pumping away in his breast as if it wanted to enjoy the activity left to it until that frightful final day. Because Ovide had no more illusions. The whole world seemed to be insisting on it: he would die on the scaffold. It was a matter of weeks. Pacifique Berthet, his odious partner, the real criminal, would never give himself away. And what if it wasn't Berthet? A Russian agent might have put another mysterious package on the plane, to exterminate three American capitalists! Or an enemy agent could have found out that Ovide Plouffe was shipping a metre-long parcel in the DC3! This hypothesis didn't stand up well: it was his package that had contained the explosives! It was he, Ovide Plouffe, who had bought fifty sticks of dynamite! And Pacifique said he knew nothing about it! Ovide had wrung his hands so much that his knuckles cracked and his wrists were rubbed red. But at the moment when Ovide might have tilted into the very madness Gédéon desired, he was granted a reprieve. The guard announced another visitor. There was a long silence during which their eyes met.

"Denis Boucher! Oh, thanks for coming. Thanks! Denis!"

"I'm here, as you see," the reporter said softly, dismayed at finding Ovide in such pitiable condition. It was worse than anything he could have imagined.

In four years Ovide had aged eight. Denis tried to recognize his old friend, but it was not easy. The proud Ovide Plouffe, reduced to a rag!

"Awful, isn't it?" murmured the accused. "I'm so ashamed. You, the best friend I ever had, I wanted to be a success when I met you again so you'd be proud of me, and here you see

353

me in prison accused of a murder I didn't commit. You look so fine, Denis, free and successful and happy! I should have gone to New York, too, and lived there."

"What's that bandage on your neck? Did you hurt yourself?" asked Denis, unable to find the fraternal bond that had linked them before.

"Er . . . just a bit of tonsillitis. It's damp here at night. And stifling in daytime. All this stone!"

"Just like in the war, damp and unhealthy. But every war has to end, Ovide."

Embarrassed by the vacant stare of this man who had guided his adolescence, Denis almost felt like leaving. He had been vaguely sceptical as he arrived, and now he paid minute attention to everything the accused man said and did, watching his reactions to detect the spark that would reassure him completely of Ovide's innocence. But this poor creature was not Ovide! The conversation was unbearable. He set down the basket of provisions done up in little be-ribboned packages.

"Your mother sent you some food. She says you're to eat it all. There's pork paté, smoked salmon, cookies, jam – and a letter signed by the whole family. You'll like this: there's a message from your daughter."

"Arlette!" cried Ovide, trembling. He grabbed the envelope and ripped it open. On one sheet he saw a drawing in coloured crayon of a dilapidated house and an immense orange sun. She had signed it in capital letters: "I LOVE YOU DADDY. ARLETTE."

"Look at that, Denis!" he said, and collapsed onto his cot, weeping.

The reporter held back the tears that welled in his eyes and handed back the drawing, which Ovide stuffed inside his shirt. Denis sat down on the stool in front of the prisoner and took both his hands.

"Your family and friends are all on your side. They're saying mass every morning in Guillaume's flat, with everybody there. You know that. I'm the altar boy. If you could see how they pray! It's beautiful. And I'm staying at your mother's place and tonight I write my first story. *Time* has ten million readers, Ovide. Do you realize that? You'll see how I write about you, how intelligent you are, and open; and about your lofty sentiments."

Ovide drank in these welcome words.

"You're the only one who can turn public opinion around! You're the only one who can really help."

Denis didn't dare tell him about his visits with Berthet and Stan Labrie or the secrets confided by Cécile and Guillaume. The poor man needed more than that.

"I'm carrying on my own little investigation. By the way, I saw Marie Jourdan today."

"Marie?" murmured Ovide. "You know about her already! Oh, how I've harmed that girl, Denis! What did she say?"

The white lie came all by itself:

"I only spoke to her briefly. Journalists aren't allowed to see her, but she was able to give me a message for you: she says, keep up your courage, I believe in your innocence!"

"Oh, that dear Marie!" Ovide exulted. "That's just like her. And you believe, too, don't you Denis? That's so important to me, you know. I swear, I'm the plaything of the damnedest circumstances, a real spider's web. Berthet got me to buy him the dynamite and now he denies it. And my lawyer wants me to plead insanity! I'm not crazy, Denis! You can see that? If you believe in me, I'm saved. Do you believe? You have to!"

Struck by the tone of this supplication, Denis stood up, suddenly transfigured, took Ovide by the shoulders, and said with words that came out like hammer blows:

"I believe you, my very best friend. And we're going to save you. I swear it."

They embraced impulsively, then the reporter listened to the extraordinary tale, the incredible odyssey of this monstrous accusation of murder. But Denis noted that not once did Ovide allude to Rita's escapades. Respect for her memory or prudent omission? He opted for the former. Caught up by a contagious enthusiasm, he transmitted it to Ovide. For the moment, what he could do was make his typewriter rattle this evening. He'd be famous at once and would do a masterly portrait of Ovide, filled with sympathy and sincerity. Two long-lost friends meet at last! As Denis left, he said:

"Try to eat all that good stuff, and sleep well tonight. Think about your daughter's drawing and the sun over the house. That sun's for you!"

Their interview had lasted three hours.

355

41

The murder trial began the following Monday.

For the Plouffes, pale with anxiety and suffering and from living like shut-ins since the fourteenth of July, their martyrdom now reached an inhuman, intolerable pitch. Their state of nerves provoked all kinds of twitches and tics, which seemed to affect even the objects around them, making them tremble with fear. Without the blind faith of Monsignor Folbèche, Denis Boucher's optimistic presence and the animal obstinacy of Napoléon, the Plouffes would have been crushed in the convulsions of despair. The immensity of this tragedy could not be encompassed in the narrow framework of these lives that were made for everyday joys and sorrows. The Plouffes were crumbling under the weight of this immeasurable trial. Ovide, the pride of the family, was threatened by death on the gallows! Joséphine never talked now, but her lips, constantly trembling, mumbled prayers that were unintelligible even to herself. Guillaume and Napoléon, helpless and resigned, were like two felled oaks lying on the earth with all their branches. Cécile was barely eating, her face was emaciated, and she paced agitatedly to and fro in the kitchen.

Prostrate with grief, the Plouffes were now but the wreckage of a family once-happy. Monsignor Folbèche continued to say mass every morning for Ovide, but now refused to talk to other parishioners who came around for news. Totally devoted to the Plouffes and to his Saviour, he refused to let his confidence flag. His faith in a just God, his stubborn hope, would see him through any trial, he thought. One thing was certain: the Plouffes would all be there, at every moment of the trial, united with Ovide, sustaining him with their love and their hope, and sharing his suffering.

Denis Boucher was providing strong support. The impact of his reports seemed to be the sole glimmer of hope for the accused. His first *Time* article had appeared three days before.

It was a story that sparkled with life and colour and unusual details that were fascinating and at times challenging. His immediate boss in New York called to congratulate him on the piece and encouraged him to keep it up. Denis had written authoritatively, describing the Plouffes, Ovide, Rita, Berthet, Monsignor Folbèche and Quebec province with astonishing penetration, explaining many things of importance, which made other newspaper articles pale by comparison. Keeping his word to Duplessis, he refrained from describing his visit to Ovide. But Ovide's extraordinary, authentic account remained his main source of inspiration. At the Press Club he was assailed by perplexed and astonished questions. Yes, perplexed: why, in this choice article, from both a journalistic and literary point of view, in which he vaunted the riches of Quebec province and the special characteristics of the population that had remained French – why did he insist so much on the personality of the Honourable Duplessis? He emphasized the fact that the premier, under a crust of apparent autocratic rigidity, was a sensitive, kind, visionary man devoted heart and soul to his province. Wasn't *Time*, as a rule, more severe in its judgements?

In the same breath Denis sketched a warm portrait of Ovide Plouffe, describing him as a Don Quixote who understood nothing of the sordid devices of the world. And why did he so casually ask so many questions about Pacifique Berthet's ambiguous role, about his handicap, his unwillingness to talk and his past in Grenoble?

He described Rita Toulouse as a charming, flighty bird, whose sprightly beauty and rippling laughter made one think of the beauty of a hummingbird. He had enthusiastic adjectives for the lovely Marie Jourdan: a young French girl, daughter of an actress liquidated by the Resistance, now taking refuge in Quebec. Readers were moved by the tale of how the Monsignor had been expelled from his parish, and how he had hastened back to stay with the Plouffes and say mass every morning for the accused, Ovide! His article showed such mastery of his subject and the surroundings, and hinted at a love story so complex and a situation so tangled, that the opening of the trial, already headline news in papers the whole world over, was confirmed as a suspense story of international scope.

Denis was ecstatic. Wasn't this the plot for the novel Ovide had advised him to write in earlier years? Now he was eager to attack the next episode: whatever happened, he must see Stan Labrie. Twice the reporter got no answer at his door, and finally learned from a neighbour that the pander had gone away and left no forwarding address. Denis was not surprised, but was furious just the same. What a coward, what a contemptible swine!

The week before, in the presence of an almost-absent Ovide, they had chosen the jury. There had been none of the usual difficulties. No one had refused, and they all met the requirements of the law. In this City of Quebec, where apparently nothing ever happened, being chosen to decide on the guilt of the accused was like winning at the races. This case with all its world-wide attention would no doubt cause these little jurors to go down in history. What an event in their lives! They'd be able to talk about it for years, with their friends, their children and their children's children.

Ovide, seeming totally indifferent, did not take advantage of his right to object to the choice of some of them, who were openly aggressive toward him. Never did a defence lawyer have such a recalcitrant client. Ovide was angry at him and would barely speak to him after his suggestion of a plea of insanity. Had Ovide decided to give up the struggle, to sink rather than swim? In any case he gave that impression.

The crown attorney was already rubbing his hands. This was going to be his big chance! It wouldn't be hard to confuse this poor fellow who was responsible for Ovide's defence. The crown would show such talent, such pitiless logic in his inculpation of Ovide Plouffe that his summing-up for the jury would surely be published in *Famous Trials*. It would be mentioned in the hall of fame of criminal law and would create precedents.

In the public's mind, the accused was already convicted before the first day was out. Each one had his reasons for making Ovide his very own hanged man, as if the music clerk turned jeweller had been guilty of multiple crimes and caused everyone's misfortunes – a universal scapegoat.

This Ovide Plouffe was more than a fellow citizen about to be judged. First and foremost he was the incarnation of the diabolical, haughty and contemptuous murderer venting his spleen on good common folk. It was said that he actually claimed as his principal defence the incomprehension of imbeciles for such an exceptional man as he pretended to be! But now virtue and justice were about to settle the hash of this prince of presumption who believed his superiority entitled him to commit the foulest crime with complete impunity. The romance of Ovide's life was now being written by the illiterate, all of whom chose the same ending: hanging! And shame on those who dared to go against the common interpretation!

Thus Denis Boucher, after fully savouring the sweets of success at the beginning, now began to detect some mistrust of himself. He saw himself subtly accused of sensationalism, yellow journalism, prejudice and doubts cleverly planted to influence public opinion or the judge and jury. At first this troubled him, then he rebelled: let them wait for his second article! Then they'd see something!

It was nine forty-five. The court opened in fifteen minutes. Hundreds of onlookers were cooling their heels on the courthouse steps to get a look at and boo the manacled monster, who was to arrive in an armoured van. The building, already packed, was bubbling with unusual activity. Everyone was posing or taking a turn behind the camera so as to be immortalized on this historic occasion.

On the other side of the street, at a corner table in the Old Homestead restaurant, Uncle Gédéon and Denis Boucher were talking quietly but intensely. No, the farmer would not go to the trial. No, he did not believe Ovide would get off. On the pretext of an asthmatic allergy he declared he was unable to breathe in the courtroom of a murder trial. The fact that the accused was his nephew didn't help matters! When he had explained to the family his reason for staying away, the Plouffes turned their backs on him.

From this corner table the old farmer would follow the ups and downs of the case and keep an eye on the strategy of Ovide's lawyer, this young whippersnapper with his flowing robe, as sensitive as a tender plant. Why in hell had this ignoramus gone in for criminal law? Badgered by Gédéon's constant phone calls and surprise visits, bewildered and trapped by the old man's trickeries and arguments, pestered by his suggestions of witnesses to be called, Ovide's attorney arrived in court in a lamentable state of mind.

Denis glanced at his watch and got to his feet. The trial began in five minutes. The tragic show was about to start. Gédéon repeated:

"Don't forget the smallest detail. Write everything down. Come and see me here at noon. And tell Joséphine I'm right with them all, just like I was there inside."

Denis nodded. He knew that Gédéon's refusal to go to the

trial had deeply wounded the Plouffes, even though the old man was helping out with the lawyer's fee and worked hard getting sympathetic witnesses.

"I hope by mid-day you'll change your mind, anyway. Remember, Ovide is innocent and we're going to save him."

The reporter ran out. Gédéon continued sipping his coffee, alone at his table, sad and a little ashamed not to be in the courtroom. But he couldn't disgrace the whole of the Beauce by showing up as uncle and godfather of the accused, or could he? What good would it do Ovide? As a wise, responsible man he had to choose the common weal before family solidarity. He wasn't proud of himself, Uncle Gédéon wasn't. He even tried to persuade himself that his godson Ovide was innocent, victim of a terrible miscarriage of justice. Denis seemed so certain! He made a decision: he himself would pay the whole fee.

In the packed courtroom, already overheated, Denis was scribbling feverishly. He listened with irritation to the first witnesses, glancing fraternally from time to time at the accused, who seemed to be hearing nothing, as if he had taken refuge in his inner world, misunderstood and indifferent to all others – with whom it was, in any case, too late to communicate.

He observed the row of seats where Ovide's near and dear ones sat: Joséphine, Cécile, Napoléon, Guillaume and Jeanne, as well as Monsignor Folbèche, who kept his eyes obstinately directed over the judge's head at the crucifix on the wall. Denis noted that the Plouffes behaved here as they did in church. Grave, humble and frightened by the tragic drama of the court, their hearts fluttering like a bird escaped from its cage and pursued in a closed room by men's enormous, monstrous hands, the Plouffes were experiencing a kind of communion through the martyrdom of Ovide. They trembled at the hellish speed of the trial, in which all the witnesses seemed almost to be pushing Ovide more swiftly toward the gallows. Soon they had ceased to listen, and, like Monsignor Folbèche, stared at the crucifix, hardly daring to cast a glance at Ovide, who sat pale and motionless, his neck bound in an immaculate bandage. If he intercepted their glances too often he might perceive their heart-breaking adieu, unspoken but poignant, before his climb to the hangman's rope.

Quebec City had never seen a more gripping murder trial. Papers sold like hotcakes, people were glued to their radios to catch the special bulletins and announcers put on their breathless voices to sum up the highlights. How horrible, this Machiavellian procedure by which Ovide Plouffe had rid himself of his pretty wife! For fifty thousand dollars he had sent twenty-three people to eternity, and there he sat, imperturbable, in the prisoner's box! Clearly we have here a fearful beast, bereft of all humanity and sense of decency! How could this exemplary Plouffe family (son Guillaume, war hero, champion pitcher recruited in 1940 by the Cincinnati Reds, mother Joséphine, president of a sodality and champion church worker of the parish) – how could such a family have produced such a monster? And that Monsignor Folbèche who hung around with them, you'd think he was their father! But no wonder: wasn't he the rebel priest who'd been run out of his parish by the Archbishop? He'd even had the nerve to testify in Ovide's favour, describing what a good-hearted, honest fellow he was, and his one-time aspirations to the monastic life. This apology had rubbed the wrong way at the public's pristine conscience, since they had the criminal by the collar and didn't want to lose him. But justice was following its pitiless path; exciting moments were still to come before the judge passed sentence, and hair-raising revelations were to be expected. Thrilling, the trial ran its course like a devilish game in which all the dice were loaded. Even the defence counsel cross-examined witnesses in a half-hearted way, as if he agreed with them. The simple-mindedness of his questions even got a laugh from the audience at times, such as his query to Ovide's former boss, the owner of the Royaume du Disque:

"It is true that the accused often fainted while listening to classical music?"

"My store is not a clinic!" he had said. "I wouldn't have kept Ovide Plouffe around if I had to pick him off the floor every other minute. He was a good salesman and he knew his music inside out. I lost a good man. After he left, my business dropped off. I might even say that this expert in everything you could mention talked like a prophet. He told me that one of these days records would all be 33 rpm and that even the 78s were a thing of the past. He explained to me scientifically how all that was bound to happen, but I don't rightly remember."

The witnesses filed past. The nun who had looked after Ovide in the hospital said he was an exemplary patient, gentle and certainly inoffensive. The doctor in charge, explaining Ovide's fainting fits, called them "psychological spasms due to a sensitivity exacerbated by a paroxystic imagination." The star witness, the elegant Claude Saint-Amant, perfectly at ease before his public, seemed annoyed at having Ovide Plouffe's name associated with his own. Yes, he had met him on the fourteenth of July at the French consulate; yes, he had received a phone call from the radio station announcing the plane crash, but he had not told the news to the accused, he merely advised him to go home, there was an emergency. Yes, the prisoner had been nervous, anxious and had left at once. What about the rôle of sponsor-editorialist that Ovide had played each week for several months? Claude Saint-Amant emphasized the accused's talent and popularity. Excited by the interest his testimony had aroused, the announcer grew pompous and sketched a psychological portrait of Ovide that was breathtaking, as if he had come from the planet Mars.

Then came several of the accused's travelling salesmen from the North Shore. Surly in manner, they nevertheless spoke in highly laudatory terms of Mr. Plouffe, who described his watches as "finely chiselled poems." A very pleasant fellow, and at meals he'd pay for aperitifs and wine.

Obviously, these were witnesses for the defence. But then, for the crown, along came the roughnecks with whom Ovide had tangled at Chez Gérard. They described the scene: this madman with a gun had threatened them. A dangerous lunatic, a maniac! And the clerk from Paquet's store also testified, telling how Ovide had picked out the St. Christopher statue, a kind of merchandise normally sought by priests and old ladies. As he paid for it, the accused had remarked cynically: "With a saint this big, even a catastrophe hasn't got a chance." And the purchaser had gone on his way whistling "I'm forever blowing bubbles," bearing his package under his arm, as nonchalant as if it had been a doormat.

Then Pacifique Berthet's turn came around. Laboriously, his head hanging, he made his way to the witness stand. Napoléon nudged Guillaume:

"Look at that damned hypocrite. He's using his old crutches to make people sorry for him. Son of a bitch!"

Pacifique was a disquieting, moving witness. The questions of the defence about his delinquent boyhood in Grenoble turned to his advantage. Young and unfortunate, he had fled the scenes of his childhood to start a new life in Quebec, this charming city with its warm and hospitable population. Here he practised his beloved trade, which allowed him to lead a normal, honest life. Then this stupid accident came and turned him into a lonely cripple, chronically handicapped. What did he think of Ovide? Well, of course he had been glad to become his partner. Everything had gone swimmingly. But what he had since discovered left him baffled.

And alas, the business was ruined! The store was closed because of the scandal. As there was no future left for him, Pacifique confessed to the court that he wished only for a prompt release from life.

In Denis Boucher's second article he revealed a little more clearly his bias in favour of the accused, cleverly citing this or that incident to draw his readers' attention to the past of Pacifique Berthet. He insinuated that Ovide's partner had been very adroit in inspiring pity but not overly convincing. He drew attention to the effectiveness of the crown's presentation and deplored the weakness of the defence attorney. He described Ovide as crushed by this one-sided trial.

In New York they slashed a few paragraphs, in spite of which the article, when it appeared, triggered an outcry against its author. It was known now that he was staying with the Plouffes and that Ovide was a childhood friend. *Time* was informed of the fact, and Denis's colleagues were not slow to denounce his lack of objectivity. It was intolerable that the representative of the most widely read magazine in the world should abuse his position to try and clear a buddy, while arousing sinister doubts about a poor handicapped foreigner! *Time*'s upper echelons reacted. They sent off a senior reporter and Denis was demoted to doing research for his older colleague. Humiliated, the young reporter saw himself sucked down by the sinking ship of the Plouffe fortunes. This opportunity, supposed to make his future, had turned into his Waterloo. And all because he liked the Plouffes, to be sure, but mainly because he wanted to prevent a grave miscarriage of justice. He was convinced of Ovide's innocence and Berthet's guilt. But alas! Because he had tried too hard to help, he had, in his subjectivity, done more harm than good to the cause he was trying to defend. But Denis Boucher was not about to give up! Champing at the bit, he sought a way of swaying public opinion. He needed evidence! Where was the thread that could lead him to the truth? If he found it, what a victory for him, and what joy for the accused!

The atmosphere surrounding the trial now became more tense.

The testimony of the hardware clerk made a great impression on the jurors and drew the rope a little tighter around Ovide's neck. He had, said the clerk, come to buy fifty sticks of dynamite in the store. He knew Mr. Plouffe by reputation, and even admired his radio talks. That was why he had not hesitated to sell him the dangerous materials. The customer had vaguely indicated they were to be used for clearing stumps. And he had incidentally sung the praises of Alfred Nobel, inventor of dynamite, but with a touch of cynicism, as being the greatest benefactor of the arts, letters and sciences: this Nobel, who, through his prestigious Prize, put his fatal invention at the service of rewarding exceptional intelligence. All eyes turned to Ovide. What a psychopath! The witness went on:

"When I gave him his two parcels, one of the sticks and one of the detonators, warning him again to be careful with them, he replied, very sure of himself, 'Don't worry, I've had experience. It won't be my first explosion!' And he laughed, very pleased with his wit. No, your Honour, he never mentioned it was bought for someone else. I remember, he just said, 'It's to blow up some stumps at a cottage.' No, he never mentioned his partner."

The next witness to be called was the travel agent whom Ovide had seen on the eve of the murder. His statement seemed to the crown attorney to be of the greatest importance. Yes, the accused had asked about the price of two return tickets to Paris in a four-engined North Star. He had then looked up the listings for left-bank hotels and had settled on the Hôtel des Saints-Pères, very reasonably priced but located not far from the church of Saint-Germain-des-Prés. He was talking about staying a few months. "With your wife?" the agent had asked. And he seemed to remember that the accused had replied with a mysterious smile and perhaps a wink.

This deposition staggered the audience once more. As the trial went on the evidence became more and more damning. Here was the taxi driver who had taken Ovide and Rita to the airport. With the parcel on his knees, the client had warned him to drive slowly and avoid all bumps, he was carrying a very fragile statue. Then came the baggage clerk, of whom Ovide had demanded the same caution; and the Canadian Pacific Airlines experts, who had located the explosion as having taken place in the left rear portion of the baggage bay, the place where Mr. Plouffe's parcel had been stowed. Brother Léopold, whose deposition got a laugh from the public, told of the reasons and circumstances behind the drubbing Ovide had given him in 1940.

When Marie Jourdan was called to the stand there was a murmur of admiration in the crowd. What a beauty! Her eyes downcast, pale faced, barely audible, she took the oath. Visibly given an easy time by both the crown and defence attorneys, she was not asked any questions that were too brutal or indiscreet. She told how she had met the accused in the record store: when he made her a present of "Les Chemins de l'amour" by Poulenc, he had fainted dead away. She had afterward seen him at Chez Gérard with his wife and Napoléon and Jeanne. Months had gone by without another encounter. Then, suddenly this spring he had reappeared at the club and created an incident because of her, brandishing an empty revolver. By mutual agreement with Gérard Thibault she had then left her job. Ovide, when he heard of this, appeared at her apartment and offered her the position of secretary for the summer. As this involved accompanying the accused in his travels she had hesitated, but finally accepted. Ovide Plouffe seemed so honest! And during the whole tour he had behaved as a perfect gentleman. But on their return, aware of the disapproval of Ovide's family, she had asked him not to see her again. Suddenly the crown attorney seemed to remember a forgotten question, and asked point blank:

"By the way, Miss Jourdan, did the accused ever suggest a trip to Paris with you?"

She paled at the recollection of Ovide spinning dreams aloud at the bow of the coastal boat.

"He mentioned it, yes, but as if it were a dream that would never come true. He seemed unhappy."

She was allowed to step down. Guillaume watched her with hungry eyes. He was reliving with great intensity their scene of love beside the Jupiter. Not once could he catch her eye. Ovide, brought back to life by her voice, had begun to tremble. For a moment he was terrified that they would exhibit the snapshots. But no! Were they keeping them for later?

Ovide's lawyer, under the impression that he was calling an important witness for the defence, brought out the Commander-in-Chief of the Order of the Knights of Columbus. This great man affirmed that the accused, because of his merits, his dynamism, his devotion, had quickly climbed the first three levels in the Order's hierarchy, the Catholic answer to the Freemasons of France. He had been, in fact, scheduled soon to pass to the highest distinction, the fourth degree. No one at the Knights had ever seen a man rise so quickly through all the steps to honour and success.

Ovide in the prisoner's box was horrified at the number of people he had met who were able to talk about him. He saw himself as inoffensive, without importance, not well known, and here were dozens of people who had an opinion about his virtues and his faults. He thought most people came to this realization only at the end of their lives.

The testimony took days on end. Halfway through the second week Pacifique Berthet was called back for a second time, and was more closely questioned on this occasion. He had been held in reserve, Denis realized, as the last blow designed to lay the monster low. Humbled as he shadowed the senior *Time* reporter – who was beginning to share his convictions on the case – he was glad now that Stan had disappeared. His testimony would have given even more weight to the supposed motivation of Ovide in disposing of his wife. But Stan, just the same, must know something important for Ovide's acquittal, Denis was sure of it.

Buttressed by his crutches, Berthet again aroused the public's sympathy by his pallor and the grimaces of pain caused by his diseased hip. He repeated for the jury how the trial was causing him increasing suffering. How had he met Ovide? In the hospital, of course, where he had at once been struck by the curious personality of the accused, who had emerged from such an ordinary milieu.

"What I remember very well today is that Mr. Plouffe was much taken by my name, Berthet, which reminded him of a criminal of that name in Grenoble a hundred-odd years ago. He told me that Berthet had inspired a famous novel, *The Red and the Black*, by a certain Stendhal."

The French reporters scribbled like mad, delighted by the anecdote.

"Is it true that you aroused the accused's admiration by your radio, which came on at the desired time by virtue of wires attached to your alarm clock?"

"That is true. But there's no great trick to it. In fact, I explained to the accused exactly how it's done. And he caught on at once. I'm sure he could have done it without any problems."

Ovide listened with terror as the cripple lied. The man was a demon! How had he, in his innocence, fallen into his toils? He, Ovide, an adroit mechanic? What an outrageous lie! The main reason he had never bought a car was his total incomprehension of motors. They remained for him an impenetrable secret. Only once had he raised the hood of Rita's white convertible, but he had closed it at once. His awkwardness was the despair of his family. It had taken him days to learn how to knot his first tie. His mind was quick but his hands could not keep up with it. He managed only to crush the poor cravat into ridiculous malformations. He thought of the rope that would strangle him and break his neck, and how the hangman would make a perfect knot without further practice. Then Ovide began again to listen to Pacifique's testimony, quite convinced now that Berthet was the murderer, but equally certain that he wouldn't give himself away. Pacifique was not accusing him directly. He simply described his association with Mr. and Mrs. Plouffe, and their joint decision to sign up for a three-way insurance policy. Ovide travelled a lot, and their business, in which Rita was an extremely useful helper, depended on the participation of all. The disappearance of one member of the trio would almost paralyze the other two. Ovide's lawyer asked Berthet an interesting question:

"You told us just now that you thought Ovide Plouffe must have died along with his wife, and that you almost fainted with astonishment on seeing him turn up at the store. Is this true? Can you be a little more precise?"

"Certainly. Put yourself in my place. I thought he had left with her."

Pacifique had been expecting the next question ever since the trial began:

"If he had not turned up, you would have been a hundred thousand dollars richer, yes or no?"

Berthet, prepared, replied calmly:

"Correct. That was the agreement. What should I do about it? But if it meant blowing up twenty-three people to collect the money – that's not my style. Imagine! Could I go on living after such a massacre?"

His only remaining reservations about Ovide Plouffe concerned his high travel expenses and excessive public relations bills. Ovide always had delusions of grandeur, but Berthet had taken him on as partner anyway.

"Did you, yes or no, ask Ovide Plouffe to go and buy for you a large St. Christopher statue?"

Berthet nodded:

"Yes, Monsignor Folbèche had come to see me before leaving the parish, reproaching me for not practising any religion, and asking me to pray for him anyway after my own fashion. I consented. As Monsignor likes statues I thought that instead of praying I would make him a present of a St. Christopher. In the North with all those bad roads and big trucks and bush pilots, an absent-minded man like Monsignor Folbèche is more accident prone than he was in town. Oh, I just remembered: Ovide said something to me about accidents, that in the Bible, in Ecclesiastes, it's written – and I looked it up, it's true – that ' . . . time and chance happeneth to them all. For man also knoweth not his own time.' I found that very striking. When the statue was brought in its box, I laid it on the work bench in my repair shop waiting for my partner's next trip to the North Shore. On the Fourteenth of July, the French national holiday, he intended to go and see Monsignor Folbèche with his wife. It was their chance to make up again, an idea that pleased me, for I'd been the first to suggest it and the family chimed in. I was very happy that day, for one thing because of their departure like a couple of lovebirds, but also because I celebrated the Fourteenth by treating myself to an automobile. And I took the opportunity of asking Ovide to bring my gift to the Monsignor. What I'd thought was going to be the finest Fourteenth of my life turned out to be the worst ever. What a shame!"

The examination continued. How had he got along with Rita during her time behind the counter? He explained that he barely saw her, as a partition separated his workshop from the store. She brought in the watches to be repaired. She was kind and pleasant, he liked her very much. Then she stopped working in the store and he saw no more of her. He thought he had heard violent arguments upstairs. About what? He didn't know. But Berthet said he was convinced of one thing: Rita must be furious about Ovide's trip with Marie Jourdan. Denis caught Cécile's eye. She sprang to her feet and, pointing at the cripple, shouted:

"Now tell them how you tried to kiss my sister-in-law, and how she pushed you off and called you a lousy cripple!"

What a bombshell! The crowd rustled and goggled. . . .

The judge ordered Cécile to sit down, but changed his mind and called her to the stand, dismissing a furious Pacifique. She took the oath, almost pounding the Bible. "I swear!" she said, loud and clear. Cécile told how her sister-in-law Rita, all at sea, had told her of the incident, insisting that she keep it a secret so as not to create a breach between the partners. As soon as Cécile realized that the crowd was hanging on her every word, she lost her self-assurance, fumbled, bumbled and stammered until her first statement lay in doubt. Was she not the accused's sister, ready to tell any lie that would save him, lost soul that he was? Her interruption had been the act of desperation of a gallant girl ready to invent the Lord knew what. Then she grew silent, almost ready to faint. The audience, launched on a fresh track, had been shaken for a moment. Ovide's lawyer asked him in a whisper if his sister had told the truth. "Not that I ever heard," said Ovide curtly. But he was upset by the revelation. This, then, was why Rita had refused to go on working in the store! Oh, Berthet, that monster!

Berthet was brought back. Like a master watchmaker he was aware of every movement in the crowd. He spoke slowly, his voice threatening to break:

"What the accused's sister just stated is horrible and completely false. Mrs. Rita Plouffe was very attractive, that is true. No normal man could be immune to her charms, but in my case . . . my case especially . . . I gave up the idea of conquering any woman. I respected my partner's wife, she was a real ray of sunshine in the shop. I don't understand how the sister of the accused can invent such a thing. It is so cruel! Oh, my God!"

He sobbed, really sobbed, but briefly. He had made Cécile hateful to the audience. There was a pause for the cripple to grow calm, then the questioning continued. Had Pacifique taken the parcel with the statue to his cottage?

"Why would I do that? With these damned crutches? Impossible. The parcel lay the whole time on my work bench. In fact, it was the accused who brought it from the shop out to the taxi, on the morning of the fourteenth of July."

The key question came next:

"Did you, yes or no, ask Ovide Plouffe on June 12 last to

buy you fifty sticks of dynamite to blast stumps at your cottage?"

Pacifique's face became a marble mask:

"I swear that I never asked him to buy dynamite and knew nothing of this purchase."

Ovide, foaming, almost shot out of his box:

"You're lying! Lying! I swear to God, on the head of my child, that this man asked me to buy those sticks of dynamite and detonator caps!"

The two police guards could barely hold down this gesticulating, frothing madman. The tense and tragic atmosphere in the courtroom gave each murmur from the crowd an apocalyptic depth. Joséphine stood up, her eyes staring:

"You believe my Ovide, your Honour! He never lied in his life!"

They made her sit down, gently, for everyone understood the despair of this good mother. The silence weighed heavily while Ovide, dry eyed, his body jerking spasmodically, sat down, one hand to his bandaged neck. They were nearing the end of the tunnel. The crux of the trial: it was Pacifique's word against Ovide's, a prisoner overwhelmed with circumstantial evidence. Pacifique, ashen faced, grimacing, pitiful, found his way laboriously back to his seat.

"I'd kill that bastard!" rumbled Napoléon.

Ovide's conviction seemed to approach ineluctably. Napoléon was holding Guillaume back, because the giant, coiled for the attack, was capable of leaping at the police and the judge and the crown attorney, to hit and hit and hit them. . . . Why hadn't he a good number thirty-six grenade to blow up this wretched courtroom where the Plouffes were in the process of dying in their deepest selves, for utter shame!

42

The day arrived for the summations to the jury. Everyone was certain, after so much overwhelming evidence, that Ovide would be convicted. The crown attorney began his show like an experienced actor. The whole world was his audience, he was going down in the history of criminal law. For three quarters of an hour he developed a summary of Ovide's acts leading up to the crime, recalling precise facts and endowing them with motivations, arranging all this in such a way that the public in the courtroom drank in his words, a crystal-clear story from which Ovide emerged revoltingly guilty. The family and the prisoner himself seemed unnerved. At times Ovide would shake his head as if to banish these semblances of truth. But for the great lawyer this brilliant exhibition was the virtuoso part of his performance. He also wanted to prove his erudition and the breadth of his analytical mind. In the last three weeks he had consulted psychologists, respected psychiatrists and all kinds of documents dealing with the temperamental behaviour of famous murderers of history. What luck he had had, friend as he was of a famous Parisian lawyer, to ferret out an accused like this one in Quebec City! After this trial he would no longer be received in Paris as a colleague from the backwoods! Stretching an avenging arm toward the accused, but with his eyes directed at the press table where the foreign reporters were scribbling furiously, he was working up to the crescendo that would climax his deadly peroration.

"We have before us a dangerous man, a megalomaniac with a split personality, a reincarnation of Dr. Jekyll and Mr. Hyde. In his afternoons he swoons to the melodies of Francis Poulenc, tears in his eyes, but at night, while his wife and child are sleeping, he tiptoes down to his partner's repair shop and constructs a delayed-action bomb that will be the death of his wife and twenty-two others. What's the difference? He is pursuing his obsession, his dream of fleeing to Paris with another woman, Marie Jourdan. That honest girl, scenting danger, refuses to see him again. He pursues her anyway. He hopes that he can persuade her to run away with him, but for that he needs a small fortune. His wife is insured for fifty thousand dollars. Let her die, then! What went on, what can go on in such a perverse and complex mind remains a mystery.

"A monster such as this in human form appears only seldom on earth. Destiny decreed that this should happen in Quebec City in a highly respectable family. But God's designs are unfathomable to us. As a child Ovide Plouffe was sickly. He was a constant dreamer, reading indiscriminately any books that came to hand and listening entranced to classical music and the opera. His family treated him like a budding genius. His mother could refuse him nothing. Having become spoiled and

371

demanding he would brook no obstacle to his desires. In public school he almost killed a playmate who called him a sissy. Later, in revolt against life, he entered a monastery as a lay brother. He was expelled for having given a knockout blow to the monk who woke him too early. Married, with one child, our man grows bitter, living from hand to mouth on his meagre salary in a record shop. There he meets one day a very beautiful customer, Marie Jourdan, who asks for 'Les Chemins de l'amour' by Francis Poulenc. It is love at first sight, so violent that he falls in a faint. He is taken to hospital.

"For some time he has been thinking of leaving his wife, with whom he is on bad terms. She, a flirtatious girl, evades his authority and has an unfortunate knack of thwarting him at every turn. Did she not, against the formal prohibition of her jealous husband, agree to become Miss Sweet Caporal? There are violent scenes between them. We have seen to what point the accused is obsessed with the myth of France. In the hospital where Ovide Plouffe is under observation his bed-neighbour is Pacifique Berthet. Berthet is of special interest to him, not only because he is French but particularly because he reminds him of the criminal Berthet, who inspired Stendhal in the creation of his famous novel *The Red and the Black*. What triggered the mysterious process then begun remains an unexplained phenomenon. Unknown to himself, Ovide Plouffe begins to turn into Julien Sorel, the hero of the novel and himself a criminal – Julien Sorel, who kills out of love and frustrated ambition. From the moment of his first meeting with Berthet, Ovide Plouffe is in the grip of an indisputably split personality. He becomes Berthet's partner, and their jewellery business is launched. Berthet, confined to his repair shop in the back of the store, leaves Ovide Plouffe as free as the wind and encourages him to travel the province, with generous expenses. The accused soon dreams of monopolizing the sale of watches in the whole country, but this is not all: at the same time he is aiming at other conquests.

"You see the psychological process of this self-taught megalomaniac, consumed by ambition, trying to hoist himself to the level of intellectuals with university degrees – and this word is important, because Ovide has no degree. This is his greatest frustration. And so he begins writing to the papers. He even gets published in *Le Devoir*. To advertise his jewellery business he buys five minutes a week of radio time, and uses part of it to express his anti-government political opinions or to talk about literature and music or moralize on all kinds of subjects. He barely mentions his business, to the great discontent of Berthet. He is a fanatical social climber. He joins the Knights of Columbus and pushes his way up to the fourth degree, an ideal springboard for his unbridled ambition. Beneath his affable and ingratiating exterior is hidden an immoral creature, dangerous in his pride and egotism. He accepts no trammels to his power. The acts of violence he committed throughout his life are peccadillos compared to the foul murder he is about to commit. What is the nature of these fainting fits that lead to his hospitalization? The doctor states that they are psychological spasms. But what if we go a little deeper? Are these indispositions not caused by the birth of the second Ovide Plouffe, the one who will be a killer? After his meeting with Pacifique Berthet his health takes a spectacular turn for the better. No more fainting fits! He did not even faint in prison. This wretched man's conscience crumbled at the moment of this fatal split in his personality.

"The commercial venture is a success. This former leather cutter turned record-store clerk turned businessman cum intellectual is unleashed upon the world. His lucubrations, his wild emotions, his pretentions, his urge to violence know no bounds. One night, after an argument with his wife, he runs down and takes the revolver from the cash drawer of the jewellery store as if he wanted to kill somebody. But whom? He goes to the Chez Gérard restaurant and sees Marie Jourdan, who works there as a waitress. Some half-drunken customers tease her. This gives the accused an ideal opportunity to impress the girl. Chivalrous as a movie hero, he strikes the man who insulted her, then brandishes his weapon, which luckily is not loaded. We know what happened after that. Now he cannot wait to conquer the lovely French girl and go live with her in Paris. This is when the criminal in Ovide Plouffe reveals itself entirely.

"When his partner asks him to buy a statue of St. Christopher for Monsignor Folbèche, the accused's sinister project takes form. The package with the statue – what an ideal receptacle for a home-made bomb! The victim of unsystematic reading that his mind could not digest, and having read all the Nobel Prize winners, he is obsessed with the word dynamite. That same day he makes a second trip, this time to the hardware dealer Samson and Filion, dazzles the clerk with his erudition, buys fifty sticks of dynamite and detonators with no questions asked. People have perfect confidence in him! Ovide Plouffe is a celebrity! He even pushes his criminal frivolity to the point of stating the dynamite is to be used to blast stumps on a summer cottage lot, no more details.

"Ovide Plouffe, a great reader, who knows much about many fields, had perfected his knowledge of clock-making as Beaumarchais and Voltaire had done before him! Late at night, on the eve of the murder, he goes down to the repair shop, opens the parcel containing the statue and stuffs its hollow places with dynamite sticks and detonators, which he connects to a Big Ben, of which there are several in the jewellery shop. Alas, Ovide Plouffe has only too well absorbed the lesson he learned from Berthet's radio in the hospital. He sets the explosion for ten thirty sharp, at which time he knows that the DC3 will be flying over the St. Lawrence River – he has often made the trip himself.

"The mysteries of human psychology are marvellous. We are seldom even aware of them. But we are forced to observe in the present case that the symbols of 'la mer,' the ocean, and 'la mère,' the mother, play a preponderant rôle in the destiny of the accused. Over-protected, coddled by his good mummy, he never in his subconscious forgot the water in which he lived for nine months. This is why 'Les Chemins de l'amour,' the pathways of love, whose first verse begins, 'The paths that go down to the sea,' sung by Yvonne Printemps for whom Poulenc had written it especially – Ovide Plouffe is also a great admirer of her husband, Sacha Guitry, the famous playwright – this is why the water must receive the debris of the exploded plane and the remains of the dismembered passengers without leaving any significant trace. Richer by fifty thousand dollars, he will be free to flee with Marie Jourdan, who knows nothing of all this, taking off for Paris, the city that occupied his imagination since his early childhood. Why had he become so nervous at the airport? Because the plane's departure had been delayed ten minutes. It was fated to crash on land, at Saint-Joachim! The perfect crime does not exist, Ovide Plouffe!

"Two days earlier, the accused had consulted a travel agent, under the impression, no doubt, that his crime would never be discovered and that he would be able to enjoy with impunity the fruits of his unspeakable crime. Can one imagine such a thing? On the very morning of the fatal day he goes with his wife to the airport, the statue on his knees. Quiet and kind, he warns the driver that the package is fragile. Everybody hopes and believes that the couple will be reconciled during this trip. At the last moment Ovide Plouffe cancels his flight and lets his wife leave alone. He has invented a good excuse, in case questions are asked later. The accused was in touch some days previously with the superior of the White Fathers of Africa, begging his permission to make a three-day retreat in his old cell so as to rediscover and plan his life. And what does he do? He draws sketches of naked women beside a river. A man is lying between them, Ovide Plouffe himself! His double personality is shared between two women. He is not even a bigamist! But then he becomes overwrought. The thought of the explosion of the plane becomes heart-rending, he cannot stay another moment in this cell, he leaves it by leaping out the window. To go where? To the Fourteenth of July garden party at the French consulate, where Marie Jourdan is. Have you seen the photo of the accused grinning broadly while his little wife and twenty-two other passengers are dying by his hand? Strange, he does not seem to feel guilty, not having been at the site of the crime. This is odious, this is frightful: this unawareness, the cynicism and cruelty of the murderer pass all understanding.

"Ovide Plouffe, you have refused to be examined by psychiatrists, because my colleague, with whom I sympathize, hoped to get you to plead insanity. It was not so much out of pride that you refused, but because you knew these specialists in mental illness would discover in you the monster I have just described and the psychological motives that pushed you to such infamous behaviour."

Ovide's accuser whipped the tone of his oration to such a degree of infectious indignation as he demanded the death sentence for the accused that he expressed the wish of every heart and the word that was on the tip of every tongue.

Most unnerved of all was Ovide's lawyer himself. He walked limply to the bar and in a timid voice without conviction tried to establish that there was no evidence that Ovide had put the dynamite into the parcel. A disapproving murmur put him completely out of countenance. Without looking at his client, who was smiling contemptuously, he delivered a flabby address to the court that was more like a postscript to the crown attorney's summing up.

He returned to his seat under the pitying gaze of the public. Then came the recommendation of the judge to the jury. Its tone and content foreshadowed a conviction. The magistrate, a man of letters, had been completely charmed by the literary qualities of the crown attorney's oratorical flight. He insisted, however, that each juror make his decision in all fairness in his soul and conscience.

The half hour the jury took to reach its decision seemed interminable. The Plouffes, in their grim solidarity, barely dared to breathe as they watched Ovide, gasping but resigned like the lamb at the slaughter. Then the foreman of the jury pronounced the verdict:

"Ovide Plouffe, guilty of murder in the first degree!"

This awful pronouncement was delivered as if muffled in cotton wool. Yet in Ovide's skull and all his being it reverberated like a roll of thunder coming from the dawn of time. As in a fog he saw the judge slip on his black gloves and pronounce the fateful words:

"Ovide Plouffe, I sentence you to be hanged by the neck until dead!"

Supported by the policemen, Ovide uttered a wild cry:

"I am innocent! I am innocent! I committed no murder!"

In the general commotion Joséphine, followed by her children, Monsignor Folbèche and Denis Boucher, pitched and rolled to the box where Ovide was struggling and succeeded in grabbing him:

"Ovide, Ovide, my little boy!"

Ovide, wild eyed, shouted as the policemen, touched, tried to detach him from his mother:

"It's a lie! It's a lie! I'm innocent! Oh, mummy!"

Ovide Plouffe was about to pay with his life for the privilege of being a super-dreamer.

While the news of the death sentence was flashing toward the four corners of the earth, and the public in Quebec, relieved, went back to everyday life with a clear conscience (had not the law of retaliation triumphed? An eye for an eye?) Ovide had been taken back to his cell as they were preparing his transfer to Bordeaux Jail in Montreal. He would be hanged in a month if there was no appeal within fifteen days. His only possible grounds: the judge had erred in subscribing almost totally to the crown attorney's thesis. Uncle Gédéon was studying this possibility with Ovide's young lawyer, but without much conviction. If only the prisoner had co-operated! But not a bit of it!

Ovide couldn't move, he remained in bed all day, refused to eat. His beard grew, and he didn't even raise his hand to the sore on his neck, still wrapped in a bandage, where a throbbing pain kept reminding him of the rope. He wished this infection would rise to his brain and bring him a quick death before they could hang him. His poor head swarmed with all the details of the trial. He, Ovide Plouffe, was supposed to be a Jekyll and Hyde case? Two personalities, one good, one bad, and each unaware of the other? Could it be true? Confused, Ovide now wondered if he had invented the story of buying the dynamite for Pacifique. Maybe the bad Ovide had schemed up the whole thing unknown to the good Ovide! Could he perhaps have sneaked downstairs while Rita slept and stuffed the statue with explosives wired to an alarm clock? It was true, he used to be a sleepwalker. One night when he was a kid he had climbed out of bed, sound asleep, opened the drawer where Napoléon kept his few clothes carefully folded and peed abundantly all over them. His mother had found him in the act and put him to bed. In the morning Napoléon, on hearing the tale from Joséphine, had given him a horrible dressing-down. But young Ovide had remembered nothing. Perhaps a similar fit of somnambulism had enabled the bad Ovide to do his evil work?

What a diabolical series of incriminating circumstances! Should he appeal? He would never be able to extricate himself from the web of facts against so many witnesses. Gradually he began to believe in his guilt, but each time this madness possessed him a voice came howling to his aid: "It was Pacifique Berthet who asked you to buy the dynamite. Never doubt it!" Then he twisted and turned more feebly on his cot. But an echo came, a horror emerging from his deepest self:

"You are innocent of this murder, yes, but guilty of something worse: of having cultivated what was second-rate in you and made the fate of those who love you subordinate to that. You brought misfortune on them by sending your wife to her death. That is your crime Ovide Plouffe! You deserve the rope!"

He groaned. No, he didn't want a new trial.

At the Plouffe house, Denis Boucher and Monsignor Folbèche were helpless witnesses to the despair that now overcame the whole family. Joséphine had even given up praying and stayed in bed, prostrate and wordless. Cécile and Guillaume crossed paths like two puppets as they paced up and down the kitchen. Napoléon came by several times a day, fierce as a wild boar, then left again. Denis, who didn't give up hope, went several times to see if Stan was back, or skulked around Pacifique's cottage and its vicinity. Who knows? A clue might turn up that would unearth the truth, quite unexpectedly.

Napoléon was the first to do something. He arrived in a rush at the house and called Guillaume out on the veranda.

"Be on your toes. Ti'-Mé's in Matane. He just phoned me. He's waiting for our instructions. My plan's going to work."

"At last, we can do something!" said Guillaume, standing tall again.

"Can you count? What's seven from twenty-one?" said the plumber.

"Fourteen, why?"

Napoléon grumbled:

"Just asking. But I like your answer."

That same morning Monsignor Folbèche obtained permission to see Ovide in his cell. Holding his hands paternally he heard his full confession and Ovide told him things he had never told anyone: the whole truth about Rita, Marie, Pacifique Berthet and Stan Labrie. The priest had him write a letter to his family asking their pardon for the pain he caused them and telling them of his love and crying out his innocence. He was the victim of a colossal miscarriage of justice, but dreaded a re-trial, he would never have the strength to go through that punishment again. He asked the mercy of heaven to let him die first. In this same missive he thanked his sister-in-law Jeanne in advance for being a mother to little Arlette and asked her always to protect the child and talk of her father as of an honest man unjustly struck down by society. He warned her about the probable spitefulness of the world around them.

With a sure step Monsignor Folbèche left the prison. No one was in the kitchen when he reached the Plouffes' house. Whispers reached him through the half-open door to Joséphine's bedroom. Cécile, Guillaume and Napoléon stood pale and silent as they watched the family doctor taking Joséphine's pulse. She was breathing irregularly.

"We're taking her straight to the hospital," said the doctor to the trio, with a look that said, "She's not putting up a fight."

Monsignor Folbèche approached the bed and took his parishioner's hand, holding it tightly:

"Joséphine, I just saw Ovide. Do you hear me, Joséphine?" She acquiesced feebly.

"Now listen to this: I know that Ovide is not guilty!"

She opened her eyes, tried to get up, rested on her elbow.

"This is no time to go to the hospital," said the priest. "We have to save Ovide first. And you have to be there! We must persuade him to appeal. You'll get your last rites some other time. How are we going to save him? I don't know yet. But the Good Lord is watching and justice will triumph. I'll go shout his innocence on the street corners if I have to."

"And we're going to give the little Jesus a hand," growled Napoléon. "He's not fast enough for my taste."

The Monsignor read them the note Ovide had written in his trembling hand. They all wept, then a healthy anger set in. The Plouffes were ready to take to the barricades to defend Ovide. They breathed more normally and a new light gleamed in their eyes. Joséphine sat up on the edge of her bed and commanded:

"Cécile, heat the soup!"

Helped by her two sons, she stood up and made her way to the rocking-chair. Noisy and energetic, they set the chairs around the table. The doctor listened again to Joséphine's heart, took her pulse and scratched his head:

"Well I'll be consarned! It's normal again!"

"See, now?" said the Monsignor, smiling. "We're going to rescue everybody!"

Napoléon, his face glowing, squatted beside his mother's knee.

"You're going to get a surprise! A nice surprise! Listen, mama, in your wedding trunk, do you still have the two white cassocks Ovide brought back from the monastery?"

She nodded weakly.

"Fine! Guillaume, it's all okay. It'll work!"

Joséphine was so overwhelmed, so penetrated by the confidence emanating from her oldest son, that she automatically began to rock, and asked Cécile to bring her a Sweet Caporal.

43

Everything was ready by nine in the morning. There were still three days in which to appeal, but Ovide was to be moved the next day to Bordeaux jail in Montreal, where medical care would be better, in view of the prisoner's weakened condition.

Guillaume, his jaw set, his gaze fixed, as in the days when his commando group was about to attack the enemy position, was waiting for his brother in the plumber's van identified as Napoléon and Sons, Plumbing and Roofing. Napoléon's older children had just left for the playground. He had shouted several times at them from the window, "Have a good day, kids! Be good, now!" Guillaume thanked his stars that no one at the house suspected the real purpose of their expedition. Only Ti'-Mé, Napoléon and himself were in on the secret. But Napoléon would have to tell his wife.

And she was sitting, pale as a ghost, in front of the big canvas bag her husband had laid on the table. Jeanne feared the worst. Napoléon, for a change, had slept badly all night, turning and tossing beside her. He came out of the bedroom carrying his trumpet, and stuffed the instrument into his bag. Then he took her hands in his.

"I'm afraid, Napoléon. What have you got up your sleeve?"

He looked at her, deeply moved.

"Thanks for not asking questions, dear Jeanne. Tell me you still love me."

"Of course I do! Even more than ever!"

"Are you ready to give your okay to anything I do to save Ovide?"

"Anything at all!" she said, in a surge of blind confidence.

"If Ovide dies of weakness or gets hanged, we're finished. And we're pretty close to that anyway. We've not a minute to lose. You don't regret joining our family?"

"If I hadn't, I'd be dead."

He spoke with terrifying seriousness:

"I'm going to ask you to be brave, even more than when you were in hospital. Guillaume and me, we're goin' to try and get

Ovide out of jail. Whether we succeed or not, I'm going to be arrested."

She couldn't hold back a horrified gasp.

"I thought that was it," she whispered.

"You're with me, we have to do it, eh? If we don't, my brother Ovide's going to die."

She nodded. He was close to tears. Seeing his wife's submissiveness, he would have liked to kneel and worship her. Any other woman would have gone into hysterics and tried to keep him from this exploit. But he controlled himself and said firmly:

"Thank you, Jeanne Duplessis, my good wife, now and forever. Nothing should change here while I'm away. I don't want you getting discouraged. You get up every morning like a real champion. Take on the jobs, keep the books, keep the house on the rails."

"And I'll keep my head up!" she said. "I'm with you a hundred per cent, Napoléon!"

He took her face in his strong hands and slowly kissed the middle of her forehead, a kind of communion kiss for this woman without whom he would not have wanted to go on living.

In the van that bore off the Plouffe commando force, Napoléon in his excitement was thinking that God had made him a plumber and then a contractor so that he could get the contract for the Quebec jail, for the sole purpose of springing Ovide, the predestined one. This conviction gave the expedition a touch of sanctity, remote controlled by the Divinity Himself.

Napoléon by now knew the Quebec jail right down to its last details, better than he knew his own house. He went there to do his repairs and make his inspections whenever he pleased and had made many friends. Last June he had even been allowed to play his trumpet for the guards and prisoners during their exercise period. He had received a standing ovation. People had grown used to seeing his thick-set form and his innocent joviality. Napoléon's popularity had, in fact, procured some relief for Ovide in his treatment by the guards, and the stopping of the death gasps performed by prisoners through the wicket in his door.

The contract was a smooth-running one. The roof, made of solid copper plates, needed little care except for the replacement of nails eaten away by rust or snapped by the winter's cold. The eavestroughs took more attention. Fallen leaves, acorns, bits of grass or twigs accumulated in them and rotted the metal and corroded the joints. Every time Napoléon suspended his swing stage by cables from the roof, prisoners appeared behind the bars and Napoléon would slip them cigarettes or treats, and bottles of soft drinks.

There was never much talk about the Quebec jail. Designed to fit the landscape, it harboured mainly petty thieves. The interior and the narrow cells had been built according to a romantic conception of the middle ages. It was not surrounded by high walls with towers for armed sentries ready to shoot down fugitives, there were no guards with machine guns or searchlights to foil escapes. Near the Provincial Museum and in the midst of one of the finest public parks in the world, people often wondered why this had been chosen for the site of this sombre building destined to cramp the style of a collection of poor devils, and overlooking the St. Lawrence River.

The warden of this operetta jail, a debonair, peaceable public servant, was patiently waiting for his retirement. The sight of prisoners demoralized him. He tried to meet them only on the day they were set free, satisfied the rest of the time to fill out and sign innumerable forms and reports. The guards came mainly from the same working-class background as the Plouffe family and obtained their jobs thanks to their member of the Assembly, as did the officers of the provincial police, who had more prestige than the guards because of their motorcycles equipped with sirens. The guards thought nothing of it when they saw Napoléon flanked by his giant brother Guillaume hang the pullied cables from the edge of the roof and slowly lower his catwalk along the metal drainpipes as he always did. They were not even surprised that Napoléon and Sons should choose that day to inspect the building. Of course they all knew that Ovide was Napoléon's brother (he must have had some drag to keep his contract!). And they knew he'd be dropping past Ovide's window. Sure, they'd be able to say a last word to each other, a brother's a brother even if he is going to hang. And a Plouffe was a Plouffe, childhood friend, catcher on the baseball team, sitting at the next desk in school. As the narrow platform was put in place two guards gave the brothers a wink and turned their backs. A prison guard has a heart, too, after all.

He closes his eyes to certain irregularities and respects family troubles.

Facing the river, where a trans-Atlantic liner was slowly sailing toward the Gulf, near the centuries-old trees and the luxuriant vegetation of the Plains of Abraham, peaceably, as if man and Nature had become accomplices of the Plouffes, the catwalk descended close to the wall, bumping against the irregularities of its stones. The prisoners behind the bars were respectful as the brothers passed their windows, expecting no treats that day. They said, "You have our sympathy, guys." The platform reached Ovide's level. Guillaume kept tapping on the drainpipe, pretending to inspect the metal. Napoléon, after checking the compressed-air cylinder at his feet, looked furtively around, grabbed the bars and called:

"Ovide! Ovide!"

The wasted form shifted on the cot, its face haggard, its beard grown long, then opened fevered eyes. Paralyzed with astonishment, he thought he saw his older brother. He rubbed his sore eyelids. The mirage was still there! Was he delirious? Or out in the desert? Then he heard a strange whistling sound, a hissing sound. A tongue of fire was eating at one of the bars, the middle one, seven inches away from its two neighbours. A man could get through. . . . Napoléon, armed with his acetylene torch, the latest style, was attacking the metal, getting nervous, puffing, his eyes protected by special goggles.

"Go to it! Nobody's coming!" whispered Guillaume, calm as a cathedral and leisurely tapping the drainpipe. In less than a minute the iron bar, its tips still red hot, fell into the cell with a dull clang. "Here, help me, Ovide, you poor bugger!" said Napoléon impatiently, and finally he was able to get through the window, taking with him a pair of overalls, a plumber's hat advertising Napoléon and Sons, and his trumpet.

"Come on, now, hup! Get up, put that on your carcass, you're escaping from here."

Like a rag, his muscles useless, without the slightest strength, Ovide was slumped on the edge of his cot.

"Get a move on, you're escaping, I tell you!"

Ovide's teeth began to chatter. This was pure madness. But with a fever of 39°, to be expected: his end was approaching. Napoléon, sweating, got him into the overalls and jammed the hat on his head. He pulled his brother like a bundle and passed

him through to Guillaume, who stood him up and closed his
hands around the cables. Then slowly, carefully, he lowered
the swing stage to the ground, as if this was a routine operation.
When Napoléon, looking out of the gap-toothed window, saw
them take off in the van, leaving the platform on the ground,
his face lit up like an angel's and he heaved a long sigh of relief.
Then, squatting by the bed he wept for joy. A guard made a
routine check through the wicket. But Napoléon's back was
turned. The more time passed, the more the knot he'd had in
his stomach since yesterday relaxed. An hour went by. Ovide
was safe! He was on his way to the hideout! A key turned in
the lock. Napoléon stood up to attention, holding his trumpet.
To the two astonished guards he said with a hearty laugh:

"Well! Yes, it's me! My brother's gone. You can't hang me,
I didn't do a thing!"

And he played *O Canada*, his cheeks puffed out like balloons.

The van was speeding to freedom.

"I'm not dreaming, am I, Guillaume, eh? Am I?" mumbled
the feverish bearded passenger, disguised as a plumber, sitting
beside a tense but triumphantly smiling Guillaume.

"Just like the war!"

He was vibrant with life, he felt himself strong as ten men.

"No, you're not dreaming, old Ovide, they won't catch us
now, not the Plouffe boys, they won't! Don't talk, now. Save
your strength. Pretend you're sleeping, put your face in your
hands. Mustn't show that damn beard."

They crossed the Plains of Abraham, drove down Gilmour
Hill (which Wolfe and his army had climbed in 1759 to conquer
Quebec), holding speed down so as to attract no attention,
stayed alongside the river as far as the Lévis ferry, left the van
in front of the harbour-station and, carrying a large bag and a
suitcase, threaded their way (as Ovide almost collapsed, his
legs barely able to carry him) toward the public lavatories, where
they disappeared.

Ten minutes later they emerged, transformed into monks of
Ovide's old order, in immaculate cassocks with hoods over their
faces. Guillaume was carrying the bundle of clothes and the
suitcase. Ovide, arms crossed, hands tucked in his sleeves,
wearing an old pair of his father's gold-rimmed spectacles, was
trying to hide his beard. They walked a hundred yards or so
and Guillaume, finally satisfied, said:

"When they find the van here they'll think we took the ferry and headed for the American border."

"I'm tired!" said the escapee, weakly.

"This is no time to fold. Give it a last try. I can't carry you on my back in public, eh?"

Guillaume considered hailing a taxi, but thought better of it. All the drivers were in cahoots with the police. They took a city bus, almost empty at this time of day, and got off at the Provincial terminal. Guillaume bought the bus tickets. They'd be hugging the North Shore up to Baie Sainte-Catherine. In the early days of his business Ovide had often travelled this route. As he prospered he had switched to planes. They climbed aboard. Ovide recognized the driver, but Guillaume, taking charge, got them safely aboard. Ovide merely followed, bent, his head hanging. How could anyone recognize him in this monk's frock, with a beard, and these ridiculous glasses on his nose? Those already seated saluted the two monks with courtesy. They proceeded to the very back of the bus, and Guillaume made him sit by the window, on the right, where he could admire the river. Hunched in the corner, he could sleep unrecognized in the shelter of his cowl. As Ovide sat down he fainted, exhausted. Guillaume saw that his brow was sweating and his hands were moist. He touched them and noted the fever. Frightened, he felt Ovide's pulse, which was weak. From a pocket of his cassock he took a mickey of gin and shook Ovide, who at last opened his eyes, haggard as if he were coming out of an epileptic fit. He whispered:

"Where are we?"

"In the bus, Father. In the open air. Here, have some."

Ensuring that no one was looking, Guillaume gave his brother a mouthful. Ovide's colour improved.

"Where are we going?" he murmured.

"Shhh! To Anticosti!" whispered Guillaume. "Look, there's your old monastery!"

The bus was passing the retreat where Ovide had once spent a decisive year in his life. But he was too weak to make the connection that – today as then – the cassock had always symbolized escape for him.

"Try to get some sleep," said Guillaume. "We have a six-hour bus ride in front of us."

Exhausted, Ovide curled up like a fetus and, his face turned toward the river, luckily missed the hills of Saint-Joachim where

385

Rita died. Alas, the driver recalled it for him, announcing in a funereal tone: "On your right, ladies and gentlemen, is the place where the DC3 crashed killing twenty-three people."

The news of the escape exploded like a bomb! As sensational as the explosion of the plane and the arrest and conviction of the accused, it had an additional element of ironic humour: Napoléon Plouffe, the plumber, had burned out the middle bar and taken his brother's place in the cell, triumphantly playing *O Canada* on his trumpet!

The photo of the three brothers hit the front page of all the papers that afternoon. Everyone recognized the war hero, the champion pitcher, the handsome, athletic Guillaume Plouffe. Pursuers should be wary of this sharpshooter, this formidable warrior, no doubt armed with several .38 revolvers as well as grenades and a whole arsenal. With him they saw the fugitive criminal, an expert with dynamite. Therefore, the danger was extreme, and they were to be shot on sight. But Napoléon's hearty laugh, his happy face in the photo, and his toot on the trumpet quickly gave the fugitives the appeal of modern Robin Hoods. The Plouffes became legendary.

The public goes wild for heroic feats and the mysteries of adventure – and they love to see a condemned man escape. Just as they had wished for Ovide to be hanged, now they secretly wished him a successful getaway. After all, the business with Berthet was a murky one, and since the family of the condemned man had shown such courage in setting him free, perhaps he wasn't guilty after all!

On that same day several guards from the Quebec jail were given a month's leave without pay, and the warden was pensioned off. At the Justice Department there was fury and frustration. The bloodhounds of the provincial police rushed to the American frontier crossings or toward Montreal, for the van abandoned near the Lévis ferry must be an important clue. On the radio a description of the fugitives was broadcast: one of them a strapping fellow, the other puny and bearded, no doubt in disguise. People phoned in to say that they had seen the pair taking to the fields, or sculling off in a rowboat.

But nobody noticed the two monks. Toward four in the afternoon Ovide and Guillaume arrived in Baie Saint-Catherine and took the ferry for Saint-Siméon. Leaning on the rail, their backs to the other passengers, the two false Brothers seemed to be admiring the sea as they prayed, their heads brushed from time to time by a low-flying seagull.

"Better now?" asked Guillaume.

"Yes, I think the fever's almost gone. The sea air is so healthy. But I'm still tired, so tired. I'm not dreaming, am I, Guillaume?"

"No, you're not dreaming. We got you out of jail and we're going to hide in our cabin on the Jupiter. You can have a good rest there and get your health back. Nobody's going to catch us. The main thing is to gain time, as much as we can. Denis Boucher seems sure he can pin down the real villain."

Ovide smiled, still dazed. He didn't yet dare be happy, but a warm contentment overcame him. The water was choppy but he wasn't sick. A while ago he had devoured the three ham sandwiches prepared by Jeanne and stored in the bundle stuffed with food. His glasses perched low on his nose, seeing very little through these thick lenses, Ovide thought of his trip on this same ferry with Marie Jourdan.

"I suppose Marie's gone back to France," he murmured.

"Guess so. Anyway, we'll talk about all that when we get you to the Jupiter."

Guillaume was nervous and constantly on the lookout, observing the behaviour of everyone that passed. The prisoner Ovide's escape was already known here and was talked about by the groups of passengers, farmers, tourists and lumberjacks.

"We mustn't attract their attention. Turn your back, keep lookin' at the water, and let's shut up."

They arrived at Saint-Siméon in the late afternoon. Ti'-Mé was waiting on the dock at the bottom of the gangway. His hat was shoved back on his head and he was looking around the surroundings with a suspicious eye. He didn't recognize the two ecclesiastics. Guillaume whispered, grabbing his arm:

"Who are you looking for, my son?"

"I'll be damned!" said Ti'-Mé.

But it was no time for chatter. They hopped into the nearly empty bus for Matane and sat in the back. They spoke softly, in snatches.

"You didn't shave your beard? That makes a bigger change than the robe. Everybody's talkin' about your escape. I can't wait to get off the Shore," said Ti'-Mé.

"That damned beard, we hadn't time to shave it off," Guillaume whispered. "It's very bad. Have you got the boat?"

"Yeah. My old fisherman, big Yvonne's dad. I was a good

boy, she's in Montreal and I haven't had a drink. He'll take us across tonight. It'll take at least twenty-four hours. I offered double his price. I said you had to be in Camp Twelve tomorrow to confess the guys and say mass in the morning, day after tomorrow. No trouble gettin' leave from the boss."

Ti'-Mé leaned over and examined Ovide, whose eyes were closed, his hands on his missal. He whispered:

"Poor old Ovide, what a wreck! Like a corpse with a beard. Looks bad. Never mind, I'll fatten him up at the hut. If we only had Marie. . . ."

"There never was a family had to go through a thing like this," sighed Guillaume, his powerful hand gripping Ti'-Mé's biceps.

And like the hackney-coach in the song, the old bus jolted off toward the dock at Matane where the old sea-dog sat smoking his pipe. His beard was white, his skin was wrinkled like a prune, yellowed and dried by the ocean winds. A powerful odour of fish came from his boat.

The broad-beamed Gaspé fishing boat, like a saucer with a stern, propelled by a gasoline motor, putt-putted monotonously through the dark, splitting the St. Lawrence's choppy waves, and sped along toward the Gulf. The moon shone down on Ovide's waxen face, where he lay curled up near the prow. They had covered him with woollen blankets and a heavy tarpaulin. Everything was going fine so far. Now they were on the heading for the Jupiter. Guillaume, at the stern of the boat, took deep breaths of the sea air. He was relaxed and happy. Had he not succeeded in his exploit?

The fisherman was proud of his boat. It must have been necessity that drove the Gaspésians to design their boats in this shape, which made them more seaworthy than any modern construction. Just as the *habitants* had created their houses, steep roofed, with low ceilings, adapted to the snow and the rigours of winter. This land, immense and intractable, this brutal climate, this pitiless, great river – the French Canadians had tamed and civilized these challenges of Nature, just as the Plouffes were trying now with fierce determination to force the hand of destiny. Guillaume did his best to avoid being seen full face by the fisherman, staying motionless and silent, his hands thrust into the wide sleeves of his cassock. He had a woollen blanket over his shoulders, as the night was chilly. He was glad to realize that after a year's glory as a baseball star and five years of war in which he had come close enough to death, he had not yet been captured by the daily grind of life. When he first came home he had experienced great distress and extreme boredom. Then, suddenly, this tragedy of Ovide's, and this spectacular escape! That's what he was made for: action! Danger! Today for the first time he felt completely alive. Of course they'd be discovered sooner or later. Ovide was a hanged man living on borrowed time. And Guillaume wondered whether he would give his life defending his big brother Ovide who was innocent of any crime. But tomorrow was tomorrow, and his champion's temperament caused him to live out totally and without question every instant of his mission. After so many years, his pulse was still beating sixty. He thought of his father Théophile and missed him acutely. If only he'd been there! Family solidarity would merely have been strengthened: hard as granite!

Twenty hours later, amidships where the engine and the rudder were, Ti'-Mé was chatting with the old fisherman. The latter, in a pea jacket and woollen toque, his pipe in his gap-toothed mouth, his grey eye scanning the skyline, was trying to spot the horizon of Anticosti. Ti'-Mé was waxing eloquent – perhaps too much so. He was explaining things to the sea-dog, who was astonished at the weakness of the White Father lying in the prow of the boat:

"That's just what you see. But when those cookies there start workin' for the Lord, they can stand anything. You take the Holy Martyrs of Canada. They may have been Jesuits, but they were all thin men. And when the Indians started torturing them, they took a while to die. Can't go by appearances."

"You bet," said the fisherman. "What you don't know! Small wonder my Yvonne thinks the world of you!"

"Well," Ti'-Mé strutted, "I've always been a good Catholic. Did you ever see my crucifix I got tattooed on my arm?" And he pulled up his sleeve.

"Yvonne told me about it. It's real nice. I mainly pray when the cod don't bite," he explained.

On this calm sea, Ti'-Mé was starting to moralize:

"You gotta pray all the time, never lose sight of the big hoof prints, what they call the devil. Keep an eye on him all the time."

389

The fisherman spat, then crouched to relight his pipe, hands around the match.

"The devil on Anticosti? Bah! Nothin' there but deers an' salmon."

"Don't say that, Pop. The American tourists, they're mostly Protestant English. Sometimes they bring women and drink like fish. The guides start doin' the same and even go to bed with the 'touristesses.' It's only normal. There's no priests, no mass, no confession. That's why I brought up two White Fathers of Africa. They're used to the jungle. And wild animals. And they can't get there too soon, by Christ! I'm tellin' you, Pop!"

Guillaume heard him, and grew angry and anxious at once. How could he stop Ti'-Mé's stupid chatter? He coughed.

"Aimé, my son, excessive talking in the Gulf air can result in damage to the vocal cords."

Ti'-Mé, in full flight, did not understand at once.

"Nothin' wrong with my throat. Don't you worry, Father."

"No doubt about it, it's fine of you to bring in priests like this," said the old sailor, a good friend of his parish priest, and a man with no idea of the excesses practised by Ti'-Mé and his daughter Yvonne. "You goin' to bed down at the mouth of the Jupiter?"

Ti'-Mé replied with the dignity of a bishop:

"No, we must waste no time. We'll jump into the canoe and paddle up to mile twelve, the big camp. There's no time to spare. The Yankees have brought in some actresses from the Ziegfeld Follies. Those girls almost have their ass in the air when they dance. Very bad for our boys. It gets them all worked up and they can't find the fish. But our White Fathers are goin' to look after all that. High mass by the riverbank. Right beside the fishin' hole. It won't convert the Yanks or the dancin' girls, but they'll see it all from the veranda and that'll make 'em think of heaven."

"My son, you tell too many tales," said Guillaume threateningly.

But the old helmsman gave a little chuckle that came to them through the fine salt spray, while Ti'-Mé turned with a hangdog look toward Guillaume, who could have choked him.

"Well," said the old man, "they'll get a good collection. Heh, heh! They have themselves a time, those tourists of yours. You got to be an American to have fun like that. Dancin' girls with their ass in the air! And good scotch on top o' that! In Menier's day that wouldn't a been allowed. When'll I come and pick you up?''

Ti'-Mé was less exuberant now.

"We don't know yet. It could take a while, tryin' to convert all them people. I hope it won't take months, with two experts, two good priests like them. We might just go back by the company boat from Port-Menier.''

The fisherman smiled into the dark as he thought of the dancing girls. His whole life, in the solitude of the sea, he had thought about women as he hauled in his nets filled with cod and mackerel.

Set on land at the Jupiter's mouth after a day at sea, the trio watched the boat disappear. It was nine o'clock at night.

Guillaume and Ti'-Mé, holding Ovide up, then lifting him right off the ground, ran to their freedom hut, lit a fire, munched a few biscuits, drank forty ounces of gin and fell into the sleep of the just.

44

In Quebec City the Plouffes were relishing the stunning news that had so excited the population. Joséphine's house was again a centre of attraction, but this time not as a contemptible, quarantined habitation. The exploit of the three brothers, standing united as the three musketeers, was a splendid example of family solidarity, recalling the cloak-and-dagger romances. A wave of sympathy and admiration swelled for them, as if Ovide, in his match for freedom and against death, had managed to get the crowd on the side of those champions, the Plouffes, just like the old days of the horseshoe contests, the baseball games and the bike races. Napoleon's honest, hilarious face in prison, his cheeks puffed out as he played solos for the other prisoners, the sacrifice he had made in abandoning family, business and freedom to replace Ovide in his cell, and the spectacular escape of his two brothers, made the Plouffes into heroes again.

After two days had passed, despite a frantic search by all the police forces, there was not a single clue. The fugitives had evaporated. Groups of curious passers-by and neighbours gathered in front of the Plouffe house, and Joséphine, like a female pope, appeared at the window. The crowd applauded her and she smiled proudly. To the police, who bombarded her with questions, she swore high and low that she had no idea where her boys had gone: they weren't "big talkers," she said. But she was sure of one thing: they hadn't been armed when they left. So there was no need to shoot on sight. Such good boys! She said the same thing to reporters, though Denis Boucher tried to prevent all interviews.

Joséphine, informed by Jeanne, knew quite a bit by this time. The two accessories after the fact giggled and winked and nudged each other to the disgust of Cécile, on whom her mother now took a sweet revenge by keeping her out of the secret, which Denis too tried in vain to penetrate. In such circumstances, thought Joséphine, you can easily talk too much, even to friends. The two women, in fact, knew where the fugitives were hiding and were delighted to know that they were sheltered by so many trees, like a pair of squirrels.

In the Quebec jail, Napoléon's presence in his brother's place had confused and embarrassed the authorities. They had ordered a hasty preliminary inquiry, no bail, and continued incarceration. At Napoléon's office the phone didn't stop ringing: business was never better. Every day Jeanne went to see her husband and was received at the jail like a VIP. Ovide was not cleared of the charge, he was still hunted like a wild animal, but the wind of public opinion slowly veered. Cécile decided to go back to work at the factory decked out in her finest feathers. The foreman allowed her into the shop, where she was actually greeted by cheers!

Oh, they were tough, those Plouffe women: they resisted all the questions of the police, showing as much force of character as the three brothers. They knew a secret and defended it fiercely. Uncle Gédéon, in temporary disgrace because of his absence from the courtroom, reappeared from the Beauce, where he was surrounded by fresh adulation from his fellow citizens, who saw the escape as "pure Gédéon!" – and he did nothing to disillusion them.

Below, in the ground-floor flat, Monsignor Folbèche, who nowadays was giving a victorious ring to his mass, shouting Hallelujah in triumph, saw the hand of God behind this wave of hope that was breaking over the whole clan. He was convinced he would soon be reappointed to his old parish, for his successor was not much liked. What could that man and even the church do against a Folbèche who was cheered when people saw him in the street?

Denis Boucher, who had received no new requests for material from his New York editors, had wired a breath-taking account of Ovide's escape. They phoned him, re-assigning him to the story, this time asking him to be as subjective as possible. His star was rising again. He had set up his typewriter on Monsignor Folbèche's altar table and was banging away like a madman, propelled by a new found, fantastic energy. *Time* had lost confidence in him? He'd show them, he'd win back the brass's esteem and this time become really famous. At the moment when Denis, in his text, was describing Napoléon as a "provincial Louis Armstrong" – a terrific touch for American readers – Monsignor Folbèche, at the other end of the table, was going through the accumulated mail that his vicar on the North Shore had sent along. There were church documents, magazines, newspapers and letters from parishioners. Suddenly, he stared in stupefaction at one of the envelopes, turning it this way and that, and cried out, interrupting the reporter:

"Goodness gracious! What's this? Denis, look! A letter from Pacifique Berthet!"

"What?"

Denis had leapt to his feet and was looking over the priest's shoulder. "From Pacifique Berthet to Monsignor Folbèche." Postmarked July the fourteenth, the Day of the Crime! The priest tore it open and pulled out a single sheet of paper. The two men stared: nothing was written on it! A blank page!

They looked at each other. The envelope and the blank page were an insoluble mystery! How could it be explained? They must see Berthet! No, not Berthet, the Chief Justice, and this very minute! In utter secrecy! A new piece of evidence! It seemed extremely urgent. They called a taxi at once and drove to the courthouse.

The august personage, himself surprised, called in the chief of the provincial police, before whom Denis swore that he had witnessed the opening of the wordless message. Why would Berthet have sent a blank page to Monsignor Folbèche on the day of the crime? The excitement of the others spread to the chief. He asked them not to mention their find. The police would drop in on Pacifique, immediately. Denis thought of Stan Labrie. Oh, if only he'd come back from his trip, the swine!

Berthet, gloomily sitting on his veranda, nibbled at his fingernails. What if the fugitive, Ovide, decided to assassinate him? He had asked the police for protection, he slept badly, and drank no gin, determined to stay alert so as to face the worst, which he felt was inescapable. Ever since the trial he had been watched, this he knew. Certain husky individuals, never before seen in the neighbourhood and passing themselves off as real-estate agents, would wander past his cottage, their hands in their pockets. He had even caught one of them observing him from behind a bush. Policemen, of course! Were they watching him or protecting him? Chilled through and through with fear, Pacifique seldom went out, and sprinkled his geraniums only once a day. Then there was the insurance company – why didn't they get in touch with him? He had submitted his claim, but he didn't dare phone to prod them. Yet they owed him fifty thousand dollars, no doubt of that! Very suspicious. . . . What's more the papers were hinting that the crown attorney would dearly love to turn up some accomplices in Ovide Plouffe's crime, so as to win even greater glory from this fabulous murder. Pacifique clenched his fists. He was smarter than all of them. They'd never get him! The cripple started: a police car skidded to a stop in his driveway, brakes squealing, pebbles flying. The two torturers who had interrogated him the first time were approaching the hut. He tried to subdue the beating of his heart. But they swaggered toward him and sat down casually on the veranda, their legs dangling, with a calm and detachment that contrasted with the urgency of their arrival.

"Er . . . Mr. Berthet, on July the fourteenth, do you remember writing a letter to Monsignor Folbèche, to his presbytery on the North Shore?"

He gripped the arms of his chair. The letter! That damned letter! Take care, now: what do they really know? He pretended to be searching his memory. How he detested these cops with their long, powerful legs dangling in the air, legs that could in a few minutes be marching him off to . . . what? He remembered perfectly Ovide's insistence, just before they left for the airport, that he, Pacifique, write a little note accompanying his present to Folbèche. Ovide had slipped it into his jacket pocket.

But hadn't he given it to his wife? Why had the police arrived in such a rush? To intimidate him? Who could have told them about the letter? Didn't it blow up with the plane? Was it the taxi driver who . . . Yet Ovide's lawyer hadn't mentioned it all through the trial. He was groping . . . but finally he whined:

"Why don't you leave me alone? This is harassment! You've got your murderer. When are you going to lay off?"

They played innocent:

"Oh, you know, we're never finished with a murder like this. But say, did you, yes or no, send a letter to Monsignor Folbèche on July the fourteenth?"

"Yes, I remember now, I gave it to Ovide to hand over to the Monsignor with the statue."

Pacifique was in a cold sweat and had a cramp in his solar plexus. Had they found that letter in the wreckage? Or had Ovide found it in his pocket and handed it over to them?

"Why didn't you mention it at the trial?"

The cripple cleared his throat, trying to fill in beforehand the gaps that might appear in a hasty answer.

"I didn't think it was important. Nobody mentioned it!"

The two men turned toward him at once, terrorizing him with their fierce, angelic eyes.

"And what did you write in this letter?"

He sucked at his saliva. If he said, "Nothing," they would suspect him of assuming Ovide would go down with the plane. Damn that Ovide! No doubt he had written out an explanation before his escape, with unmentioned details in it, including this business of a letter. Then Pacifique committed his first big mistake.

"I don't really remember. A few words, I guess, good wishes or something like that. Nothing special."

"Did you ask him to pray for you?"

"I don't believe in prayers."

They got to their feet and said, almost together:

"You should have!"

And one of the policemen continued:

"A very good day to you, Mr. Berthet, take care of yourself. Just for your information, Monsignor Folbèche got this letter in the mail."

They laughed boisterously and left without another word. Their car moved off very slowly, like a hearse leaving the church. Pacifique, his face ashen, was shivering in the torrid air. The whine of outboard motors on the lake seemed to come from within his head. . . . What a horror!

Meanwhile, the police were wondering who could have mailed the letter to Monsignor Folbèche. If it had been Ovide, did it help to prove his innocence? It meant he didn't know the plane was going to explode! Or if he knew, had he exchanged Pacifique's note for a blank page, thus preparing his alibi and incriminating Berthet? And why had no one mentioned it at the trial? This evidence would have been useful to Ovide. Very complicated, indeed! But one thing was sure: Berthet had just lied. Oh, how they would have liked to catch the fugitive!

After two days in the "happiness cabin" as Ti'-Mé called it, Ovide could still not get over the feeling of unreality into which his escape had plunged him. Calm and taciturn, Guillaume looked after him like a mother, trying to provide him with absolute peace for a few days. Guillaume had a premonition their hideout was about to be discovered. Everyone knew he was a guide on Anticosti in the summertime, and from that to looking there. . . . Ovide allowed himself to be spoiled, huddling into the warmth of a delicious freedom that he had never before appreciated as being essential to mankind.

Several times a day Ti'-Mé did the rounds in the forest nearby, but had come across no trace of an intruder. The fishing season was almost over, deer hunting didn't start for another month. He would come back from his forays with armfuls of plants and wild herbs. They made dressings for Ovide's neck and teas for him to drink. The fugitive recovered his strength quickly and his sore neck was healing. He ate sumptuous meals of game, fresh fish, shrimps and lobster. On the third day they dragged him to the Jupiter and dumped him in naked, afterwards soaping him abundantly and splashing him with the crystalline water. Regaining his strength, Ovide laughed for the first time, as if the soap and this pure water had washed away his anguish. Then they dressed him hurriedly, because there was a grumble of thunder in the distance. But before going back to the hut Ovide wanted to look at the sea and admire the black clouds streaked with lightning, coming from the Gaspé shore. Black waterspouts striped the sky like the bars of his cell, and he was sad and frightened again. But then came a perfect rainbow, brilliant and extraordinary. His heart beat faster, and he was flooded with a great hope that came without reason, like a mystery. His step was lighter as he returned to the cabin, the two others following. He sat down by the stove, his face in his hands, and stared at Guillaume and Ti'-Mé with a look of intense ecstasy.

"Don't look at us like that, Ovide," said Guillaume, "you'll make us nervous."

"You look real pleased all of a sudden!" said Ti'-Mé. "That's just fine!"

Ovide, who had uttered nothing but monosyllables since their arrival, suddenly felt like thinking out loud for hours on end.

"I wonder what's happening to Napoléon in jail!"

"He'll be all right, he knows all the guards. Don't you worry about him," said Guillaume.

Guillaume and Ti'-Mé had agreed not to let any news filter through to Ovide. But they kept well informed through their short wave radio, and knew everything that was going on in Quebec City. Ovide was clear headed now, emerging from limbo, recovering from his lethargy, and aware of a joy that penetrated him more and more. He was also more voluble.

"You know, Guillaume, this escape at first seemed to me like sheer madness. And don't forget that the three of you are going to have a criminal record for the rest of your days."

"So what the hell!" said Ti'-Mé, laughing.

"Right! What the hell!" confirmed Guillaume. "We're in the right because you're innocent. Aren't you glad we did it? You're not in Bordeaux jail, your health is coming back and you're free. Free, d'you hear? And we'll see about the rest later, all in good time. You worry too much. You try too hard to think what's goin' to become of you, and then it never happens the way you thought. So don't get your guts in an uproar. Live from day to day."

"Bull's-eye," smiled Ti'-Mé. "If we can keep you happy and free for a while, it's paid off already. Who the hell cares about a criminal record? The fact is, we were right to build this cabin. Hey, guys, what about a little game o' cards?"

Ovide coughed to hide his feelings, but managed to say:

"This is the first time in my life that I really knew what it meant to be loved."

His voice broke in a long lament like the howl of the wolves that could be heard addressing the moon after dark.

"Go ahead, bawl, it'll do you good!" said Ti'-Mé.

He tapped Ovide gently on the back as the sobs continued. "Don't you know we did it for our mother, too?" asked Guillaume.

"And for justice," said Ti'-Mé quietly.

45

The old fisherman who had brought the three to Anticosti was so impressed by Ti'-Mé's most Christian concerns and his desire to exorcise the American demons on the Jupiter by importing at great cost two missionary fathers straight from the African bush, that he mentioned the matter to his friend the village priest.

The priest, edified in turn, made this the subject of his Sunday sermon. Before his flock, excited, bemused and fascinated by this raid of the monks on the dancing girls of Anticosti, the priest proclaimed:

"Yea, my dear brethren, in this world assailed by debauchery on all sides, it warms my priestly heart to think that a humble fishermen's guide of our people touched by the grace of God, brought in on his own initiative two missionaries of the White Fathers of Africa to say mass on the Jupiter and spread the Good Word, confessing the guides and perhaps even the tourists, and above all to ensure that the dancing girls from the Ziegfeld Follies are encouraged to dress, so that their languorous and sensual bearing does not lead our good Gaspésians into temptation and foul frequentations which, like alcohol, make man resemble the beasts and often lead to his death!"

This homily did not have the precise effect the priest expected. Far from sharing his horror of the flesh, the men, most of them lumberjacks separated for long months from their families, began to dream that these dancing ladies might come to end their solitude in the forest shanties. Normally they had to settle for pin-up girls ripped from American magazines and plastered on the bunkhouse walls. The wives of fishing and hunting guides, chaste from June to October, bit their lips in anxiety. If that was how things were on Anticosti, what was going on elsewhere? Their husbands were careful not to mention these things on arriving home. Female tourists after a drink or two would certainly try to make conquests of the handsome men of the Gaspé, tanned, muscular and vulnerable, hungry for companionship!

But the man who was most intrigued when he heard the curate's sermon was the game warden for the region. He had just come back from inspecting the Jupiter and had seen neither White Fathers nor dancing girls. In fact, the Anticosti region was nearly deserted, as the salmon season had ended. What kind of tale was this, of a guide and two monks? And the African bush was nothing like the forests of Anticosti! Could it be that Ovide Plouffe, the famous fugitive, had something to do with Ti'-Mé Plouffe, the guide? And hadn't the papers mentioned that the famous Guillaume Plouffe was also a guide on Anticosti?

Now, game wardens, like all inspectors, end up thinking like a cop. The zealous employee of the state hastened to the regional chief of the provincial police and shared the story with him. And the Matane-Quebec City phone line began to hum. A coast-guard launch with twelve policemen armed to the teeth sped at once toward the mouth of the Jupiter to the place where the fisherman had landed the fugitives. They hadn't far to search. Good old Ti'-Mé, who was too anxious to cook a fine hot meal for Ovide! The thread of smoke that rose from the cabin chimney at the "happiness camp" quickly drew the attention of the patrol.

The condemned man had been free for eight days. They brought the three conspirators back to the Quebec jail, which, for the first time in its history, held three brothers and a cousin, all with the same name: Plouffe!

The crescendo of sensation had not peaked! Ovide Plouffe, the re-captured murderer, continued to make news as melodramatic as his crime and his escape. But what was going on? The attorney general seemed less in a hurry to have Ovide executed. His departure for Bordeaux prison was delayed for several weeks. And his hanging was postponed *sine die*!

Against all expectations, Joséphine Plouffe these days was continually singing to herself in the kitchen. Her three sons were safe in the Quebec jail, near enough to visit. As for Ovide's hanging, so much was certain: it would never take place. It was Berthet that they suspected now. Denis Boucher, with his article in *Time*, was once again in the spotlight with a fabulous scoop:

Pacifique's letter to Monsignor Folbèche–a blank page! Implacable suspicion hovered over Berthet. And the priest had actually had the courage to visit Pacifique, who had run him off his property, showering him with blasphemies.

For Joséphine, Denis now was more than the friend of the family: what with his magic articles and his constant phone calls to New York he had become the source of all her hopes. This was why she had again persuaded him to type his despatches under her attentive eye.

"You're so hot. Have a little rest! How about some good home-made wild strawberry jam and fresh-baked bread?"

She coddled and spoiled and venerated him, because he was writing the truth and saving Ovide and the family. Absorbed in his writing, the reporter shook his head and went on hammering his typewriter, obsessed with the thrilling aspects of his story. Fugitives disguised as priests, the freedom cabin, the Ziegfeld Follies dancers, the Gaspésian curate's sermon, the capture of the prisoners, their popularity, Napoléon's triumph in the Quebec jail, the three Plouffe brothers and cousin Ti'-Mé incarcerated in separate cells, Jeanne's self-sacrificing heroism (on her visits to the prison she was hailed as the family's gentle mascot), the embarrassment of the government in the face of public sympathy, all that had been for Denis, installed at the very heart of this tragi-comedy dominated by that great lady Joséphine, a source of material unique in the history of North American journalism. A fabulous story! Now Denis wanted to repeat his triumph. Suddenly he stopped typing and stroked his chin, hesitating, searching for the right detail. Joséphine, who had insisted that he work upstairs again in her domain, turned toward him anxiously:

"What's the matter? Are you stalled?"

"Just one little thing missing."

He got up and swiftly made for the door, impelled by an instinct peculiar to great reporters. He said mysteriously:

"I'm going out to get it."

He was gone. Joséphine, her face marked by a new anxiety, began to read the page that was in his typewriter. Nothing there that she didn't know. Did this gap in Denis's information mean that Ovide was still in danger? She sat down in her rocking-chair and began saying a rosary, begging the Blessed Virgin to help the reporter find the solution. Her expression as respectful as if she had been gazing at the tabernacle itself, she stared at the typewriter and the blank paper that awaited the truth Denis was seeking.

He walked quickly toward Stan Labrie's apartment. His intuition told him that with the Plouffe brothers caught and imprisoned, Stan might have decided to come home. His suspicion was borne out by the fact. Stan Labrie, tired of biting his nails on the beaches of Old Orchard, where from behind his sunglasses he no longer even sized up the charms of the young ladies in their bathing suits, had taken a chance and returned to Quebec City as soon as the Plouffe brothers were in jail. A prey to persistent pangs of guilt and waves of fear that came back like a fever, but still hoping the whole business would blow over without his name being mentioned, Stan yearned for his former peace of mind. But he had lost weight and aged in the meantime, and wandered around like a lost soul, without even the courage to operate his network of "escorts." Fortunately he had not lost his love for flowers, which no one had watered while he was away. He was tenderly making the rounds with his watering can when Denis, who had found the door unlocked, bounded out onto the balcony like a mischievous goblin, whistling "The next day she was smiling." Stan turned around, hardly surprised at all:

"That's fine, I was just thinking about you. I wanted to give you a call."

"I thought as much!" said Denis politely, quickly switching his strategy.

They went inside. The reporter kept an eagle eye on his victim.

"You've lost weight," he said.

"Yeah. If you knew what I've been through. You were looking for me, eh? I was at Old Orchard. But it was no vacation, it was torture. I followed the trial down there. I read your articles. You kept your word, you didn't mention me. Thanks, that was okay of you."

"Do I understand you're ready to help me now?"

Stan shook his head, but in resignation.

"I am, but I'm sure now it wasn't Ovide. I'll swear to tell you the truth as long as you don't say it came from me."

"I promise."

"You'll tell the Plouffe brothers I helped, won't you? Without saying how?"

"Sure. They won't touch you when they get out. I can promise that, too. Go to it, now."

Stan spoke in the toneless voice of a weary evil-doer confessing his crime:

"After the burial, when I saw Berthet scud off between the gravestones while they were arresting Ovide, I followed him in my car, right to his cottage. I hid behind a bush an' watched him. He looked nervous. He checked to see if anybody was looking, and first he took a shovel from under the veranda, then he threw it back in there and went to a little square of dug-up garden near the back fence, and then he picked up a spade that was lying there and started breaking clods and marking little rows in the earth. I was wondering why in Sam Hill he'd start gardening on a hot day like that."

"A square garden plot! With geraniums in it?" Denis exclaimed.

Stan shook his head.

"No. But ever since I've been wondering if he hadn't buried something there. He looked so nervous."

"Why the hell didn't you tell me this before?" shouted Denis. "You could have saved a lot of people a lot of trouble! Do you realize that?"

The reporter, in a frenzy, ran off to his typewriter as fast as his legs could carry him. Very soon, on the appearance of his article-in-progress, the police would learn (along with the general public) about these new facts concerning a garden plot, now covered with flowers. This time he'd reach the apotheosis of celebrity. On condition, of course, that the gendarmes found something unusual under the geraniums! Nothing ventured, nothing gained!

At eleven in the morning, two days later, millions of copies of *Time* reached the news-stands of the world. What was most unusual was that the director of the provincial police received half a dozen copies by special messenger, two hours before the general public. The chief, reading Denis Boucher's latest story, opened his eyes very wide as he came to the following passage: "Our reporter, during his visit to Pacifique Berthet's summer cottage to get a statement from him on the capture of Ovide Plouffe, was most intrigued, during the interview, by Berthet's furtive glances toward a garden plot covered with geraniums. It was later established that these flowers were planted after the murder of July fourteenth. As for Ovide Plouffe, interrogated immediately after his capture, covered in our last issue, he simply stated that immediately after he left the monastery on that day, he had mailed Berthet's letter to Monsignor Folbèche. He admitted quite frankly that during the trial, because of his general state of distress, he had completely forgotten this incident, which would have helped him to establish his innocence."

The phone lines again began to hum, and there was action in police circles. Denis Boucher, imbued with the spirit of this legendary affair of a time-bomb that killed twenty-three people, succeeded in shaping his strategy with a similar diabolical precision. Just as his report reached the Quebec police and the readers of the world, Denis arrived at Berthet's cottage in time to witness the climax of this frightful adventure. Berthet, in a lumberjack shirt, was absent-mindedly staring at the cracks in his veranda floor. He was lying rather than sitting in his rocking chair, and let loose a string of curses on seeing Denis. His face, distorted by hatred, turned white with rage.

"Where did you crawl out of, you dung beetle? Little bastard, you want to kill me with your stories!"

Denis had no stomach for making sport of the man. He knew the truth now and examined with pity this unhappy creature slouched before him, his gaze feverish and his limbs trembling, a two-day stubble on his face.

Berthet began to speak, heart-rendingly:

"Little killer! You're all a bunch of killers. All the Rita Toulouses are killers! Do you have any idea, a fraction of an idea, what it's like to drag yourself around on crutches with no hope of a cure? When you wake up in the morning, the first thing you look for is – crutches. All day long you have to think about leaving them within easy reach. You never take your eyes off them. They're your salvation and damnation. Shackles and legs at the same time. Look at my fingers! Calloused forever! Napoléon Plouffe was the only one that understood. Oh, yes, I should have gone aboard with Rita and died along with her! Why don't you go away? Just go!"

His hard eyes had softened and he began to weep. The reporter, embarrassed, didn't know what to say. He tried to apologize:

"Oh, I understand all too well. I'm sorry, Mr. Berthet, and this is the last time we'll meet. My work is ended. You mustn't

403

hold it against me. I did my duty as a reporter and as a friend of Ovide Plouffe."

Berthet repressed a grimace of pain. His hip was hurting more these days and he had to change his dressings twice a day. In fact, the fever had settled in and never left him now. Denis had one ear for the traffic: the police should arrive any moment. He was trying to gain time. He spoke gravely, kindly:

"Monsieur Berthet, give yourself up to the police, for God's sake. You are the guilty man. It would be so much simpler for you and everyone else."

"Let them prove I made him buy the dynamite!" he screeched.

Berthet felt the chill of horror on him. Since the blank letter to Folbèche had been discovered, investigators had questioned him several times, and he had actually contradicted himself. From that time on he had felt that thousands of enemies were creeping toward him for the final attack, in which Denis appeared to be the leader of the host. And the reporter kept furtively glancing over at the geranium bed. Suddenly Berthet jumped, uttering a terrified "Hah!"

Two police cars had entered his lot and driven right back to the geranium beds where they screamed to a stop. The two long-legged inquisitioners who had arrested both Berthet and Ovide and questioned them repeatedly and mercilessly emerged spryly from their cars followed by four men with shovels. They began to dig, and dig, and dig. Denis was avidly watching Berthet's reactions. His lips were pale and trembling. Grasping his wooden crutches he went inside, and emerged almost at once, his hair carefully combed, in a tight black jacket, swinging on his aluminum crutches, resigned at last to being taken away. Denis went closer to the police. The men were still digging. The torn geraniums lay half covered by loose soil.

"There's something," said one of the diggers.

Slowly they uncovered a statue of St. Christopher and several sticks of dynamite, mingled with aviation magazines and a large photo of Rita Toulouse as Miss Sweet Caporal. Denis Boucher did not follow the two policemen as they ran toward Pacifique Berthet, who stood ready to give himself up.

They came up on both sides of the man.

"Berthet, you are under arrest!"

The cripple smiled sadly, then, with a grimace, pressed simultaneously with both index fingers on the switches Napoléon had built into the crutches to light their "seeing-eye" bulbs.

The devastating explosion that followed left only shards of flesh and bones.

Berthet had left no confession. It was concluded that he had made the bomb in his cottage several days before the crime. On the morning of the fourteenth, he had gone early to the jewellery store and, without witnesses, quickly exchanged the packages – child's play for the murderer. But on discovering that the plane had left ten minutes late and crashed on land, with a strong smell of dynamite emanating from the wreckage, he had panicked, and doubly so on seeing Ovide alive. He had at once rushed to his cottage where, totally distracted, he took the real statue from his car and buried it with his papers, the bits of wire and the remaining dynamite, from which he rescued a few sticks to insert in the hollow of his crutches.

Ovide and the Plouffes were saved, justice was done, but two of Quebec's finest had died in the course of duty.

Epilogue

Two months later, on a golden October Sunday in 1949, Ovide Plouffe, sitting on the third landing of the great stairway linking the lower to the upper town, where he had kissed Rita Toulouse for the first time many years ago, was listening sadly to the din of the churchbells celebrating the end of high mass. Ever since he was released from prison he had lived in a solitude as complete as that which he had experienced in his cell. Even as a free man he could not accustom himself to everyday life or his family and surroundings.

Yet his innocence had been completely established! He was in no way an accessory, and even the blank page sent by Berthet to Monsignor Folbèche showed only the fingerprints of the cripple and those who had touched it since. Ovide's were not to be seen.

His escape from prison had, however, created an imbroglio unequalled in the annals of justice. Aimé, Napoléon and Guillaume, all accomplices, deserved to be tried. But the forces of law and order had gone so far astray, and the Plouffes had become so popular – and other political events occupied the province's rulers so thoroughly – that they liberated the mischief-makers without prosecution.

Denis Boucher was certain to be named Reporter of the Year

by *Time* magazine, and he had already been rewarded with an assignment to the Paris office. In a long letter to Ovide recounting his good fortune, he told him that he had lunched a few times with Marie Jourdan. He and Marie got on very well, and even . . . he suggested . . . perhaps . . . were in love?

That Sunday Joséphine had invited all her children and grandchildren over for the mid-day meal. Ovide descended the great stairway and walked toward his mother's house past the church, which seemed to vibrate with new life now that Monsignor Folbèche was back in his parish. Ovide was living with his mother these days and had only a gloomy glance for his former jewellery store, now occupied by a grocer.

He had gone through a frightful inner cataclysm and could not yet enjoy his new-found freedom. Without Rita he was nothing. But the family, solid as a rock, was rediscovering its old happiness. In her gratitude to the Lord, Joséphine had stopped smoking and sent Major Ephrem about his business. Cécile, appointed foreman of her department at the factory, had gone so far as to offer a sweater she had knitted to the handsome assistant foreman from Montreal. Guillaume and Ti'-Mé, now co-owners of a forestry concession Uncle Gédéon had wrung from the government, were leaving this week to organize their first lumbering operation. Napoléon's business was prospering again. His wife was pregnant with twins, but didn't know it yet. The plumber had been so happy to get out of jail that he had served up double portions, unaware of the divine dispensation: the year of our Lord 1950 was to see the greatest crop of twins in the history of humanity. Success descended on Napoléon, barely leaving him time to practise the "Skater's Waltz" on his trumpet. That winter he was to join a trio playing for the neighbourhood rink. But that was the least of his successes. Those fatal crutches with the seeing eyes had attracted the attention of the minister of Veterans' Affairs, as being suitable for disabled veterans. The federal government was interested in his invention! Handicapped people were coming to see him, looking for better prostheses. He gave up patching drainpipes and devoted himself to the the disabled!

But what was to become of Ovide? He had a child, little Arlette, who was being raised by Jeanne and already called Napoléon "Papa." Yet he must try to live for her and see to her education. Ovide suddenly thought of Stan Labrie and made a face. What had brought him to mind? The pimp had turned over a new leaf and often went to see Napoléon, who thought well of him since Denis had made a mysterious comment to the effect that he had helped unmask Berthet and save Ovide. Stan even confided to the plumber that he was working on a book about pimping, in which he would reveal various recipes for sexual gourmets, including that of the butterfly system. Innocent Napoléon, still unaware of the late Rita's escapades and the role Stan had played, promised to let his brother Ovide check the manuscript. To his great surprise Ovide flew into a terrible rage. He certainly would not correct the French of that bum! Was that Stan Labrie going to hang around *ad nauseam* in Ovide's life? What was more, the ex-pimp was playing the part of Rita's "widower" to the hilt. Twice when Ovide had gone to the cemetery to pray at his wife's tomb he had had to beat a retreat, as the prie-dieu was occupied by Stan! What a persistent louse he was! Ovide thought perhaps he should go into exile. But where?

An American publishing house and another, more prestigious, in Paris, were competing for his memoirs of the incredible adventure. He had refused, reacting as Guillaume had reacted to writing his account of the war. He was not inclined to make literary use of his unhappiness and that of his family, who had already suffered enough on his account. Yet the Americans were making him a good offer! Ovide was drifting, hoping for a little push from fate to get him going again, and actually looking to the future. He thought of his godfather, Uncle Gédéon, who had married again last week.

Already he could hear the screeches of the Plouffe youngsters sitting at the table by Joséphine. The moment he showed up everyone would freeze in an embarrassed silence. Even now that he was proven innocent, he would always remain an ex-accused murderer, dragging that indelible stain in his wake forever.

"Don't stop talking, go on laughing! What's the matter?"

They tried to act naturally. But their heart wasn't in it. Suddenly Joséphine remembered something and walked with her heavy step to her sewing machine. She opened the drawer and took out a letter.

"It's for you! The mailman brought it yesterday. I forgot to give it to you."

He examined it and tore it open. Everyone was watching: who could be writing to him?

Gaping, he looked at the cheque for fifty thousand dollars from the insurance company. At once he had a vision of himself as an older student, beginning his classical studies in a foreign city, courses that Rita Toulouse had paid for with her life.